JOEL KOTKIN was born in Heidelberg, West Germany, and grew up in Brooklyn and Long Island. He was educated at Washington University in St. Louis, and graduated from the University of California, Berkeley, in 1975. He has spent more than five years reporting on California and the West for the *Washington Post*, and has written for *Esquire*, *The Village Voice*, *California Magazine*, *SoHo News* and the *Los Angeles Times*. He will publish his first novel, THE VALLEY, in fall 1982.

PAUL GRABOWICZ was born in Springfield, Massachusetts, and graduated *Phi Beta Kappa* from the University of California, Berkeley, in 1973. He has written for the *Washington Post*, *Esquire*, *The Village Voice* and other publications, and is currently a reporter for the *Oakland Tribune*.

CALIFORNIA, INC.

JOEL KOTKIN
and
PAUL GRABOWICZ

 A DISCUS BOOK/PUBLISHED BY AVON BOOKS

Portions of this book in different form have been published
in the following magazines and newspapers: *Esquire*, the
*Oakland Tribune, Newsday, New Times, TWA Magazine,
The Village Voice,* and the *Washington Post.*

AVON BOOKS
A division of
The Hearst Corporation
959 Eighth Avenue
New York, New York 10019

The Rawson, Wade Publishers, Inc. edition contains the
following Library of Congress Cataloging in
Publication Data:

Kotkin, Joel.
  California, Inc.

  Includes index.
  1. California—Civilization. 2. California—Economic
conditions. 3. California—Politics and government—1951— .
I. Grabowicz, Paul. II. Title. F866.2.K67   979.4′05   81-40270
                AACR2

First Discus Printing, March, 1983

Contents

Acknowledgments

The origins of this book lie in the authors' unending fascination with California, its land and its people. Without the many years we spent working in the state as journalists, and living as Californians, we could never have gathered the myriad strands which together make up the following effort. Along the way we met many people who freely and with good cheer offered their insights, stories, and feelings to the authors. Their numbers are so great that many unavoidably remain unmentioned, but their help is nevertheless appreciated by both of us.

But there are certain individuals whose contributions loom over this book in ways which demand they be named specifically. Of these, we offer our most heartfelt thanks to Richard Kahlenberg, our agent, who labored mightily, at great personal cost, to sell this project on the often unfriendly sidewalks of New York. It was our good fortune that Richard was able to link us with James O. Wade, executive vice-president of Rawson, Wade Publishers, a man whose foresight, criticism, editorial grace, and unbridled enthusiasm turned California, Inc., from a mere concept into a reality. We also are deeply indebted to Jim's assistant, Charles McCurdy, and others at Rawson, Wade for their large doses of aid and comfort to two strangers from the West.

When, on occasion, the authors broke the restraints of common sense and historical accuracy, we were fortunate to have the generous advice of numerous friends and colleagues. Of all these, special mention must be made of Mark Benham, an exemplary native Californian currently a student at the University of Chicago School of Business, who combined his painstaking criticism of the early drafts of this text with much needed encouragement. We also wish to thank Joel Garreau, our former editor and protector at the Washington *Post,* and Lou Cannon, former west coast bureau chief and now White House correspondent for that paper, for their insights, suggestions, and occasional *caveats*. In addition, the book was improved by the thoughtful comments of John Harrigan, an Oakland attorney and longtime friend.

Several other individuals made special efforts to help us during the research and writing phases of this project. Among the most notable are Gray Davis, chief of staff for Governor Edmund G. Brown, Jr.; Don Livingston, vice-president for intergovernmental relations for Carter-Hawley-Hale Stores; Peter Hannaford, president of Deaver-Hannaford public relations firm in Los Angeles; Hank Koehn, Conrad Jamison, and Tom Lieser, all of Security Pacific National Bank; John Popovich, vice-president for Consumer Affairs at First Interstate Bank; Bob Arnold, director of the Center for Continuing Study of the California Economy in Palo Alto; K. W. Lee, editor of the *Koreatown* newspaper in Los Angeles; Miguel Garcia, attorney and chairman of Californios for Fair Representation; Al Ortiz, expert on Mexican-American youth and trusted teacher; Harry Hamparzumian, of the Los Angeles Area Chamber of Commerce; John Mack, chairman of the Los Angeles Urban League; Paul Hudson, attorney and president of the Los Angeles NAACP; Kathy Macdonald of the Washington *Post*'s Los Angeles Bureau; the staff of the Data Center in Oakland; Congressman Robert K. Dornan of Santa Monica; Regis McKenna, president of Regis McKenna Public Relations in Palo Alto, California; Ralph Carson, of the Entrepreneurship Program at the University of Southern California; and Robert Gnaizda of the Public Advocates law firm in San Francisco.

While all the above-mentioned persons contributed to the writing of the book, we extend our special thanks to Susan Hershman and Julie Schwerzmann, who put up with the authors' long hours, occasional absences, fits of depression, and constant *kvetching* during the life of this project. Without their love and support, we would never have made it.

Joel Kotkin
Los Angeles, California

Paul Grabowicz
Berkeley, California

June, 1981

"What do we want with this worthless area, this region of savages and wild beasts, of shifting sands and whirlwinds of dust, of cactus and prairie dogs? To what use could we ever hope to put these great deserts and these endless mountain ranges?"

—U.S. Secretary of State Daniel Webster in 1852, speaking about the American West

I.
The California Ascendancy

In the last dispirited months of the Carter administration, a Presidential Commission for a National Agenda for the Eighties issued its report, in which the first item of the proposed "agenda" was a stark amplification of Horace Greeley's famous exhortation—"Go West, young man." The Commission recommended that virtually everyone flee the aging industrial cities of the East and Midwest in favor of the prosperous states to the west and south. The invitation to leave behind the bitter cold of winter, to abandon the infarcted mass transportation systems, the oppressive burdens of an unemployable welfare class, the crime, dirt, noise, and diminished prospects of the older half of America, was both rational and attractive. Clearly, the federal government faced a decision: it could either spend vast sums bailing out the economies of the aged cities or, as the Commission proposed, encourage people to move out west. There, it was suggested, ambitious new generations of Americans could still pursue the classic American dream, hacking out personal fortunes from a rich, developing frontier. Nowhere was this essential American dream more vibrant than in California, the nation-state of the emergent Sunbelt, the place where the rainbow ends.

For most of its first two centuries, the culture, economic development, and political life of the American Republic were dominated by the great cities of the East and, after the Civil War, those of the Midwest as well. Americans from all across the vast continent received their information from books, newspapers, and later radio shows and television programs that were produced by the great megalopolis of the Northeast and Great Lakes states. American industrial power was concentrated in the red brick mills of that region, manufacturing the ships, trains, cars, and appliances that constituted the steel backbone of the world's mightiest economic power. The nation's financial affairs were controlled in the boardrooms and stock exchanges of New York's Wall Street and Chicago's Loop. Political power, too, flowed from this rich, seminal America, whose intellectual elite saw themselves—and were largely seen—as the mind of the nation.

The 1970s marked the twilight of that familiar, reassuring world. After years of steady industrial growth, cultural self-assurance, and worldwide political hegemony, suddenly the American industrial heartland was sent reeling by a series of economic shocks. The OPEC oil producers flexed their economic muscles and thrust drastically higher prices upon the industrialized world; the manufacturing giants of the Northeast staggered like aging, punched-out boxers, fearing the final knockout blow. Desperate for the resources necessary to sustain the creaking industrial centers, the nation's leaders found themselves seemingly at the whim of strange, upstart powers like Iran, Saudi Arabia, Nigeria, and Libya.

Even among the family of industrialized, oil-consuming nations, the manufacturing centers of the East and Midwest seemed particularly ill-equipped to deal with the rapidly changing world economic order. Uncontrollable inflation and persistent recession, accompanied by one of the highest unemployment rates since the Great Depression of the 1930s, wracked the once proud, aging urban centers. The steel industry was deemed hopelessly antiquated. The entire consumer electronics industry, including such key products as televisions and radios, fled the American industrial heartland. The auto industry (traditionally the bellwether of America's economy) developed a chronic case of obsolescence. The Japanese, the Germans, the French, and even such comparatively poor nations as Korea and Taiwan moved in, outperforming and replacing the Americans both at home and abroad. Factories closed, towns died, prices skyrocketed, and productivity plunged. After two hundred years of dominance, the America of the East has faded and a new America, centered in California, has risen to take its place.

Long the nation's top agricultural state, California is now its leading industrial power as well. By 1978, California boasted the nation's largest commercial bank, the top six savings and loan companies, the biggest retail food chain, the largest construction engineering firm, and the leading producers of both gold and television films. With the greatest concentration of technical and scientific personnel in the United States, California also dominates the most promising industrial fields of the future, including the commercial exploitation of outer space travel, semiconductors, microcomputers, genetic engineering, and laser technology.

Not since the gilded age of the robber barons has there been such a rapid, massive accumulation of wealth and power in one place. While the recessionary spirals of the 1970s ravaged most of the country, California's major industries—aerospace, electronics, high technology, entertainment, and agribusiness—were recording banner years. Between 1970 and 1980 California's manufacturing employment increased at a rate more than five times that of the rest of the country. In 1979, the real gross state product expanded at a pace three times the national average, and by the end of 1980 it was expected to reach $311 billion. California ranked fourth among the 50 states in per capita income in 1979, behind its two sparsely populated western neighbors, Alaska and Nevada, and Connecticut in the East. As a nation, California would rank as the world's eighth leading industrial power.

California's economic ascendancy is inseparable from a traumatic reordering of world economic power, brought on by the increased strength of the oil-producing nations and by the rise of Japan and other Asian countries as major manufacturing centers. While the Northeast and Midwest have been devastated by the OPEC price rises, California, a major oil producer that depends on overseas imports for only one fifth of its petroleum, has been less severely affected. At the same time the state's young industrial economy has grown in symbiotic tandem, not conflict, with the emergent manufacturing giants of Asia.

"The center for economic and cultural activity used to be in Europe," explains Richard Silberman, a San Diego banker, fast food and electronics tycoon, who served as a cabinet officer and top campaign official for California's Governor Edmund G. Brown, Jr. "But now the center of gravity is changing. You have masses of people in China; the industrial power of Japan. There are new markets, powerful nations there." Under the leadership of both governors Brown and Reagan, California has moved aggressively to exploit this shift in "the center of gravity." Without a sizable steel or auto industry, California has not been harmed by imports from Japan and Korea. Meanwhile the state's large agricultural, aerospace, and high technology electronics industries have found lucrative markets in the newly rich Asian nations of the Pacific Rim.

Throughout the 1970s these Pacific Rim economies—notably Japan, South Korea, Taiwan, Singapore, and Hong Kong—expanded at two or more times the rate experienced by the East's traditional trading partners in Europe. Largely as a result of this Pacific boom, the value of California's foreign trade increased by 681 percent between 1965 and 1976. In 1981, California's exports (some two thirds bound for Asian destinations) grew by an estimated 27 percent, compared to a national export growth of only 16 percent.

This sense of being part of the Pacific Rim, the world's emerging economic powerhouse, has created an excitement among Californians of virtually all political persuasions. "Out here there's a sense of being where the action is, with Japan and the Pacific," remarks Peter Hannaford, a former Reagan staff member and leading public relations adviser. "In Europe you get this sense of ennui, like nothing's going on." This belief in the shift in power from the Atlantic to the Pacific underlies the conviction, common among California political and business leaders, that the state will effectively dictate the future direction of the United States.

THE INVISIBLE HANDS

The change in "the center of gravity" in the world economy has provided California with the necessary preconditions for its ascent toward national and international prominence. But perhaps as important has been the character of the men who have steered the state's exploitation of those changes. From the days of the great Gold Rush of the 1840s, California has lured the adventurous, the innovative, as well as the ruthlessly ambitious, to its shores. These men, many of them failures, refugees from justice or political oppression, noncomformists, left the stodgy eastern seaboard, the flat Midwest, or the poverty of old Europe and Asia to find a new way of life in California. Brought up to believe that they live on the far edge of the frontier, Californians have been characteristically more willing than perhaps any population on the planet to experiment, to break with tradition. This Californian will to innovate has made the state the world's greatest mecca for far-out cults, deranged political sects, and bizarre lifestyles. To many people in the East and around the world, craziness defines California, making it difficult to take the place seriously. But it is precisely this willingness to try new things, to look at sagebrush and mesquite and see farms and cities, which has pushed California to its current position of national dominance.

While foreign and eastern seaboard pundits alike have usually chosen to focus on the Charles Mansons and other aberrations of the California character, the most important exponents of the state's innovative tradition have been found among the entrepreneurial class. Cyril Magnin has been for decades a leading member of the political and business establishment of San Francisco, the epitome of what passes for the old order in California. But Magnin, an enthusiastic investor and octogenarian chairman of the Joseph Magnin clothing chain, is no traditionalist:

California has recaptured what America once had—the spirit of pioneering. People in business out here are creative, they're willing to take risks.

We have a great pool of very able scientific minds here. That's what makes things happen ... because those kinds of people are here.

I have invested in projects that are new. I've got a hunch that the biggest opportunity is going to be in electric cars—that's the thing of the future. If you came off the street and showed me plans for a new source of energy, I'd be willing to talk to you about it and put money in it. I'm eighty years old but my thinking is probably younger than [that of] men in their forties, especially my friends back east.

The belief that technology and innovation can solve any problem, cherished by entrepreneurs like Magnin, has been the key to California's breathtaking rise to economic prominence over the past century. It began with the state's drive to control water and energy resources—the basic building blocks upon which its industrial and agricultural supremacy are constructed.

While most of the cultivated land and population centers lie south of the Sacramento River, the overwhelming bulk of California's water supplies are locked in the mountainous northeastern section of the state. Los Angeles, for instance, has local water supples at best adequate for several hundred thousand residents. The San Joaquin Valley, today the state's and the nation's richest farming area, is by nature arid, suitable mainly for grazing.

But like Cyril Magnin, the men who built California were not traditionalists. They used new strains of crops that could be grown in the dry soil and a steam-powered tractor to harvest their increasing yields. Wells and canals for catching underground water supplies were built all over the state, allowing for the early growth of both San Francisco and Los Angeles. Long before California's entrepreneurs dreamed of assaulting the Eastern welfare state, their water and power projects were among the greatest "welfare clients" of all. Through the construction of these technological wonders, California became the nation's leading agricultural state. But to become more than a farming state, California's business leaders recognized they would need power as well as water. In 1936, the state's industrial economy received a giant boost with the completion of the massive Hoover Dam, a project pushed by the state's corporate and business establishment, the engineering masterpiece of its decade.

The state's business and government leaders are today in the forefront of exploring other new, innovative technologies. Under Governor Jerry Brown, California has embarked on a large-scale drive, financed with tax rebates, to encourage conversion to alternative energy—a move that could provide up to a third of the state's energy needs by the year 2025. At the same time the San Francisco–based Pacific Gas and Electric Company and Los Angeles's Southern California Edison have each sponsored projects to explore the state's promising geothermal energy potential.

California corporations and utilities are also turning to a totally new industry, synthetic fuel, to meet their future energy needs. California-based corporations, notably Standard Oil of California, Getty Oil, Champlin Petroleum, Atlantic Richfield, and Occidental Petroleum, have been at the forefront of developing new technology to tap the huge energy resources located in the "Overthrust Belt" in the satellite states of Arizona, Idaho, Utah, and Wyoming. Yet another California-based company, Fluor Corporation, is building the nation's first workable, large-scale synthetic fuel plant.

As the center of advanced technology, home to the majority of the Western states' population and base of its largest financial institutions, California is in a powerful position to dominate the region's energy development. The West, with less than 20 percent of the nation's population, possesses nearly half of all American oil reserves, as well as nearly 90 percent of the uranium ore and two thirds of the coal. These vast resources, most of them barely tapped, represent an energy potential on the scale of the Middle East, according to some estimates. "Over the next few decades, those Californians are going to be all over us," predicts Roger Markle, corporate vice-president of the Valley Coal Company in Price, Utah. "Wherever you look in the region, you'll find Californians looking to develop our energy resources."

To some Rocky Mountain state officials, such as Phil Burgess (who is executive director of the Colorado-based Western Governors' Policy Conference), California banks, energy companies, and utilities have adopted a classic "colonial" attitude toward the comparatively underdeveloped Western hinterland. California utilities, led by Southern California Edison Company, are already pulling power to the state from the enormous 2,085-megawatt Four Corners Power Station near Farmington, New Mexico, where a once pristine environment is polluted largely for the benefit of California homes and industries. Another project to bring natural gas from Sage, Wyoming, to California via a 583-mile gas pipeline is being proposed by California energy companies. Numerous other huge projects are on the drawing boards of California corporations and utilities, all designed to make sure that their state maintains adequate energy supplies. This relentless drive to subdue other regions and nature for California's benefit, says Tom Lieser, a young economist at Los Angeles's Security Pacific National bank, lies at the heart of the state's economic ascendancy: "The history of this area is one of overcoming tremendous obstacles. Look at the water and power problems and how we overcame that. This place just can't stop growing no matter what. This is fantasy land and nothing will be able to put a stop on it."

THE GREAT DIVIDE

In the years before World War II, California was still primarily an agricultural powerhouse; its industrial economy was essentially regional, providing products for the Western market. Following the attack on Pearl Harbor, however, a massive military buildup, designed to provide the base for the great counterstrike against Japan, transformed the state almost overnight. Aircraft factories rose out of the pea fields and orange groves of Southern California, while in the north quiet fishing villages along San Francisco Bay suddenly became the shipbuilding centers for the war in the Pacific. Between 1940 and 1950, California increased its population by 53 percent, while total personal income leaped a remarkable 240.7 percent.

After the war, the Korean conflict, the "space race" with the Soviet Union, the Vietnam War, and the current Carter-Reagan military buildup all helped the fledgling California aircraft and electronics firms to flourish and turned the state into the uncontested national leader in military and technological production. In 1980, California firms won 44 percent of all NASA prime contracts, totaling over $1.6 billion, while also garnering a nation-leading 25 percent of all prime Defense Department contracts, worth another $8.8 billion.

With these dollars California firms like Hughes Aircraft, Lockheed, and Northrup have hired vast numbers of highly trained, innovative personnel. Between the 1940s and the 1970s, California's population of professional and technical workers jumped over 200 percent, five times the rate of the East. The new technologies these specialists have perfected will assure California a key position in the future of American industry. Larry Horwitz, vice-president for regional economics at Chase Econometrics, the forecasting arm of New York's Chase Manhattan Bank, notes: "The fruits and nuts are important but what keeps California going are the military and the electronics. It's not so much a question of so goes the United States, so goes California. Actually, it's the other way around. They are on the cutting edge of technology."

California's aerospace and electronics industry dominates the state's industrial economy. Between 1976 and 1980, employment in the aerospace and electronics fields increased by more than one third while backlogged orders from 1977 to 1979 grew by an incredible 224 percent. One major Los Angeles aerospace and electronics firm, Hughes Aircraft, has received so many new orders for sophisticated military and commercial gear that since 1976 it has nearly doubled its work force, to 53,000. The company currently claims to employ more electrical engineers than all the college staffs in the country, and Hughes employment development director Don Horton has tripled his recruitment budget in order to lure new workers to the company. At a time when 200,000 auto workers were out of work in the Midwest, Horton and other aerospace officials were engaged in desperate combat over potential new employees. "I know it's weird to say this in the middle of a recession," Horton, a soft-spoken engineer, says, "but it's the hardest job around to get new people. There's so much competition among aerospace, high technology companies in California that people steal from each other, do anything to get people."

The confidence, even arrogance, of California's aerospace leaders is characteristic of the state's entrepreneurial community. Long criticized by Eastern economists for their overdependence on military and space procurement, California corporations sustained their growth despite the massive aerospace layoffs of the post-Vietnam period. Instead of being consumed by gloom, as Detroit has been since the decline of the American auto industry in the late 1970s, California entrepreneurs chose to seek out new opportunities, branching into the computer, semiconductor, entertainment, and recreation industries. By 1973, for instance, at the height of the aerospace recession, California industry, through large-scale reinvestment and innovation, had taken the lead from New York as the state with the highest average hourly value added by manufacturing—a basic measurement of productivity.

Since the mid-1970s, California industries have consistently outperformed their Eastern competitors. Between 1974 and 1978, for instance, the earnings of California's major banks grew at a rate more than twice that of the fifteen largest U.S. banking institutions, predominately located in Boston, New York, and Chicago. In 1979, the profits of California's one hundred largest publicly held corporations increased by more than 40 percent, far outdistancing the 27 percent growth of the Fortune 500. Despite rising immigration, California, for the first time since 1967, experienced an unemployment rate consistently lower than the national average. By 1978, the state was home to six of the country's thirty-two wealthiest people, nearly twice its proportion of the population. More than half of the fifteen highest paid executives in the country were with California companies.

While much of this prosperity flowed into the coffers of the state's established, large companies, a significant proportion of the new wealth was created by recently formed, smaller enterprises. Whereas small business staggered through the 1970s in most regions, in California the spirit of entrepreneurship predominated. Between 1975 and 1979, new business formations in California increased at almost two and a half times the national rate. Even in the midst of the 1980 recession, which brought gloom to Wall Street and businessmen across the country, nearly 60 percent of west coast businessmen expected their enterprises to improve over the previous year, according to one insurance industry poll.

Most economists agree that this vigorous growth will continue well into the future. In 1981, the Bank of America predicted that California's growth rate would be quadruple the national average. Investment capital, both foreign and domestic, will flood the West in the 1980s but largely bypass the East and Midwest, according to a report in the *Wall Street Journal*. Manufacturing will continue to drift out beyond the Mississippi, away from New York and toward cities like Los Angeles. Employment growth in California, according to projections made by Wells Fargo Bank, will be 10 percent higher than in the rest of the nation between 1976 and 1990. The state's gross product during the decade of the 1980s is expected to soar over 70 percent, nearly 13 percent above the national norm, a recent study by the Palo Alto–based Center for Continuing Study of the California Economy concluded.

These figures encourage the men who run California's economy to feel that the future is indeed theirs. From his high-rise office in the Bank of America building in San Francisco, Walter Hoadley, the bank's vice-president and chief economist, foresees the development of a "two tier" economic system, in which the West continues to grow independently and even at the expense of a stagnating East. Looking over the magnificent San Francisco panorama, Hoadley prophesies a role of permanent decline for the East in the American economy. "The country's lagging so far behind us," he says. "We're backing into a period of tremendous growth in the 1980s out here. The West has a lot of potential resources and a dynamism which simply doesn't exist back east."

Few California business or political leaders believe the government should take any action to save the east coast from its place on the lower rung of the two-tier economy. Men like Silicon Valley electronics manufacturer W. J. Sanders III, who made a fortune through innovation, insist that sluggish, uncompetitive east coast industrial plants should be allowed to meet their fate:

We have been going the wrong way in that we are trying to shore up unproductive industries like steel. America has lost the steel battle. It's like if you've got five children to support and you can only support four, you should only support the four most productive children. We should be investing in the productive aspects of the economy where we have leadership position.

To me, the Chrysler thing is a perfect example. We shouldn't indemnify failure, we should incentivize success. The future of this country is in technology.

Overtaking the massive industrial complex of the East and Midwest has been a dream nourished in the hearts of Californians for decades. Early visionaries like Harrison Gray Otis, editor of the Los Angeles *Times,* saw this growth potential in the California vastness even before the turn of the century. Others, more spiritually inclined, looked at the state's majestic mountains, deserts, and the placid blue Pacific and almost instinctively sensed, as Aimee Semple McPherson told her followers, that in California one could find "God's great blueprint for man's abode on earth." In the decade of the 1970s such visions have all but come true. As New York has declined, Los Angeles has flourished. In the past 10 years New York's metropolitan area lost 330,000 manufacturing jobs, while Los Angeles's region generated a quarter of a million new positions. During the same decade the rate of personal income growth in Los Angeles was a full 55 percent better than New York's, 30 percent higher than Chicago's. In the 1980s, according to projections made by Chase Econometrics, employment in Los Angeles should grow 1.5 percent each year, compared to a 0.5 percent annual decline in New York. "I don't think there's any question that New York simply isn't the dominant city," concludes Andy Moody, director of metropolitan forecasting at Chase. "The whole point is there's a shift away from New York and to Los Angeles."

Much of this "shift," significantly, has taken place in precisely those areas that determine the location of the national nerve center—fashion, publishing, entertainment, and finance. In each of these crucial areas New York lost jobs while Los Angeles gained dramatically throughout the 1970s. Between 1972 and 1978, for instance, New York's famed garment district lost over 32,000 jobs while Los Angeles's booming apparel market, boosted by a docile and largely illegal immigrant work force, added 21,000 new workers to its rolls. The nation, meanwhile, increasingly deserted New York's more formal styles for the look of California casuals.

THE DREAM PACKAGERS

New York's demise during the 1970s marked the end of an era over two hundred years long in which the city dominated thought and culture. As opportunities dried up in New York and its surrounding metropolis, many bright New Yorkers migrated to other regions, particularly California and the West. By the end of the decade, New York and other Eastern industrial states had become California's leading source of immigrants, with New York alone accounting for over 16 percent of the total. Critically, among these New York exiles were some of the city's brightest entertainment lights, including Johnny Carson, Gore Vidal, Neil Simon, Bob Dylan, and Norman Lear. With the loss of these and other creative people to California, New York began to lose its entrenched position as the sole home of society's cultural elite, the breeding ground for the songs, books, and screenplays that entertain the fancy of millions across the country. The control of mass market entertainment now is a greater prize, for those who value real power, than any rewards from the old, established artistic and intellectual aristocracy.

As many of the nation's creative minds converged on Los Angeles, the native California movie, television, and recording industries exerted an almost hypnotic control over the national consciousness. By the end of the decade of the 1970s, television and movies were completely under California domination. In 1978, nearly 63 percent of all movie and television production workers lived in Southern California. More remarkably still, more than 90 percent of the world's recorded entertainment production now takes place in the Los Angeles area. For even the most pro-Eastern entertainment executive, the lure of California has become irresistible. David Salzman, chairman and chief executive officer of Group W Productions, producer of the "Mike Douglas Show," "Everyday," and others, explained why the Westinghouse affiliate chose to move its corporate headquarters from New York and Philadelphia to Los Angeles:

If you want to be an important force in TV production today—and probably for a long time to come—you have to be in the entertainment capital. Here's where you have the most personalities and stars, today and tomorrow. What's more, you have a resource pool of creative talent that runs the whole panoply from idea people to the actual executors: the writers, the directors, the producers.

Los Angeles is where you have the best and most facilities. The state of the art technology and production techniques are all here. ... Those in the industry who have said they would never leave New York and other cities are now in Los Angeles. ...

Los Angeles is the ideal locale to do TV shows because the people who mount and shape the shows are influenced by the values, mores, lifestyle, and environment in which they live. I think that New York has become atypical. Los Angeles today is not only representative of the country, but is in some key areas what America will be like tomorrow. People everywhere like to see and to identify with that.

Even the last great bastion of Eastern culture, the book industry, has fallen under Hollywood's inexorable sway. Today, as many as three or four of the top fifteen best-selling nonfiction titles are either written by media celebrities or about them; paperback publishing has become increasingly reliant on such confections as "movie novels," which turn film scripts into instant literature. The "commingling of the media" has done little to improve the quality of film or television, but it has succeeded in transforming much of the book-publishing industry into a second-rate adjunct of Hollywood. Many publishing executives, some of whose companies are owned outright by studios or vast entertainment conglomerates, consider the movie or television "tie-in" more important than the inherent quality of a literary property. Indeed, in 1980 one top publishing executive, Simon and Schuster President Richard Snyder, admitted: "In a certain sense we are the software of the television and movie media."

Unlike New York's or Boston's elite, California's cultural commissars tend not to be heavily influenced by the classic literary values and political ideals of the past. Their world, for the most part, began shortly before yesterday: its status symbols not Harvard degrees or the ability to read Latin, but the expensive cars, youthful physical appearance, and other manifestations of the "fast-lane" lifestyle endemic to Southern California. Perhaps even more important, these individuals live in a city where wealth and poverty are usually separated by enormous distances and monstrous freeways. Los Angeles is a city of individualism and rootless anonymity; you can easily avoid thinking about the realities of American society back east while commuting between Beverly Hills and Universal City, gliding from air-conditioned tower to air-conditioned tower along the great concrete slabs of the freeway system. In New York, on the other hand, even the highest ranking executive is daily treated to the gritty street reality of the urban scene. Richard Gingras, a television executive who has worked on both coasts, believes that the location of the new media center profoundly affects the men controlling the nation's mass culture:

> Clearly there's an element who control the entertainment industry. People make their decisions based upon their values, which come from living in Southern California. These people get only a certain exposure to the world. They get in their Mercedes with their car stereos and go on the freeway. They don't see the problem areas. At least in New York you see the people on the streets. If you live here [in California] you have no real concern about what the country is like. There is a media world in which people are completely enclosed. The experiential force is what is going on in the Los Angeles media celebrity world.

With this shift toward Southern California culture and ethos comes a gradual easing of the sense of social responsibility, the inherent sense of interdependence that marked the New Deal, once the central commitment of New York's intellectual and cultural elite. "New York's decline has given the country over to the know-nothings who are against the New Deal traditions," believes George Sternlieb, director of the Center for Urban Policy Research at Rutgers University and an expert in the shift of regional power. "It is sad because New York had achieved the highest level of social consciousness in American history. Los Angeles is triumphing precisely because it is so primitive. They have had the great advantage of coming last. That has given them the future. . . ."

II. The Entrepreneurial Spirit

Back in 1972, an obscure thirty-five-year-old engineer named Jim Pinto quit his job at a San Diego sophisticated instrument manufacturer. He felt his career had reached "a dead end"; he yearned to fulfill his American dream, to be his own boss, to become an entrepreneur. Taking $5,000 from his bank account, Pinto spent his first year as a businessman alone, tinkering with blueprints in his "office"—a spare room in his suburban home.

On the surface, Pinto's prospects seemed very poor. Massive military cutbacks were undermining the basis for the state's electronics industry; unemployed engineers swarmed around San Diego, taking jobs as cabbies and waiters to make ends meet. Pinto, an immigrant from India, had never owned a business before and was virtually without contacts. Yet in those dark days, when Eastern writers were smugly criticizing the "artificial" nature of California's defense-oriented economy, Pinto never gave up his faith in the power of innovation and technology. He was convinced of the long-term demand for the new products emerging from his blueprints—a series of unique, high-precision measurement instruments designed to increase industrial productivity. Even the presence of Eastern corporate giants like Honeywell in the same field failed to discourage him. Alone in his room, Pinto kept working doggedly, paying local machine shops to manufacture the prototypes for his new product line. Finally, a local banker offered to lend Pinto enough money to start his new company, Action Instruments, in a tiny ramshackle 700-square-foot office.

Nine years later Pinto was directing his company from a sprawling office complex in Kearny Mesa, a booming new industrial area in the barren foothills northeast of San Diego. Since its early days in that spare room, Action Instruments' sales volume had grown more than 50 percent annually; in 1980, it logged over $8 million in sales, its customers including such giants as Exxon, Dow Chemical, and Kodak. Dressed casually in a red plastic windbreaker and tan workman's pants, the bearded Pinto calmly predicted that Action Instruments would enter the *Fortune* top 500 list of industrial companies by the end of the 1980s.

Pinto described himself as part of an ascendant new class of California entrepreneurs, men who will use their command of technology to dominate the American economy in the waning days of the current century:

> Look, man, the entrepreneur here has already produced dazzling results. Our wealth has been produced by individuals who are not part of the Rockefellers—not the old club. We come out of a new seed, a new plant grown out of this ground. We weren't born of inherited capital, but from our own brains and guts....
>
> The old-style capitalists are heading for a brick wall. The east coast dinosaurs will soon be fighting for their lives. The key difference between them and us is people orientation; we believe the individual can still make a difference, that people can do wonders if left to their own devices.

Stories like Jim Pinto's have been repeated in California on farms, in factories, at movie studios, throughout the state's economic past. Nor are these stories merely Horatio Alger tales, poor boys making good; the peculiar genius of the California entrepreneur has been his ability to create things that are new, that have not been tried before. It is that extra element of innovation, the seizing of technological initiative, which has made the state the heartland of the future.

The explosion of the high technology electronics industry in California represents the most recent triumph of this entrepreneurial spirit. In the late 1960s and early 1970s, large cutbacks in military orders created a deep recession within the state's large aerospace/electronics industry. Between 1967 and 1976, the aerospace industry's employment dropped more than 25 percent, losing 157,000 workers. California's unemployment rate soared above the national average; in 1971, the state's population growth fell to the lowest level in over 30 years. In that same year Burbank-based Lockheed Aircraft, one of the nation's aerospace giants, staved off bankruptcy only by receiving loan guarantees from the federal government.

Yet even as the large aerospace companies were languishing, new companies like Pinto's Action Instruments were sprouting up in nonmilitary, high technology fields. These new entrepreneurial companies—notably in the areas of semiconductors, computers, and precision instruments—would pace the state's economic recovery. Domestic shipments of the U.S. semiconductor industry, half of it based in California, jumped 484 percent from 1971 to 1980. Between 1972 and 1978, largely through this sudden explosion of entrepreneurism, California's rate for creating new manufacturing jobs was more than three times the national average.

Through innovation and new applications of technology, such as home computers, California by the late 1970s had greatly reduced its once critical dependence on federal government contracts. "And we're not going to them to get those contracts," said W. J. Sanders, president of Advanced Micro Devices in Sunnyvale, "in fact we're trying to limit our contracts with them." In the early 1970s, high technology electronics had helped lead California into a deep recession; by the late 1970s those same technologies, put to different uses, allowed California to enjoy unprecedented prosperity in the face of recurring national economic downturns.

Small, entrepreneurially oriented electronics firms were the essential elements in this remarkable transformation of the state's economy. Companies like Pinto's Action Instruments, run by determined men with technological skills and vision, were able to adjust to changes in the marketplace far more easily than large, bureaucratic corporations, particularly in traditional industries like automobiles and steel. In 1980, high technology electronics companies represented nine of the nation's 25 fastest-growing small publicly held companies; of those nine, more than half were headquartered in California.

Like Action Instruments, many of these small, fast-rising companies were founded in the midst of the aerospace recession of the early 1970s. The founders of these firms shared Jim Pinto's inherent sense of destiny about their inevitable triumph over the old, lumbering industrialists of the East. Robert Kleist, an engineer who founded Printronix—a firm in Orange County that manufactures computer printers—in 1974 with $50,000 and two employees, believes that the 1980s will see the rise of the "technological businessman" from California to the top ranks of America's business leadership. From his spacious office in a modern industrial park, Kleist, whose company had 1980 sales of over $37 million and was the nation's eleventh fastest-growing small company, observed: "Old-fashioned east coast big business is inefficient. The manager has no real interest. For the entrepreneurial guy, the man who started it all, it's a big challenge. Big business gets bureaucratized, that's what they get compensated for. The president of Chrysler makes twenty times what I do, but I doubt he's doing as good a job."

By the beginning of the 1980s, California's high technology and electronics enterprises maintained 3,700 different business facilities with a total payroll of over $6 billion annually, including some 400,000 workers, 23 percent of the state's total manufacturing labor force. High technology and electronics firms, the vast majority of them companies with less than 500 employees, accounted for more than one third of the state's entire industrial expansion over the years 1963–79 and, according to one projection, are expected to produce nearly 100,000 new jobs in California from 1980 to 1983.

Today, California's electronics industry dominates the burgeoning high technology field, which by the end of this decade could rival automobile manufacturing as the world's leading industry, according to a 1980 Worldwatch Institute report. In 1979, for instance, California produced $2.7 billion worth of integrated circuits, the basic building blocks for many high technology products—a production level that surpassed that of the rest of the United States and dwarfed the output of any other country in the world, including Japan. With 34 percent of the world's integrated circuit production, California's electronics companies have become the model for all aspiring high technology companies. Japanese and other foreign industrialists today often visit the firms of the Santa Clara Valley on their trips to the United States, much as American industrialists make inspection tours of the modern Tokyo steel and automobile plants.

In many ways the current high technology businessman, like Pinto or Kleist, shares the same characteristics as the men who, in earlier decades, tamed the San Joaquin Valley, created the Hollywood fantasy factory, and first built the aerospace industry. Like these California industrial pioneers of the past, the high technology entrepreneur often comes from a modest background, not from the ranks of inherited wealth; he is frequently a Jew or an immigrant or simply an iconoclastic parvenu. It is this individual, possessed by California's unique entrepreneurial spirit, who has forged the state's current electronics boom, according to one leading industry expert, Don Valentine. Valentine, whose Capital Management Company has helped fund over thirty-five successful new California high-tech companies since the early 1970s, observes:

> There are guys who are so aggressive that it's ridiculous. All you need to start a company and make it go is a free idea, a little money, and a running start. You have to be able to go on the fast track. You have to have brass balls. . . .
> There's a lot of people here who have made a lot of money in small companies. This is still the frontier. It's still the frontier. It's like Frederick Jackson Turner revisited. Substitute computers for land.

THE CONQUISTADORS

Turner's thesis of the frontier as the shaping force in American history had not even been postulated when Henry Miller arrived in San Francisco. The year was 1850 and the port town was crowded with fortune-seekers, lured by the gold deposits discovered two years earlier at Sutter's Mill outside Sacramento. California's population swelled in the decade 1850 to 1860 from slightly under 100,000 residents to almost 380,000. While most of them came in search of the gold in the streams, Miller decided to make his gold from the earth.

The general lack of interest in farming was not just due to "gold fever"; the state's climate and chronic lack of water discouraged the traditional "yeoman farmer" approach to agriculture common in the Eastern and Midwestern lands from which most of these new Californians had come. But Miller, a German immigrant with but six dollars in his pocket, believed there was vast potential in California's land. Raw exploitation, or what some might call entrepreneurial guile, was the method Miller used to achieve his goals. With his partner Charles Lux, Miller rode around the great barren lands of California, purchasing future deeds from the heirs to Spanish land grants. After abusing the grazing privileges included with those future rights, Miller slowly coerced the owners into selling their entire estates for prices as low as $1.15 an acre. In addition, the wily "Clemenceau of the Plains," as Miller would later be known, sought after land with key riparian rights; by seizing the scarce water sources, he was able to force smaller farmers to sell out to him.

Once Miller and Lux had achieved their ruthless gains, they set about building the massive irrigation works that would later characterize virtually all of California's large-scale agriculture. To work his vast fields, Miller used large numbers of "tramp" laborers imported from the East during the era's periodic financial panics. This sorriest of innovations would later be repeated with numerous other forlorn groups. Thus a permanent class of virtual "wage slaves" was imposed on rural California—a situation that persists to the current day.

Whatever the morality of Miller's actions, the sharpness of this entrepreneur's insight paid off. By 1910 the value of California foodstuff production was more than double that of the entire state's mineral production. Miller, the former near-destitute immigrant, and his partner Lux, ruled an empire nearly as large as the kingdom of Belgium. Over a million head of cattle grazed on it. Miller's success was just the most spectacular of several stories of businessmen-farmers who built massive empires on the land. Dr. Hugh Glenn, known as the "Wheat King" of

Colusa County, owned a 57,000-acre wheat ranch during this same period which, at the time, was the largest single cultivated field owned by one man in the world. Other major landowners included William Chapman, known as "the scrip land speculator," who acquired more than a million acres of land, in part through the buying up of properties issued by the government to Indians in exchange for their tribal lands. Government surveyors themselves shared in this shameless land bonanza. One California state surveyor managed to buy 350,000 acres for himself before leaving government service, while a federal surveyor purchased a similarly immense stake including the Tejon Ranch, which eventually was controlled by the Los Angeles *Times*'s Chandler family.

What arose on the land of California was an agriculture different from anything yet seen in the rest of the country. In 1870, the average size of a California farm was three times greater than the national average. In that year California had only one tenth the number of farms then existent in New York State but two hundred times the number of farms of 1,000 acres or more. Some five hundred men in California during that decade controlled 8.6 million acres—a land mass greater than the combined states of Massachusetts and Connecticut.

But the huge land holdings of Miller, Chapman, the Chandler family, and others paled in comparison to the massive feudal kingdom controlled by the Southern Pacific Railroad. The SP owned over 11.5 million acres of land in California, largely composed of real estate that had been granted by the federal government in exchange for laying down its rail lines in the West. It represented one-fifth of the total privately held land in the state—an area significantly larger than the entire country of Switzerland.

The building of the Southern Pacific empire began in the fall of 1860 when four men—Leland Stanford, Charles Crocker, Mark Hopkins, Collis P. Huntington—gathered in a room over a Sacramento dry goods store. All four men were immigrants from the east who had grown up in modest surroundings and become successful merchants in California during the gold rush era. The "Big Four," as they later became known, started with a total investment of $15,800 and constructed their railroad lines with the aid of government loans, grants, and other subsidies as well as 10,000 poorly paid Chinese laborers. Ultimately their combined fortune was estimated at $200 million.

The Southern Pacific also emerged as the single most powerful political influence in California during the latter part of the nineteenth century. Leland Stanford was elected governor of the state in 1861, and later to the U.S. Senate. But the railroad's domination of politics did not start in earnest until 1879 when a state commission was established to regulate the railroads. The SP's response was to promptly bribe two of the three commission members and effectively block any interference in the monopolistic performance of their business. The "Southern Pacific Political Bureau" doled out free rail passes and campaign contributions to California legislators, subsidized local newspapers, and provided investment opportunities as well as outright bribes to politicians on every level of government throughout the state.

Through its manipulation of rate charges, the railroad also achieved a virtual stranglehold on the economic life of the state, extending discounts to favored industries while ruining those who opposed its power. Particularly hard-hit were farmers who were at the mercy of the SP to ship their goods to eastern markets. Watching the "iron horse" of the Southern Pacific rumble through vast stretches of the San Joaquin Valley, a character in Frank Norris's novel *The Octopus* was awe-struck by:

> ... (this) symbol of a vast power, huge, terrible, flinging the echo of its thunder over all the reaches of the valley, leaving blood and destruction in its path; the leviathan with tentacles of steel clutching into the soil, the soulless Force, the iron-hearted Power, the monster, the Colossus, the Octopus.

Soon the greedy practices of the "Octopus" had created some equally powerful enemies. Besides the farmers, manufacturing and lumber interests were chafing under the SP's rate-setting system. In Los Angeles they and other reformers began the Non-Partisan Committee which, in the words of its first secretary, Meyer Lissner, sought to "bring together the businessmen who are interested in good government." After defeating the SP-backed slate in the 1906 Los Angeles municipal elections, the reformers started the Lincoln-Roosevelt League and launched a statewide campaign to break the SP's virtual stranglehold on political and economic life in California. Their efforts came to fruition in 1910 with the election of Hiram Johnson as governor, marking the end of the three-decades-long domination of state government by the railroad.

THE GREENING OF CALIFORNIA

While frequently brutal and ruthless, California's landed gentry also advanced agricultural technology to unprecedented levels. They put to use the work of such brilliant innovators as Luther Burbank, a plant breeder who came to California from Massachusetts in 1875. After working on a Northern California farm cleaning chicken coops, Burbank started to experiment on new strains of plants adaptable to California's dry climate. His pioneer breeding methods created new varieties of lilies, plums, roses, berries, tomatoes, potatoes, corn, and squash, many of which greatly enriched the fortunes of California's agricultural businessmen. By the late 1880s the state's farming business was by far the nation's most industrialized, pioneering the use of such new technologies as the refrigerated railroad car, the steam tractor, and the "Stockton gang plow." This last invention used multiple plowshares attached to a beam pulled by a team of horses; at huge farms like the Glenn Ranch, sometimes as many as one hundred of these plows were in use at one time, each pulled by a team of eight. Such techniques on enormous ranches, employing vast numbers of wage laborers, made some of these early California farms seem more like factories than pastoral estates. Frank Norris, in *The Octopus,* captured the industrial regimentation of one of these ranches around the turn of the century:

> The plows, thirty-five in number, each drawn by its own team of ten, stretched in an interminable line, nearly a quarter of a mile in length, . . . Each of these plows held five shears, so that when the entire company was in motion, 175 furrows were made at the same instant. At a distance, the plows resembled a giant column of field artillery.

While many sensitive observers of the time were shocked by the mechanistic approach to farming, the results for California's agriculturalists were staggering. Between 1860 and 1890, wheat production jumped nearly 600 percent, making California the second-largest wheat producer in the nation. Later, the state's farmers diversified their crops and established dominance over scores of fruit and vegetable products. Shortly after the turn of the century the state was growing two thirds of the United States's orange crop, 90 percent of its lemons, and 80 percent of its wine. In the early part of the century, Los Angeles County emerged as the nation's leading agricultural county, to be replaced later by Fresno County in Henry Miller's San Joaquin Valley.

THE INHERITORS

As would occur later in such fields as electronics and aerospace, California's agricultural dominance owed much of its success to innovation—scientific, technological, and entrepreneurial. From the founding of the University of California in 1868, farmers have applied their political muscle, as well as generous donations, to the university's extensive agricultural research program, which in 1980 spent an estimated $72 million. Much of the university's agricultural research currently is focused on developing mechanized mass harvesting of some thirty-four

crops—including tomatoes, wine, lettuce, and peaches—that could ultimately reduce the farm labor force by an estimated 128,000 workers.

Equally important, California's agriculturalists have followed Henry
Miller's lead in approaching their farms as industrial enterprises. The
yeoman farmer in California today is even less of a factor than he was
in the days of the "Clemenceau of the Plains" or "the Wheat King."
Mechanization, vast irrigation projects, an intricate pattern of finance
capital, and corporate ownership have combined to produce a giantism
in agriculture on a scale more familiar in El Salvador than in traditional
Jeffersonian visions of America. In 1977 forty-five California corporations farmed 3.7 million acres, more than one third of the state's acreage
farmed that year. ". . . farming," the historian and journalist Carey
McWilliams noted in 1935, "has been replaced by industrialized agriculture, the farm by the factory." California's farmers, working on
about 3 percent of the country's farmland, produce over 9 percent of the
nation's gross farm income and 12 percent of its farm exports.

California agricultural enterprises today are among the wealthiest
and most powerful of the state's businesses. They control the largest industry in the nation's dominant state; their political power, although no
longer absolute, is still sizable in both Sacramento and Washington.
Many have become international conglomerates in themselves, applying their advanced techniques in faraway lands, exercising worldwide
influence over the prices of such products as almonds, lettuce, and
cotton.

Typical of today's California agricultural enterprises is the J. G. Boswell Company. The company was founded in 1924 by its namesake, a
crippled retired colonel from Georgia, on 440 acres in the San Joaquin
Valley. Through intensive irrigation and the lending of money to other
farmers, Boswell expanded into one of the world's largest cotton-grow-
ing and -ginning empires. Boswell now owns over 140,000 acres of prime
California agricultural farmland and also stands as the largest cotton
grower in Australia. From its modest start Boswell has become a $130
million corporate giant, its worldwide farming, marketing, and processing operations directed from a computerized headquarters located
on the forty-sixth floor of a Los Angeles highrise.

Yet even in its current corporate form, Boswell has not lost the ability
to innovate when faced with new challenges. In 1969, for instance,
floods threatened to break a levee in the San Joaquin Valley and inun-
date hundreds of Boswell-owned acres. Rather than surrender to nature, Boswell officials came up with a unique solution. They bought
seven thousand junked cars and crammed them into a weakened levee,
saving it from collapse. Asked about this highly unorthodox maneuver,

a characteristically pragmatic Boswell official simply shrugged, "There are times you just do what you have to do."

Facing the challenges of an environment vastly different from that of the familiar Eastern states, California's entrepreneurs have seen themselves as a class apart, "a new seed," in Jim Pinto's words. When the first pioneer businessman came to the largely unoccupied state, they were faced with severely limited water resources. Used to the four seasons of Europe and the East, they were now confronted, particularly in the south, with a short, rainy season and a long, dry period lasting from March until December. Three thousand miles from the sources of capital and government, these early California entrepreneurs found themselves in the midst of a long-established Mexican population with a decades-long legacy of decline. Roads, dams, farms, ports were all in disrepair, if they existed at all. The commercial infrastructure of the state was practically nonexistent.

All these conditions cried out for the formation of a new kind of entrepreneurial elite. Class pretensions, old loyalties meant little in this unique, desolate environment. Since the old solutions to problems rarely worked, expertise and credentials from the "old country," whether Europe or the Eastern United States, did not impress members of this elite. From the days of the American conquest of 1848 on, Californians were primarily concerned with getting results. Thus, from these early days, California's entrepreneurial community has been built largely by men with heavy accents, hard-bitten immigrants, dropouts from more polite societies. At a time when Jews were being systematically excluded from the upper echelons of New York and Boston society, Jewish families—Newmark, Lazard, Strauss—were welcomed into the early social elites of San Francisco and Los Angeles. Even an alleged former pirate, Joseph Chapman, could migrate to Southern California and, by the 1850s, be fully accepted. Los Angeles management consultant Dave Norris, himself a product of a century-old San Francisco family, believes that California's entrepreneurial community today still lacks the sort of rigid social structure characteristic of the Eastern part of the country. A former Kaiser Steel Company executive and consultant to scores of California entrepreneurs, Norris observes:

> Over the years most of our entrepreneurs became entrepreneurs because they had to. There was no opening for them so they created new ones.
> The guys here have always had a "go to hell" attitude. There's not much class consciousness in the Los Angeles business community.

The social registry of this town is about one step removed from the bandits.

MANIFEST DESTINY

What the conditions of California called for were not men of breeding but men of determination. From the Gold Rush days on, California's entrepreneurs have bolstered themselves with a particularly fanatic belief in their manifest destiny; faced with tremendous obstacles, as well as a land of unquestionable promise, the Californians chose to *will* themselves to greatness. Unlike other westerners, they objected almost immediately to being a mere economic resource colony for the imperial centers of the Northeast. The California businessman wanted to be his own boss, to create his own civilization along the pristine shores of the Pacific. As General Harrison Gray Otis, the editor of the Los Angeles *Times*, declared on March 1, 1887: "Few Californians of today have any adequate conception of the magnificent future that lies before their state. Its destiny is high and its future assured; only let them be worked out to their fullest by the fortunate men and women whose lots are cast on these western shores."

When Otis wrote this bold proclamation of manifest destiny, California still was essentially a colony of the great Eastern centers, trading foodstuffs and gold for Eastern manufactures. More remarkable still, Los Angeles, the centerpiece of Otis's vision, was at the time little more than a sun-drenched, lazy cowtown. Since its founding by a handful of pioneers from colonial Mexico, escapees in fact from that economically static society, the city had grown slowly, sleeping through the early phases of the industrial revolution, passing in obscurity from Spanish, to Mexican, and, finally, American control. At the time of Otis's pronouncement, the city had no more than 50,000 residents.

But Otis, an ambitious real estate speculator and risk capitalist beneath his thin journalist's mask, believed his little provincial town could transform itself into a great metropolis. A product of an Ohio farm, Otis knew what it was to pull oneself up by the bootstraps; he first learned the newspaper business as a printer's apprentice and quickly gained other journalistic experience, including a stint as an editor for the *Grand Army Journal* after a distinguished military career in the Civil War. He had struggled to become what he was and he expected those in his adopted city to do the same. He believed the Los Angeles of the 1880s, home to more cowpunchers than foundrymen, could evolve into an industrial power as great as Cleveland or even New York. "No city in the United States," Otis insisted, "can offer superior inducements to Los Angeles as a field for manufacturing enterprises."

Despite the persuasion of the *Times,* Los Angeles, indeed all of California, showed little promise of becoming a manufacturing center. The state was far from known coal and iron reserves, at that time the essential building blocks for the civilized world's industrial centers. While San Francisco was blessed with a fine natural harbor, Los Angeles's port at San Pedro was a 30-mile ride from downtown and consisted of little more than a few piers. Worst of all, Los Angeles and most other California cities were chronically short of water; the springs and rivers of Southern California could slake the thirst, at best, of several hundred thousand residents.

Yet like Boswell's men at the crumbling levee, Otis and the other hard-driving businessmen of Los Angeles would not accept the commandments of nature. Around the turn of the century the former mayor of the city, an engineer named Fred Eaton, started exploring the possibility of constructing an aqueduct to tap runoff water from snow on the eastern slopes of the Sierra Nevada and transport it nearly 250 miles south to Los Angeles. In 1904 the city's chief engineer, a self-educated, outspoken Irishman named William Mulholland, began work on the project, including raising money through a local bond issue to finance what became known as "the Panama Canal of the West." After a bitter struggle with the hapless farmers of the Owens Valley, whose water supplies were siphoned off by the Los Angeles project, the aqueduct was opened in 1913. It ushered in a new era in the history of California.

The aqueduct made Mulholland a near-deity in the eyes of Los Angeles entrepreneurs, many of whom, including Otis, reaped enormous benefits from landholdings suddenly made immensely valuable through the importation of water. Civic leaders proclaimed Mulholland "California's Greatest Man." Otis and other business leaders offered Mulholland the chance to be the city's next mayor, an offer he refused in no uncertain terms. "I would rather give birth to a porcupine backwards," Mulholland told admirers in his pronounced brogue, "than be mayor of Los Angeles."

The worship of Mulholland and his rather offhanded rejection of the city's highest political post affords some insight into the relative importance of the various key figures in California's development. While most historians concentrate on the careers of the state's political and literary figures, it has been the engineers and entrepreneurs who have literally created California out of wasteland. (Today in the age of high-tech the engineer and entrepreneur have largely become one.) While its politicians have grabbed headlines and its writers touched the reader's imagination, California's ascendancy was arranged by men who *built* things. Few politicians in California history—even the prominent reformers Hiram Johnson and Earl Warren—have been even remotely as influential in the rise of California as engineers like Mulholland and the entrepreneurial elite.

Indeed, even with water supplies assured by the aqueduct, Los Angeles might not have grown as far or as fast had it not been for another visionary, Henry Huntington. A native of the East, Huntington came to California in 1892 and ten years later settled in Los Angeles where, like Otis, he was soon captivated by the city's potential:

> I am a foresighted man and I believe that Los Angeles is destined to become the most important city in this country, if not in the world. It can extend in any direction as far as you like. Its front door opens on the Pacific, the ocean of the future. Europe can supply her own wants; we shall supply the wants of Asia. There is nothing that cannot be made and few things that will not grow in Southern California.

Huntington knew that the Los Angeles area—then a collection of some forty-two autonomous, only loosely connected municipalities and districts—could never become a major urban center until the pieces were bound together, in his words, "in one big family." To accomplish this enormous task, Huntington, an heir to the Southern Pacific Railroad fortune, in the first decade of the twentieth century, constructed his extensive Pacific Electric mass transit system. Along with the Owens Valley water supplies, Huntington's rail system, which had more cars than his five largest national competitors combined, took Los Angeles out of its horse and buggy era and into the ranks of major metropolitan areas. Los Angeles's population soared from 100,000 in 1900 to nearly 600,000 in the early 1920s.

THE OIL-FIRED ECONOMY

Despite engineering triumphs and exponential growth in Los Angeles, California in the years after World War I remained predominately a resource colony for the dominant Eastern interests. Steel production, the measure of industrial strength at the time, was negligible. Agriculture was still far and away the state's dominant industry; the food-processing plants, particularly canneries, were the largest manufacturing employers in California until the early 1920s.

The discovery of large oil deposits in California during the 1890s greatly expanded this resource-centered economy. As a result of major finds in the San Joaquin Valley and the Los Angeles area, California in 1903 became the nation's largest oil producer, with an annual production of over 24 million barrels. In 1910, explorers for the fledgling Los Angeles–based Union Oil Company made a breakthrough discovery near Taft in the San Joaquin Valley. The gusher exploded with such fury that it literally blew apart the derrick standing above it; ultimately that one deposit yielded nearly 10 million barrels of oil. Soon other discoveries were made throughout Southern California, producing along with them a whole new generation of entrepreneurs. "Oil fever" seemed to seize the whole population: a gusher in the backyard became the latest version of the "pot of gold." Among those swept up by the tide was a young Los Angeles millionaire who had planned an early retirement and a life of ease. But John Paul Getty could not sit still. As he later recalled:

> . . . I observed the rapid growth of new derrick forests in beach-areas, on hillsides and amidst orange groves. Other men were boring down into pay sands, bringing in gushers, opening up new fields. For my part, I lolled on sandy beaches and opened up nothing that could possibly gush except far too many champagne bottles. This state of affairs first nagged, then gnawed and finally became intolerable.
> I un-retired.

By 1923, California's oil output had reached 263 million barrels, a ten-fold increase in production in only 20 years. Out of this boom would emerge the tycoons and the companies that would play a major role in California's remarkable economic and political development, including Getty, Union Oil's E. L. Doheny, and Thomas Bard, a U.S. senator and a founder of Union Oil. Oil companies would constitute the five largest industrial corporations in California by the late 1970s: Standard Oil of California, Atlantic Richfield, Occidental Petroleum, Union Oil, and Getty Oil. Along with the established agriculture and railroad interests (predominately the Southern Pacific), these oilmen have helped shape the careers of many California political leaders, including Richard Nixon and Ronald Reagan.

As in agriculture, California oilmen have long been leaders in developing innovative technologies. John Paul Getty built a sprawling oil business by integrating refining, transportation, and exploration on an international scale. His successors at Getty Oil today are leading in the new technologies for processing tarlike "heavy oil," the largest deposits of which lie in the San Joaquin Valley. In the 1930s, Western Geophysical Company run by Henry Salvatori, a major sponsor of Ronald Reagan's political career, pioneered new scientific methods for increasing the efficiency of oil exploration. Since the mid-1960s the Los Angeles–based Atlantic Richfield Company has been in the forefront in developing the previously unexplored Arctic wilderness of Alaska.

But perhaps the most visionary of today's California oilmen is Dr. Armand Hammer, who took over a small, declining Los Angeles oil company called Occidental Petroleum in the early 1960s and transformed it into the twentieth largest industrial company in the United States. Hammer, eighty-two, traveling around the world in his twenty-passenger Gulfstream jet, has cultivated vast business and political contacts in such countries as Libya, the Soviet Union, Romania, and Poland. He was among the first to advocate the use of new techniques to recover oil from shale rock, a process being refined by Occidental engineers. Hammer in recent years has insisted repeatedly that oil shale deposits in the "Overthrust Belt" of the Rocky Mountain states hold the key to solving the nation's energy problems: "There are two and a half times the oil reserves of the whole free world locked up in three Western states—Colorado, Utah, and Wyoming. We have perfected our methods of processing oil shale underground, and if we get the incentives, the oil crisis could be solved by the middle of this decade [the eighties]."

Such claims have been derided by many industry and government officials who maintain that oil shale technology has not advanced to the high levels suggested by the peripatetic Dr. Hammer. But with a self-assurance characteristic of California's corporate class, Hammer calmly predicts his course will win out. "Somebody has to be first," he explains. "The industry will follow."

BUILD WE MUST

In the first four decades of the twentieth century, the supposedly unmixable elements of oil and water established the foundations for California's future industrial economy. Oil keyed a rapid 30 percent jump in export trade from the West's four principal ports between 1901 and 1911, a figure nearly double the increase enjoyed by the four leading harbors of the Eastern states. By 1925, oil refining had replaced food processing as California's leading industry by far, generating $369 million in revenues that year. The demands of this quickly expanded industry created new opportunities for California's engineers and entrepreneurs.

Among those plunging into the oil exploration and refining boom was John Simon Fluor, a Swiss immigrant who started an engineering and construction firm in Santa Ana, California, in 1912. In part through its work for the oil industry, the Fluor Corporation quickly developed a reputation for getting the job done whatever the obstacles. Like Henry Miller or William Mulholland, neither John Simon Fluor nor his nephew and successor, J. Robert Fluor, came to Los Angeles as men of consequence; they created their own success through determination, constant innovation, and the development of superior technology.

Today, Fluor Corporation, with over $4.8 billion in sales in 1980, ranks as one of the nation's largest engineering and construction firms. Although the company's current chairman, president, and chief executive officer, J. Robert Fluor, lacks a college degree, his company has emerged as one of the most respected engineering firms in the world. Since its founding Fluor has helped train more than 100,000 foreign nationals in the company's construction techniques. The company's current projects include a $5 billion gas refinery in Saudi Arabia, a $2 billion coal liquefaction plant in South Africa, and an $800 million copper-mining project in the People's Republic of China.

In November 1980, Fluor invested $12 million in Genentech, Inc., the California-based firm pioneering in recombinant DNA research. The investment is an effort to apply possible breakthroughs in genetic engineering to shale oil development, in which Fluor has been active. At fifty-nine, Robert Fluor blithely explained: "The idea is, we turn some bugs loose in coal and then they chew like hell and turn out oil."

Fluor also recently tendered an offer to purchase St. Joe Minerals Corp., which owns mines in Argentina, Chile, Peru, and Australia, as well as some of the most promising land in California's old mother lode gold area.

At the firm's annual meeting in 1981, J. Robert Fluor stood before the stockholders, pulled some money out of his pockets, and proclaimed: "Here is a hundred dollar bill, a five dollar bill, a one dollar bill, a dime, a nickel, and four pennies. And $106.19 is what this 1960 dollar would be worth today if you had invested it in Fluor stock."

The emergence of Fluor in Southern California paralleled the rise of another construction engineering giant, the San Francisco–based Bechtel Corporation. The company's founder, Warren Bechtel, was a German immigrant mule skinner who in 1898 began to hire out animals for railroad construction work. A pioneer in the use of the diesel-powered shovel for road construction work, Bechtel, like Fluor, developed a reputation for getting results quickly and efficiently. Bechtel's son, Steven, led the company to a position as the world's leading construction engineering firm and amassed a personal fortune estimated at $700 million, making him one of the world's five wealthiest men.

Men like Warren Bechtel and John Simon Fluor represented a new brand of businessman, particularly adapted to the ambitions of California business leaders. Seeking an imperium, the state's elite, from the days of Harrison Gray Otis and William Mulholland, has depended on engineering solutions to its problems. This familiarity with massive projects, be they freeways, rail systems, or oil refineries, has made companies like Bechtel ideally suited to the needs of modern societies. As the pioneer and behemoth of the construction engineering business, Bechtel in recent years has won such prized contracts as the engineering of the rapid transit systems of San Francisco and Washington; the construction of the 1,100-mile trans-Arabian pipeline and a $20 billion industrial seaport project in Saudi Arabia; and a $190 million 10-acre world trade center in Moscow. Due to its involvement in such "megaprojects," Bechtel between 1970 and 1978 nearly tripled its annual revenues to $6.4 billion.

But it was back home in California, where early dreams demanded the presence of large engineering concerns, that companies like Bechtel and Fluor first developed their reputations. In 1931, Warren Bechtel and his friend, the Oakland industrialist Henry Kaiser, were instrumental in putting together the famous "Six Companies" whose original task was to build the Hoover Dam. Kaiser, like Bechtel, a hard-bitten entrepreneur, had started out modestly, building roads. Encouraged by the state's expanding oil- and food-based resource economy, Kaiser wanted to establish a true industrial infrastructure for the state.

The son of an upstate New York shoemaker, Kaiser had left school before his thirteenth birthday and ended up owning a photographic studio. In 1906, at age twenty-four, Kaiser struck out west, settling in Spokane, Washington. He worked as a salesman for a hardware company and later for a sand and gravel firm. Kaiser started his own road construction firm in 1914, and soon gained a reputation as a highly efficient, innovative contractor. After building roads from British Columbia to California, he moved his business to Oakland and started expanding his scope of operations. Without any formal engineering education, Kaiser built up an enormous construction company with interests eventually extending into the manufacture of such basic building materials as sand, gravel, aluminum, and steel, and the ownership of communications and health-care concerns as well. But at heart Henry Kaiser remained a builder, a man whose vision of California's future greatness was tied inexorably to the construction of the largest possible infrastructure of concrete and steel:

> ... Necessity is the great creator. All of our facilities are inadequate. Housing, communications, highways, transportation, and all of the institutional life which modern living requires, are taxed far beyond their capacity. Furthermore, there are many essentials which we have never enjoyed. So vast were the resources of the west that we seemed incapable of organizing them for the good which should have been our portion.
> And so the stage is set, and now let the play begin.

The Hoover Dam provided Kaiser with one of his first opportunities to seize that "portion" from the rich but rugged country of the West. Working on a road project in Cuba, Kaiser became obsessed with the dam project as soon as he heard about it. "Word of the project got down there," he later recalled, "and I lay awake nights in a sweltering tent thinking about it over and over." To divert water for the dam, Kaiser, Bechtel, and the other contractors for the federally sponsored project had to blast four tunnels, each a mile long, through Arizona canyon walls. To contain over 10 trillion gallons of water in the dam's reservoir, walls over sixty stories high were built. Under the leadership of Kaiser, the "Six Companies" completed the dam in 1936, a remarkable two years ahead of schedule.

During the ensuing years of the Roosevelt administration, Kaiser oversaw the construction of other key Western dams, including Parker, Bonneville, and Grand Coulee. With these projects California at last garnered sufficient water and power to allow for full-scale industrialization.

The rapid rise of such industrialists as Kaiser required, in its turn, the development of a home-grown financial community. Through the 1800s California, like the rest of the nation, remained a financial dependent of the established banking houses of the East and Europe. Small financial institutions, such as Wells Fargo in San Francisco and the Farmers and Merchants Bank (later Security Pacific) in Los Angeles, can trace their origins back to the Gold Rush era; but for large sums of capital, Californians were forced to look east.

Yet even as Henry Kaiser prepared to build the dams that would help transform California and the West, he found a California-based bank able to match resources with the conservative New York bankers. Kaiser's banker was Amadeo P. Giannini, whose Bank of America would extend an enormous (for that time) $43 million line of credit to the Oakland industrialist.

Like many of the other major business giants of the pre–World War II era in California, Giannini was a thoroughly self-made man. Born in 1870, the son of Italian immigrants, he was already a successful San Francisco produce merchant when, at age thirty-four, he opened his Bank of Italy in California in 1904. Uninhibited by formal education in the stately craft of banking, Giannini ran his bank with the homespun guile learned in the produce trade. Precisely because he was a newcomer, Giannini was able to adapt his loan policies to the unique conditions of California. He pioneered the use of branch banking in the state's highly mobile society and made numerous loans to working-class people, practices considered anathema back on the east coast. Combining his numerous branches around the state with his ample knowledge of agricultural markets, Giannini was able to shift his loan funds to match the seasonal needs of different types of farmers in the various regions of the state.

Giannini's bank flourished, becoming the state's largest by the 1920s. At the end of that decade the old man retired and placed his bank, now called the Bank of America, under the control of a manager from the East. Quickly, the new head man scuttled Giannini's innovative methods and returned the bank to traditional, staid business practices. Soon the Bank of America was in deep trouble; in 1932, an ill and aged Giannini felt compelled to return to San Francisco from his convalescence overseas. Resuming control of the bank, Giannini reimposed his California-bred concepts. The bank recovered. By staying true to its founder's novel conceptions, in 1945 Bank of America took its place as the nation's largest bank.

Today, California ranks second only to New York as the nation's banking and financial capital. Five of the country's fifteen largest banks are now located in the state, as well as four of the ten largest diversified financial companies. By the late 1970s, California banks had nearly 65 percent of the combined assets of the long-dominant New York banks, while California's savings and loans had triple the assets of their New York counterparts.

Equally important, since the rise of Giannini, California's financial institutions have established themselves as the trendsetters in new banking techniques and procedures. The state's banks have pioneered the mass branch banking system, the use of automated tellers and credit cards, the aggressive "hustling" of loans by local managers. California is the home for the nation's largest interstate bank-holding company, the $30 billion Los Angeles–based First Interstate Bancorp. "West coast banking," concluded a top New York bank consultant, David Cates, in 1981, "is the forefront of American banking."

Throughout this century California's aggressive, nontraditional financial institutions have helped accelerate the state's remarkable development. In the 1920s and 1930s, bankers like Giannini provided the capital that established the San Joaquin Valley as the nation's richest farming area. During the 1950s California-based savings and loan institutions, including the nation's largest, Los Angeles–based Home Savings, financed much of the new construction needed by the state's fast-growing population and new businesses. Today California's financial institutions, ranging from venture capital funds to more traditional commercial banks, have shown a marked interest in helping entrepreneurs in such areas as motion pictures, garments, and high technology electronics. Conrad Jamison, a student of the state's banking history and chief economist for Los Angeles's Security Pacific National Bank, believes that the California banker long has shown a markedly stronger tendency to back the newcomer, the guy with entrepreneurial vision, than his counterparts on the east coast: "We have always been different here. This is an area that's responsive to new business. The economy is growing and can accommodate new companies. Back east a new company has to cut into someone else's business. There you have old relationships—it's hard to break in. You have to belong to the club to get a foothold. Here change is accepted, even by bankers."

THE WAY WEST

California's reputation as a land for fresh starts helped lure some of the 2 million Americans who migrated to the state between 1920 and 1930. While oil and agriculture continued to expand, those resource-based industries could not hope to provide the jobs necessary to employ this massive influx. The state's economy—despite the grandiose visions and brilliant accomplishments of the engineer-businessmen—still was in its industrial infancy, particularly in Southern California, where more than 70 percent of the new migrants chose to settle.

The Great Depression accentuated those problems both by reducing employment and by pushing millions more toward California's shores. Between 1920 and 1940, Los Angeles became the focus of this great migration, its population jumping from 577,000 to over 1.5 million people. Refugees from Oklahoma, Arkansas, Texas, and other regions of the great "Dust Bowl" crowded into unsettled canyons and deserted pea fields, sometimes unable to find any sort of work for years. One frightened observer wrote: "Like a swarm of invading locusts migrants crept in over all the roads. . . . Often they came with no funds and no prospects, apparently trusting that heaven would provide for them. . . . They camped on the outskirts of town, and their camps became new suburbs."

Civic leaders like Harry Chandler, who succeeded his father-in-law Harrison Gray Otis as publisher of the Los Angeles *Times*, made efforts to lure heavy industry to employ this huge work force. But few manufacturers, particularly in the depressed thirties, wanted to chance the move to California. Mulholland, Kaiser, Bechtel, and Fluor had helped construct the foundations of an industrial economy with their refineries, dams, and hydroelectric power stations; all that was missing were the factories. California was still, as the novelist and political reformer Upton Sinclair had written in 1920, "a parasite upon the great industrial centers of other parts of America."

The only industry to move into California on a large scale before World War II was one not solicited by the likes of Harry Chandler. In 1908, Colonel William Selig, a pioneer filmmaker, had photographed the historic *The Count of Monte Cristo*, California's first commercial film, in Los Angeles. Soon other filmmakers trekked to the desert city, where they received a tepid welcome at best. They came for reasons early pioneers like Henry Miller or Joseph Chapman would have understood. For the most part, these were men without large capital resources, poorly educated, often immigrants with thick accents. They deserted New York, where the film business originated. Also, in New York the movie people had lived a second-class life, in the shadow of a glamorous Broadway. In Los Angeles there was no such competition.

If ever there was a "new seed," these men were it. William Selig, for instance, had been an upholsterer; Sam Goldwyn, later one of the great moguls, got his start as a glove salesman; the Warner brothers were sons of a butcher.

Like the other key entrepreneurs of California, however, these men were possessed with vision, an instinct for the future. Almost alone among their contemporaries, they understood the nation's desperate need for fantasy, entertainment on a vast scale. "The demand was ahead of the supply," another of these brash film-making pioneers, Adolph Zukor, later wrote. Anything could be sold and "nobody took the business seriously."

By 1915, the film business payroll had jumped to $20 million and within five years was Los Angeles's leading industry. The movie business expansion transformed the once obscure Hollywood section of the city from a quiet suburb of 166 in 1903 to a crowded, nerve-wracking, bustling urban community of 235,000 by 1930. By 1938, the film business ranked fourteenth among America's industries in terms of volume of business and was eleventh in assets.

Equally important, the film industry put Los Angeles and California on the map in a way that all the machinations of Otis, Mulholland, and Huntington could never hope to do. The stars created by the new industry—from Mary Pickford to Charles Chaplin—were among the best-known Americans in the world. In twenty short years the movie moguls had transformed Los Angeles from a staid town of oilmen and produce dealers into a flashy center of international society.

Today, with over 83,000 employees, the entertainment industry is an important, although hardly predominant, factor in the economy of California. It has served over the years to make the Los Angeles region the nation's mass cultural capital and more recently the fabricator of much of our political mythology. But back in the 1930s the movie business so overshadowed everything else in California as to become the source of most information about the state in the world beyond the Sierras.

This concentration on Hollywood did not work all to California's advantage. The movie community tended to lend a bizarre image to the entire state with its wild parties, sordid scandals, and fantasy-land atmosphere. Rather than seeing California as the land of entrepreneurs, as Henry Kaiser and Amadeo Giannini had done, most Americans perceived California as being basically a lotus land, an unreal place not to be taken seriously like, say, Chicago. These negative images were often supplied by visiting literati, among them F. Scott Fitzgerald, William Faulkner, Sinclair Lewis, and Nathanael West, who came to make money from the movie industry and left cursing the foibles of "tinsel town." In a typical assessment, William Faulkner wrote off Los Angeles as little more than "the plastic asshole of the world."

WAR AND PEACE

The transformation of California from lotus land to industrial giant began with the outbreak of World War II. What gold, land, oil, engineering marvels, and visionary entrepreneurs had failed to bring about, fear of Imperial Japan accomplished in short order. With no equivalent of England standing between the Axis and the Pacific Coast, California suddenly became the immediate staging area for the great Allied counteroffensive. Between 1940 and 1944, over $800 million was invested in some 5,000 new industrial plants in Southern California alone; the value of Los Angeles's manufacturing output jumped during the war from $5 billion to $12 billion. From the fog-shrouded Northern California coast to the Mexican border, a vast army of workers tore up fields and forests, building the essential infrastructure for the state's future industrial dominance. Total personal income in California tripled during the war years.

For the brilliant, innovative industrial pioneers of California, the war presented unprecedented opportunities, which were duly taken. Although Henry Kaiser had virtually no prior experience as a shipbuilder, in 1942 the Oakland industrialist took upon himself the task of directing one of the most ambitious shipbuilding programs in world history. Setting up new shipyards in the Bay Area harbors of Richmond, Oakland, and Sausalito, as well as at San Pedro in Southern California, Kaiser developed a novel method of ship construction using prefabricated parts and new welding techniques. Working twenty-four hours a day, Kaiser's crews by 1943 were launching a new "Liberty ship" every ten hours. In all, Kaiser's West Coast yards accounted for the production of some 1,490 "liberty ships," 35 percent of the nation's total merchant fleet construction during the war. In the same period Kaiser also built the West's first steel plant, located at Fontana, on the high desert plateau 50 miles east of Los Angeles. After four years of war, Kaiser was no longer a strange maverick industrialist in "lotus land"; he became known as the model entrepreneur of his age, the man who *Fortune* magazine would later claim "created the role of the executive who could master [diverse] industries."

The war also provided exceptional opportunities for California's struggling young aircraft industry. During the 1920s and 1930s, many of the pioneers of the industry—John K. Northrup, Donald Douglas, Howard Hughes among them—had established themselves in Southern California largely because of the area's ideal climatic conditions. But before the war, the aircraft business was little more than a plaything; despite the efforts of men like Billy Mitchell, even most military officers failed to perceive the central importance of flying machines in the modern age.

The destruction of much of the nation's air- as well as seapower at Pearl Harbor, and the evident might of Japan's aerial forces, led to Washington's demand for massive airplane production. Suddenly a previously indifferent government wanted thousands of new, advanced planes—many times the number built in all the years since the Wright Brothers' initial flight. With a large concentration of aircraft firms already in Southern California, Los Angeles became the focal point for an instant large-scale industry: the region filled fully one quarter of all the government's airplane orders between 1941 and 1945.

At war's end California, at last, was an industrial power. Manufacturing employment by 1947 was 66 percent higher than it was in 1929. Population continued to swell: in 1942 alone, California gained 640,000 new residents, accounting for nearly 90 percent of the nation's total population increase that year. Peace brought no end to this tide of immigration. Many of the estimated 7 million servicemen who had been through California during the war now wanted to settle in the state. Between 1940 and 1947, California gained a total of 3 million people, rising from the fifth to the third most populous state in the country.

But many wondered if the state's new industrial economy could adjust to peace. By early 1946, cutbacks in military contracts brought a quick increase in California's unemployment rate. In Los Angeles, "the arsenal of democracy," gloom reigned. "Peace," Mayor Fletcher Bowron warned darkly, "threatens industrial dislocation in this area which might throw thousands out of work. . . . The good Lord didn't intend this to be an industrial city."

Yet while politicians and Eastern economic experts were predicting a long-term slowing of California's growth, the state's corporate leaders were determined not to lose the precious momentum provided by the war. The heady successes in the wartime production of aircraft, electronic instruments, and shipbuilding had instilled a new confidence among industialists. The technological advancements these men had made in war—new aerodynamic designs, advanced circuitry, radar, among others—were now seen as providing the tools for dominating the peace.

At the center of this ambitious group of businessmen was Howard Hughes, the son of a Texas oil-bit manufacturer, who had come to Los Angeles in the 1920s to make his name as a filmmaker. Although born to a sizable fortune, Hughes spurned the lifestyle acceptable to the establishment gentlemen of the East. He chased starlets, notably Jean Peters and Katharine Hepburn, with a most unaristocratic vigor; and he ignored conventions, in social life, in business, in politics.

Outside of Hollywood, Hughes's greatest interest was in airplanes and the technology that made them work. Almost as a lark, he established his Hughes Aircraft Company in 1936 at the Union Air Terminal in Burbank. His entire staff consisted of twenty-four engineers and craftsmen. In 1938, while Hughes was preparing for his record around-the-world flight, this group designed and built a special radio communication device that was waterproof, unsinkable, and self-contained. It was his first step into what would ultimately become the main business at Hughes Aircraft—electronics.

Believing war with Japan was inevitable, Hughes on the weekend of July 4, 1941, moved Hughes Aircraft, now grown to over five hundred employees, to a far more spacious site at Culver City. During the war that started the following December, Hughes's Culver City facility became a beehive of activity. Specializing in aircraft weaponry, Hughes Aircraft played an important role in establishing American technological supremacy over the Axis powers.

While the innovations designed at Hughes came in handy for defeating the Japanese and the Germans, few easterners saw much long-term potential in Hughes and his Los Angeles–based circle of technicians in the postwar economy. They calmly expected that, with the war boom over, grass would grow on the streets near the massive hangars in Culver City.

But Hughes, following an already well-established California entrepreneurial pattern, refused to accept the conventional wisdom. Perhaps the first American capitalist fully to comprehend the industrial potential of electronics and other advanced technologies, Hughes in the late 1940s brought in thousands of scientists, technicians, and skilled laborers to his Southern California plants. While the Eastern giants smugly returned to building cars and toasters, Hughes brought Los Angeles the keys to the future. As Charles ("Tex") Thornton, one of Hughes's top assistants after the war, would later recall: "When Mr. Hughes brought me out here we were alone, starting this high technology business. It all happened in a flicker of the eye. The leaders of the East were in a different environment, absorbed by current demands, by tomorrow's situation. They couldn't see the future. They let us take the best people from under RCA and GE. We made the commitment when no one else would."

Just as he had anticipated war with Japan, Hughes realized that the military would continue to be dependent on advanced technologies in the tense "peace" that followed the Allied victory. The emerging "cold war" with the Soviet Union—so the ferociously anti-Communist Hughes believed—would prevent the United States from returning to the "normalcy" of the post–World War I era. From now on, he predicted, the United States would need to maintain enormous "forces in standing," a permanent miliary establishment with an industrial equivalent, in order to counter the Soviet threat. Thus in 1946 Hughes set up one of the world's first "think tanks" to develop new high technology military products. Among the early initiatives of this new enterprise was the development of the world's first air-to-air guided missile, the three-dimensional radar system and the operational laser.

In the late 1940s, California's aircraft giants—Hughes, Northrup, Douglas, Lockheed, and North American Aviation—started reaping the benefits of new military contracts, as Hughes had predicted. As a result of their technological superiority, by 1948 Southern California's aircraft manufacturers had established complete supremacy over their Eastern competitors, winning more than 55 percent of all the Pentagon's airplane contracts, twice their percentage during the war. This was the beginning of the first sustained peacetime defense boom in the nation's history, accounting for more than half of California's economic growth between 1947 and 1957.

But Hughes's vision extended far beyond military concerns. Hughes, according to Thornton, believed that the devices first developed for the military would eventually spawn a whole new series of civilian-oriented technologies and products. "Technologies exploded," Charles Thornton later recalled, "technologies that first went to the military would then spill into new products like computers, calculators, and other devices."

In 1953, Thornton left Hughes to establish his own high technology company, Litton Industries. A West Texas native who once chopped cotton for 10¢ an hour, Thornton ignored the old-line industrial pattern and concentrated on developing such new technologies as data processing, aircraft guidance systems, digital computers, and scores of other advanced electronic devices. Today Litton stands as one of the giants of American industry, employing over 76,000 workers, with 1979 sales of over $4 billion.

Largely as a result of the vision of men like Hughes and Thornton, California has emerged as the nation's dominant center for high technology. Companies like Hughes have spun off such giants as Litton and TRW, started by former Hughes engineer Dr. Simon Ramo; Litton itself in the twenty-seven years between its founding and 1980 trained executives who now head up some twenty-seven companies, mostly in the high technology field. Today, one third of the state's fifteen largest industrial firms are involved in advanced technology and its applications.

ARSENALS OF DEMOCRACY?

From the days of Luther Burbank's pioneering experiments in genetics to today's latest advances in electronics, California's entrepreneurs have sought to exploit the fruits of the most recent scientific and technical innovations. This passion for achieving the "state of the art" has led the state's business leaders to foster the development of California's colleges and universities.

In education, as in so many other matters, California businessmen have been obsessed with getting results. Since few of the state's entrepreneurs were shaped themselves by the traditional academic institutions of the East, California's top colleges and universities were not built on the old Ivy League model. Where schools like Harvard and Princeton have stressed the training of leaders, with a strong emphasis on the humanities and moral values, California's schools have tended to be focused more upon the sciences and engineering fields so crucial to the state's economic development. All three of California's most respected institutions of higher education—the University of California, California Institute of Technology, and Stanford University—have sought to establish their excellence in the "practical" scientific and technological fields dear to their corporate sponsors.

This concentration has helped make California the nation's leading center of advanced work in such economically applicable areas as the natural sciences, mathematics, biology, chemistry, physics, and engineering. By the early 1960s, California became the home to far more Nobel laureates than any other region of the country, a trend that has continued to the present day. The state has also consistently enjoyed wide leads in its representation in such prominent groups as the National Academy of Science. In 1980, for instance, Californians won seven of the twenty Medals of Science awards granted by President Jimmy Carter.

Although the old-line Ivy League institutions continue to hold an upper hand in such fields as law, philosophy, history, and English, California's schools predominate in the more practical (i.e., ultimately profit-making) areas. A 1977 study by Professors Seymour Martin Lipset and Everett Carll Ladd, Jr., showed that California's schools held three of the four most highly regarded graduate faculties in chemistry; three of the top six in engineering; two of the top four in mathematics; and three of the five leaders in physics.

George Sternlieb, director of Rutgers University's Center for Urban Policy Research, believes that the technological orientation of California's education system has given the state a tremendous advantage over the Eastern states with their more traditional academic institutions. California, Sternlieb observes, was the first state fully to recognize the connection between new technologies and economic growth in the modern era: "California came to fruition and grew along with the new technological changes. The educational system in the east is antiquated. It doesn't have the inter-relationship with high technology. That's why Silicon Valley is here [in California] and not in the east." One cannot overlook the established centers of research in the East and Midwest (MIT, Harvard, Chicago, etc.), but on the sheer numbers California wins.

This close interrelationship between the needs of the business class and academia started with the state's publicly supported University of California. Founded in 1868 with 10 faculty members and 38 students, the school in its early history developed a reputation as a leading center for agricultural research. Ranchers, businessmen, lawyers, and engineers were all among the school's early boosters. The university's second president, Daniel Coit Gilman, recognized from the beginning that California's educational needs were different from those of the East. In 1872, Gilman declared that practical concerns would be paramount at this new institution: "It is not the University of Berlin nor of New Haven which we are to copy ... but it is the University of this State. It must be adapted to this people, to their public and private schools, to their peculiar geographical position, to the requirements of their new society and their undeveloped resources."

Pleased with the functional orientation of Gilman and his successors, California's corporate community has been generous in its support of the university. In 1896, Phoebe Apperson Hearst, widow of Senator George Hearst (a self-educated engineer who had made a fortune in mining and started the Hearst newspaper empire), gave the endowment to construct the university's school of mining building. Members of the Berkeley campus's engineering school would later design and construct such major projects as the Hoover and Shasta dams, the Golden Gate Bridge, and, with engineers from Bechtel, the San Francisco–Oakland Bay Bridge. More university-trained personnel would help build irrigation systems, oil refineries, and other foundations of California's economy.

Although a public university, private interests (notably the Bank of

America's A. P. Giannini) provided close to half the funds for the university's building program in the years before World War II. In 1923, Berkeley became the world's largest university, with 14,061 full-time students. Due to generous support both from the business community and from the corporate-dominated Board of Regents, the school soon became the nation's model public university.

But it was in the physical sciences that Berkeley made its name as a world-class university. "Science," Gilman had stated, "is the mother of California." In the mid-1920s, a brilliant physicist named Ernest Lawrence began putting together a coterie of scientists who, in 1931, invented the cyclotron, one of the major steps toward the development of atomic power. Lawrence, a hard-driving Nobel Prize winner, would eventually establish Berkeley as a top scientific institution, with such famous professors as Dr. Edward Teller, one of the principal architects of the first atomic bomb. Under Lawrence's tutelage, the first eleven artificial atomic elements heavier than uranium were discovered by Berkeley scientists. Today, the University of California operates three huge laboratories—one at Berkeley, another near the suburban town of Livermore, and a third in Los Alamos, New Mexico—which remain among the world's leading scientific research facilities.

In the late 1950s, the university adopted a "master plan," which included nine separate university campuses around the state. From its inception this expansion was designed to stimulate further the scientific and technological sectors of the California economy. Its greatest advocate was Clark Kerr, appointed president of the university system in 1958. A true disciple of Gilman, Kerr rejected traditional Eastern notions of academic "ivory tower" isolation from the world of business. In his aptly titled *The Uses of the University*, published in 1963, Kerr wrote:

> Universities have become "bait" to be dangled in front of industry, with drawing power greater than low wages or cheap taxes. . . .
> The university and segments of industry are becoming more alike. As the university becomes tied into the world of work, the professor—at least in the natural and some of the social sciences—takes on the characteristics of an entrepreneur.

The dehumanizing impacts of this approach to education, combined with the system's rapid expansion to accommodate over 100,000 students, helped incite bitter protests that rocked Berkeley and other University of California campuses in the decade between 1964 and 1974. But after surviving the assaults of that turbulent period, the university appeared, by the late 1970s, to be returning to the role assigned it by Gilman, Kerr, and the state's corporate elite. In 1978, the University of

California was the nation's number one recipient of private donations. The University of California graduates making headlines as the 1980s began were not rioting students; they were trained biologists who have made California the headquarters for the two leading enterprises in the fast-growing field of genetic engineering, Genentech and Cetus Corporation. (Harvard University released a "trial balloon" to form a "research and development" corporation in 1980, but retreated in the face of fierce criticism from alumni and the press.)

A perhaps even more symbiotic relationship exists between California's elite and its two leading private schools, the California Institute of Technology and Stanford University. Founded in 1891, CalTech gained prominence because of the support and financial largess of a handful of millionaires in the Pasadena area, including the energetic Henry Huntington. Still virtually unknown outside the Los Angeles area, the school began to take off in 1921 when its business-oriented president, Robert Millikan, organized sixty local millionaires into the California Institute Associates, which required all members to contribute at least $1,000 annually to the school. In the 1930s and 1940s, these generous grants reaped enormous returns. The oil industry benefited from geological research at the campus's seismological laboratory. Later, work in advanced aerodynamics proved crucial to the evolution of the aerospace industry in Southern California.

Like Clark Kerr, Robert Millikan believed passionately in the interlocking interests of the academy and the state's entrepreneurial community. Southern California, Millikan realized, was an artificial oasis, its very existence possible only through the wonders of engineering. In 1948, on his eightieth birthday, Millikan proclaimed:

> Southern California faces a challenge. She has no coal, which has in general been considered the basis of the great industrial developments. In her semi-arid climate she has not the natural hinterland commonly considered essential for the support of such a huge population as wants to live here. In order to meet the challenge of these handicaps she must of necessity use more resourcefulness, more intelligence, more scientific and engineering brains that she would otherwise be called upon to use . . . its supreme need . . . is for the development here of men of resourcefulness, of scientific and engineering background and understanding—able, creative, highly endowed, highly trained men in science and its application.

CalTech—and its Los Angeles business boosters—followed Millikan's advice. During the 1940s, a resurgent aircraft industry sponsored the development at CalTech of an experimental "wind tunnel," which greatly enhanced the technological capabilities of the local aircraft industry. Later, CalTech emerged as a forerunner in space research, which led to the location of NASA's Jet Propulsion Laboratory in Pasadena.

HARVARD WEST

But no school in California has been so intertwined with the business community as Stanford University. The university itself was founded in 1891, by Leland Stanford in memory of his only son, Leland, Jr., who died the year before of typhoid fever at age fifteen. Stanford himself had left his rural New York origins behind him, emigrated to California, and along with Charles Crocker, Mark Hopkins, and Collis P. Huntington, set up the Southern Pacific Railroad in the 1860s.

With what was for that time virtually unlimited resources, Stanford funded the construction of his school on 8,200 acres of rolling countryside south of San Francisco, all designed by Frederick Olmsted, the architect of New York's Central Park. In its early history, Stanford University was known as a sort of school-cum-country club for the sons and daughters of the state's elite who shunned the more prestigious institutions back east.

But shortly after the turn of the century, Stanford began to make waves; as in the case of Berkeley, science and technology quickly became its most cherished domain. In 1909, Stanford President David Starr Jordan invested $500 in a company sponsoring the pioneering work done by a local Palo Alto engineer, Lee De Forest, who three years later perfected the vacuum tube, one of the key early inventions in modern electronics. By serving as an amplifier and generator of electromagnetic waves, De Forest's vacuum tube would later act as the technological basis for such future developments as radio, television, radar, computers, and tape recorders.

Stanford's emergence as a center for electronics research was accelerated in the 1920s by the appointment of Frederick Terman as professor of electrical engineering. Terman had a peculiar knack for discovering promising engineers and steering them toward entrepreneurship. Among Terman's early students were William R. Hewlett, a designer of the audio-oscillator, and David Packard. With Terman's urging, the two founded a new company in 1938 in the garage of Packard's home in Palo Alto. Today their creation, Hewlett-Packard, is the world's leading manufacturer of electronic measurement equipment. In 1980, it employed 57,000 workers and had sales of over $3 billion from a list of nearly 4,000 separate electronic products.

After wartime research work at Harvard, Terman returned to Stanford to assume the post of dean of engineering. Over the years that followed, he helped to instigate the world's greatest explosion of innovative electronic companies, transforming the once lush orchard lands of the Santa Clara Valley around Stanford into the high-tech hothouse known as Silicon Valley. Out of it have come most of the modern giants in the electronics field, including Ampex (1980 sales: $469 million), Varian (1980 sales: $621 million), National Semiconductor (1980 sales: $980 million), and Intel Corporation (1980 sales: $855 million).

Largely due to Stanford, the Bay Area has established its industrial supremacy in such fields as computers, semiconductors, sophisticated instruments, and bio-technology. This has attracted unprecedented financial support for Stanford from the state's business community, including such successful graduates as William Hewlett, David Packard, and Russell Varian. Stanford's endowment, now estimated at $550 million, is the nation's second largest among private universities, exceeded only by Harvard's. Much of this funding comes from generous donations from such non-alumni as Cecil Green, co-founder of Texas Instruments, and out-of-state corporate powers like IBM, which recognize Stanford and California as the focal points for the current high technology industrial revolution. In 1974, Frederick Terman, looking back over his school's and his state's remarkable progress across the last four decades, quipped: "... there wasn't much here and the rest of the world looked awfully big. Now a lot of the rest of the world is here."

WHERE THE MONEY IS

That sense of a new Western scientific and industrial preeminence, as expressed by Terman, has today spread to all sectors of California's entrepreneurial community. In 1979, for example, a proposed reciprocal banking bill with New York State brought howls of protest from business leaders who scorned the potential market in the East.

The legislation, sponsored largely by New York's Citibank, would have opened California to New York branch banks, and vice versa. California's bankers vigorously opposed the measure, charging that the opportunity of doing business in New York was not worth opening up booming California to the out-of-state interests. "I wouldn't trade two blocks of Fresno for all of New York City," complained John J. Duffy, executive vice-president of Los Angeles's Security Pacific National Bank. "... I resent New York being chosen as my market."

Washington bureaucrats, however, rather than New York's old-line bankers, have been the source of greatest annoyance to California's business community. Having "won" the economic battles of the 1970s, few California entrepreneurs look with favor upon federal proposals to redistribute some of their wealth to the distressed sectors of the national economy. As the beneficiary of profitable trade with Japan and other foreign nations, California's business community has lined up solidly against attempts to limit foreign imports—a position in marked contrast to that taken by the beleaguered automobile and steel manufacturers east of the continental divide.

Congress's efforts during the 1960s and 1970s to expand the scope of the New Deal welfare state intensified the political alienation of California's entrepreneurs. Faced with rising taxes and increased regulation, they began to look upon government as their enemy, a bloated monster whose appetite needed to be curbed. To men like Randy Knapp, founder of Wespercorp (a fast-growing Orange County computer component manufacturer), government intervention has served only to slow down economic progress, to discourage the aggressive and innovative businessman. Knapp, who founded Wespercorp in 1976 with $160,000 scraped from several investors and turned it into a company with sales in 1980 of nearly $10 million, calls for a return to laissez-faire economics, unleashing the full force of the entrepreneurial spirit:

> We have a different attitude towards life here. I don't think the government needs to be putting restrictions on people or businesses. I sure the hell don't need help competing with IBM, Japan or anyone. . . .
>
> I couldn't function in the kind of welfare state that we've been heading towards. Things like this company just don't happen if there's no incentive to go out and raise hell in the marketplace. I'll tell you, this country will be finished the day people start thinking success is a government paycheck, a Saturday football game and a can of beer.

The great political struggle of the late 1970s and the 1980s has involved the attempt by California's entrepreneurs to impose their anti–New Deal ideology upon the rest of the country. Backed by differing, but on economic issues compatible corporate factions, Brown and Reagan in 1976 each tried to bring the California political approach into their respective parties. In 1980, with the election of Reagan, the dominant, more conservative elements in California at last seized control of the despised national government.

But one election, even one President, cannot bring about the complete triumph of this new political vision. While entrepreneurs like Randy Knapp share Ronald Reagan's faith in the free market system, leaders in other regions have much less reason to feel so sure. California's private sector, with its healthy high technology base, was able to boost employment 20.6 percent between 1974 and 1979; Pennsylvania managed only a 3.4 percent jump; New York a mere 5.4 percent; and

Ohio 5.9. Even Massachusetts, the much-ballyhooed "success story" of the northeastern industrial states, managed a job growth slightly better than half that of California.

Looking at these and other economic figures, some Midwestern and Eastern observers fear that free market trends could turn their states into permanent economic backwaters. Already many of the major engineering schools in the Midwest—Purdue, the University of Illinois, the University of Michigan—fear a steady "brain drain" of technical talent to California and other Western states, ominously similar to the "brain drain" that afflicted England as it fell into decline in the 1950s and 1960s. Perhaps the most immediate victims of the loss of technical and scientific personnel are the automobile companies. At one major auto-industry source for top engineers, the University of Michigan's Dearborn campus, the number of graduating seniors in engineering staying in the state dropped from 85 percent in 1977 to a mere 15 percent in 1980.

With their industries facing technological obsolescence and murderous foreign competition, Eastern and Midwestern officials in recent years have looked increasingly toward Washington for help. Federally guaranteed loans, such as those keeping Chrysler and New York City from bankruptcy, could prove the only practical salvation for scores of the declining regions' corporations and governments. In the late 1970s, the Carter administration, under pressure from congressional liberals like Ohio's Senator Howard Metzenbaum, granted record aid to these depressed areas in such fields as summer jobs, transit subsidies, and re-development grants. Without increased assistance from the federal government over the decade of the 1980s, some local officials believe, whole sections of the Northeast-Midwest industrial belt could become little more than giant slums. Harry Meshel, chairman of the Ohio State Senate's Finance Committee and representative from the depressed steel-producing town of Youngstown, warned in the bitter fall of 1980: "If we don't stem this tide, we'll have a region here that will be a megalopolis of low income, wage earning people. It will be a reversal of the role played by us after the Civil War. We fed the nation, we built the ships and factories and automobiles. We built up the rest of the country and now those parts of the country are benefiting while we suffer."

The regional despair expressed by Meshel was intensified by the release later in 1980 of the presidential commission report on the eighties, which called for the encouragement of the shift in wealth and population to California and the states of the West. The report's laissez-faire conclusions, not surprisingly, gained widespread support among most Western entrepreneurs and politicians, while attracting much bitter criticism in the East and Midwest. In a major attack on the report's findings, Felix A. Rohatyn, head of the Municipal Assistance Corporation in New York, claimed that such benign neglect by the federal government would create a nation "half suburb, half slum," with the Midwest and Northeast playing the unfortunate latter role. Rejecting the "supply side" economic solutions offered up by the Reagan administration, Rohatyn called for a comprehensive federal effort, largely financed by the new wealth of the West, to lift the depressed Eastern industries from their "self-eviscerating cycle" of decline. The Wall Street banker even suggested reconstituting the New Deal era Reconstruction Finance Corporation to direct this massive effort to prop up the failing industries of the East. "What we have to do is turn the losers into winners, restructure our basic industries to make them competitive," Rohatyn wrote in early 1981, "and use whatever U.S. government resources are necessary to do the job."

Rohatyn's proposals run smack against the sensibilities, interests, and values shared by most of California's corporate elite. Having struggled to achieve ascendancy over the marketplace, they can be expected to resist any attempts to redistribute the fruits of their triumph through the tax system or federal spending. Their viewpoint is that of "winners" who have seen their entrepreneurial spirit create one of the world's most vibrant, advanced economies. This proud elite has no intention of sharing its riches with the "losers" of the East. As one top Fluor Corporation executive bluntly explained:

> We've had enough of "what's mine is mine and what's yours is mine." That's what has been going on in this country for the last fifty years. We should go back to "what's mine is mine and what's yours is yours and if you step over the line, I'll blow your brains out." That's the Western way.

III. The Rise of Reagan

Henry Salvatori, his face suntanned and deeply wrinkled, sits in his well-appointed Century City office, reminiscing about his ascent into the ranks of California's self-created privileged class. The son of Italian immigrants, Salvatori rose from working at his family's grocery store in Philadelphia, to school at the University of Pennsylvania and Columbia, where he earned a master's degree in physics. Like most of the pivotal figures in California's corporate elite, Salvatori made his fortune from innovation, by seizing the initiative from the established industrialists of the East. While working in the oil fields of Oklahoma, Salvatori developed a new method of oil exploration, vastly increasing the accuracy of the surveying process. In 1932, at the age of thirty-one, Salvatori founded the Western Geophysical Company. Later, with his Grant Oil Company, he played a key role in the discovery of oil fields near Wilmington, south of Los Angeles, and in the San Joaquin Valley. These finds helped provide the energy for the postwar boom in California.

But the innovation of which Salvatori is most proud, and for which he is best known, came in the field of politics. Like most self-made businessmen, Salvatori always repudiated the New Deal liberalism imposed from the east coast. A firm believer in the industrial wizardry of free enterprise, Salvatori felt that American world supremacy could only be maintained by stemming Washington's relentless drive toward a regulated, bureaucratic welfare state. By the early 1960s, Salvatori had given up on convincing the old east coast Republican establishment to take on the task of dismembering the Rooseveltian state. A new breed of President, nourished by Western money and Western ideas, was needed to inject the vital force of the entrepreneurial spirit into the White House.

In 1964, Salvatori made his first successful thrust against the entrenched Eastern powers. As California finance chairman for the presidential drive of Arizona Senator Barry Goldwater, Salvatori spearheaded an almost religious crusade against presidential hopeful Nelson Rockefeller of New York, the living symbol of Eastern establishment accommodation with the welfare state. Goldwater overwhelmed Rockefeller in the crucial California primary and went on to win the Republican nomination that summer in San Francisco.

Only months after the convention, however, it became clear to Salvatori and most other Goldwater backers that the crusade was heading for a humiliating defeat at the hands of President Johnson. Yet just as things looked their bleakest, Henry Salvatori saw upon the television screen the ultimate instrument for carrying out his political dream: a ruggedly handsome actor named Ronald Wilson Reagan. The brother of Neil Reagan, a prominent media strategist for Goldwater, Ronald Reagan had been chosen to make a last-minute appeal to the conservative faithful. The speech Reagan gave was called "A Time for Choosing." Over the next fifteen years it would be delivered, with some alterations, hundreds of times in hundreds of places. Eventually known simply as "The Speech," it captivated Salvatori the first time he heard it. Fifteen years later, the old oilman would remember: "After that speech we decided we better keep that fellow on TV. We realized that Reagan gave the Goldwater speech better than Goldwater. He seemed steadier, less inclined to fly off the handle than Goldwater. He had more self-control, he could say the same things but in a more gentle way."

The themes enunciated by Reagan in that speech were dear to the heart of Henry Salvatori and other members of his generation of California businessmen. The choice facing America, Reagan said simply, was between the dark forces of big government and the saving light, the innovative brilliance, of free enterprise. It was a wholesale, no-nonsense assault on the New Deal politics that had been initiated by Roosevelt and carried forward by such men as Rockefeller, Johnson, Adlai Stevenson, and the Kennedy family. The same message had characterized Goldwater as an extremist; yet conservative Republicans realized that, because of the skillfulness of the former actor's delivery, the identical principles now seemed more plausible, less extreme, and above all, more saleable to the American people.

A few months after Goldwater's devastating loss at the polls, Salvatori and a handful of his fellow fundraisers gathered for a meeting. There, A. C. ("Cy") Rubel, chairman of the board of Union Oil Company, Holmes Tuttle, a Los Angeles car dealer, and Salvatori formed the core group that would initiate Ronald Reagan's drive for power. The objectives were unchanged from their Goldwater days: the undermining of the New Deal political ethos and its replacement by a faith in the power of capitalism's invisible hand to reward those deserving rewards. Yet these men were different from the know-nothings and turnback-the-clock reactionaries who had long dominated the right wing in America. These men lived in the future: they saw the solution to problems emerging from the application of rational business management principles that had made them rich, powerful, and self-assured; their eyes fixed on the creation of a stable new corporate order, dominated by the technology and innovative genius that characterized the California entrepreneurial elite.

A decade and a half later, a triumphant Salvatori set forth the values of this new America. It would not be based upon liberalism or Christian charity but upon modern, unsentimental concepts that had more in common with the stern ideals of Plato than with those of Rousseau or Jefferson. It centered on the protection of the privileged status of the most successful and clever members of society:

> Nothing's sacred, so nothing's excluded, this is the trouble we have in this country. We have to have a new consensus. We have to cement together the social order. In the history of man everyone has talked about expanding rights, having more and more freedom. But we have found if you let people do what they want to do, you have chaos. No, I think we can't restore moral values, that's hopeless. What we have to do is restructure society, set minimum standards of respect and order. Frankly, we need a more authoritarian state. I don't mean a dictatorship but something like de Gaulle. We need to preserve our business, our society because this nation is the light of the world.

THE GRASS ROOTS

The men who gathered together to form the "Friends of Ronald Reagan" in 1965 were all well acquainted with the world of business and politics. Most had previously played important roles in the careers of politicians like Nixon, Goldwater, and the recently elected senator from California, George Murphy. These men were hardened corporate operatives who, in the two decades since the end of World War II, had helped transform California into the nation's most populous and industrially advanced state. Their thinly veiled contempt for the values of the East was manifest.

The chairman of the group was a well-connected Pasadena attorney named Robert Mardian, who would later serve as Assistant U.S. Attorney General under Richard Nixon and play a role in the Watergate scandals. In addition to Salvatori, Tuttle, and Rubel, other key members of the clique included the motion picture executive Jack Warner, Reagan's longtime theatrical and political mentor and a major backer of Nixon's unsuccessful 1962 run for governor; Walter Knott, owner of the Knott's Berry Farm tourist spot in Orange County, and veteran backer of right-wing causes; Ed Mills, a vice-president of Tuttle's Los Angeles Ford dealership, and director of a half-dozen California businesses; and Stanley Plog, president of the Van Nuys–based Behavior Science Corporation, a conservative research organization.

"We raised a little money and sent him on his way speaking around the state," Salvatori recalled. "The reception was so great we decided to run him for governor of California." The clique believed that then democratic Governor Pat Brown, running for a third term, was vulnerable. Unrest amid such groups as the Berkeley campus students and the state's minority community had created dissension within Brown's party. The problem facing Reagan, so Salvatori and others in the group decided, was one of establishing credibility as a candidate. While he was a smooth, convincing speaker, Reagan had little grasp of the complex issues facing state government. "We knew then, as we know now, that Reagan didn't have any depth," Salvatori admitted frankly. "But he was sure good on his feet."

Stanley Plog's Behavior Science Corporation was assigned the important task of educating and shaping the new standard-bearer. Through Plog, Reagan for the first time learned how to be briefed and pumped full of quotable statistics, which soon became a Reagan trademark. An experienced political hand, Lyn Nofziger, formerly a reporter for the conservative San Diego–based Copley News Service, was brought in to steer the new man through the rapids of the California Republican primary. In some ways he replaced the legendary Kyle Palmer of the Los Angeles *Times* as a newspaperman with real political clout.

But perhaps Reagan's greatest problem lay in his lack of a personal political image. His major primary opponent, San Francisco Mayor George Christopher, was well known and a leading moderate within the party. Reagan's film career had already passed into near oblivion; he was primarily known as a competent supporting player for bigger stars. In fact, when Jack Warner first heard that his old protégé was about to make the gubernatorial plunge, he is said to have quipped: "No. Jimmy Stewart for governor, Ronnie for best friend."

Reagan, clearly, was a candidate in serious need of an individual identity. A fundamentalist preacher supportive of the Reagan effort,

Reverend William S. McBirnie of Glendale, came up with an appealing campaign slogan, "the creative society," which captured the sunnier side of the candidate's faith in the productive capacity of the free enterprise system. The dynamic public relations firm of Spencer-Roberts seized upon one of the candidate's worst supposed flaws, his lack of governmental experience, and crafted the image of Reagan as "citizen politician"—a man who could rise above the normal concerns of such traditional politicians as Christopher and Governor Brown.

The policies advocated by Reagan in that first campaign revealed a sophisticated reading of the mood of middle-class voters in both parties that spring of 1966. The growing rebellion on the college campuses and the black riots in Watts during the previous summer had irritated or frightened most white, middle-aged, middle-class California voters. Reagan stood firmly against these dissidents, appealing to a popular appetite for what Salvatori would call "a more authoritarian state." At the same time Reagan used the promise of lower taxes to seduce an electorate that already believed its earnings were being diverted to pay for the education of unruly radicals and the welfare of riotous blacks.

But the true key to Reagan's success, it turned out, was the candidate himself. "The most manageable candidate you could ever ask for," according to Lyn Nofziger, Reagan took instruction easily. Although at first they were nervous about how their man would fare with the news media, Reagan's cautious advisers were eventually convinced by Neil Reagan to let his brother face the cameras and reporters as much as possible. Neil, later a senior vice-president at the McCann Erickson advertising agency, always believed his brother's greatest gift was his engaging, earnest personality. During his years as an actor, Neil explained, Ronald's most successful roles were those where he played a character similar to himself:

> Ronnie always played Ronnie. He was typecast—the young American, the boy from the Midwest. He was always a good guy. . . . He still plays it today. If he played a gangster, it would have ruined his box office.
> . . . I knew how to sell him. I sold [him] not as my brother but as a piece of soap.

The primary campaign—both its issues and its candidates—electrified the conservative grass roots of California's Republican Party. In the friendly, homespun persona of Reagan, "the citizen politician," the state's right-wing loyalists found an attractive successor to their recently fallen hero, Barry Goldwater. Thousands of these zealots walked precincts, made phone calls, donated small contributions to the already well-financed effort. They sensed that here was someone special, the man who could carry the conservative banner to victory. To these people—to someone like the articulate Reverend McBirnie—Reagan took on the aura of an almost religious hero: "It's a sense of mission. He wants to drive the barbarians out. He's El Cid. He's the guy who could have taken it easy but instead chose to come out and fight."

While right-wing enthusiasts played an important role in the defeat of George Christopher in the spring primary, the Reagan strategists realized they would need the support of the state's moderate Republican business establishment in the coming attempt to unseat the entrenched incumbent Pat Brown. Reagan's top corporate backers, notably Salvatori, Tuttle, and Rubel, were not interested in wasting their money on simple ideological crusades; their goal was to effect change, to seize power. They knew Reagan would need the financial backing and the patina of respectability that the state's business establishment could provide. If these leaders stood on the sidelines, as they did during the Goldwater fiasco, the Reagan candidacy would be in deep trouble.

Most of these corporate moderates at first viewed Reagan's candidacy with a combination of amusement and alarm. Many had backed George Christopher in the primary; they feared Reagan's right-wing image would lead the party into a repeat of the 1964 disaster. Reagan's business backers worked to persuade these men that their candidate was not an intemperate ideologue. They stressed the pro-business side of his program. "We had to convince them," Salvatori would recall later, "that we weren't a bunch of kooks."

To the dismay of Reagan's more fanatic supporters in groups like the John Birch Society and the United Republicans of California, the corporate establishment forces joined the campaign. Men who were considered Rockefeller stooges and even Soviet sympathizers by Reagan's fundamentalist conservative supporters suddenly joined the inner circle of the candidate's "friends." Most prominent among these new heavyweight backers were Justin Dart, head of the DART Industries conglomerate and thereafter a top Reagan stalwart; John A. McCone, a cornerstone of the state establishment, ex-business partner of Steven Bechtel, director of the United California Bank, and director of the CIA under Kennedy and Johnson; the industrialist Leonard Firestone, a backer of Nelson Rockefeller in 1964; Taft Schreiber, Reagan's old Hollywood agent and vice-president of the Music Corporation of America; and William French Smith, a corporate attorney with the Los Angeles firm of Gibson, Dunn and Crutcher, and director of Pacific Telephone and Pacific Lighting companies, who would later become Reagan's personal attorney and then U.S. Attorney General.

With the resources of California's largest corporations behind them, Neil Reagan and other Reagan strategists, aided by the public relations firm, Spencer-Roberts, unleashed a brilliant, high-visibility media blitz against Pat Brown. Cleverly linking the incumbent governor to the forces of unrest, they exploited public indignation over the turmoil at Watts and Berkeley. They promoted Reagan as an almost nonideological "citizen politician," whose only interest was to save the state from overtaxation, over-regulation, and left-wing anarchy.

In the end the generous financial backing of the corporate community, the appeal of Reagan's message, and the effectiveness with which he delivered it spelled disaster for Pat Brown. A new day was dawning in California and national politics; buried by nearly a million votes, Brown became its first victim.

Ronald Reagan's election as governor marked the political maturation of California's brash new class of entrepreneurs. Other successful politicians from California, notably Herbert Hoover and Richard Nixon, had achieved their national prominence only *after* leaving the state. But Reagan became a presidential contender almost immediately upon being elected the state's chief executive. As leader of the nation's now most populous and economically powerful state, Reagan did not require the blessing of the established forces on Wall Street or Washington. He was and would remain essentially a California-created, home-processed product, who spoke, first and foremost, for his Western business constituency. In fifteen years, that constituency would see its man in control of the ultimate goal, the American presidency.

FROM HARD TIMES TO EASY STREET

Little in Ronald Reagan's early life suggested his future role. Born in 1911 in the small Illinois town of Tampico, growing up in nearby Dixon, a placid community of 10,000, Ronald Reagan was nurtured in an atmosphere more befitting a populist hero than a leader of the corporate right. His father, Jack, was a gregarious, hard-drinking Irish Catholic who worked as a shoe salesman. His mother, Nell, was a staunch, church-going Christian who often gave away the family's meager possessions to the poorer families in town.

Despite his family's often strapped finances, Ronald Reagan's childhood was essentially a pleasant one—a time for daydreaming along the banks of Rock River, which ran through town, or playing football on the front lawn with friends and his older brother Neil. The mind of the young Reagan was filled with the stuff of pure American mythology—a steady diet of Tom Swift and Horatio Alger books. It was, as Reagan himself would later write, "one of those rare Huck Finn–Tom Sawyer idylls."

The Depression of the 1930s brought hard times to Dixon. Although

Reagan's reminiscences overwhelmingly focus on the sanguine aspects of small town life, the reality was in fact quite harsh. Unemployment helped engender sporadic outbreaks of racial hatred as gangs of local white toughs took out their frustration on the small black population. The atmosphere in the Reagan home was sometimes tense as well; constantly shifting jobs, Jack Reagan was periodically drunk and depressed. Yet through it all the Reagans maintained their basic, fundamental New Deal liberalism. The family actively opposed racial discrimination and the two brothers went out of their way to help their black friends during times of harassment. Jack Reagan himself, through his connections as a rare Democrat in a conservative town, eventually took a job with the New Deal–inspired Works Progress Administration (WPA), handing out free clothes to the needy.

Throughout these difficult times, Ronald Reagan remained the quiet, unassuming daydreamer. He was every mother's ideal son, who went to church on Sundays and avoided the gruff men who hung around the speakeasies and boarding houses in the rougher section of Dixon. "Ronnie hung out with the northside kids, who we considered a bunch of sissies," Neil recalled. "I don't think Ronald ever saw the inside of a poolroom."

This reluctance to deal with the seamier side of society would remain a Reagan characteristic throughout his career. While millions of Americans grumbled on breadlines and joined movements to the far left and far right, Ronald Reagan attended school at local Eureka College, where he played football, was a cheerleader, and acted in school dramas.

It was his developing love for drama, not any sort of burning political ambition, that led Reagan to leave his midwestern home for the first time. In the mid-1930s, Reagan worked as a sportscaster for WHO and WOC, twin radio stations in Iowa. Known as "Dutch," Reagan soon became famous for his fanciful, colorful, play-by-play descriptions of Chicago Cubs' games, based on teletype reports that came into his studio from Wrigley Field hundreds of miles away.

In the early spring of 1937, Reagan followed the Cubs on a trip to Southern California. He had a vague notion of getting a shot at a Hollywood acting career. Through a singer he knew in Los Angeles, he met a local movie agent. One screen test later, the kid from Dixon landed a seven-year contract with Warner Brothers at the then sizable sum of $200 a week. As in adolescence, so in adulthood Ronald Reagan managed to avoid staring into the unhappy face of America, one that most of his fellow Americans saw only too clearly.

Reagan soon got many parts in the B-pictures being mass-produced at the time at big studios like Warner's. His image reflected his actual persona—the clean-cut nice guy from the Midwest—and established him as a significant, although hardly major, box-office draw. As the 1940s began, Ronald Reagan was one of the rising second-line stars in Hollywood. In 1940 he co-starred in *Knute Rockne—All American*, playing the now famous role of the Gipper, the terminally ill football player George Gipp. His career reached its zenith in 1942 in a fine performance as a victim of medical sadism in the highly acclaimed *King's Row*.

Yet even at his high point, Ronald Reagan stayed aloof from the more sexually liberal and hedonistic behavior of the fast set in Hollywood. Frank McCarthy, who met Reagan shortly after his arrival in Hollywood and remained a good friend through the years, recalled:

> Ronnie was always a stalwart, a man of very strong principles. He was more serious than anyone else in the movies. He was not as much fun as the others. If there was drinking to be done, he wasn't around to do it. He wasn't into womanizing. I mean everyone got off and got laid every once in a while but Ronnie, well, he never made a career of it.

Ronald Reagan's prolonged period of innocence was shattered by World War II. He was bitterly disappointed when he was refused overseas military duty because of his poor eyesight. Reagan found himself on the sidelines, spending the entire war behind a camera as a propaganda and training filmmaker.

The war and Reagan's inability to participate actively in it intensified his patriotism and helped motivate him in his search for a serious role in public affairs. He started to follow world events closely, joined political groups, and plunged into the affairs of his union, the Screen Actors Guild (SAG). "I found him totally changed after the war," Frank McCarthy would recall over three decades later. "Something had happened. He had gotten so serious to the point he was talking about the world and politics all the time. People started listening to him at parties."

This concern and involvement, however, did little to revive Reagan's acting career. The war had turned America into a more sophisticated, worldly-wise nation; the good guy Midwestern image no longer played well in the new postwar era, with its deep economic troubles and the looming conflict with the Soviet Union.

While the nation turned to a new set of heroes on the screen, events unfolding beneath the surface in Hollywood provided Reagan with his opportunity to wave the flag on high. From 1945 to 1947, the movie industry was torn apart by a bitter battle between the International Alliance of Theatrical Stage Employees, a union with a past history of organized crime connections and collusion with studio owners, and the rival Conference of Studio Unions, a more militant, left-leaning group. The key issue at the time concerned the right to represent the construction laborers on the sets, a conflict that led to actual brawls at the studios. The role of SAG (and Ronald Reagan, elected union president in 1947) was crucial in this struggle. An alliance between SAG and the Conference of Studio Unions could have resulted in a strong, hard-line union front in the movie industry, a prospect that terrified the major studio heads like Louis B. Mayer at MGM and Jack Warner, Reagan's boss.

With anti-Soviet and anti-Communist paranoia on the rise throughout the nation, Mayer, Warner, and other moguls zeroed in on the involvement of alleged "reds" in the Conference group and tried to destroy the troublesome union. They courted Reagan, the SAG president, who at the time described himself as "a near hopeless, hemophilic liberal." To the surprise of the left and liberal forces that had helped elect him to the SAG board, Reagan chose to side with the studios and their favored union. Soon after assuming the SAG presidency, Reagan had clearly cast his lot with the emergent right-wing forces within the union, organized by Robert Montgomery and George Murphy.

Suddenly, for the first time since the opening of the war, Reagan found himself the toast of the Hollywood bigwigs. Instead of being another actor on the way down, Ronald Reagan was now the honored guest at parties of the rich and famous of corporate Hollywood. Robert K. Dornan, a youthful nephew of comedian Jack Haley and close to the Warner family at the time, recalled that period some thirty years later:

> He was often at the Colonel's [Jack Warner's] place up on Angelo Drive. They lived up in this castle—big movie theater, huge ceiling, hell, you felt like a chess piece. The Colonel—you had to call Jack Warner that—and Ronald Reagan would be in a room talking a lot, even at parties, about how to keep the Communists out of Hollywood.

By then Ronald Reagan was an unabashed spokesman for anti-Communist Hollywood. He cooperated with the FBI in its Communist-hunting forays in the film industry, supported mandatory loyalty oaths and the public (although not the secret) blacklisting of left-wing actors. In the fall of 1947, Reagan testified as a friendly witness before the House Un-American Activities Committee, then probing the influence of communism in the motion picture industry.

Although he always struggled to maintain his image as a fair-minded union chief, Reagan's coziness with the blacklisters earned him the enmity of many former liberal friends in the industry. Some saw him as an opportunist, using the "Communist" issue to promote his flagging career; others felt he was simply manipulated by men of stronger will. Karen Morley, an established actress in the 1930s who was ruined by the blacklist, knew Reagan through this crucial period. Recalling those days, she insisted that Reagan joined the anti-Communist forces more out of convenience than any deep, ideological commitment: "It isn't that he's a bad guy really. What's so terrible about Ronnie is his ambition to go where the power is. I don't think anything he does is original, he doesn't think it up. I never saw him have an idea in his life. I really don't even think he realizes how dangerous the things he does really are."

Whatever friends Reagan might have lost among his old liberal associates were more than made up for by his new social circle, the emergent right wing in Hollywood. Gathering around the banner of superpatriotism and devotion to capitalist ethics, the leaders of this new set were actors like John Wayne, Adolphe Menjou, Gary Cooper, Irene Dunne, and George Murphy. These stars associated more and more with their studio bosses or the fast-growing entrepreneurial community in Southern California. For the first time in his life, Ronald Reagan entered the world of the business elite and began to be exposed to their view of the world. The comradeship of these new friends became deeply important to him personally, particularly after his 1948 divorce from his wife, actress Jane Wyman.

The separation from Wyman cut Reagan's last tie to his prewar, liberal Hollywood past. In 1951, the producer Mervyn LeRoy, who was a leading figure on the Hollywood right, introduced Reagan to a young, struggling actress named Nancy Davis. They quickly fell in love and on March 4, 1952, were married. Through Nancy, the adopted daughter of a wealthy and staunchly conservative Chicago physician, Reagan slipped completely under the gilded covers of the local upper crust, never again to travel in the society of men of modest means.

THE BOYS IN THE BACK ROOM

From the early 1950s on, Reagan became associated with a tight-knit social clique that consisted of former Hollywood greats, aging corporate executives, and members of Southern California's landed gentry. It was from among such people that Reagan, over the next thirty years, would select his friends and seek advice and political support. Known today as "the Reagan crowd," these wealthy individuals played an important role in Reagan's metamorphosis. Jack Wrather, the son of a Texas oilman and producer of such classic 1950s television shows as "The Lone Ranger" and "Lassie," has been a key figure in the "crowd" since its inception. He believes that by associating with people like himself, Reagan came back into touch with his own fundamentally conservative Midwestern values. Sitting in his Beverly Hills office, Wrather explains: "He woke up to the fact that there was a conspiracy of radical liberals in the industry. He woke up to the fact that their values weren't his."

The "crowd"—according to Wrather—brings together the conservative elements of Hollywood with successful Southern California businessmen. Wrather, for instance, first met Reagan through his wife, former actress Bonita Granville, a close friend of Nancy Davis's during her brief career in Hollywood. Other crowd members, like the New York department store heir Al Bloomingdale and Sears heir Armand Deutsch, are Eastern rich who migrated to California in the thirties and forties to dabble in moviemaking. Irene Dunne was an actress contemporary of Reagan's and later a director of Technicolor Incorporated. Justin Dart migrated from Chicago to Los Angeles and has associated with the upper-crust Hollywood society, as has developer William Wilson, the son of an old California oil family and owner of a vast ranch in Sonora, Mexico, where crowd members gather for periodic vacations.

While people connected with Hollywood had traditionally been regarded by Southern California's business establishment as parvenus and libertines, this select group joined in an early alliance with such prominent entrepreneurs as Henry Salvatori, Charles ("Tex") Thornton, and supermarket executive Ted Cummings. Through dinner parties, private screenings, and elaborate joint vacations, the crowd found that they shared values with some of the top corporate forces in California. As Wrather describes it:

> We're all business people who have been associated with the motion picture community on the west side of Los Angeles. . . . The common factor is that we've all been very successful and we have a strong sense of fiscal responsibility. We like economic stability and in essence we all like to live lives—it sounds dull—like quiet family people.

This Los Angeles social elite, Ronald Reagan's home base for nearly three decades, differs drastically from the established old families of the east coast. Formed in the postwar California boom, these people have few associations with the grim realities of the Depression; unlike the Eastern society leaders, they do not feel any sympathy with the objectives of Roosevelt's New Deal. In addition, few of these wealthy Southern Californians interest themselves in the traditional intellectual pursuits common among the Boston or New York upper class. The crowd's cultural life is built more around television, movies, and sporting events. Large bookcases full of well-worn tomes are rarely seen in their palatial homes or spacious high-rise offices. The home screening room has replaced the library.

Rather than attend the opera or symphony, these people regard as an ideal evening a quiet dinner, lightweight banter, a couple of glasses of wine, and a movie screened in a private projection room. It is a narrow little world, bounded by the affluent neighborhoods of Bel-Air, Beverly Hills, and Pacific Palisades; contact with other "elements" of society is extremely limited. There appears to be little ideological passion among the crowd members and even less intellectual curiosity. As the tall, aristocratic-looking William Wilson, who is Reagan's best friend, explained: "I don't read much, none of us do. We like to ride, look at Western art, Andrew Wyeth, that kind of thing.... None of us are really politically minded. Most of us just play tennis, ride horseback. We don't over-indulge...."

While essentially nonideological, the members of the crowd do possess a firm idea of their own interests. Like their friends within the more hard-nosed entrepreneurial elite, Reagan's close-knit social set has long been obsessed by the maintenance of the free enterprise system and their privileged place within it. While zealots of the far right have passionate concerns on social issues such as abortion, homosexuality, and drugs, the clan concentrates its attentions overwhelmingly on the economic and foreign fronts.

"Let's face it, each person is formed by their circle and their friends," says clan member Armand Deutsch. "People around Ronnie care about the economy, the loss of American power around the world. We do not talk about marijuana or gay rights and those things. We are not interested."

Even Ronald Reagan's new friends among the rich and powerful could do little to save his faltering theatrical career in the 1950s, however. Although a hero to the moguls, their gratitude was severely tested by such horrible films as *Bedtime for Bonzo* (1951), *She's Working Her Way Through College* (1952), and *Hellcats of the Navy* (1957). Soon his acting career was irreversibly on the skids, resulting in economic hard times. He could barely keep up the mortgage payments for his spacious new home in Pacific Palisades. Reagan, according to one associate, began complaining about his money problems, and placed much of the blame on the bite taken out of his modest income by taxation.

While the crowd and the moguls could not help him with his film career, corporate America came to Reagan's rescue. In 1954, General Electric offered him a generous $125,000-a-year contract to host its "G.E. TV Theatre" and serve as the company's goodwill ambassador.

For the next eight years Reagan toured the country, meeting what he later estimated to be almost a quarter million G.E. employees. This experience honed his skills as a public speaker and developed his political philosophy further along conservative lines. Under G.E.'s tutelage, Reagan created the outlines of what would later be known as "The Speech."

The message of "The Speech"—a blend of business boosterism and dire warnings about the growth of big government—impressed many conservative businessmen. They began using him at political fund-raising events for such favorite candidates as Richard Nixon. But in 1962, just as Reagan was starting to achieve some notoriety as a spokesman for conservatism, he lost his G.E. job when the show went off the air. He retreated to his ranch and his home in Los Angeles.

At this stage of his life, according to Neil Reagan, the middle-aged actor could very easily have slipped into a comfortable lifestyle with his genteel friends in the crowd. But Neil was convinced his younger brother had a promising political future ahead of him. He persuaded Ronald to take a marketing test for a new Western series then being put together for U.S. Borax Corporation: "We brought these women off the street and let them see the commercial. We asked them what they thought of Ronald. They said they'd buy anything from him. They even said they'd vote for him for office and we didn't even ask them that." Four years later they did just that, and Ronald Reagan was elected to his first governmental post as the thirty-third governor of the state of California.

THE BUSINESS OF CALIFORNIA

The selling of Ronald Reagan did not cease after the 1966 election. From the day he arrived to take office in Sacramento in January 1967, his supporters were determined to lend an aura of almost regal splendor to his ascension. With all the fanfare appropriate to a conquering hero, Reagan rode in a heavily guarded motorcade through the downtown streets. The lavish inaugural program, designed by Walt Disney Studios, included a huge ball with five bands and a full chorus singing a stirring rendition of "America the Beautiful."

In contrast to this privately financed pomp, Reagan's inaugural speech promised a new day of stark limitations on government services. "We are going to squeeze and cut and trim until we reduce the cost of government," Reagan boldly promised the crowd of 15,000 people attending the spectacular. Within two weeks Reagan unveiled an ambitious plan to cut the state budget 10 percent across the board. "Any major business can tighten its belt by ten percent and still maintain the quality and quantity of its operation," he insisted. "So can government."

Reagan's reference to business procedures came naturally since, from its inception, his administration was dominated by the state's business leadership. While the extreme conservatives claimed credit for the Reagan landslide, the operational control of the new regime was firmly in the hands of Reagan's affluent and pragmatic friends and allies. Basic government policies came under review by a "businessman task force," composed of some 250 top corporate executives. In the first years of the Reagan administration, these task forces made hundreds of recommendations that provided basic policy direction for the new governor.

Perhaps even more influential was the emergence of a "kitchen cabinet" of advisers, including the original corporate core group of supporters as well as members of the Reagan crowd. In addition, Reagan solidified his ties to the state's moderate business elite by inviting several of their leaders into the powerful inner circle. William French Smith, Taft Schreiber, Leonard Firestone, and Justin Dart—all previously cited—were joined by such heavyweights as Leland Kaiser, retired San Francisco insurance securities company executive and member of the national Republican Finance Committee, and Arch Monson, another San Francisco corporate official and a past supporter of George Christopher and Nelson Rockefeller.

These wealthy men, playing a central role in screening Reagan's appointments and policy options, wanted—and got—a government run with a central commitment to corporate priorities. As a result, Reagan's administration took on the character of a full-scale merger of private and public sectors, the ultimate businessman's government. The former head of the California Real Estate Association, for instance, was appointed state real estate commissioner; a former lumber company executive became state Director of Resources; an executive at a savings and loan company emerged as head of the business and transportation department; a onetime utility industry consultant was placed on the state's Public Utilities Commission; and two horse breeders found themselves on the track to the state Horse Racing Board.

Such appointments represented a blatant rejection by Reagan's backers of the notion that government's primary role was to balance the public's interest against powerful corporate forces. To the Reaganites, with their unbounded faith in the entrepreneurial spirit, public and private interest were essentially one and the same. Any government attempts to restrain business objectives were viewed with deep suspicion. Al Bloomingdale, charter member of both the crowd and the "kitchen cabinet," once described the Reaganite attitude toward business and government regulation rather colorfully:

When you can stop a project because of a snail darter, that's ridiculous. Hell, put it in an aquarium. . . .

This whole country is based on the business community. These guys who attack business, these Naders, are full of it.

Once in power, the Reaganites found their pro-business approach to government challenged by the entrenched, proud civil servants in the state's regulatory agencies. For years employees of these agencies had tried to maintain a scrupulous distance from political considerations; California's public boards and commissions achieved a solid national reputation for professionalism, honesty, and defense of the public interest despite outside pressures.

One special target of the Reagan administration and its big business backers was the state Public Utilities Commission (PUC), the agency regulating California's large utility and transportation interests. During the previous Brown administration, the PUC had developed a strongly pro-consumer orientation; Reagan's appointees quickly sought to reverse the process, relaxing tough regulations and approving massive rate increases. Only five months after taking office, the governor himself openly declared that the PUC "is going to have to be more realistic in its approach and its permissions to the phone company."

This remark created a storm of controversy at the Commission, which was designed to operate without any interference from the governor's office. Bill Dunlop, then secretary of the PUC and a top veteran civil servant, recalled: "No other Governor in the history of California has ever made such statements. [Reagan] was trying to dictate, so to speak, something to the guys he appointed. Obviously, something must have happened between the Governor and the phone company to make a statement like [that]."

Although Reagan's appointees on the PUC strenuously denied any direct gubernatorial interference, they approved over $193 million in rate increases for Pacific Telephone over the next five years, allowing Pacific's profit rate to jump by 23.8 percent. In an even more controversial move, Reagan's commissioners in 1970 and 1971 allowed Pacific to retain what would have amounted to $1.5 billion in federal tax savings rather than passing them on to the consumers. In a third decision, the Commission tried to deregulate the California operations of Western Electric, the phone company's manufacturing and supply unit. Both of these latter two decisions came over strenuous objections of PUC staff and were subsequently overturned by the state supreme court.

Watching their long-established public interest reputation collapse before them, PUC staffers like Dunlop were enraged by the coziness of the relationship between the utilities and Reagan's inner circle. The informal head of a Reagan advisory group that screened state appointees, William French Smith, hailed from a Los Angeles law firm that had represented Pacific Telephone and several other companies regulated by the PUC. In 1967, Smith joined the board of directors of Pacific Lighting, a holding company that controlled one of the nation's largest gas distribution network, and two years later he added a seat on the board of Pacific Telephone to his already impressive list of corporate directorships. In 1970 three directors, five vice-presidents, an executives' political trust fund of the phone company legally contributed a total of $25,000 to Reagan's reelection effort. One Pacific director, Charles Ducommun, served as vice-chairman of Reagan's 1966 state campaign committee. Asked to explain the utility's backing of Reagan, Ducommun answered: "Reagan undoubtedly got support from the utilities because they felt he had a better perception of their problems. That's why they put their chips on him."

Reagan's "better perception" of business concerns extended to other of his major corporate backers. In 1972 DART Industries, controlled by longtime Reagan bankroller Justin Dart, was building a 25,000-acre residential community in the Tehachapi Mountains of Southern California. PUC regulations required the developer to place utility lines underground, but DART requested an exemption from the PUC, claiming that laying underground lines would eliminate the profitability of the project. The PUC staff reviewed DART's argument; they branded it "misleading" and "contrary to the facts." Yet despite staff objections, the PUC commissioners granted DART its exemption.

Some top PUC civil servants came to believe that their professional judgment was secondary to the corporate needs of Justin Dart, a prominent member of Reagan's "kitchen cabinet" and a Reagan delegate to the 1968 GOP National Convention. In addition, Holmes Tuttle, along with Salvatori, one of the original Reagan creators, also sat on the DART board of directors. In 1970, DART contributed $14,367 to the Reagan reelection effort, while Tuttle himself gave $5,000 more. Tuttle also chaired the Committee for a Greater California, which funneled $123,000 in anonymous contributions to the 1970 Reagan effort. In 1974, shortly before leaving Sacramento, Ronald Reagan himself acquired $7,000 worth of DART stock and two years later appointed Justin Dart as a trustee managing his personal finances during his unsuccessful presidential run in 1976.

Within the eight years between January 1967 and January 1975, the California PUC, an effective institution for several decades, was completely emasculated, its staff demoralized and powerless. Disgusted, several of these proud professionals left state government in the late 1960s and early 1970s, among them Casimir Strelinski, head of the

PUC's finance and accounts division in Los Angeles. The quintessential professional California bureaucrat, dedicated, soft-spoken, and strait-laced, Strelinski later charged: "The big utilities had Reagan in their pocket. They sure made us push those babies through. I could have stayed at the pig's trough and gotten my retirement, but I just couldn't take it."

This pattern of lax regulation and reflexive pro-business decision-making characterized the entire Reagan administration. Perhaps one of the most far-reaching instances of the administration's corporate orientation involved the Irvine Company's attempt to develop its 120-square-mile ranch in Orange County into the world's largest planned community.

Part of Irvine's scheme was a proposed residential marina complex along the shoreline of surrounding scenic Newport Bay. Irvine needed the approval of the State Lands Commission (SLC) to swap 450 acres it owned on the upper part of the bay in exchange for a stretch of valuable state-owned shoreline. In August 1966 the SLC, still dominated by Brown administration cabinet members, turned down the proposal after the staff concluded that the swap would be "a distinct loss in value" to the state.

But with the election of Ronald Reagan, the Irvine Company's proposal suddenly started looking better to the state. In September 1967, only thirteen months after the original decision, the three Reagan cabinet officers on the three-member SLC board reversed the decision and approved the swap. A subsequent report by the state's independent Auditor-General's office charged: "The [SLC] approved the Upper Newport Bay exchange . . . in spite of warnings by counsel that public access along the entire west side of the bay would be so inadequate after the exchange as to raise a substantial question as to even the legality of the exchange."

Just three years later Irvine again benefited from the Reagan administration's solicitude for big business. In 1970, the Irvine Company unveiled a modified master plan for the area surrounding the new University of California campus located on its Orange County ranchland. While earlier versions of the plan called for a "cap and gown" community of 100,000, the new scheme called for an expanded, incorporated city with twice the acreage of San Francisco and a population of over 430,000. The new proposal immediately was denounced by officials of several surrounding local communities and conservationists for its severe environmental and economic impacts.

The new scheme required the approval of the University of California Board of Regents, whose ex-officio president was Governor Reagan. Joined by his own appointees, Reagan voted to approve Irvine's request despite the vigorous opposition of one Regent, the multimillionaire Norton Simon, who had denounced the plan as "detrimental" to the new campus. Norton also openly charged that "the Regents were avoiding the issue because of the interests of some Regents in the Irvine Company."

One target of Simon's broadside was the ubiquitous William French Smith, a Reagan appointee and chairman of the Regents, the governor's personal attorney and, coincidentally, a lawyer for the Irvine Company. When the proposal came to a vote in 1970, Smith abstained, although the other Reagan appointees joined their governor in helping to provide a lopsided 18 to 2 vote in favor of Irvine. That same year, as the governor's men geared up his reelection campaign, two trustees of the Irvine Foundation (which controls the Irvine Company) contributed $1,000 each, and William Pereira, the master planner for the company's grandiose scheme, and his architectural firm chipped in another $7,000.

The patterns established at the PUC and the SLC were paralleled by Reagan's own office. In 1967, for instance, Reagan signed a bill into law that exempted oil and gas royalties from property taxes, thus giving a $2.7 million windfall to eighteen oil companies. The action came at the urging of several oil company executives and over the objections of some leading members of Reagan's own staff. Three years later, during his 1970 reelection run, Reagan received tens of thousands of dollars from the oil companies benefiting from the bill, including $10,000 from Atlantic Richfield (ARCO), one of the original forces behind the legislation.

In another case during his first term, Reagan signed a bill increasing the profits of horse owners by millions of dollars. In 1970, Reagan received nearly $70,000 from the state's major horse-racing associations. Similarly, in 1968 Reagan signed a bill—vetoed only six years earlier by his predecessor—that gave the motion picture industry a multi-million-dollar tax break on its inventories. Top Hollywood executives—including Jack Warner, Taft Schreiber, and Jack Wrather—had been among the earliest supporters of Reagan's political career.

The generosity of Reagan's corporate sponsors extended far beyond mere campaign contributions. Within eight years after his election as governor, Ronald Reagan was provided the wherewithal to become a multimillionaire for the first time. Central to his elevation in financial status were two land deals involving a ranch that Reagan had originally purchased during the 1950s for under $300 an acre. Shortly after his election, in December 1966, Reagan sold 236 acres of his ranch, located in the Santa Monica Mountains above Los Angeles, for more than $8,000 an acre to Twentieth Century-Fox Corporation. This transaction, when completed, yielded Reagan a return of nearly $2 million off an original investment of only $85,000. Four years later, during his re-election campaign, Reagan's Democratic opponent, Assembly Speaker Jesse Unruh, claimed that Fox had, in essence, given Reagan a million dollar "bonus" for being elected governor. While denying any wrongdoing, Fox executive Richard Zanuck later admitted the transaction was indeed "a good deal" for Reagan. Just how good was made clear in 1974, the last year of Reagan's administration, when the State Parks and Recreation Board purchased the same property and some adjacent Fox-owned acreage at an average price of only $1,800 an acre.

Reagan's beneficent backers even ended up providing their hero with the very roof over his head. Upon arrival in Sacramento, Nancy Reagan loudly announced her intention not to stay in the old, charming, but dilapidated State Mansion, home to generations of California chief executives. Aware that Nancy yearned to live in the style to which they themselves long had been accustomed, fourteen wealthy Reaganites stepped forward in 1969 with $150,000 to buy a Sacramento home, which they leased to the Reagans. The mansion purchasers included such familiar names as Henry Salvatori, Homes Tuttle, Justin Dart, J. Robert Fluor, and Leland Kaiser.

When he wasn't living in this charitably provided home, Reagan spent much of his time throughout his two terms visiting yachting harbors, homes, and exclusive clubs inhabited by these and other loyal supporters down in Southern California. On important decisions, Reagan staffers recall, the advice of these men often outweighed the contrary opinions of political aides and technical experts. Largely because these well-heeled folk so dominated the chief executive's personal trust and private time, some aides believe that input from other classes and viewpoints—notably minorities, laboring people, and liberal intellectuals—rarely reached Reagan's ears. As one longtime Reagan political operative recalled:

> They are the only people [Reagan's] truly comfortable with, the only ones he really cares about. . . . Back in Sacramento we always got scared whenever he met with those people. They are so cloistered, so enclosed. How the hell can they understand the problems of some jerk making $18,000 a year? It seemed he'd change every time he'd come back from L.A. There would always be some new idea, like cutting welfare ten percent or something. Around the office we'd joke, "Oh shit, the Governor's been talking to his grassroots again."

Reagan's loyalty to his "grassroots" did not extend, however, to the legions of far right true believers who worked so hard for him in the early days of his career. Although many of these zealots stuck with Reagan all the way to the White House, they have proved consistently unable to influence their hero once in office. In every Republican primary fight since 1966, Reagan has opened his drive by playing the "El Cid" of the right, only to turn increasingly moderate as he faces the general election and then the realities of power.

Once in office in 1967, Reagan attempted to stop the growth of government by ordering an immediate 10 percent cut across the board in state spending. Initially, this approach won broad support from both the hard-core right wing and the corporate moderates; Reagan abandoned it only after Democratic opposition and the impracticality of such arbitrary cuts became clear. Throughout his administration the far right, philosophically opposed to all but a handful of state programs, attempted to revive the across-the-board budget-cutting strategy. The corporate moderates, fearing the impact draconian cuts would have on such beneficial (to business) programs as higher education and state water projects, opted for the more gradual practical approach. By his second term Reagan was fully in line with corporate thinking; the high rate of govenmental growth spawned by the Brown administration was only slowed, not stopped or reversed. While Reagan would later make much of the $5.7 billion he claims to have rebated to California taxpayers, state income tax collections almost tripled during his two terms in office. The annual state budget also jumped from $4.6 billion to $10.2 billion, an increase of 122 percent.

Even more distressing to the rightists was Reagan's failure to stand his ground on several of the moral issues to which he committed himself in the early days of the 1966 campaign. Here the cleavage between entrepreneurial Reaganites and the faithful of the far right has always been sharp. While issues like abortion can whip the fundamentalists into an almost messianic fury, few of Reagan's businessmen backers consider such "moral" issues of great importance. Although Reagan has always claimed to be a devout Christian, he showed little inclination to impose fundamentalist principles while governor of California. As William Wilson, Reagan's best friend, and now his envoy to the Vatican explains: "Ronnie believes in God, but for him it's a personal, dignified thing. Ronnie's tendency is not to legislate morality. He really isn't interested in protecting people from themselves."

As early as 1967, the right wingers discovered Reagan's moderate "tendency" when he refused to veto narrowly passed legislation that liberalized the state abortion law—at the time the most progressive measure of its kind in the nation. Over the next eight years, hard-line moralists watched in horror as over 600,000 legal abortions were performed in California. Also in 1967, Reagan balked at supporting a bill introduced by Orange County State Senator John Schmitz, a member of the John Birch Society, which would have repealed the state's fair housing law. Reagan instead endorsed a watered-down compromise bill that left standing many provisions considered close to communistic by his erstwhile right-wing supporters.

Even welfare reform, one of Reagan's favorite issues when talking to ultra-conservative audiences, turned out to be more of an illusion than a reality. While Reagan later claimed to have saved California taxpayers some $2 billion by his toughminded "crackdown" on welfare, most independent studies place the actual tax savings at only one fiftieth of that figure. Most of the reduction in the welfare caseload during Reagan's term, in fact, resulted from the upswing in the California economy and, ironically, from the state's liberalized abortion law. In addition, much of the Reagan welfare program was thrown out by the courts and the remainder largely scrapped after the administration left office. Reagan's most famous draconian measure for welfare recipients, the Community Work Experience Program, dubbed the "work or else" law, ended up placing only a handful of destitute people in jobs. After a gush of publicity, the program was gradually phased out because it was ineffective. Jack Veneman, a former California state legislator and later undersecretary of HEW under President Nixon, concluded after studying the Reagan welfare record: "He was trying to do things that were contrary to federal law and his figures on caseload reduction just don't hold up. It was very popular but the whole thing, I think, was a phony."

By the time Reagan left Sacramento, some thoughtful right wingers no longer trusted their one-time hero. A number of them even became staunch critics during his ensuing presidential runs, including the leaders of the far right United Republicans of California (UROC). In 1975, UROC issued a detailed position paper on Reagan that accused him of making "eloquent conservative speeches while his deeds have served the liberals." They attacked Reagan for having "betrayed" conservative ideals on such issues as property rights, income tax withholding, gun control, crime control, and welfare reform.

Anthony Hilder, a young record producer who put together a "Stars for Barry" album for the Goldwater forces in 1964 had been among the first ultra-conservatives to jump on the Reagan bandwagon. In December 1964, he mass-produced "Run Ronnie Run" bumper stickers and promoted them throughout the state to pressure Reagan into politics. But by the end of Reagan's two terms in office, Hilder was looking back bitterly at his former idol: "I thought he was terrific, a knight in shining armor, a hero to save the troops. But what did we get from him? Higher taxes, abortion laws. There's got to be a question mark about him for any conservative with any sense."

While Reagan's moderate record in Sacramento disappointed zealots like Hilder, it was generally applauded by the state's business leaders. When Reagan left office in 1974 and prepared for his first full-scale run at the White House, many of his longtime businessmen supporters stressed that the former actor had matured from his Goldwaterite past into a truly responsible statesman. This middle-of-the-road assessment was ratified by Reagan's closest friends, such as Al Bloomingdale. Sitting in his Century City office, Bloomingdale expressed frustration with the "Eastern establishment" which, he claimed, failed to understand his friend's essentially pro-business, level-headed approach to government:

> He's right on some things but when Ronnie leads the government, when he has to run things, he goes down the middle.
>
> If the Ku Klux Klan or the Christian groups want to support him, you have to be politic about it. What are you going to do—ask them to support the other candidate?
>
> ... I have no real ideological position. This is a personal thing for most of us. We have only a few [right-wing] idiots.

Despite his record as a pro-business moderate in Sacramento, Ronald Reagan had an exceedingly difficult time winning corporate support during his initial attempts for the White House. Many businessmen, even in California, feared Reagan's nomination would bring about a repeat of the 1964 Goldwater debacle. Longtime supporters wondered whether the country was ready to accept the former actor and his Western entrepreneur backers as the nation's new leaders.

The 1968 Reagan for President drive had been little more than a trial run. The California governor, after just two years in office, had little business support outside his own state and a national following only among the right-wing fringe of the old Goldwater forces. The 1968 Republican Convention in Miami belonged to another Southern Californian, Richard Nixon, who had a long lead in building a national constituency. Nixon, who had moved to New York after being trounced by Pat Brown in California's 1962 governor's race, conceded his home state to Reagan, and instead concentrated on winning delegates in the other regions of the country. A veteran of the Washington scene, Nixon represented an earlier, as yet not self-confident era of California politics; he still relied heavily on Eastern power and approval, Wall Street connections, and farm state Republicans for his political base.

In 1976 it was Gerald Ford, Nixon's stand-in, who inherited the disgraced former President's corporate support. Even such past Reagan boosters as Robert Fluor, the industrialist David Packard, and Henry Salvatori rallied to the Ford banner, hoping to avert a divisive primary fight within the party. This corporate pressure was designed to keep Reagan out of the race and nearly succeeded.

Backed against the wall, Reagan turned increasingly toward his old core supporters in California—the crowd, Hollywood, and the ideological right. He expanded his constituency by appealing directly to the "white shoes crowd"—the car dealers, oil jobbers, and land developers who had made their fortunes during the post-1960 Sunbelt boom. Cast aside by the traditional Republicans, Reagan fell under the influence of a new group of young conservatives led by Jeff Bell, later a candidate for the U.S. Senate, University of Southern California economist Art Laffer, and other devotees of what became known as "supply side" economics. Built upon an almost mystical faith in the creative power of the entrepreneurial spirit, these activists called for a program of reduced government spending and lowered tax rates, which, they claimed, would spur private industry, boost productivity and employment.

Reagan had publicly endorsed these new principles at a speech in Chicago on September 27, 1975, which called for cutting "the Gordian knot" of federal control over economic life. The message, essentially a recitation of "supply side" concepts, was largely dismissed as heretical by the east coast–dominated media and conservative academic establishment alike. Most corporate executives, particularly outside the West, also rejected the new Reagan program. But the clarion call for a return to fundamental entrepreneurial capitalism—a combination of old-fashioned Adam Smith economics and Kennedyesque optimism—got an enthusiastic reception among the new entrepreneurs and grassroots Republicans, particularly as the 1976 primaries moved into the Southern and Western sections of the nation. After a series of humiliating defeats, Reagan overwhelmed Ford in North Carolina, swept through the Rocky Mountain states, and won a lopsided victory over the President in Texas. In the June California primary, Ford was unable to mount little more than a token opposition.

By the late spring, many top corporate leaders were ready to join the Reagan effort. Rather than dismissing him as a potential Goldwater, a number now saw him as a new improved version of their old favorite, Richard Nixon. Although the former President felt compelled to give token support to the man who pardoned him, Nixon confided his growing admiration for Reagan to Pat Hillings, a close friend and former Republican congressman. After a visit to Nixon's San Clemente estate, Hillings reported: "Nixon is worried about Ford. He feels Ford didn't take advantage of his position. It is just so terribly botched. . . . Nixon is an admirer of Reagan's style. He likes it because it's Nixon's own."

By the opening of the Republican convention in Kansas City, Reagan was completely surrounded by Nixonite veterans, including campaign manager John Sears and political operative Lyn Nofziger. Other old-time Nixonites financed the burgeoning Reagan effort, including the Whittier oil family of Los Angeles, Southern California steel magnate Earle Jorgensen, and the Coberly family of Los Angeles—all of whom had contributed to Nixon's infamous 1952 "slush fund." Sears and other top Reagan strategists hoped that, if a deal could be struck with Eastern moderates, the nomination might be won. Sears attempted to carry out this plan by offering the vice presidency to Pennsylvania Senator Richard Schweiker. It was classic Reagan, a Fabian thrust to the center; but the move came too late. Ford's early primary victories and the power of his office proved just a little too much for the California candidate.

THE RETURN OF THE NATIVE

Ronald Reagan and his growing core of supporters approached the 1980 elections with a renewed sense of determination. Up until his defeat by Ford at Kansas City, Reagan had seemed willing to play the role of the good loser, the ideological hero who gladly suffers for speaking the truth. But Ford's triumph and the subsequent disasters of the Carter presidency stiffened Reagan's resolve not to end up as the William Jennings Bryan of the right. As one top adviser put it:

> Defeat changed him. Ronald Reagan has always been a little bit of a fatalist, believing that help would come over the hill at the last moment. He used to feel God looked over the country and nothing was going to happen to it. Now he realizes God doesn't usually get involved and the cavalry usually arrives late. He decided if he wanted the presidency, he'd have to go and get it.

Reagan's new-found vigor was greatly reenforced by the dramatic shift in national economic and cultural power that took place during the late 1970s. While the Eastern half of the country suffered from recession and high unemployment, the Western states enjoyed an accelerating economic boom. The "two tier economy," predicted by the Bank of America's chief economist Walter Hoadley, began to take irrefutable shape; the once proud East was clearly relegated to the "lower rung" of the new economic totem pole. California corporations consistently enjoyed two to three times the profit rate of their Eastern competitors. In the corporate community the new success stories increasingly came out of the West—from the brainy engineering wizards of Silicon Valley to hard-driven oilmen like Occidental's Armand Hammer, ARCO executive Thornton Bradshaw, and Denver energy mogul Marvin Davis.

This accumulation of wealth in the West engendered an increasing national fascination with Western viewpoints, lifestyles, and fashions.

The symbols of American status and success, from J. R. Ewing of the "Dallas" television series to Farrah Fawcett-Majors and Cheryl Tiegs, largely came off the Hollywood assembly line, which exercised an unprecedented dominion over the national consciousness. For the first time, Western fashion became national high fashion; stores selling high-priced pseudo-cowboy gear sprouted on the streets of New York and other centers of Eastern sophistication. Even Western music, now controlled largely by Hollywood recording companies, broke from its traditionally limited markets and emerged as a dynamic new force on the national pop music charts.

Behind these outward cultural manifestations lay a profound national shift toward the values and attitudes long associated with the Western states. After forty years of the east coast code of noblesse oblige liberalism, Americans in the late 1970s turned increasingly toward the frontier ethic of individual self-reliance. If liberal social programs had failed to correct the nation's problems, many Americans concluded, perhaps the solutions promoted by the Western entrepreneurs—essentially leaving the fate of the poor and minorities to the workings of the marketplace—deserved a chance. Rampant inflation and soaring tax burdens accelerated the electorate's attraction to these new, less costly approaches.

Similarly, the morality-laden internationalist foreign policy advocated by Carter's east coast and Southern advisers failed to keep pace with the changing national mood. Devotion to international cooperation seemed ridiculous to many Americans at a time when the national economy was being undermined by OPEC price rises and foreign industrial competitors. When Iran seized fifty-two American hostages in the winter of 1979, it intensified the nation's hunger for a more aggressive, even jingoistic foreign policy.

As Carter and his administration stumbled from crisis to crisis, Ronald Reagan, with his craggy face, Western clothes, and individualistic credo, seemed ever more attractive. Fed up with the pietistic Carter, Americans yearned for a return to the vigorous spirit of the nineteenth-century entrepreneurs, for the days when the country's leaders seemed sure of the nation's destiny and moral correctness. Peter Hannaford, a veteran Reagan public relations adviser, theorizes that these shifts in the national psyche prepared the nation for the elevation of his former client to the presidency. Sitting in the Los Angeles office that once served as Reagan's headquarters between elections, Hannaford observed: "Ronald Reagan represents a Western optimism, a great surge in national feeling. There's got to be a stop to all this guilt. We shouldn't feel guilty for being a rich and powerful country. We don't need to wear a hair shirt all the time. Reagan doesn't carry that awful burden of guilt which has destroyed Carter and other Presidents."

The Reaganite assessment of the national mood received a tremendous boost from the passage in California in June 1978 of Proposition Thirteen. Howard Jarvis's tax-slashing effort, similar to a measure sponsored by Reagan during his gubernatorial administration, captured the imagination of middle-class voters around the country. Within a few months, over twenty-three states had active campaigns for tax-cutting measures, and by November 1978, twelve had passed some major tax reduction legislation. Even some prominent Democrats, such as California's Governor Brown, Massachusetts Governor Ed King, and New York City Mayor Ed Koch, became staunch advocates of fiscal belt-tightening.

Equally heartening to the Reagan strategists, Proposition Thirteen did not cause the governmental collapse predicted by many of its critics. Instead, California's economy seemed to flourish from the stimulus of the tax cut, an affirmation of the "supply side" theories of Art Laffer, key economic adviser to both Reagan and Jarvis. With the nation catching "tax revolt" fever and the "supply side" faith, the Reaganites sensed that their triumph was just over the horizon.

Impelled by the self-confidence of men convinced of their destiny, the Reagan forces marched into the 1980 campaign unconcerned with lingering east coast opposition. They were no longer dependent on the men of Wall Street, Chicago's Loop, and Washington's Dupont Circle, who rallied behind such candidates as John Anderson, George Bush, and John Connolly. Even in the face of the California experience with Proposition Thirteen, the Reaganites learned, the establishment Republicans were still opposed to the "supply side" creed; George Bush, who proved the most viable of the traditionalists' candidates, denounced Reagan's endorsement of the Kemp-Roth tax cut bill as "voodoo economics."

Such attacks on the Reagan program in 1980, however, lacked the sting they had held back in 1976. This time, the Reagan strategists realized their opponents on the east coast were divided; there was no President Ford to rally around. Equally important, the events of the last four years had, in large part, discredited the old power centers. It was *their* cities, from New York to Detroit, and *their* industrial companies, such as Chrysler and U.S. Steel, that were clearly failing. As the Carter administration and its Eastern-dominated State Department struggled with the Iran crisis, Reagan boosters grasped the power slipping from the hands of the ossified traditional establishment. As Ted Cummings, a veteran Reaganite and ambassador-designate to Austria, explained: "Those of us who have backed Reagan feel we need a new leadership for America. Since the death of Nelson Rockefeller the easterners have lost their sense of leadership. We need to regain our prestige in the world, our respect for ourselves. We cannot allow America to be pushed around anymore."

As Cummings suspected, the east coast old-line leaders no longer possessed the will or the strength to stop the rising Reagan tide. Some prominent Eastern Republicans, such as Pennsylvania's Richard Schweiker and New York's ambitious Congressman Jack Kemp, actively backed Reagan from the start. Even the Eastern media seemed prepared to ease up on the California candidate; throughout the primary campaign, liberal papers like the Washington *Post* and the *New York Times* repeatedly stressed Reagan's "moderate" record as governor and his adherence to pragmatic campaign strategies.

After his triumph over Bush in New Hampshire, Reagan fired campaign manager John Sears in order to stem rising factionalism on his staff. For a replacement Reagan reached into the heart of New York's corporate establishment and plucked William J. Casey, a sixty-seven-year-old attorney and former chairman of the U.S. Securities and Exchange Commission under President Nixon. Casey, now director of the CIA, lent his own considerable prestige to the Reagan drive and, by late spring of 1980, was fully confident that the Eastern leadership would ultimately accept leadership from California:

> I know my friends in New York will reconcile themselves to Reagan. They know he took over California and turned it into a state with AAA bond ratings. They know that the country is losing strength and respect around the world. They know we must change our economic policies. They want leadership back for this country and they realize, finally, that Reagan is a lot more than just an actor. He's a leader.

Casey's prediction proved correct—Reagan easily won his party's nomination, and in November 1980 beat incumbent Jimmy Carter by one of the largest margins in presidential campaign history.

The men who made Reagan have created new industries and new wealth and formulated the basic premise of Reaganite philosophy: that private enterprise, unencumbered by govenment regulation, can solve most of the nation's problems. This is far more than a simple recitation of traditional conservative homilies. Reagan's backers have dared to break with both the Republican and Democratic pasts; their program of tax cuts and massive spending reductions goes considerably beyond traditional conservatism. As Laffer explained shortly before the election:

> I look at the primary role in economics of incentives. Traditional Republican policies of raising taxes and reducing spending—that's

what Jimmy Carter is doing. He's right in that tradition of Hoover, Nixon, and Ford.

In both parties the leaders have been interventionists. Nixon was a tax increaser and government interventionist. My perception is Reagan is something different. Reagan is truly free market.

As he did in Sacramento, Ronald Reagan upon arriving in Washington clearly established the pro-business, anti-welfare state nature of his administration. He immediately froze federal hiring and speeded the deregulation of oil prices. Following the Sacramento pattern, he pleased his entrepreneurial backers by promising to cut back the regulatory power and the professional staffs of such troublesome agencies as the Securities and Exchange Commission. In line with "supply side" concepts, he advocated major tax cuts and reductions in federal expenditures, particularly in social welfare. His program clearly represented the wishes and aspirations of the ascendant West. The Eastern states stand to gain little from higher domestic oil prices; social service cutbacks will be more painfully felt in declining cities like Detroit, Cleveland, and St. Louis than they will in boomtowns like Houston, San Jose, or Los Angeles.

Not surprisingly the Reagan cabinet, like his early policies, has reflected the values of these well-heeled men. The key players in the new administration are devoutly free market in approach and anxious to dismantle the rusting remains of the old New Deal edifice. The placing of virulently pro-development James Watt as Interior Secretary, for instance, represents part of a long-cherished dream among Reaganite entrepreneurs for an end to federal controls over land development, particularly in the West. At the same time Reagan's inner circle has taken care to deny the far right zealots of the Moral Majority access to the key levers of power. None of the key cabinet officers—Treasury Secretary Don Regan, Secretary of State Alexander Haig, CIA Director William Casey, Defense Secretary Caspar Weinberger, and Attorney General William French Smith—has been associated in any way with the fundamentalist Christian political movement.

The reason for this shutout of the far right lies in the attitudes prevalent among Reagan's California boosters. Men like Charles Thornton, Henry Salvatori, Ted Cummings, and Al Bloomingdale are embarrassed by the moral rearmament preached by the Reverend Jerry Falwell. Most express the hope that, as happened in Sacramento, the far right during the Reagan presidency will turn into little more than an ineffectual cheering section. "We don't buy that kind of approach," revealed Thornton, standing next to a picture of his old friends, the Reagans. "You shouldn't, you can't legislate morality. We did that before and all we got out of it was organized crime."

The Reagan presidency means far more than a temporary changing of the ideological guard. It ushers in the beginning of a whole new era of American politics, one dominated by the societal values, culture, and economic forms of California. The state's political message may shift, but essential patterns have been set down with the acceptance of the individualistic credo of the California entrepreneurs. Nathan Shapell, a developer and longtime supporter of Reagan, predicts that California has just begun to fulfill its destined role as the new center of the American Republic. In politics, in culture, and most of all in business, Shapell maintains, the day of the Eastern elite has passed and a new era, dominated by the entrepreneurial spirit of California, has come into being.

Like many of the California businessmen, Shapell's faith was born out of his own personal success. He came to Los Angeles in 1955, a survivor of the Auschwitz death camps and the postwar displaced person camps. Through hard work and drive he has built a $217 million real estate and construction empire. Looking out from his high-rise window, Shapell feels a deep pride at his city's progress over the last twenty-five years, a progress he played a major role in creating. Today, Shapell maintains, the nation must turn to the West and adopt the very spirit that spurred himself and so many makers of the California ascendancy:

> Out here we know what the nation needs. Reagan knows it because this approach has already worked here. All this country needs is to get back to the fundamentals of capitalism. Leave the entrepreneur alone and let him survive if he can. . . .
>
> You know, California used to be a joke. We were always criticized by Wall Street for not being diversified enough. But after Proposition Thirteen, we showed the way. Nobody knocks us around any more. We're finally getting respect.

IV.
Jerry Brown
and the New Class

Perhaps even more than Ronald Reagan, Jerry Brown was brought up in the bosom of the New Deal. His father Pat, the son of a San Francisco gambler and theater operator, was a native Californian and a politician of the old school. As district attorney in San Francisco in the 1940s, and State Attorney General in the 1950s, Brown was close to all of the key constituents in the New Deal coalition of minority communities and interests, labor, and the liberal corporate gentry. In 1958 he was elected governor of California, the first Democrat to gain that office in twenty years.

Under Pat Brown, California had its New Deal, Fair Deal, Square Deal, New Frontier, and Great Society all rolled into one. During most of his eight years in office, California prospered, its per capita personal income increasing by more than a third. On some days the state's population gained 1,000 new residents and, overall, California's population swelled from 15 to 19 million during the Brown years. In October 1962, Brown, bubbling with enthusiasm, announced to the press that, according to his calculations, California had surpassed New York as the nation's most populous state. "As the momentous shift of population from the Atlantic to the Pacific has come about, we have met it with the vision and determination characteristic of our people," he proclaimed immodestly.

In many senses, Brown's gratuitous claims were justified. Under his administration, California furthered its reputation—born in the days of Hiram Johnson, Culbert Olson, and Earl Warren—as the nation's center for progressive government. The number of state employees jumped nearly 50 percent and expenditures more than doubled during that noninflationary era, far outdistancing the increases in population. Unemployment, welfare, and workmen's compensation benefits were all raised to record highs, as were state taxes. The state's mental health and developmentally disabled care systems were considered models for the nation. The civil service, particularly at such key state agencies as the state Public Utilities Commission, carried out the highest ideals of Hiram Johnson and his Progressives.

But to Pat Brown, his greatest accomplishments were those enshrined in concrete. Under Brown an enormous, advanced economic infrastructure, unparalleled in any state, was built up. By the end of the 1960s the state had 1,650 miles of freeway, over 1,000 of them paved during Brown's eight-year administration. Brown provided the university system with the most generous backing in its history: three new university campuses and six new state colleges were built during his tenure. Brown's greatest achievement, the State Water Project, begun in 1960 with a $1.75 billion price tag, took water from the Feather River in the wet, mountainous northern reaches of the state and delivered it to the dry, flat, fertile farmlands of the San Joaquin Valley and the rapidly expanding suburbias of the Southern California coastal plain. Thousands of acres in new lands were brought into productive use; at the same time, thousands more disappeared before the onslaught of bulldozers in the spreading metropolitan areas of the state.

THE LAST HURRAH

In the Sacramento of Jerry Brown's youth, there were, in effect, two Democratic parties, one that carried on the social idealism of the New Deal and another, more opportunistic faction that represented the contractors, architects, and agricultural interests, benefiting from Brown's building mania. As the administration settled into its rule, this latter group became more dominant, with favor-seeking contractors gaining ever more influence over the governor and the state legislature. Watching his father and his cronies engage in smoke-filled-backroom big money politics made a strong impression on young Jerry Brown. His long-time aide Tom Quinn recalls:

Jerry's attitudes developed all the years watching the political activity around his father. This build, build, build, build thing was just prevalent. He could remember seeing the cement builders at former Democratic National Committeeman Eugene Wyman's house applauding loudly about paving over the state.

It all began a real questioning of the values of the Democratic Party, questioning all the programs and the money. He wanted people to prove things to him. It was a real break with the Humphrey-Johnson approach. Jerry was probably the first Democrat in the country to question that. Of course, now that's become commonplace.

Brown's revulsion against the consumption-oriented, materialistic world of his father at first drove him away from politics. In the fall of 1956 he entered the Jesuit Seminary in Los Gatos, high in the hills between Santa Clara and Santa Cruz in Northern California. There he lived in a world distant from the wheeler-dealers, cement-mixers, and cigar-chompers of Sacramento. Instead of the Governor's Mansion, his home was now a small cubicle, with straw mattress and no running water. It was a life of privation—renunciation of worldly goods, long periods of silent meditation, enforced conformity of dress, celibacy, and mortification of the flesh.

After four years at the seminary, Brown decided to reenter the world. He enrolled at the University of California at Berkeley in 1960; but the effect of the Jesuit years had been profound. His revolt against materialism had grown under Jesuit auspices into a missionary passion to impose a more disciplined, leaner order of things on the world. The "era of limits" was born inside the prisonlike walls of the seminary. Brown would later recall:

Life was very simple. A bell would ring at five in the morning and we would get up and then, until nine in the evening, would follow a strict schedule that was basically the same each day—meditation, Mass, Latin, waiting on tables, sweeping floors, working in the fields, reading spiritual books: Thomas à Kempis, the history of the Jesuit order and a three-volume work on ascetic virtues.

. . . It was very engrossing and it was where I wanted to be. It was very disciplined all right, but for a purpose.

When Brown left the seminary for the University of California at Berkeley campus, he entered a strikingly different world. Even before the famous Free Speech Movement in 1964, the campus area was a hotbed of political and cultural revolt against American society. But Brown retained his distance from the revolution brewing around him; he was not really involved in Berkeley's subculture or the intense Marxist-tinged politics of the campus. Like Reagan during the Great Depression, Brown at Berkeley seemed to live in his own world, separated from the passions of the day. To him, Berkeley in the early sixties was not the fountainhead of a new era, but a "depressing" place, lacking meaning or restraint. "There was a wasteland quality about experiencing the Berkeley campus in 1960," Brown would later recall, ". . . the impersonal rules and bureaucracy, the lack of direction, the drift, the fragmentation, the void."

Brown graduated from Berkeley in 1961, and went on to Yale Law School, gaining his degree in 1964. It was the year that saw the start of the Free Speech Movement back in California, and many of his generation were plunging into political activism—using their legal training in the nation's ghettos or filing actions against the interests of the corporate elite. Brown instead became a clerk for a justice of the California Supreme Court, and in 1966 joined the prominent Los Angeles corporate law firm of Tuttle and Taylor, working on small civil and criminal cases.

Throughout this period, when his father was still governor, he remained aloof from politics. The reclusive, philosophically inclined Jerry Brown continued largely to ignore the great political storms around him until 1968, when he joined the insurgent anti-war presidential campaign of Senator Eugene McCarthy, as a member of its California slate of delegates to the Democratic convention in Chicago. In McCarthy, Brown found a kindred soul—a reserved Catholic intellectual, who, while the darling of the American left, was still an iconoclast and conservative in many of his attitudes. Brown's support of McCarthy represented yet another break with the Humphrey-Johnson political traditions of his father, who, two years before, had been trounced at the polls by Ronald Reagan.

That defeat had further solidified young Brown's belief that the New Deal emphasis of his father's party was doomed to destruction. He watched as the smooth actor from Southern California picked apart his father, the seasoned politician. Reagan got tremendous political mileage out of attacking the spiraling government spending in California and the runaway costs of the welfare state. Equally telling was Ronald Reagan's ability to saddle Jerry's father with the onus of being soft on the radicals at Berkeley, and failing to curb the licentiousness that was casting fear in the hearts of middle-class Americans all over the country. They were lessons that would have a profound impact on a young lawyer (then twenty-eight) who believed that new ideas and a new consensus were essential for anyone wishing to survive in political life. The ease with which the minor Hollywood figure disposed of Pat Brown created a lasting impression on Jerry. Later, he would model his political career not on his father's achievements, but more on the accomplishments of the man who so skillfully ridiculed them. Asked fourteen years afterwards what "model" most appealed to him in building a political organization, Brown responded:

Reagan. And Reagan does have a coherent ideology . . . a view of an era that's dying. . . . Reduce government spending, and regulations to free up individuals and corporations—whatever their size—to do whatever they want as long as it doesn't violate traditional morality. . . . That's a coherent view. And it fits in with the liberal view of our tradition that there is a central power that is the cause of our problems. Weaken that power, whether it is a monarchy or the government, and we will become liberated. That's his view. Now whether you're talking about Exxon as well as the individual [sic], it's still within the tradition.

THE RISE OF GOVERNOR MOONBEAM

In 1969, with his father retired from office, McCarthy defeated at the polls, and his interest in law waning, Brown himself began to consider a political career. His first effort was modest: in the spring of 1969, he decided to run for the Los Angeles Community College Board. He had by now largely broken with the party traditions of his father, but the old man's political friends, and the widespread recognition of the Brown family name, remained at his disposal. With 14 places open and a field of 133 candidates, Brown ran an independent campaign and came in first. "He was a loner then, just as quite frankly he is a loner now," commented political consultant Joseph Cerrell, an old hand in Pat Brown's administration, who lent his support to Jerry's first campaign. "He ran as Edmund G. Brown, Jr. If his name was Edmund G. Green, I wouldn't have wanted to bet on his running in the top fourteen."

Aided by Tom Quinn as his media adviser, Brown adroitly used any and every opportunity to gain press attention. While often awkward in personal interactions with people, he made up for it with his skill at using the media—particularly television. Within a year Brown, at age thirty-two, and Quinn, just twenty-six, were ready for bigger and better things. Brown announced his candidacy for the office of Secretary of State. It was a low-key race for an obscure state office, and Brown again benefited from his well-known family name. In November 1970, Jerry Brown—in the face of Ronald Reagan's reelection landslide—won his first statewide race by over 300,000 votes.

As the Community College Board had been a mere dress rehearsal for another show, so too was the Secretary of State's office. This time the goal for Brown and his coterie was the governor's office, from which Reagan was retiring in 1974. Brown used the Secretary of State's office as an official pulpit, attacking "special interests," gaining a reputation as a reformer. In the meantime his father's old cronies, assuming that the son would carry out the traditions of the old man, supported Jerry's ambitions, wallets at the ready.

It turned out 1974 was a fine year to cloak oneself in the garb of the reformer. The scandals swirling around the Nixon administration led to a general reaction on the part of voters against the "old politics" of sleazy backroom deals. That year Brown was the chief proponent of ballot Proposition Nine, a statewide initiative calling for campaign-spending reforms. With Quinn manipulating the press, Brown ran as a Mr. Clean candidate against his two leading Democratic Party opponents, Assembly Speaker Bob Moretti and San Francisco Mayor Joe Alioto. Italians and New Deal politicos of the old school, the two campaign veterans were helpless against the Brown/Quinn deluge of press releases and television campaign commercials. Desperately, they tried to force Brown out on other issues. "Jerry Brown continues to campaign in the closet," Alioto complained loudly at the time. But Brown kept to his script and on primary day, 1974, triumphed along with Proposition Nine.

Although they were queasy about young Brown's strident attacks on political fat-cats, Pat Brown's old contributors held firm through the general election. Brown received large donations from such longtime Democratic financial stalwarts as Lew Wasserman, chairman of the Music Corporation of America (which had previously supervised Ronald Reagan's acting career), oilman Edwin Pauley, Los Angeles financier John Factor (who formerly was linked to underworld figures in Chicago and was a big financial booster of Hubert Humphrey), and Southern California land developer Richard O'Neill. Pat Brown himself helped more directly, with $4,500 in donations from his Beverly Hills law firm and another $21,000 from an oil-marketing concern partly owned by the Brown family. Joining the old guard were less seasoned members of California's entrepreneurial class, including Eli Broad, co-founder in 1957 of the huge Kaufman and Broad construction firm; theatrical agent Jeff Wald; and S. Jon Kreedman, a founder of American City Bank in 1963 and chairman of the campaign.

Against Brown's well-financed and expertly run campaign, Republican challenger Houston Flournoy's prospects seemed to be grim at first; he was behind in the polls from the start. But Flournoy, the state controller and an attractive moderate Republican, campaigned vigorously, accusing Brown of ducking direct debate and avoiding taking positions on virtually every political issue. Brown, meanwhile, laid low, relying on crafted commercials written for television by the gifted Quinn. A passive strategy, Kreedman later admitted, was adopted in order to keep Brown's lead from collapsing too quickly. Virtually unknown apart from his television image and famous last name, Jerry

Brown had little to gain by coming out into the sunlight. The voters, Kreedman observed, were "not too sure of what [was] there. Jerry had the lead, and why fight it, why make the one big mistake?"

Ultimately the strategy worked. Promising little more than to bring "a new spirit" to Sacramento, Jerry Brown defeated Flournoy by slightly over 175,000 votes. California, for the second time in eight years, had elected a near political novice to the state's highest office. Few people knew what Jerry Brown actually believed or what he planned to do, least of all the old warlords of the Pat Brown era who had so generously supported the campaign of the strange young prince of California's Democratic Party.

Jerry Brown arrived in Sacramento in January 1975 bathed in spot-lights. Not much more than a shadowy, televised figure to most people, he had almost no political past and few debts—he was virtually a free agent. Mickey Kantor, law partner of Democratic National Chairman Charles Manatt and a longtime Brown strategist, believes this lack of a political past allows California media candidates to avoid the dead-ening process of trade-offs and compromise that is the realpolitik of the East. In California the party structure has been notoriously weak for decades, far removed from the world of the well-healed ward boss coralling votes on a street corner, or the experience of national political candidates jockeying for support among power groups in their parties. With little sense of obligation to smaller constituencies—particularly on the lower rungs of the social order—California's political leaders can move more freely, trying out new ideas, limited only by the demands of their own image and the needs of the monied classes that sponsored their careers. It is a situation particularly suited, in the cases of Reagan and Brown, to the formation of a political ideology based on the visions of the state's entrepreneurial elites. As Kantor observes:

> Jerry Brown came to Sacramento without a lot of excess baggage. Both he and Reagan didn't have to fight their way up through an Assembly seat. They didn't have their images washed away along the mashed potato circuit. They were able to become identified with young ideas. If you go from G.E. and Borax to Governor, it's easy to keep your ideas foremost. Jerry did the same thing, he went in six years from Community College Board to Governor.
>
> There has been less emphasis for years here on paying dues. There's much more emphasis on communications technology and big money. The question here is not whether the labor leader is backing you but who is doing your media. This is the way things have gone in California, and now it's how politics will be done in the East as well.

While Ronald Reagan, upon entering office, already possessed a well-defined ideology and a set of big money supporters, Jerry Brown lacked either. His financial boosters were largely holdovers from his father's era; his campaign slogan, promising a "new spirit" in government, was about as specific as ad copy for a Pepsi commercial. He had observed and been affected by the late 1960s and early 1970s revolt against military adventurism overseas and the wanton destruction of the natural environment at home. What he finally settled on as the theme of his administration was the "era of limits." This concept would prove the cornerstone of Brown's political persona, the ideological basis for his calculated response to the increasingly popular Reaganite concept of an unfettered free enterprise "Creative Society."

The "era of limits" grew out of Jerry Brown's fundamentally conservative notion that America's government spending, consumption patterns, and military-industrial complex had overreached the nation's productive capacity. Brown's new vision tapped into eclectic sources; it blended the "small is beautiful" utilitarianism of E. F. Schumaker with California's future-oriented technological determinism; Jeffersonian liberal idealism with the austere logic of Jesuit social values. "I think that order, and values and dignity are very important for a civilization," Brown once explained. "The self-indulgence and mindless consumption can erode human dignity and democratic order." Like Savanorola, he came to rid Venice of *superbia* and *luxuria*.

Brown saw the huge, cumbersome government bureaucracy at the federal and state levels as the main villain undermining the social order. Government, he believed, had become too intrusive in people's commercial and personal lives, rendering them weak, unproductive, and irresponsible. From the beginning of his administration, Brown sought to reduce the government's role as guarantor of individual welfare; he preached that the family, the church, neighborhoods, and business should assume control over many social functions now assumed by the government. He firmly believed in government's role as a spur to greater productivity and the guardian of natural resources, but he largely rejected the "social contract" obligations that had grown out of the Roosevelt era. After taking office, Brown shocked traditional Democrats with declarations like:

> ... The whole Jeffersonian ideal was that the people are temporarily in government. Government is not the basic reality. People are. The private sector. And government is just a limited power to make things go better. Now we're inverting that, and government is all-pervasive. Every time you turn around, there's government. I think that's not part of the American character. I'd like to reverse that [pro-

cess]. I think it's an uphill battle, given technology, mobility and information flow. To put government on a smaller scale and still make it work is a pretty good trick if you can do it.

Government isn't a religion. It shouldn't be treated as such. It's not God; it's humans, fallible people, feathering their nests most of the time.

Almost immediately, Brown started to scale down government in California. He refused to move into the ultra-modern new Governor's Mansion, denouncing it as a "Taj Mahal" symbol of the era of overspending; he practiced personal asceticism, slept on a mattress on the floor of his spartan apartment near the Capitol, and drove around in an unobtrusive Plymouth. He took a tough, "zero base" approach to virtually every item on the state budget.

Like Reagan, Brown concentrated much of his early fire on the huge University of California system. It was still unpopular from the days of the Berkeley and Santa Barbara student insurrections, so it provided a convenient target. While Brown's anti-university rhetoric lacked some of the bloodthirstiness of Reagan's outbursts, Brown was equally resistant to the blandishments of the system's entrenched bureaucracy. He put the whole university system on a strict budgetary diet, claiming the elite institution was not putting back into the economy what it was taking out. Before Proposition Thirteen, Brown kept the university's annual rate of budget increases roughly equal to that under Reagan; after the passage of the Jarvis measure, controls became even more severe. "The problem with the university is that it's out to lunch," declared Brown's chief of staff, Gray Davis. "A decade ago the university had a blank check and there was no greater claim on the government's coffers. They want everyone to be studying Greek and Latin. Well, today you've got to do better than that."

While the university's president, Albert Bowker, loudly complained about the "cheap shots" taken by the Brown administration against the U.C. system, the cutbacks on the campuses were just the first in a broad range of "deadwood" that fell before Brown's budgetary ax. The budget restraints under the Brown "era of limits" exceeded even the most draconian steps taken by the Reagan administration. Whereas the nation's leading conservative had cut the annual rate of state employee growth nearly in half from that during the Pat Brown regime, Jerry Brown trimmed Reagan's rate of employee increases per year an additional 55 percent. "If you ask the people in the university and other bureaucracies who was a worse governor," claims former Reagan cabinet member and later Brown appointee to the regents of the state university, Don Livingston, "they'll say Jerry Brown. Ronald Reagan was not as far right as people thought and Jerry Brown was not as far left. There was a lot of similarity between the two."

SMALL IS VERY BEAUTIFUL

If anything, Brown's budget cutting was more vigorous and successful than Reagan's. As governor, Brown has carried on his predecessor's assault on Sacramento's government bureaucracy and the state's entrenched social welfare programs. Even before the passage of Proposition Thirteen, Brown adopted Reagan's basic anti-New Deal political formulation: reduce government, cut regulation, allow the economic forces to run their course. To the vehement protests of traditional Democratic constituency groups, Brown has vetoed increases in pay for state workers and blocked more state funding for education and welfare programs. "When Jerry Brown talks about lowering expectations," remarks Dr. Jerome Lackner, Brown's former director of health, "he is really talking about lowering expectations for the poor, the mentally ill and the disabled."

One of Brown's most controversial cutbacks involved the state "homemaker chore" program, which provided low-paid workers to help care for disabled citizens in their homes. While funding for the program was supposed to be set according to federally mandated guidelines, Brown in his first year in office blithely slashed $13 million out of the "homemaker chore" budget proposal. The result was sharply reduced services in many counties and a total elimination of support for hundreds of disabled people. While Brown's tough talk about the "era of limits" impressed the mass of voters, his willingness to reduce care for these helpless persons seemed to many draconian and heartless. Robert Oden, a thirty-nine-year-old Tulare County truck driver who was paralyzed in an auto accident, was among the hundreds of recipients to have his home chore worker removed due to Brown's cutbacks. Utterly dependent on his helper for such vital functions as preparing meals and helping with personal hygiene, Oden sued the Brown administration to retain the state-mandated service. Interviewed from his bed, the invalid complained: "Brown's people are very indifferent, very cold and callous. They look at the figures and wait for the pins to light up and they cut. It looks good for them to be cutting money. They don't see the human beings who are suffering."

Brown's reductions in the "homemaker chore" program were symptomatic of his desire to cut back government-sponsored care for society's needy citizens. Brown also targeted such traditional "sacred cows" as regional community centers for helping the retarded, autistic children, and the handicapped for reductions. Asked about these un-precedented cutbacks, Gino Lera, Brown's legislative consultant at the time, explained that under the new "era of limits," even the most distressed citizens "have to sacrifice something too."

Brown also cut deeply into the budget for the state's mental hospitals. Due to restraints imposed by both Brown and Reagan, five of the state's mental hospitals lost their national accreditation in 1976. At the same time money-saving moves to reduce patient beds at the hospitals and smaller facilities forced the "dumping" of some 30,000 mental patients into inadequate nursing homes, critics charged. State investigators traced scores of deaths of patients still within the faltering hospitals during the 1970s to staff negligence and over-drugging. Like university administrators, those responsible for the state's disabled population began to look back on the Reagan regime with feelings of nostalgia. As Dr. Richard Elpers, Los Angeles County director of mental health, put it: "Things went fairly well under the Reagan administration. It wasn't pie in the sky, but there was genuine concern for people. Now [under Brown] I don't see much concern for people at all."

Despite such criticism and occasional exposés in the media, Brown expanded his tough approach toward these social welfare programs. In recent years he has favored cuts in aid to the elderly, the elimination of cost of living increases for the indigent, and restrictions on compensation for workers injured on the job. While legislators of both political parties often objected to these cuts, Brown deflected his opponents by using his ample media skills. If there was a particularly poignant exposé on deteriorating conditions at a state hospital, Brown would arrange a highly publicized "surprise" visit to a mental ward, shaking hands with some retarded patients under a flood of camera lights. When representatives of the state's poor and minority communities complained about welfare cutbacks, Brown countered by trotting out long lists of minority officials appointed to high positions in his administration.

He was particularly aggressive in recruiting from the state's Hispanic community, California's dominant minority group, which will constitute a full third of the state's population by 1990. By 1978 Brown had appointed over thirty Mexican-American judges, compared to only three on the bench at the end of Reagan's regime, and placed two hundred Mexicans on state boards and commissions.

These appointments helped insulate the Brown administration from carping liberal critics. Placing Mario Obledo, a politically well-connected Hispanic lawyer, as secretary of the sprawling Health and Human Services Department muted criticism of Brown cutbacks from the state's largest, and poorest, minority group. Similar manipulation, particularly of details of Brown's bizarre private life, also diverted attention away from the impact of the governor's actions. Indeed, by the end of Brown's first term his liberal opposition had been essentially rendered harmless through the governor's adroit use of symbolism and imagery. He managed to keep taxes low, cut programs, and still retain the support of the Democratic Party's core constituencies. As one liberal member of the state legislature's Democratic leadership put it:

> He is a master of the symbol. Appoint a black or gay figurehead and no one will complain. Everything seems to be a big distraction with Brown's aides—they distract you with satellites so you don't think about nursing homes.
>
> The Plymouth is a distraction, the bed on the floor is a distraction, [Brown's friendship with singer] Linda Ronstadt is the ultimate distraction. And none of it means anything.

While Brown was successful in neutralizing his liberal critics, he had more serious problems with the state's powerful business community. They generally approved of the budget-cutting mania of the "era of limits"; what bothered them were the environmental ramifications arising out of the same doctrine. Convinced that overconsumption was not only immoral but impractical, Brown in his early years worked hard to slow down the rate of growth that was devastating the environment of the state. Business leaders, used to the far more permissive policies of the Reagan administration, protested loudly when their developments were slowed, or even stopped, by Brown's environmental policies.

This conflict between the state's business leadership, often allied with labor, and the "New Spirit" government in Sacramento, came to a head in 1977 when the Brown administration's regulations halted the construction of a massive $500 million Dow Chemical Plant in rural Solano County. The vehement protest by Dow and construction unionists stung Brown deeply, as the administration developed an extreme anti-business reputation.

The energy policies of the new governor exacerbated this conflict. One of the first American politicians to perceive the environmental dangers of nuclear power, Brown delayed the licensing of future plants. "Era of limits" quickly became a hated expression among the businessmen of the state; it was associated with the "no growth" ideologies of the young ecology-minded remnants of the 1960s political and cultural left. Joseph Rensch, president of Pacific Lighting Corporation, a $3.4 billion natural gas and utility holding company, recalls early business meetings with Brown. "He would come into these meetings very hostile and arrogant, like we were bad guys or something," Rensch, later a convert to the Brown cause, remembers. "There was a real antagonism in the business community toward Jerry. He was closed off from us. But as he's evolved, he's grasped the significance of a sound economy."

THE GURU

If Brown's "liberal image" was acquiring a slightly off-color complexion in some circles, men like Richard Silberman saw him as the answer to creating a Democratic Party wedded to the values of California's newly emerging entrepreneurial forces. The son of a Russian-Jewish immigrant junkman, Silberman grew up traveling from city to city in Depression era California, first to Los Angeles, then San Francisco, before his family settled down in the then sleepy coastal town of San Diego. From his struggling, itinerant merchant father, he learned the essentials of entrepreneurship, how to make a buck on the run. His first job was selling peanuts on San Francisco's Embarcadero while he was still in grammar school. "I came off the streets and I was always working to try and earn some money," Silberman recalls. ". . . My life's been a very lucky, rocky road."

Like so many California entrepreneurs, Silberman has been driven by an obsession to seize the initiative, to benefit from the nascent future. While other kids in San Diego were out playing football, the science-oriented Silberman worked alone in his room, fixing radios. His youthful future orientation was reflected in the title of his high school valedictory address: "Now Is Tomorrow." Characteristically, while still in school at San Diego State, he started his first significant business venture, the Video Service Corporation, which capitalized on the new market in television repair. Later, he established himself as a leading electronics manufacturer and a financier for new, innovative high technology firms. In the 1960s he increased his already considerable fortune by becoming an executive in the Foodmaker Corporation, owner of the original Jack-in-the-Box hamburger chain. Shortly after selling off Foodmaker to Ralston Purina in 1968 for $58 million, Silberman and another business partner took control of the Southern California First National Bank. In 1975, he sold the bank to the Bank of Tokyo for nearly $70 million.

For the peripatetic Silberman, success served only as a spur for enlarging his area of exertion. Nearing his fiftieth birthday, wealthy beyond his means and recently divorced, he looked for some way to increase his influence on the world around him. He was a visionary without a champion, a man needing a star to which he could attach his vast resources and energies. The Republican Party, controlled in San Diego by men of Henry Salvatori's generation such as financier

C. Arnholt Smith, seemed indifferent to the promise of the future that consumed Silberman. Its members were largely oblivious to the new forces that were beginning to dominate the nation's economic life. Yet the Democrats, too, appeared out of touch with Silberman's entrepreneurial vision; most clung instinctively to old political formulas dating to the days of FDR.

But, in 1976, Silberman became acquainted with Jerry Brown. Although few of his peers in the business community then agreed with him, Silberman saw in the eccentric young governor a man capable of grasping the realities and needs of California's fast-changing economic environment. Three years after joining with Brown, he observed:

> I doubt if there's a person in political life who has a better understanding of economics than the Governor.... What he is arguing about is seeing more business directed toward investment, more high technology, less emphasis on consumption. By stimulating consumption, all we do is stimulate foreign employment....
>
> He does not believe that the future of the country will be well served by major corporations which are unwilling to adapt to change.... He started talking about things like "an era of limits," and they in the business community were afraid of it. [But] younger people in their 20s, 30s, and 40s don't have the same perceptions of people in their 50s and 60s who are running a lot of these big corporations. The younger vice-presidents in these firms like what Governor Brown is saying. They will be the business leaders of the 1990s.

From the time Silberman took on the job as Brown's chief fundraiser during the governor's presidential drive in 1976, he cultivated this new generation of businessmen. Later, serving Brown as secretary of business and transportation, finance director, chief of staff, and 1980 campaign co-chairman, he continued to enlist the backing of this emerging "new class," preparing for the day when they, like Salvatori's group before them, could take the reins of power.

These businessmen of the "new class" spring largely from the generation that came to maturity in the 1960s and 1970s. Having experienced the drastic military cutbacks of the post-Vietnam era in their prime, they did not share the same enthusiasm for the defense-centered economy of men like Charles Thornton. Instead, most of the fortunes of these pro-Brown businessmen came from newer enterprises in high technology, real estate, banking, and entertainment. Following his humiliating defeat in the 1980 presidential primary campaign, Brown put together a powerful coterie of these leaders and invited them into a new "kitchen cabinet," modeled on the earlier Reaganite model. Joining Richard Silberman in this new inner circle were Northern California developer Jack Brooks, also chairman of the Fremont Bank; record industry executives David Geffen and Joe Smith; August Coppola, brother of the filmmaker Francis Ford Coppola; Don Gevirtz, a founder in 1969 of the $141 million Foothill Group, one of the nation's fastest-growing large financial institutions; and San Francisco attorney Jeremiah Hallisey, who has represented such major corporate interests as Standard Oil of Ohio. Products of an age of rapidly diminishing American resources, power, and technology, these men believe that government must play an important role in encouraging new, innovative, productive industries in order to compete with well-planned industrial nations like Japan. As Silberman puts it: "There will be an increasing role for government in the future but it's a different role. The whole complaint over too much regulation doesn't address the real issue, which is the need for a closer relationship between government and business. It's naive to say we need less government. We have to redirect what government does."

In consultation with such business leaders as Silberman, Brown has increasingly identified himself with this new vision of government's role. During his abortive 1980 presidential campaign, he tried to raise these issues in his call for the "reindustrialization" of America, only to find them largely ignored as his sputtering campaign fizzled ignominiously. But with the smashing triumph of Reagan, Brown seems sure to offer himself again as a future-oriented alternative. In Sacramento, the testing ground for Brown's ideas, the governor in 1981 proposed the formation of such cooperative state/private projects as a new Microelectronics Innovation and Computer Research Operation at the University of California and a new state-funded California Corporation for Innovation Development, a nonprofit agency designed to help fund new technology companies. While other Democrats have attacked Reaganism for its insensitivity to the needs of the poor, Brown, counseled by his entrepreneurial advisers, chastised Reagan for failing to meet the goals of the business community. He lambasted Reagan for his inability to balance the federal budget or to aid American business in the struggle to remain competitive in the world marketplace. In March 1981, Brown wrote:

> This nation did not become the world's leading economic power by merely manipulating its money supply. Our strength has been built with the world's most sophisticated tools, and we continue to lead the way toward a new information era in which investment in the products of the human mind replaces our past emphasis on resource exploitation.
> To meet this challenge, it will not be sufficient for the government simply to "get off the back" of business. Our nation, like our major

corporations, must practice strategic planning. A new national consensus among business, labor, and government will be needed, in which government becomes a *partner* in the creation of new wealth.

Within months of Reagan's triumph, forces allied with Brown and California's "new class" successfully maneuvered one of their own, Charles Manatt, into the post of Democratic National Chairman. A Los Angeles lawyer, whose firm has blossomed along with the growth of the region's new entrepreneurial elite, notably in entertainment and banking, Manatt also represents the institutionalization of California's ideological dominance over the second of the nation's two parties. Upon taking his post, Manatt, whose law partner Mickey Kantor was Brown's 1976 campaign manager, called on the Party to leave behind the New Deal traditions and move toward the more businesslike approach advocated by Brown. "No one is going to vote Democratic in 1982 just because we ran FDR fifty years before," Manatt said, in sounding the death knell for his party's half-century-old tradition. " . . . We must convince people we can manage government as well as create it. We cannot be viewed as dewy-eyed spendthrifts or incompetent administrators."

As high-tech industries—electronics in particular—gain primacy over the economy, Tom Quinn argues, they will provide the essential base for Brown's push for power. And just as the collapse of the Eastern industrial economy and financial leadership undermined the "social contract" dating from the New Deal, so the Western high technology revolution will create the new ideology of the "party of the people." As Quinn puts it:

> Until the last couple of years these new entrepreneurial types couldn't see how the government could help. I think that's now changing. A decade from now these people will be a force in politics. Jerry would like to see them as a force. He believes in what they are doing and the potential of what they could do for the country. If Jerry Brown was President, he'd be far more likely to figure out how to help the semiconductor industry than help old companies like cars and steel that are dying anyway.

A BORN-AGAIN CAPITALIST

As early as 1976, Brown had started laboring hard to repair relations with the state's business leaders. In addition to his anti-government rhetoric, Brown began advocating such pro-business policies as the elimination of the state inventory tax, the deregulation of state oil prices, the emasculation of regulatory agencies, and an easing of the federal government's 160-acre limitation on the size of farms eligible for water from federal projects. He threw his support behind legislation to eliminate licensing of real estate agents and to reduce regulation and promote technological research in the cable TV industry, and he placed a strict limit on the time state agencies could take to review the environmental impact of development projects.

At the urging of Richard Silberman, Brown began weekly regular dinner meetings with Robert Anderson, the chairman of ARCO Oil Company, the state's second-largest corporation. Other key business leaders such as industrialist David Packard and wine grower Robert Gallo suddenly found their opinions carried weight with the Brown administration. State officials, including Brown, donned buttons and put up posters bearing the slogan: "California Means Business." The new initiatives and image building even impressed some hardened Reaganites. "Brown's just great," enthused Reagan "kitchen cabinet" member Justin Dart in the spring of 1976. "He shows how both parties can be responsible."

Brown's desire to please his business critics grew as his 1978 reelection campaign approached. Alienating business was costing him support in both the legislature and the media, where he lived. His lack of organizational and labor support prevented him from building up the noncorporate political base that aided such populist-style politicians as Texas Senator Ralph Yarborough or California Congressman George Brown. "He's gone to the corporations," one disgruntled Brown aide later admitted, "because that's where Jerry thinks the power is at. It's just a simple, logical conclusion."

As part of his drive to please business leaders, Brown transformed his "slow growth" and "era of limits" administration into one that was an advocate for increased economic development in the electronics sector. In the year before his reelection bid, Brown unveiled new programs to promote two of the state's key emerging industries—space and high technology. He proposed doubling the state job apprenticeship program and gearing it primarily for the fast-growing electronics firms. He unveiled a plan for a joint venture with Hughes Aircraft to launch the state's own "Syncom 4" communications satellite and, despite his strict budgetary policies, asked the legislature to establish a $500,000 Space Institute at the fiscally ailing University of California.

Brown's increased appreciation for the politics of growth also led him, in April 1977, to travel to Japan in order to pry loose more business from the Pacific Rim's dominant power. Although Brown's requests that the Japanese build a California auto plant were courteously turned down, his calls for more and freer trade between the state and its

Pacific neighbor drew support from the expansion-minded California entrepreneurial elite. In 1979 one third of California's $40 billion annual foreign trade was with Japan which was far and away the state's leading trading partner.

In May 1978, Brown opened a California Office of International Trade to lure more Pacific Rim business to the state. The office's director, businessman Richard King, promoted California's growing symbiosis with the prosperous Japanese economy, even at the expense of the declining industrial regions of the United States: "We don't want to rely any more on the establishment of the Eastern states. They're Europe-oriented and our future is with Japan and the Pacific Rim. The Japanese see California as part of their 'Pacific Co-Prosperity Sphere' and we better be responsive to that."

Brown's international offensive also served to blunt criticism from the state's powerful oil and utility interests, which had accused him of pursuing his beliefs in alternative energy sources at the expense of nuclear power, thereby dooming the state to an inevitable "brown-out." Much in the fashion of a leader from a sovereign nation, Brown traveled to Mexico to negotiate gas agreements favorable to California's industrial interests. Even more impressive to the state's business establishment, the governor in 1978 announced his vigorous support for a planned $600 million facility to handle Indonesian liquefied natural gas at Port Conception, one of the most pristine sections of California's central coast. Although conservationists and many staffers at the PUC and members of the state Coastal Commission actively opposed the giant project on environmental grounds, Brown and Silberman helped push the project through the state bureaucracy and legislature.

Brown's support of the Point Conception project in the months before the November 1978 election represented a throwback to the "build, build, build" policies of his father. It was also revealed that Pertamina, an Indonesian gas cartel that would be a supplier of the LNG for the project, was involved in other business dealings with Pat Brown, Sr. In addition, Pat Brown's Beverly Hills law firm received legal fees from the project's utility backer, Southern California Gas Company (a subsidiary of Pacific Lighting). Brown's promotion of gas agreements with Mexico also was called into question when it was reported that the gas deals could benefit the Bustamante family in Mexico, which had been involved in other business deals with the elder Brown.

Brown's embrace of these energy deals, expanded Pacific Rim trade, lower business taxes, and more recently the state's new water project, the Peripheral Canal, represented a clear bid to become an ally of the state's ascendant entrepreneurial elite. His positions led to massive corporate contributions to his 1978 reelection drive. Although few of these powerful and traditionally staunch Republican interests were truly enthusiastic about Brown, not many could complain about the state's business climate. They realized—and Brown's aides took pains to keep reminding them through the media—that during his years as governor, California's employment, corporate profits, and per capita income had far outpaced the national average. Among the corporate giants giving funds to Brown's 1978 campaign were such establishment bastions as the Bank of America, the Irvine Corporation, Pacific Lighting, Kaiser Steel, ARCO, DART Industries, Occidental Petroleum, Warner Brothers Records, and several organizations affiliated with the sprawling Howard Hughes empire.

So pronounced were Brown's efforts to curry favor with corporate interests that many leading environmental groups, including the Friends of the Earth and the Sierra Club, no longer considered him a reliable ally. Many of his liberal supporters from 1974 and 1976 were dumbfounded. "Jerry Brown's attitude, particularly in the beginning, was often read as anti-business," explained Max Palevsky, former chairman of the executive committee of Xerox and a co-founder of Intel Corporation in the Silicon Valley. "When he first entered the [Governor's] office, he had real anti-business biases, a kind of hippy-dippy ideology. But he has become so insensitive to business he's almost gone overboard."

Brown's move toward the entrepreneurial class helped him in 1978 to become one of the few Democrats in recent California history to outspend his rival in a gubernatorial race. The embrace of pro-business positions also softened Brown's image as an impractical dreamer. Gray Davis, Brown's reelection bid campaign manager, believes the courting of the business community helped to prevent the corporate forces from coalescing behind Republican candidate Evelle Younger in the months before the crucial November 1978 election. "There are limits," Davis later admitted, "to the era of limits."

THE GREAT TAX REVOLT

While Brown was busily placating his corporate critics, he faced in the spring of 1978 perhaps an even greater challenge from the state's grass-roots voters. Over the winter Howard Jarvis, a seventy-five-year-old conservative Republican warhorse, had managed to qualify Proposition Thirteen, a property tax limitation measure, for the June 1978 ballot. Jarvis had been fighting against taxes of one sort or another for fifteen years. He had worked on several state initiative drives to lower taxes, including Proposition One, a measure backed by Ronald Reagan, which had lost by over 300,000 votes five years earlier. In 1976, a

Jarvis-supported anti-tax measure had failed to gain even enough signatures to qualify for the ballot.

But 1978 proved to be a very different kind of year, one that would shake California and then the nation to its roots. Due to soaring increases in home values, property taxes in some areas of the state had jumped over 60 percent between 1975 and 1978. Homeowners were mad as hell, and Howard Jarvis became their hero. By December 1977, Jarvis had collected over 1.5 million signatures, nearly three times the number needed to qualify his measure for the ballot, and more than had ever been collected for a ballot proposition in the history of the state.

Despite this outpouring of popular sentiment, Brown and virtually every other major politician in the state denounced Proposition Thirteen as a danger to the state's treasury. Even though California at the time was amassing a huge $4 billion tax surplus, Brown and the state legislature decried the Jarvis measure as a threat to essential public services and a disaster for the state's economy. Early in the campaign that argument even swayed the state's top corporate powers—such as the Bank of America, Atlantic Richfield, and the Times Mirror Corporation—which all went on record in opposition to Thirteen.

Opinion polls, however, continued to show the measure headed toward an easy victory as Election Day approached in June 1978. In the waning days of the campaign, many of the state's business powers quietly withdrew their financial support for the anti-Jarvis campaign. By Election Day, the opposition to Thirteen was disorganized and dispirited. Against what had initially been one of the most formidable arrays of corporate, labor, political, and media power ever assembled in California, Jarvis's measure sailed to an impressive 2 to 1 landslide victory at the polls.

The political fallout from the passage of Proposition Thirteen was pervasive and almost cataclysmic. It was as if, in one day, the legions who supported the New Deal welfare state had been assembled on the battlefield and crushed. The appeal of the "tax revolt" was overpowering for the working and middle classes. Over 65 percent of the nation's population favored the extension of Thirteen's tax-cutting approach, according to a March 1979 poll published in *Fortune* magazine. Within a month after its passage, Jarvis-like tax revolt movements had sprung up in twenty-three other states. By the following November, twelve states had already passed tax reduction measures.

For Jerry Brown, Proposition Thirteen posed direct dangers. Polls at the time showed him running virtually even with his Republican gubernatorial opponent Evelle Younger, who had given lukewarm support to Thirteen. A Jarvis endorsement of Younger, then California's attorney general, could literally have destroyed Brown's reelection chances. All over the country Democratic leaders were walking around in a daze; many of them would not survive the Republican tax cutting of 1978, or its aftershock—Ronald Reagan's anti-government sweep into power two years later.

But of all the leading Democratic politicians in America, Jerry Brown was perhaps best suited for dealing with the Jarvis challenge. Although he had opposed the measure, Brown had long identified himself with the cause of lower taxes. Keeping a lid on state spending was the most consistent part of his "era of limits" program. Having inveighed against high taxes and spending, he saw, even before its actual passage, the significance of Proposition Thirteen. Soon after the election, Brown declared: "We have our marching orders from the people. This is the strongest expression of the democratic process in a decade. . . . Things will never be the same."

While Younger sat around expecting longtime Republican Jarvis to throw the election to him, Brown assiduously courted the crusty old warrior. He worked hard to pass the necessary "bail out" bills, which transferred much of the state surplus to localities that had suffered most grievously from the property tax cutbacks. Instead of the preelection predictions of 450,000 government layoffs resulting from Thirteen, Brown's chief of staff Silberman later calculated that there were slightly more than 20,000 actual firings. Jarvis had been right and Brown wrong; the governor admitted it with the candor of a born-again believer.

As the point man directing the state's efforts to adjust to the impacts of Proposition Thirteen, Brown was able to portray himself as the measure's actual implementor. With skill, he quickly turned a major liability into a tremendous asset. A Los Angeles *Times* poll, taken one month after Thirteen's passage, revealed that most Californians actually believed Brown had originally supported Thirteen. One top Republican strategist, former Reagan campaign manager Stuart Spencer, was duly impressed. Late in the gubernatorial campaign he warned that Younger had better "wake up pretty soon and start to recognize that he is challenging one of the best politicians in America. . . . This liberal, far left figurehead of intelligentsia has become the staunch, two-fisted proponent of government economy and decreased government bureaucracy." Although he campaigned hard for other conservative Republicans across the state, Jarvis refused publicly to endorse either Younger or the governor, though he made a highly publicized appearance with Brown on one occasion. On Election Day, 1978, as scores of liberal Democrats across the country were falling before the tide of the "tax revolt," Jerry Brown won reelection by a record-shattering 1.3 million votes. Among those casting their ballots for Brown, in the sanctity of the voting booth, was Howard Jarvis.

THE ROCKY PRIMARY ROAD

The same media-wise skills with which Brown handled his various California adversaries also marked his early entrance into national politics. Like Reagan, Brown assumed the governorship with one eye on the presidency. One close friend, Federal Judge Stephen Reinhardt, claims that Brown's aspirations for the White House were discussed among his friends and allies as early as 1971, when Brown was in his first year as secretary of state.

Not surprisingly, Brown's initial entry into the presidential sweepstakes was largely prompted by his success in handling the national media in the first eighteen months of his new "era of limits" administration in California. Top national reporters trekked to Sacramento, as if to Mecca, and sat at the feet of this maverick politician with his novel ideas and lifestyle. Brown was new and exciting; the other candidates running for the White House, including frontrunner Jimmy Carter, decidedly were not. On March 12, 1976, Brown called four reporters into his office for coffee and casually announced his intention to run.

Brown's seat-of-the-pants decision was not based on any conventional wisdom. He lacked organization, money, and political support outside of the state. But more important to Brown was what he perceived to be the media's hunger for him. He had, he thought, an ideal opportunity to shock his way into the national limelight, to make a big splash. For Brown, that was enough. Mickey Kantor, Brown's 1976 campaign manager, recalled: "We had no staff, no structure, nothing. That was not only typical Brown, but typical California. The feeling was to go with nothing but media, hoping to build on people's perceptions. Jerry was different, he was exciting, he never bored you. He was enormously attractive."

Within two weeks of the announcement, Kantor started to build the one truly necessary organizational element, the finance committee. Under the leadership of Richard Silberman, the committee set up three large fund-raising events, seeking support generally from the same constituencies that had backed Brown's gubernatorial run two years earlier. Real estate developers Jack Brooks and Harvey Furgatch, corporate attorney Frank Rothman, Xerox Corporation executive Sanford Kaplan, and Joseph Rensch's Pacific Lighting Corporation's campaign PAC were all early contributors. Brown also won substantial support from Hollywood's entertainment community, including Columbia Pictures president David Begelman, Los Angeles Rams owner Carroll Rosenbloom, Paramount Pictures president Barry Diller, Warner Brothers executive Ted Ashley, actor Warren Beatty, and Jeff Wald, manager for his wife, the singer Helen Reddy.

With these ample dollars, Brown was able to take his show on the road. The results were electrifying. Brown whipped the "New South's" Carter in Maryland, Rhode Island, Nevada, New Jersey, and California, and came in a strong third, as a write-in candidate in the Oregon primary. He was pragmatic, to say the least, about the allies he picked in each state; in Maryland and New Jersey, he went into business with the old-line political machines; in Oregon, mainly through TV spots, he courted that state's big environmental vote. In most of the states he also substantially outspent the over-extended Carter. Despite his triumphs, Brown could not turn the tide against Carter, who had dominated the early primaries. "We didn't lose," Gray Davis later observed, "we just ran out of primaries."

Brown's brilliant performance in 1976 established his credentials as a national politician. His reputation was further bolstered by his enormous landslide reelection victory two years later. Brown had the feel of a "winner" and, as 1980 approached, he began to piece together a strategy for taking on the quickly fading President Carter. Brown troubled himself little with the idea of building up a strong national organization as Carter had done four years previously. He was confident that the media, needing the excitement of a challenge against the incumbent, would promote his candidacy for him once again. As he had once explained to an interviewer:

> The media needs conflict, needs contradiction, in order for there to be anything to talk about. Popular taste must be appealed to. The media cannot survive without it.
> The media has a relentless commercial obligation underlying much of its objectivity. Advertising space must be sold. Circulation must be maintained and expanded, ratings much be attained.
> ... That is the ever-present underlying reality of the entire media process. Drama creates interest. In order to have drama, you must have a protaganist and you must have conflict. You must have the challenger; you must have the incumbent. And if you're writing for a national publication, you can't write just in terms of California. You have to find a national angle. And that creates this relationship of antagonism with the President.

But this time Brown's cynicism failed him. His endorsement in January 1979 of a constitutional amendment to balance the federal budget had cost him the support of liberals both within the media and among the electorate. At the same time, his alliance with former SDS student leader Tom Hayden's Campaign for Economic Democracy and the militant opponents of nuclear power alienated most of Brown's business supporters. Attempting to bridge the gaps between left and right, environmentalist and entrepreneur, cost Brown most of his support from both sides and virtually all his credibility. He would go from a reception for conservative Texas millionaires to anti-nuclear rallies in New Hampshire, leaving each place empty-handed.

Even some of his oldest backers had argued against the race. Mickey Kantor, the brilliant strategist, maintained a strict neutrality; longtime ally Mayor Tom Bradley of Los Angeles eventually jumped aboard the Carter bandwagon, as did an old business booster, Leo Wyler. Brown's own campaign staff was deeply divided. On the one hand were the pro-business pragmatists, grouped around finance chief Silberman, who favored running on the issues of a balanced budget and the "reindustrialization" of the nation's economy; on the other side were aides like Jacques Barzaghi, a former French filmmaker, and those loyal to activist Tom Hayden, who saw the Brown drive as a crusade against nuclear power and for alternative energy sources.

These deep divisions robbed the Brown campaign of any clear-cut sense of direction or ideological consistency. In marked contrast to his performance in 1976, Brown now appeared ambiguous, confused, even incoherent. Few reporters took seriously his strange hodgepodge of fiscal conservatism and shrill, Jane Fonda–style anti-nukism. Soon satirists, like the cartoonist Gary Trudeau of "Doonesbury" and columnist Mike Royko, were having a field day poking fun at "Governor Moonbeam" and his crazy coterie of "laid back" Californians.

Reeling from this torrent of abuse, Brown was further undermined by the entrance into the race late in the winter of 1979 of Senator Edward M. Kennedy. An unreconstructed and conventional New Dealer, Kennedy became a magnet for all those liberals, thoroughly disaffected by Carter, that Brown had hoped to lure into his camp. Other wayward liberals, suspicious of Brown's support for the constitutional amendment to cut taxes, found their way into the embrace of John Anderson. At the same time Brown lost the support of many of California's top establishment Democrats, who rallied to the banner of the beleaguered Carter. MCA chairman Lew Wasserman, a Brown family friend for decades, would not help the governor. "Jerry Brown is brilliant, maybe someday he'll be President, if only he can be patient," said one MCA political operative close to Wasserman. "But the problem is, Jerry doesn't take instruction easily."

By the time of the crucial New Hampshire primary, Brown's only solid source of financial support came from the younger, less established forces in Hollywood. Sometime girlfriend Linda Ronstadt, record producer and promoter Irving Azoff, the Eagles singing group, Helen Reddy and her husband, Jeff Wald, film mogul Francis Coppola, all stood behind Brown, keeping his faltering drive alive with fundraising concerts and cocktail parties.

But in the snows of Maine, New Hampshire, and Wisconsin, organization was what Brown needed. For that he had relied on his alliance with Hayden and the anti-nuclear movement. This too turned out to be a drastic miscalculation, as Hayden could not produce more than a few hundred volunteers. Tom Quinn, who eventually quit his position as campaign director in disgust, later admitted that Hayden "simply couldn't produce what Jerry expected. The Hayden relationship clearly hurt Jerry more than it helped in the campaign."

Ridiculed, short on funds, without a strong organization or a coherent set of ideas, Jerry Brown was a disaster on the early primary circuit. In April, following a major media blitz organized by Coppola, he failed to make a decent showing in the Wisconsin primary. Jerry Brown, the man who saw himself as the candidate of the future, dropped out of the race.

In the summer of 1980, he would confess: "I didn't have a strong enough organizational base. My own ideas were not adequately or comprehensively formulated, much less communicated. My seniority in the process was not adequate. . . . I hadn't become familiar enough with campaigning as a political business."

THE GEMINI STRATEGY

Over the ensuing months, Jerry Brown watched with interest as his predecessor, Ronald Reagan, moved closer and eventually took over the ultimate goal, the presidency. It was a time for reflection, much like the months Reagan had spent following his 1976 defeat. And like Reagan, Brown emerged from his introspection with a determination to latch onto the same spirit in California that in 1980 propelled the Hollywood actor into the White House. He began the process by pulling together those parts of his program that had attracted entrepreneurs like Richard Silberman to him in the first place—fiscal conservatism, the advocacy of Pacific Rim trade, deregulation, encouragement of investment in new, innovative industry. Brown rudely jettisoned the radical dreamers of the Tom Hayden camp, whose support would only be a liability in the struggle to come. Instead, he turned fully to men like Silberman, attorney Mickey Kantor, and Foothill Group chairman and banker Don Gevirtz—men who represent the leadership of the new California entrepreneurial constituency.

After nearly a decade of searching—through "clean government" reformism, environmentalism, fiscal conservatism, and anti-nukism—Brown had finally stumbled on the secret of California's "manifest destiny." Out of the ashes of defeat, Jerry Brown may yet emerge as the spokesman of an ascendant "new class," rich and powerful enough to sustain a long-term, serious bid for national office. With the increasing shift in power to the West and the industries dominated by these entrepreneurial newcomers, asserts Don Gevirtz, Brown may still be riding on the wave of the future. In time, the current Brown "kitchen cabinet," with its preponderance of entertainment- and technology-oriented entrepreneurs, could follow the Justin Darts and Henry Salvatoris on the road to national power.

As Gevirtz sees it:

I think Brown is developing a greater ability to concentrate, to realize what is really important. His approach, I believe, will prove in the long run extremely pragmatic and businesslike. He understands high technology and venture capital better than any U.S. politician. He understands the importance of the entrepreneur in this country. He understands what is the wave of the future. Jerry lives comfortably with the prospect of a high technology, post-industrial society.

I see good in him. I see strength in him. There are still some suspicions about him but if he keeps going this way, I think Jerry Brown could be the most important politician of the last part of this century. He definitely has a shot for all the marbles.

V. The Politics of Culture

Thornton Bradshaw, dressed in a conservative brown suit, his accent distinctly upper class, seems almost out of place in his presidential office suite atop the Atlantic Richfield Towers—a stiff-looking northerner exiled amid the sun-drenched buildings of the Los Angeles megalopolis. The product of Phillips Exeter Academy, Harvard College, and the Harvard Graduate School of Business Administration, Bradshaw confesses to a longing for the vibrant theater, concert, and opera life of New York, the cultural capital of the established Eastern elite. Yet Bradshaw, who was instrumental in moving ARCO Oil Company from New York to Los Angeles in 1968, believes that the day when the nation's prevailing culture consisted of such arcane pleasures has long passed, as has the once dominant role of the East in the nation's cultural and political life. As he observes:

> There's a tremendous psychological reluctance to admit it because New York still has these wonderful advantages. But the feedback in this country has shifted, it now goes from the west coast to the east.
> We have become a nation of mass culture. I think it's great. Now, never have 220 million had it so good in sharing a culture. . . . Here the west coast has spawned that new culture. Here you have people who are not encumbered by tradition and caste. I think it's a sound culture—and a very hopeful harbinger of the future.
> Unlike the Eastern, European culture, it has not grown out of a few members of society. I think you can see a culture here that better represents the culture of the United States than did the culture of the East.

Bradshaw's interest in the shift of the nation's cultural center is more than casual. ARCO had been among the nation's largest contributors to public television, donating more than $4 million in 1980 to sponsor such programs as Jacques Cousteau's "Odyssey" series and Carl Sagan's immensely popular "Cosmos" science programs. Long an active patron of music and the arts in New York and Los Angeles, Bradshaw in the summer of 1981 became president and chief executive officer of Radio Corporation of America (RCA), one of the nation's largest communications conglomerates.

His, and ARCO's, involvement in mass culture, Bradshaw said during an interview shortly before he was appointed to the RCA position, grew out of his belief that mass communications holds the key to the nation's future social and political order. In California, Bradshaw maintained, a new society is ushering in a political and cultural revolution. In the West, the old structures of neighborhood and community, ethnicity and provincialism, have crumbled, leading to the creation of a new politics and culture unconnected to the long-established "social contract" of the New Deal. This brave new world, according to Bradshaw, will see the final breakdown of the fragmented class and racial politics of the past. What will emerge is the ideal mass society, unified by its disdain for government interference, its passion for private solutions, and its appreciation for a single, shared culture dominated by the mass media. Bradshaw offers this analysis:

The United States for a long time consisted of fairly rigid groups characterized by the farmer, the small businessman, the New York intellectual, the Jews, the Hamtramack Polish. They were expected to act as groups. That has changed. The West is now the place where history is being made. It's due largely to radio and television. We're developing a common culture. We are no longer these groups bound together. We are individuals. . . . This kind of breaking out, that's what California and the West represent.

MAINLINING DREAMS

At the center of the change lie the fantasy factories of Hollywood, which today make California the nation's—and the world's—leading center of mass culture. This cultural ascendancy has accompanied the state's great surge of economic and political power during the last several decades. From being little more than an outpost of transplanted Middle Western culture in the great American desert, California is now home base for nearly three quarters of all the nation's movie production personnel and almost 70 percent of the country's television production payroll. Within the last ten years Hollywood has also established itself as the nation's recording center; by 1980, over 90 percent of the world's recorded entertainment originated in Southern California.

This growth in the concentration of mass cultural industries in California has come at a time of rapid expansion of the entertainment field. Between 1970 and 1977, the volume of record sales increased by nearly 300 percent in the nation, and from 1971 to 1978 movie box-office grosses jumped 96 percent. New technologies, notably cable television, video cassettes, videodiscs, micro cassettes, and telecommunications satellites, are expected to increase further the market for products of the industry. With more, diverse programming becoming available, Hollywood executives foresee the day when television will be the dictator of the national consciousness. While the amount of time the average family spends watching television rose over 13 percent from 1966 to 1978, the men who run the studios believe that the market, both domestically and worldwide, has bàrely been tapped. "I'm going to talk in hyperbole, because I think the market is tremendous," remarks Metro-Goldwyn-Mayer Film's chairman Frank Rosenfelt. "I see every kid in the world with his own Tom and Jerry cartoons on videodisc."

ALL OUR CHILDREN

Perhaps no group in America has been influenced more by Hollywood than the nation's children. Already a generation of "baby moguls," in their twenties and early thirties, weaned on television, pop music, and movies, has taken over direction of the leading Hollywood studios. Unlike their predecessors in the earlier Hollywood days, these new cultural packagers often lack any frame of reference beyond the electronic world. In virtually every studio these young people have taken positions of responsibility unheard of in other industries. To them, the pablum of the 1950s and 1960s is part of America's artistic tradition, just as the earlier film executives looked to the classics of literature and the theater for their inspiration. Tom Werner, a thirty-year-old senior vice-president for prime-time programming at ABC's Los Angeles production headquarters, says: "We really are children of the medium. A number of people with whom I work here grew up with television. It was more than just an appliance in my house. I could serenade you with theme songs of shows from the fifties and sixties."

Among the younger siblings of the TV generation, the influence of television is even more devastating. A poll in the *Ladies' Home Journal,* taken at the end of the 1970s, found that 75 percent of American high school students surveyed were dissatisfied with their parents and would replace them if they could, largely with celebrity figures. Of the top choices for "new" parents, all but one, President Jimmy Carter, were Hollywood celebrities. Among those chosen were such glamorous figures as Lee Majors, Farrah Fawcett-Majors, and Raquel Welch. Such adoration of Hollywood celebrities comes in large part from their virtual monopolization of children's time. By age fifteen the average American teenager has spent over 20,000 hours watching these celebrities on the tube—more time than is spent in school or doing homework.

A child's world view becomes defined more in terms of the animated actions of those on the screen than the demanding, dreary world of real life. As Bruno Bettelheim has observed:

> Children who have been taught, or conditioned, to listen passively most of the day to the warm verbal communication coming from the TV screen, to the deep emotional appeal of the so-called TV personality, are often unable to respond to real persons because they arouse so much less feeling than the skilled actor. Worse, they lose the ability to learn from reality because life experiences are more complicated than the ones they see on the screen, and there is no one who comes in at the end to explain it all. . . .

In the 1970s the interest, even worship, of Hollywood celebrities reached a new high. Magazines like *People,* devoted to celebrity coverage, rocketed to the top ranks of American periodicals. The entire entertainment publishing industry (i.e., fiction and popular nonfiction), especially the book business, is turning ever more toward becoming a subsidiary "software" industry for the power brokers of the electronic media. By 1979, advertising revenues for the commercial television segment of the entertainment industry had reached $10.2 billion, almost $4 billion above the total sales of the book industry.

VOTING AT THE BOX OFFICE

Political life, too, has fallen under the sway of Hollywood's cultural hegemony. Once considered little more than an ornament in the country's political process, Southern California's celebrity society has developed into a major source of national power. This phenomenon began modestly with the theatrical community's participation during and after World War II in local politics. By 1950 a former actress, Helen Gahagan Douglas, could run as a serious candidate for the U.S. Senate, the nominee of the Democratic Party against Richard Nixon. Fourteen years later a former song-and-dance man, George Murphy, won admittance to the U.S. Senate, the "most exclusive club in the world." Two years after that came Ronald Reagan.

But the influence of Hollywood over the nation's political life extends far beyond the successful careers of a few individuals. Television advertising ate up 60 percent of the campaign budgets of President Carter and Ronald Reagan in the 1980 election. Other politicians, selected largely for their skills in front of the camera or their celebrity connections, have become almost commonplace in legislative bodies and executive offices across the nation. With their coiffured hair styles, carefully crafted images, and celebrity spouses, politicians like Virginia Senator John Warner (husband of Elizabeth Taylor) and Kentucky Governor John Y. Brown (husband of beauty queen/media celebrity Phyllis George) have been able to rise above less fortunately married opponents. Since the 1972 McGovern campaign, celebrities have also shown themselves to be startlingly effective fundraisers; Jerry Brown's 1976 and 1980 presidential drives received much of their funding from rock concerts and celebrity-hosted cocktail parties.

The relationship between show business and politics has furthered the erosion of the New Deal state. As the public's interest in political parties and issues is displaced by the *People* magazine imagery of Hollywood politics, the very meaning of the elective and legislative process has changed dramatically. Television, both in the New York–dominated news side and the Hollywood-controlled entertainment side, creates a single, national consciousness about candidates. Regional identification, class, community, all fade before the chimera of media politics. The individual's involvement in the political process is thereby reduced, leaving a mass who cast their votes according to which celebrity candidate titillates their private fantasies. "Electronic communication," writes the social psychologist Richard Sennett, "is one means by which the very idea of public life has been put to an end."

The substitution of media blitz for party organization and image for platform has its roots in the ascendancy of the Hollywood "star" system in the nation's cultural life. Seeing their every move enshrined on the covers of major magazines—even in such once restrained Eastern publications as *Newsweek* and *Time*—the leaders of the Hollywood community naturally assume their role as the shapers of the nation's political, as well as cultural, destiny. Politicians and actors, campaign managers and media "experts," have become almost interchangeable, and the celebrities and media moguls of Hollywood see themselves as the new power brokers, the creators of political style for the coming decades. Former NBC executive Richard Wald observes:

The entertainment people in television, Hollywood, are not just looking for a large audience, they're looking for all the audience. That kind of thinking, mass thinking, changes the way you operate. Old politicians were looking for part of the audience, for a coalition.

They were looking at problems and saying, "Look, this is a common problem for many of you. I'll represent you in dealing with it." The new politicians are looking for chords. They float above the problems. They strike responsive chords. What they really want to do is cloud men's minds.

It seems like a better idea. California, the idea of the place. You want to surrender to it.

SUNSHINE AND SOUND STAGES

The idea of Hollywood as a cultural, much less a political, power center would have seemed absurd to those who watched the first group of early filmmakers trek to the barren foothills of the Santa Monica Mountains shortly after the turn of the century. Climate was certainly one of the key reasons for the movement of the infant film industry to Los Angeles, but there were others. The Edison Company back east had a patent on the film-making process, and those who wished to avoid paying Edison's fee and make their films illegally found California's proximity to the Mexican border inviting. There was also an abundant supply of cheap labor in Los Angeles—from indigent Mexicans to unemployed cowboys—willing to whoop and holler and ride for a little extra beer money.

Given its cattle-raising and Mexican past, its broad vistas and towering mountains, it is not surprising that Western themes should have provided some of Hollywood's first major materials. Pioneers like Thomas Ince imported authentic Sioux Indians and sent them into predictably unsuccessful battle against the duded-up local cowpokes. The Western—with its plot centering on the Indian wars, battles between settlers and land barons, or conflicts between lawmen and bandits—drew deeply upon the national psyche. The mythology of the West was, and remains, an important shaping force on the collective American consciousness. The noted historian Frederick Jackson Turner believed that the settlement of the West was a great unifying force, giving character, meaning, and dynamism to American society. The West, in image and reality, provided Americans with

a safety valve for social danger, a bank account on which they might continually draw to meet losses. This was the vast unoccupied domain that stretched from the borders of the settled area to the Pacific Ocean. . . . No grave social problem could exist while the wilderness at the edge of civilizations [sic] opened wide its portals to all who were oppressed, to all who with strong arms and stout heart desired to hew out a home and a career for themselves. Here was an opportunity for social development continually to begin over again, wherever society gave signs of breaking into classes. Here was a magic fountain of youth in which America continually bathed and was rejuvenated.

The Western hero, popularized by Hollywood from its earliest days, reflected the optimism, strength, and irrepressible character implied in Turner's thesis. From silent screen stars William S. Hart and Tom Mix, to John Wayne, Gary Cooper, Jimmy Stewart, and Ronald Reagan, Hollywood's American cowboy has remained the most persistently admired figure of the American public. Born in poverty, challenged by the elements and evil men, the cowboy was a man who could, stoutly and with humor, take on all challengers and win. He was, as John Wayne said of one of his performances, "the big, tough boy on the side of right."

Like the Western hero, most of the early filmmakers came from modest backgrounds. Many were nickelodeon operators, trumpet players, glove salesmen, who came from the lower social classes of Europe or the slums of New York. D. W. Griffith, Adolph Zukor, Jesse Lasky, Carl Laemmle, Samuel Goldwyn, were unknowns to the general public when they came to Los Angeles, searching for a new frontier, their land of opportunity. At first, they were reviled by the staid folks of the city. In the early years, many lived in tents and improvised sets in the middle of vacant fields. More often than not they and their players found the doors of the city locked to them. "Over no decent threshold," wrote one observer at the time, "were they allowed to step. They were unfit to mingle with respectable citizens." On some boarding house doors a sign was hung: "No Dogs or Actors Allowed."

But the entrepreneurs of Hollywood soon were able to achieve respectability. In 1915, when D. W. Griffith's *Birth of a Nation* was released, the movie business suddenly matured. With its large budget, lavish sets, and highly controversial content—the movie was in part a glorification of the Ku Klux Klan—*Birth of a Nation* helped establish films as big business. Soon other filmmakers, notably Charles Chaplin and Cecil B. DeMille, were joining Griffith in making highly profitable pictures that won international reputations. In 1915 the film industry had a $20 million payroll, and was gaining recognition as the national headquarters for the motion picture industry.

While moguls like Griffith were achieving a grudging respectability in the business world, their stars were winning something far greater: fan worship on a national, even worldwide scale. Among the early stars was Mary Pickford, who had worked for D. W. Griffith beginning in 1909. Known as "Little Mary," she became the nation's idol, its favorite heroine. By 1913, Adolph Zukor was paying her $20,000 a year; two years later, she was commanding well over $100,000 annually. Other stars of the period, such as Lionel Barrymore, Charles Chaplin, and Douglas Fairbanks, all soon received enormous salaries as well, while countless new "pulp" magazines soon chronicled every event in their glamorous lives.

The movie stars, to a large degree, provided America with its first mass-produced royalty. Combining the luxurious lifestyles dreamed of by countless Americans with personal rags-to-riches histories, these celebrities reached deep into the consciousness of the nation. The studio bosses, aware of the nation's thirst for stars, often "created" them out of whole cloth. Twentieth Century-Fox took Theodosia Goodman, the large-hipped, curvy daughter of a Cincinnati tailor, and transformed her into the ultimate "vamp" of the period, Theda Bara. Fox helped launch one of the most illustrious careers in the early film era, as Bara's salary climbed from $75 to over $4,000 a week in just four years.

The mass adoration of such stars soon infected the social elite. By the 1930s, the stars of Hollywood were accepted not only by the matrons of old Los Angeles but by many of those in the social registries of Newport, Manhattan, and Washington, D.C. Royalty, including Prince George of Britain, Prince Bernadotte of Sweden, and the Maharajah of Indore, started to mingle with former glove salesmen and tailors' daughters. Some stars, such as Douglas Fairbanks, married into the European aristocracy; others wedded members of powerful American corporate families, such as western hero Randolph Scott's marriage into the DuPont family.

Hand in hand with social acceptability came an enormous expansion of the film business. Between 1921 and 1929, movie production expenditures jumped from $77 million annually to over $184 million, an increase of nearly 140 percent. At the same time the stars themselves began to earn almost unheard-of salaries. Charles Chaplin is said to have made over $1 million from the 1921 movie *The Kid.*

As film making passed from its initial, roughneck phase into a major industrial enterprise, the big Eastern financial interests also began to take notice. As early as 1916, Samuel Goldfish (soon to be changed to Goldwyn) began drawing heavily on a line of credit and investment capital from the Delaware DuPonts and Wall Street's Chase National Bank. Another Wall Street firm, Goldman, Sachs, secured the money to finance the early growth of Warner Brothers, while the Bank of America's A. P. Giannini helped set up Harry Cohn in what would become Columbia Pictures Corporation.

With film profits soaring, increasing numbers of wealthy investors and corporations started entering the Hollywood entertainment business—including Joseph P. Kennedy, Howard Hughes, and RCA. On occasion these powerful interests actually sought operational control of production. In 1927, for instance, Howard Hughes started work on his own picture, *Hell's Angels,* purchasing over eighty planes and hiring more than one hundred pilots for the aviation-oriented film. While Hughes would later prove a genius in manufacturing aircraft, his early performance as a filmmaker was equally spectacular. The movie was released in 1930 after costing $3.8 million in production, and was a big success with audiences and critics alike.

Although corporate and banking influence meant that most studios had New York–based head offices, attempts by Eastern financiers to control the creative process in the film industry usually met with disaster. When Joseph Kennedy probed into the finances of troubled Paramount Studios in 1936, he reported that many of the problems came from too much supervision by the "business" side in New York of the creative end in California. Grudgingly, the wealthy owners have generally been forced to admit that the movie business was like no other; the norms of the business world, particularly in areas like risk-taking and employee compensation, did not readily apply to the fantasy factory. Only the showmen/moguls, most business investors soon realized, truly understood the strange dialectics of the movie industry. "The men on the west coast are paid preposterous salaries," admitted one early film financier, "because they have the kind of mad genius that's needed to put out films."

I'M ALL RIGHT, JACK

The uniqueness of the film industry became starkly evident in the 1930s. While the nation languished in a prolonged depression, the movie business recovered rapidly from the 1929 crash and expanded during the following decade. Production costs inched upward despite the deflation in prices, increasing over $13 million between 1929 and 1937. Although the movie moguls themselves widely expected business to drop off, "hard times" actually seemed to make people more anxious to attend the movies than ever before. The director King Vidor remembers that ". . . in the crisis of 1929, the attendance at the theatres proved to be better than we dared hope and film-making was affected least of almost any business I can remember. We discovered that the mood of the people going to see the movies was not that of enjoying merely a passing fad, but that this form of entertainment had become a necessary part of their lives . . . almost a needed part of their daily existence."

While the rest of the nation suffered through one of the worst periods in its history, Hollywood in the Depression era embarked on what many consider the "golden age" of the movie industry. The introduc-

tion of sound in the Warner Brothers feature movie *The Jazz Singer*
(1927) had opened whole new theatrical forms, such as musicals and
screen replicas of stage plays. Warner's—a relatively minor concern in
the days before sound—became one of the giants of the industry, its
assets increasing in value from $5 million in 1925 to over $160 million
in 1929. In that year Warner's profits exceeded $17 million, an industry
record.

During the 1930s, Warner's turned out sixty pictures a year, ranging
from musicals like Busby Berkeley's *Gold Diggers of 1933*, to adventure
and gangster films patterned after the early cowboy sagas. For millions
of Americans, the swashbuckling Errol Flynn, the tough guy
Humphrey Bogart, the hard-nosed Bette Davis became constant, reliable companions, antidotes to the drudgery and bleakness of 1930s life.
The sociologist Caroline Ware noted in her study of Greenwich Village
in 1935 that "the movies [were] not only the most universal form of recreation but a major source of ideas about life and the world in general. . . . Movie attendance had become practically universal. . . . The
neighborhood movie house was an important feature of the life of the
community. . . . The glamour which surrounded the movie and entertainment world . . . was positively dazzling to young people."

The result was an enormous growth in the movie industry during the
1930s. Between 1933 and 1937, the very heart of the Depression, production outlays by movie companies climbed almost $80 million. Box-
office receipts were more than a half billion dollars in 1939, and over 50
million Americans attended the movies *each week* of the year. In 1939
there were over 15,000 movie theaters in the country, one for every
2,300 families, more than the total number of banks and three times the
number of department stores.

For the moguls and stars this boom created a fantasy world of affluence in the midst of widespread poverty and suffering. The nation's
eleventh-largest industry in terms of total assets in 1937, the movies
ranked second in terms of executive renumeration. Over 22 movie company executives and producers in 1939 received annual salaries of over
$150,000. In 1937 Louis B. Mayer earned over $1.29 million, making
him one of the highest paid executives in all of American industry. The
stars, too, greatly benefited from the boom, with fifty-four of them
earning over $100,000 annually in salaries. In 1937 Shirley Temple,
then age nine, earned over $307,000, making her the seventh-highest
paid person in the entire nation.

Although most actors earned far less—indeed, many were forced to
take second jobs as waiters or laborers—it was the luxurious life of the
stars that dominated the nation's impression of Hollywood. Within the

film community at the time there was an atmosphere of unreality, as the movie elite lived in gracious splendor in marble mansions, with large pools, set back in the Hollywood Hills.

In an age marked by political radicalism and attacks on the "economic royalists" of the industrial establishment, the gilded movie community largely escaped the wrath of its impoverished audience. Unlike the rich of Wall Street or Michigan Avenue, the stars were not seen as enemies of the working and middle classes; they were, in fact, seen strangely as manifestations of the basic American dream, the cowboy myth of the common man making it. As Leo Rosten observed in 1940:

Men have always loved the Cinderella story and have always dreamed of magical success. Hollywood is the very embodiment of these. One reason for Hollywood's stars becoming national idols is that they represent a new type of hero in American experience. Hollywood's children of fortune are not the thrifty newsboys of the Horatio Alger stereotype—honest, diligent, pure of heart; here instead are mortals known to be spendthrift and Bohemian, people believed to lack impressive brains and given to profligate ways. Yet they have been rewarded with great lucre and honored throughout the land. They represent a new kind of folk-hero in a society whose ethos rests upon hard work and virtuous deportment. Furthermore, the public sees the actors at their trade; it sees how they earn their living. The public never sees Morgan making money or Ford making cars; but it does see Robert Taylor making faces. The visual evidence of the films offers the waitress a chance to compare herself to the movie queen; it gives the shoe clerk a chance to match himself against the matinee idols. It provokes the thought, "Say, I could do that. . . ."

Although the fans would forgive the stars some of their excesses, their love affairs and their divorces, the moguls of Hollywood made sure the audience was not alienated by too much licentiousness. Over one third of the leading actors were divorced, yet few films during the period openly advocated such behavior. The screen personas of the most successful stars—from Robert Taylor and Jimmy Stewart to Claudette Colbert and even Ronald Reagan—maintained an image of rectitude and morality. Even "tough guy" characters like the gangsters played by Jimmy Cagney retained a basic goodness.

In many ways the Hollywood served up to the public in the 1930s remained, despite an occasional scandal, an island of innocence in an increasingly brutal world. In order to please censors—and the audience—the producers crafted their films along strictly predetermined lines. Frank McCarthy, who first came to Hollywood in 1938 as a technical adviser for the Warner Brothers movie *Brother Rat,* and later produced *Patton* recalls:

> It was Pollyanna time. The code was very strict. You couldn't do a lot of things. Every picture had to have a moral message.
> ... If you had two persons in bed together, one had to have a foot on the floor. But, you know, it worked and it was wonderful. Implicit sex shouldn't be on the screen. John Gilbert and Greta Garbo were as sexy as anyone. You don't have to take your clothes off to be sexy. It was fun but we still had discipline back then.

It took nearly two decades for the problems of the outside world to impinge on the magical Hollywood Oz. Hardly affected by the Depression, few stars had taken much interest in the political and social movements of the period. The only "ism" that Hollywood readily embraced, as Dorothy Parker observed, was plagiarism.

HIGH NOON

The first significant political stirring in Hollywood came in response to Upton Sinclair's candidacy for governor of California in 1934. After Sinclair won the Democratic nomination on a quasi-Socialist platform promising to "End Poverty in California," nervous studio heads like Louis B. Mayer of MGM and Joseph Schenck of 20th Century-Fox tried to mobilize the power of the film community in favor of Frank Merriam, the colorless Republican candidate. Threats were made to move the industry to Florida if Sinclair won the election, and the moguls tried to force their wealthy stars to contribute a day's salary each to the Merriam campaign.

The so-called Merriam Tax roused the long-quiescent stars into political action. Jean Harlow and James Cagney spearheaded a group of actors refusing to pay it. Others bitterly attacked the moguls for using film footage and actors in harsh propaganda assaults on Sinclair, who lost the election after an extremely vituperative campaign.

The attempt to foist a political conservative like Merriam on the film community was an affront to the basic instincts of most actors, writers, directors, and even many executives. While men like Louis B. Mayer and Jack Warner were doctrinaire Republicans, most of the rest of Hollywood was essentially liberal, if it bothered with politics at all. The rise of Hitler and Mussolini, in particular, and their censorship of American films, intensified liberal sentiments in the movie community.

The liberal consciousness of Hollywood led to the production of some of the most daring social-oriented movies ever produced. Such films as King Vidor's *Our Daily Bread* (1933), and screen versions of

John Steinbeck's *Of Mice and Men* (1939) and *The Grapes of Wrath* (1940), represented pervasive liberal, populist impulses in the film industry. Some actors, writers, and directors even took their new-found ideals out into the real world. Melvyn Douglas and Helen Gahagan Douglas formed the Committee to Aid Migratory Workers, an organization that some conservatives tried to brand as Communist-tinged.

The liberals, however, heatedly denied the charges of radicalism, claiming they were acting in the finest traditions of American altruism. James Cagney commented at the time: "We are accused of contributing to radical causes. When you are told a person is sick or in need, you don't ask him his religion, nationality or politics. . . . I am unequivocably opposed to subversive organizations of any kind. I am for this government and for American principles." Besides their efforts to alleviate the plight of others, members of Hollywood's liberal community also concentrated on improving working conditions in the film industry itself. In 1933, the Screen Actors Guild (SAG), and five years later the Screen Writers Guild (SWG), came into existence. Many of Hollywood's big names, including Cagney, Gary Cooper, Jeanette MacDonald, Robert Montgomery, and Paul Muni, joined SAG.

While SAG remained essentially bipartisan and apolitical, other more stridently left-wing organizations began appearing in the late 1930s. The Hollywood Anti-Nazi League, for example, was set up to combat Nazi propaganda. The organization at its height boasted some 5,000 members, but fell apart when the Communist-leaning elements within it refused to condemn the Nazi-Soviet Pact of 1939. Nonetheless the activities of the Anti-Nazi League and others like it sparked the opening round of what would become a vicious campaign to root out "Communists" in the movie industry. Congressman Martin A. Dies, chairman of the House Un-American Activities Committee (HUAC), made much of the supposed Communist influence in Hollywood, pointing to such films as *Juarez* and *Fury* as signs of the "Red Menace" lurking in Hollywood.

The entrance of the United States into World War II in December 1941, however, temporarily blunted the red-baiting attacks on Hollywood. The wartime alliance with Stalin strengthened the hand of the estimated 4,000 Communists in Los Angeles. In the spirit of the alliance, several openly pro-Soviet films were made, including MGM's *Song of Russia* (1943) and RKO's *Days of Glory* (1944). These films, Jack Warner later said, were intended "to help a desperate war effort," as part of the huge number of propaganda films being churned out of Hollywood during the war years.

With the end of the war and the alliance with the Soviet Union, Hollywood's left-leaning community once again came under fire. Even before the emergence of Joseph McCarthy, the right-wing forces in Washington were blasting leftists and "fellow travelers" in the industry for subverting American values. Some of those targeted by the revived HUAC clearly had used their positions to promote pro-Soviet ideas; many others were just innocents whose past left-wing associations would prove deadly in the new anti-Communist hysteria sweeping the nation. The red scare was also used by the International Association of Stage and Theatrical Employees in their successful jurisdictional battles with the left-wing Conference of Studio Unions.

The year 1947 saw the issuance of lists of suspected Communists in the industry, among them the famous Hollywood Ten and Hollywood Nineteen. While most of the leftists refused to discuss their political affiliations, there were many "friendly witnesses" ready to testify before Congress about the "Red Menace in Hollywood." They included such industry leaders as Jack Warner, Louis B. Mayer, Walt Disney, Adolphe Menjou, SAG president Ronald Reagan, Gary Cooper, George Murphy, and Robert Montgomery. Walt Disney claimed that the Screen Cartoonists Guild was Communist-controlled and had plotted to make Mickey Mouse step to the party line. Gary Cooper said he had turned down many scripts because they were "tinged with Communistic ideas," yet, when questioned, he was unable to recall the names of any of them.

After Congress cited the Hollywood Ten for contempt in 1947, the major motion picture companies, meeting in New York, pledged themselves to discharge the Ten from employment. Even noted liberals like RKO boss Dore Schary, who had been opposed to the blacklisters, backtracked and now permitted banning the Ten from RKO studios.

Once the moguls, and their financial backers, had decided that Hollywood must join the anti-Communist crusade, the fate of the Hollywood left was sealed. Although many in the industry had flirted with left-wing causes during its period of popularity in the late 1930s and early 1940s, the roots of the radical community in Hollywood were shallow. A fiercely individualistic business, the movie industry had never developed a strong sense of fraternalism—exactly the force that helped leftists in such industrial unions as the International Longshoreman's and Warehouseman's Union to weather the period of the purge.

Some actors, as individuals, did try to rouse public opinion. John Huston, Humphrey Bogart, Gene Kelly, Judy Garland, and Katharine Hepburn all rallied to the cause of the Hollywood Ten. Their efforts diminished, however, after the moguls made it clear that such behavior was unacceptable. Of the 204 Hollywood figures who signed the *amici curiae* brief supporting the Ten, 84 were themselves blacklisted. By early 1948, many of those who had opposed the blacklists were reconsidering their activities. Others turned against their leftist associates and started naming names. One of those backtracking from his old left-wing views, Edward G. Robinson, suggested that with the death of Roosevelt no one in Hollywood dared stand up against the forces of the right. "The Great Chief died," the tough guy of countless films admitted, and "everybody's guts died with him."

In the end, the Hollywood left—and much of the movie industry's social conscience—was obliterated. Some 250 actors, writers, and directors fell under the assault of the blacklisters. Most victims of the repression found themselves abandoned by their studios, their agents, even their friends. Principles, not surprisingly, fell by the wayside in the rush to salvage careers. The "golden age" of Hollywood, born of entrepreneurial zeal and individualism, ended in a blaze of the most abject selfishness and conformity. Three decades later, Dorothy Tree Uris, a liberal member of the SAG board during the 1940s, would recall bitterly: "These people were deserted. The guild board during the blacklist didn't help the blacklisted member one iota. The liberals got scared and for the most part did nothing. After lives had been ruined, people had died, then the unions gave them awards."

Attempts to escape the blacklist were doomed to failure. Paul Jarrico produced the now acclaimed *Salt of the Earth* in 1954 along with blacklisted director Herbert J. Biberman. The powerful film, based on the struggle of New Mexican copper miners, evoked all the ire of the new right-wing, ultra-capitalistic mentality in Hollywood. Howard Hughes, the head of RKO, wanted to ban the film's export to other countries; one of the movie's stars, Rosaura Revueltas, was deported back to her native Mexico even before shooting was finished. When it was finally released, *Salt of the Earth* was a financial disaster.

The new group in the cultural saddle in Hollywood had first coalesced as the Motion Picture Alliance for the Preservation of American Ideals, founded in 1944. Among the leading members of this group were Walt Disney, Gary Cooper, Clark Gable, Adolphe Menjou, Barbara Stanwyck, and John Wayne. Members of the Alliance had worked with HUAC in its inquisition against the left, and its ideological bent was clear: it extolled the virtues of free enterprise and pledged itself to weeding the Communists out of Hollywood.

For nearly two decades following the end of World War II, this nationalistic consciousness reigned in Hollywood. Movies stuck to the traditional American themes, and the cult of the cowboy/soldier hero reached new heights. The domestic political turmoil that had marked the era of the 1930s evaporated before the demands of an age dominated by the memory of war, and the perception of a continuing "cold war" with the Soviet bloc. The mores of the filmmakers of the late 1940s and early 1950s were direct. It was the era of the good guys versus the bad guys, the black hats against the white hats, a beguiling faith in the essential goodness and inevitable triumph of American free enterprise society. Congressman Robert K. Dornan, nephew of the comedy star Jack Haley, grew up in the Los Angeles of this period and recalls fondly:

> It was boy meets girl, lives happily ever after. There were clean-cut heroes and villains. Nazis torturing little old ladies; John Wayne landing on the beaches. It was Andrews Sisters songs. . . .
> You have to remember the times. From 1941 to 1953 it was America against the Nazis, against Communists, all the struggle—and prosperity. A helicopter in every garage.
> We all thought we were going to have a generation of Pax Americana. There was a great deal of idealism. We thought the system would end bigotry, that it was making everybody middle class. America was the bearer, the hope of the world.

HOWDY-DOODY ARRIVES

In 1947, only 160,000 television sets were produced nationally; by 1950, over 7 million of them were manufactured and sold. In 1947 alone the number of television stations jumped from 17 to 41, and 86 more came on the air the following year.

Hollywood felt the effects of the new TV market quickly. Movie attendance and revenues sank as people turned increasingly to the tube. Some of Hollywood's most powerful studios even started to feel the pinch. The number of craft workers in the movie industry plunged from 22,000 in 1946 to only 13,500 in 1949. Average weekly attendance at the movies dropped precipitously, from 90 million in 1946 to only 47 million in 1956. Hollywood's profitable free ride was being quickly replaced by "free" entertainment.

The studios realized that they faced certain disaster unless they could find a way to make peace with the new medium. But here the purge of the left hurt them badly. Since Hollywood's movies had adopted a severely limited perspective, they had little to offer that was superior to the television product then being made in New York. The screenwriter Stephen Longstreet, whose credits include *The Jolson Story*, recalls the depression and ennui of post-blacklist Hollywood:

> The 1950s saw the first decline of the great film studios. Better, more daring films were being made abroad and shown in Bel Air and Beverly Hills living rooms. Early Fellini was about to appear,

and the English were producing amusing little films with Alec Guinness and Peter Sellers.

The real killer, however, was television; if not to kill at least to deeply wound. TV products were no worse than the studios' and were for free. Its banalities were an extension of motion picture fare.

Ultimately, however, it was Hollywood's very banality that helped save its dominion over the mass culture. Even as New York ushered in what was later to be known as the "golden age of television," Los Angeles entertainment entrepreneurs were laying the foundations for today's lower common denominator, mass television. While the New Yorkers were producing excellent programs like "Playhouse 90" and "The Honeymooners," pioneers in the Hollywood television industry were coming up with the game shows, situation comedies, and Westerns destined to dominate the new media. Perhaps the key figure in this Hollywood television ascendancy was Klaus Landsberg, a hard-driving refugee from Hitler's Germany who was hired to direct programming at Los Angeles TV station KTLA in the late 1940s. Landsberg rejected the "high-brow" programming then fashionable in New York and responded with light, mass market-oriented fare. Among the programs first brought to the tube by Landsberg were the "Time for Beany" puppet show, the "Frosty Frolics" ice-skating program, the "Spade Cooley" country Western presentation, and the wildly popular "Hopalong Cassidy" Westerns.

While the New Yorkers sneered at Landsberg's pedestrian approach to television, these and other new Hollywood-produced programs eventually pushed the more intellectually sophisticated New York products off the air. As television expanded from a small metropolitan audience into a truly mass medium, the more mainstream Los Angeles approach proved to have far greater appeal. Syd Cassyd, a native New Yorker who moved to Los Angeles in 1945 and founded the Adademy of Television Arts and Sciences the following year, believes that the Midwesternism and middle American values the immigrants brought to Los Angeles alerted the early Hollywood television makers to the realities of the emerging national TV market. Men like Landsberg, appealing to pedestrian Los Angeles tastes, understood the mass American psyche far better than the skilled dramatists who dominated New York's television industry:

Back then this was the biggest midwestern city in the country. We had 200,000 people from Iowa. It was a big difference in audience because you didn't have that New York culture scene. They thought television would be this great cultural medium. . . . Their attitude was nothing happened on the other side of the Hudson. We were still a cultural cowtown.

Live TV died and New York lost its production largely because of a question of life styles. The attitude in Los Angeles, the culture here was different. We have always been a backyard society, one which could appeal to people all over the country. The culture of New York is more unique, an Italian and Jewish culture. The market needed mass programming, all different kinds and the studios proved the only place you could get it.

By the late 1950s, Hollywood-produced action-oriented dramas, such as "Cheyenne," "Gunsmoke," and "Wagon Train," were dominating the ratings. Many of New York's television writers—men like Rod Serling, Paddy Chayefsky, and Reginald Rose—left Gotham for the burgeoning California television industry. Light family comedies on the order of "Ozzie and Harriet" complemented the simple "cowboy" dramas that had long been Hollywood's dominant motif. Through television the once endangered species of the B-movie, home to such second-rate stars as Ronald Reagan, flourished again. "When television came out here in the 1950s, everyone had a TV. You had to put out a lot of crap," one longtime industry observer commented. "You went from the excellent drama of the New York days to cranking out B-movies for television. That's what television really is, a bunch of B-movies, something only the studios can make in huge quantities."

The triumph of Hollywood's "B-movie" product over New York's relatively sophisticated live drama solidified the conservative cultural hegemony that had emerged in Hollywood in the post-war era. The Los Angeles of the 1950s and early 1960s became the center of a new, mass American culture—decidedly middle class and (at least publicly) well behaved. Hollywood trumpeted to the world the values of its entrepreneurial elite: fun-loving, adventurous, dedicated to the achievement of material progress. Poor people, minorities, and ethnic whites rarely appeared in the streams of images flowing out of California. The Hollywood community of this period was an Oz without the artfulness of the 1930s.

THE WORLD ACCORDING TO WALT

Walt Disney was one of those who gave America a great deal of innocent laughter and squeaky-clean family entertainment on the screen. But by far the greatest expression of Disney's world view proved to be his Disneyland amusement park, which opened amid the orange groves of Anaheim in 1955. Within a year almost 4 million people had trekked to this $17 million Versailles for the masses. With its magic castles, idealized Main Street, make-believe Frontierland and Adventureland, Disneyland reflected the optimism, pioneer ethos, and fascination with technology that marked the ascendant entrepreneurial class in California. Disneyland, like the Hollywood film industry, offered the public a sanitized, plastic, talking, and moving model of America and its history. Full of effusive praise for such traditional values as free enterprise and individual liberty, Disneyland simply ignored such historical realities as slavery, and blacks did not start appearing in "people contact" jobs at the park until 1968. During the 1950s and early 1960s other similarly minded entertainment entrepreneurs established themselves including Walter Knott, the founder of the Knott's Berry Farm "family" amusement park in Orange County.

The beginning of the 1960s, however, also presented these cultural packagers with a threat to their peculiarly Western values. The election of John F. Kennedy to the presidency brought an unwelcome aura of sophistication to the national government. Kennedy—urbane, Eastern, intellectual—courted the high-brow artists of New York more than the popular culture-makers of Los Angeles. He also showed a strong proclivity for dealing with such issues as poverty, race discrimination, and nuclear proliferation—issues relegated to oblivion in post-blacklist Hollywood. (He did, however, enjoy the company of movie stars.)

To some of the rabid rightists in the entertainment community, Kennedy's "New Frontier" and the ensuing "Great Society" of Lyndon Johnson seemed a signal to return to the hated values of the New Deal. In 1964, the alarmed and aroused conservatives entered the political fray on behalf of Senator Barry Goldwater, the grandson of a cowboy entrepreneur and a man who shared their individualistic, ultra-nationalist point of view. Walter Brennan, Dale Evans, Roy Rogers, Mary Pickford, Rory Calhoun, John Wayne, Efrem Zimbalist, Jr., Robert Stack, Hedda Hopper, Randolph Scott, and others appeared on a "Stars for Barry" record album used in the Goldwater campaign. On Memorial Day, 1964, dozens of conservative Hollywood's finest gathered at Knott's Berry Farm for a Goldwater rally. Ronald Reagan led them in the pledge of allegiance, and John Wayne then took the microphone to deliver a speech to the faithful:

> I suppose a lot of people are wondering why an actor is acting as master of ceremonies at a political rally. Well there's one good reason. I'm an American citizen and a voter and I have something I want to say and I'm going to say it right now. Liberal columnists, both Democratic and Republican, have repeatedly used the big lie in speaking about Senator Goldwater, because he couldn't agree with

an enthusiastic, but nevertheless irresponsible civil rights bill which gives awesome power to the administration out of proportion with the concepts of the constitution. . . .

Our government, our way of life and the people of the United States have lost prestige the world over. This must be due to the incompetence of our State Department and the impractical regulations of our civil service. . . .

Do we want a president . . . who will not be frightened by rabble-rousing political self-seekers, nor be frightened by the slanted press and columnists who belong to the tired, old New Frontier . . . and most of all a man who will make decisions, and back them up with the will and power of the people of these, under his leadership, soon to be respected again, United States of America? Such a man is Barry Goldwater.

The concerted effort for Goldwater by these and other entertainment industry figures played an important role in the Arizona senator's triumph over the idol of the Eastern establishment, Nelson Rockefeller, in the June 1964 California primary. Although Goldwater was trounced in the November general election, the Hollywood right was greatly encouraged by the triumph of one of their own—former SAG board member George Murphy—in his race for the United States Senate that same year. For the first time the fund-raising and vote-pulling power of the Hollywood community had been clearly demonstrated. Then came Reagan.

Sue Taurog, wife of the film director Norman Taurog, remarked in the early days of 1980:

These relationships go back, some of them, for many years, to the thirties, forties, and fifties. They are very loyal to the Governor [Reagan]. They do a tremendous service by raising money in other states.

You bring a John Wayne or a Jimmy Stewart into a campaign because they really believe in the cause. If they go someplace, at least people will listen to the candidate. He means something to them, what he stands for is what they have always stood for. . . .

When we see Reagan up there, it makes us proud. When you get behind a candidate, you feel part of the big picture. You feel you have a piece of America in your hands, a piece of the presidency.

On January 20, 1981, the Hollywood conservatives celebrated winning their long-sought-after "piece" of the American presidency. The Reagan inaugural attracted many of the principal figures from the Hollywood of the 1950s: Jack Wrather, Frank Sinatra, Jimmy Stewart, Efrem Zimbalist. Yet beneath the glittery costumes and well-preserved figures, the signs of age were everywhere—gray hair, slow paces, wrinkled, sun-dried faces. Indeed, many of those who thirty years before had led the conservative takeover in Hollywood were no longer around to experience the grand finale. Time had claimed some true giants of the period, including Jack Warner, John Wayne, and Walter Brennan.

"The old Hollywood conservative group is physically dying out," observes Arnie Steinberg, a Republican media strategist in Los Angeles. "There's not much left. Right now most of the entertainment people are turned off [to] the Republican approach. They are much more in line with guys like Jerry Brown, even though Reagan comes out of the industry."

Steinberg and many other observers of Hollywood believe that the right in Hollywood has been on the decline for at least the last ten years. It started when, as in the 1930s, forces from the outside began impinging on the Hollywood Oz. As Disney, Wrather, Reagan, and other cultural conservatives tried to maintain their old standards, new forces of social change undermined their audience. The sexual revolution, drugs, rock music, Vietnam, all served to make the Hollywood establishment seem ossified and out of step.

Hollywood's slowness to react to these social changes hurt the entertainment establishment tremendously. By the early 1960s, movie production was less than half of what it was during the heyday of the 1930s and 1940s; by the opening of the 1970s, Hollywood was in a sharp decline, with most of the major film companies deeply in the red. In 1970 the number of movie theaters declined to 13,600, compared to 22,000 in the 1940s, while unemployment in the industry reached 40 percent. Weakened, many of the large studios fell under the control of distant conglomerates, with Gulf and Western seizing Paramount, Kinney taking over Warner's, Time Inc. and Seagrams picking up the pieces of once proud Metro-Goldwyn-Mayer.

Underlying the decline was the fact that the old Hollywood could not or did not wish to understand the changes going on in the society beyond tinsel town. The America of the 1960s was not at all like the America of the 1950s. Civil rights struggles, student riots, and social discord eroded the atmosphere of easy self-confidence and "harmony" that had marked the Disneyland era. By 1969, 46 percent of the traditional optimistic American middle-class people felt that conditions had declined over the preceding decade and, more importantly, over 58 percent believed that such decline would continue into the next decade, according to a Gallup poll. These new attitudes were particularly evident among the "baby boom" generation. The number of college students had doubled from 1955 to 1970, and young people comprised 60 percent of the movie audience.

The inability of the established order in Hollywood to respond to these changes resulted in a creative paralysis in the motion picture industry. The vacuity of the old order was demonstrated in the expensive failure of *Cleopatra* (1963), which despite a then record-shattering $24 million budget, immense hype, and the presence of Elizabeth Taylor, did not live up to its expectations at the box office. The movie, Judith Crist said at the time, was "at best a major disappointment, at worst an extravagant exercise in tedium."

If Hollywood's attempt to glitter itself back to success failed, so too did its attempts to reassert the traditional "cowboy" mentality, which stood at the core of its historical success. John Wayne's *Green Berets* (1968), which transported his prototypical hero role into the jungles of Vietnam, proved to be an anachronism, and was soon followed by a string of anti-war films. There was a growing sense in the executive suites of Hollywood that the industry needed an injection of new blood. "There is no shortage of talent," said the new head of production for 20th Century-Fox, Richard Zanuck, in 1971. "The only shortage lies in the number of men who can courageously and knowledgeably evaluate it."

Under the leadership of a new generation of executives like Zanuck, the movie and television industries began to recruit a younger group of entertainment figures—men more in line with the changing mores. Many of these new filmmakers had attended college in the 1960s, and then went to work for emerging independents. From the ranks of these new directors and producers—including Francis Ford Coppola, George Lucas, Haskell Wexler, Robert Altman, Bert Schneider, and Bob Rafelson—came the leadership that would bring Hollywood back to prosperity.

This new trend in film and television making had little to do, however, with the old ideals of the leftists who had been purged in the 1950s. Only a few of the new film industry powers, notably Jane Fonda and Haskell Wexler, did anything even close to populist films on the order of *Salt of the Earth* or *Our Daily Bread*. Most of the new filmmakers succeeded much as the early Hollywood directors had: by being innovative, challenging conventions, and, above all, by drawing strong, individual characters.

While the new filmmakers rejected the complacent middle-class standards of the Disney generation, they were not particularly interested in mass political struggles, as earlier leftists in the 1930s had been. The anti-establishment movies of the late Vietnam era—*The Graduate* (1972), *Getting Straight* (1970), *Easy Rider* (1969), *Five Easy Pieces* (1970)—dealt more with youthful alienation, dropping out of society, not challenging it directly. The heroes of all these films were, in a somewhat twisted fashion, the traditional lonesome "cowboy," hardly a revolutionary. Basically he just wanted to be left alone. "The old heroes used to protect society from its enemies," observed Paul Newman, "now it's society itself that's the enemy."

But unlike the old left in Hollywood, the new group generally was not interested in full-scale revolution to create a more just social order. When the new-style actors and filmmakers talk of revolutions, they are more likely the sexual, gay, or technological revolutions than a revolt of the masses. The focus is on the individual and how that individual can extend the limits of his or her freedom. The revolution is not political but personal and social.

THE BABY BOOMERANG

This new-style entertainment entrepreneur is not limited just to the movie business. In television and in the recording industry the younger, aggressive entrepreneurs objected not to the old order's capitalism but to its moral restrictions. Their attitudes are mainly those of merchants who believe only in the morality of the marketplace. Deena Kramer, head of television movies for NBC, commented in 1978;

> You wish you could live in a world that was all nice and won-derful, but I know you can't. I guess maybe sometimes you have to believe in evil, in being naughty....
> This job is like working as a buyer for Klein's Department Store's bargain basement. I might hate gold lamé pants but I'd order them. If the public likes them, then my job is to supply gold lamé pants.

The ascendant powers of the new Hollywood share this essentially cyn-ical view of their business. Among today's entertainment industry lead-ers, the entrepreneurial moral code has taken hold as never before.

By the mid-1970s, with the war over and sexual barriers falling even in television, the individualistic attitudes of the new Hollywood came to the fore. Social norms included a sort of comfortable liberalism, per-missive attitudes toward sexuality, and drug-taking. Some conserva-tives even complained that they were being "white-listed" by dominant industry liberals, much as they themselves two decades before had blacklisted the left. Old-time Hollywood conservative and comedy star Jack Haley complained shortly before his death in 1980: "There is a new problem in Hollywood today and it's called the closet conservative. A lot of conservatives say they can't say anything because it will hurt our careers. It's like the old blacklist has whiplashed.... It's a very sad thing in our industry when the gays are coming out of the closet and the conservatives are going in."

The chief political beneficiary of Hollywood's cultural "new class" has been Reagan's gubernatorial successor, Edmund G. Brown. Brown's strongest support in the entertainment industry has come from Los Angeles's new generation of record makers. The record industry prospered mightily throughout the 1970s, nearly tripling its sales. Chief beneficiary of this upsurge was the recording business in Los Angeles, which over the decade of the 1970s saw its share of the national record production market increase from 15 to 70 percent, according to John Sippel, director of marketing for *Billboard* magazine. This enormous boom created an extremely rich, new generation of Hollywood entrepreneur. Some of them, such as Eagles producer Irv Azoff, have also branched into moviemaking, with films like *Urban Cowboy* (1980).

As Brown abandoned the traditional liberal constituencies of the Democratic Party, he turned more and more to the entrepreneurs and stars of the recording industry. Early on he courted these powers, dating rock star Linda Ronstadt, socializing with Azoff, the Eagles, and Electra/Asylum boss Joe Smith. These wealthy individuals, Brown realized, were far less concerned with his position on economic issues like oil deregulation or cost-of-living raises for welfare recipients. If they concerned themselves with issues at all, it tended to be such things as gay rights, censorship, or fears about nuclear power. As one high-level television executive and longtime conservative activist, put it: "Brown's perfect for those guys. The Hollywood bigshots of today are social liberals and economic conservatives. They want to be free to blow pot, or go to bed with boys or whatever, but they don't want to pay taxes. They're not like the old liberals who wanted to help the poor. They just wanted to help themselves."

Brown's strong appeal to this generation of record moguls and stars is both cultural and political, argues his longtime backer Jeff Wald. Unburdened by Disney era morality, single, and a celebrity of starlike proportions, Brown can cavort with the new rich of Hollywood's music industry as an equal, just another player in the glitter game. The Hollywood community responds to Brown, Wald explains, with the admiration of one skilled communicator for another: "We need a leader who's inspirational, who's got charisma and who enjoys knowing how to use the media. Part of [Brown's] relationship with the entertainment community comes from a common understanding about the media. They are stars and Jerry Brown is a star. Carter is very naive about the media. He is no star."

Indeed, much of the 1980 presidential campaign resembled little more than a political version of television's inane "Battle of the Network Stars." The old, gray-haired Disney era establishment stood around their aging hero, Reagan. For the old-line Democrats in the industry, such as MCA chairman Lew Wasserman, President Carter was the choice. Among the ascendant powers in the new Hollywood, Jerry Brown, John Anderson, and Edward Kennedy jockeyed for endorsements.

The tendency of most Hollywood figures to gravitate toward the Democratic Party distressed some top Republicans, such as former public relations executive and now White House counselor Michael Deaver. Along with such long-term Reagan backers as Justin Dart, Holmes Tuttle, and Henry Salvatori, Deaver, in response, has helped promote the thirty-five-year-old record industry tycoon Mike Curb as the new conservative matinee idol. In 1979, Deaver warned:

> The activists within Hollywood are getting more partisan and out there doing things. We have a generation out there that supports us [i.e., Reagan] but it's getting old and we better replace them.
>
> We really need a guy like Curb. He can get support from people who might support Republicans. Maybe people will start realizing that Republicans don't have horns.

The baby-faced Curb, elected lieutenant governor of California in 1978, has worked for almost a decade to build a new conservative Hollywood base for the Republicans. His music firm has recorded such young, Disney-mold artists as the Osmonds and Debby Boone, and his own Mike Curb Congregation Singing Group has provided photogenic smiles, good looks, and clean entertainment for the generally rather staid Republican gatherings.

But Curb, who made his first million at age twenty-two, has shared some of the more permissive attitudes common to the record industry, which supported his candidacy as well as Brown's. In 1967, for instance, Curb was involved in the movie *Mondo Hollywood*—a raunchy account of the seamier side of the entertainment business. Curb provided the music for the film, which included one scene involving a young woman disrobing in front of another burly, cigar-smoking woman. Although Curb has downplayed his role in the movie, the California lieutenant governor has taken a basically free enterprise view on other so-called moral issues. In 1978, for instance, Curb (along with most of the entertainment industry) opposed the Briggs' Initiative, a right wing–backed measure aimed at banning gays from teaching in public schools. He has even taken a tolerant view toward marijuana use, telling one interviewer: "In terms of pot, I don't know. Pot is so prevalent now. We have to advise against it because it's illegal, but I don't know whether it will be two years from now. Everybody seems to think that pot leads to hard drugs, and that's ridiculous. Every young person who's on drugs today started out drinking milk. I've yet to see a harmful effect from pot. . . ."

Although some Reaganites may shudder at Curb's "liberal" views on such issues, most of the President's inner circle of supporters have pledged themselves to promote the political fortunes of California's young lieutenant governor. Already the old Reagan "kitchen cabinet" has begun raising funds for a Curb run for the Governor's Mansion, the inevitable first step toward the White House. Passing over other potential replacements, they have focused on Curb as Reagan's likely successor, finding in him the same glibness, basic economic conservatism, and celebrity appeal that catapulted their actor friend into the White House. As Gray Davis, Governor Jerry Brown's chief of staff, once pointed out:

> The day of the bosses, issues, linear politics is fading into the past. People vote their perceptions, what they know. To many of the people out there, people on television are as real as anything in their lives. When you're tired, worn out and alone in Modesto, and it's 11 o'clock, Johnny Carson is like a real friend, a member of your family.
>
> . . . Let's face it, people are more into the lives, habits, and political preferences of today's celebrities. I mean, it might sound ridiculous, but people really care about who is Suzanne Somers's favorite governor. It wouldn't have even entered anyone's mind five years ago.
>
> Who will Charlie's Angels endorse for President? That question might well be a serious one. . . .

With characteristic zeal, the entertainment entrepreneurs of California are planning to expand their dominion over the mass culture even further. MCA, for instance, has been a leader in the development of "videodisc" technology, which could turn every living room in the nation into a movie house. Similarly, California's culture-mongers are in the vanguard of the nationwide shift to cable and pay television. The state boasts three of the country's top five cable systems—in San Diego, Los Angeles, and San Jose—and, under the leadership of entertainment darling Governor Brown, Jr., enacted the first major deregulation law for cable TV in the nation.

By applying advanced technology to mass culture "software," these California entertainment interests foresee a new day in which virtually every house is "wired" into a relentless flow of programming. John Gwin, president of Southern California–based Oak Communications, a leading cable system operator, predicts that American homes will soon become "electronic cottages." "The cost of transportation, the crime rate, almost everything these days contributes to keeping people at home," Gwin believes. ". . . it's our intention to bring services to the people. Technology snowballs. The next five years will exceed the last ten in what we can do. . . ."

Even now, as the nation moves toward Gwin's "electronic cottages," the influence of the Hollywood mass culture industries continues to grow unabated. The major alternative to Hollywood culture—the east coast paperback publishing industry—is staggering from high interest costs and insufficient or flat growth in unit sales. The most elite hardcover houses in New York now scour the Hollywood headlines, signing up stars to write personal memoirs, to keep their companies solvent. Others make management decisions about what to publish based on largely electronic factors, including possible movie and television tie-ins and the screen appeal of a potential author who would appear on TV talk shows.

TWILIGHT OF THE SCRIBES

The print entertainment business came upon hard times in the 1970s. In New York City, the major center for the book and magazine industry, total employment in publishing and printing between 1970 and 1978 dropped by 30,000, a 25 percent decrease in the total number of jobs. These difficult times have been brought on by a decreasing interest in reading among the public, forcing many publishers and periodicals either to close up shop or to cut back output. Even more discouraging, many of the publications that have survived have largely been those most anxious to cater to the wishes of Hollywood's mass culture industries. Celebrity-oriented publications—"talk shows for the semiliterate," in the words of Los Angeles public relations man Bob Gibson—have dominated the magazine racks in recent years.

The success of publications like the *National Enquirer* and *People* magazine has encouraged other "news" media to focus ever more on the Hollywood celebrity. Whereas much of this coverage in the past has been sharply critical, in the current era of star adulation and star power the emphasis on sharp reporting has diminished steadily, even in august giants like *Time* and *Newsweek*, which have devoted more and more space to long, often glowing accounts of Hollywood celebrities. In some cases, the stars have become so powerful, interest in their lives so pervasive, that publications have surrendered their covers, and sometimes control over their copy, to celebrities and their hired hands.

As disturbing as this trend might seem to the romantics of the print media, to the stars and entrepreneurs of Hollywood such commercialism makes perfect sense. They believe that in the America of the 1980s, the written word has lost much of its force. The electronic image has become the power, the marketable force in a world increasingly turned off to ideas. This substitution of hype for argument, personality for substance, visual communication for books, constitutes the basis for the

Hollywood cultural ascendancy. Shep Gordon, manager of Alice Cooper, Raquel Welch, and other stars, explains with blunt logic: "In some strange way we're dealing with the inevitable here. Whether you're a Dodge salesman, a Good Humor man, an entertainer, or a member of the press, you're dealing with a product." He later added, ". . . In the end it's all manufactured. Before, news was managed by the White House with more death and despair. Now we're managing the news, but we're doing it with stars and the kind of hype everyone wants to believe in. And nobody dies."

In surrendering the cultural initiative to Hollywood, the nation has placed enormous power in the hands of a celebrity society with a peculiarity egotistic, businesslike, and morally lobotomized sense of values. From its very inception, Hollywood has been recognized as a lavishly narcissistic society, a natural outgrowth of the insecurity and star hierarchies endemic to theatrical enterprise. Even in the era of all-powerful studios and patriarchal moguls, Hollywood as one observer noted decades ago, was a society governed by the rule of "an I for an I."

HOW SWEET IT IS!

While the wealthy classes in the East have been traditionally squeamish about broadcasting salaries and possessions, in Hollywood consumption long has been among the highest of values—the more conspicuous the better. This is an obsession that cuts across the generational and ideological lines in Hollywood. And nowhere is it more amply demonstrated than in the boutiques lining Beverly Hills's Rodeo Drive. There one is as likely to see "liberal" celebrities buying the same piece of $3,000 lizard-skin luggage or $5,500 gold-plated belt as more "conservative" stars. It is all part of an elaborate social game. Donald Pliner, owner of the swank Right Bank shoestore on Rodeo Drive, whose hotselling item in 1977 was a $335 pair of satin boots, says the excessive consumption has more to do with status than with need or enjoyment. "It's not really business, it's all a show for the effect," Pliner explains. "It's just a little Fellini for the street."

Although theatrical and "leisure-class" societies throughout history have shared some of the characteristics of the current Southern California celebrity culture, few have ever attained its degree of notoriety. Many in the Los Angeles entertainment industry lack any real concern about the past, the sense of history that usually marked hereditary, industrial aristocracies. Made up predominantly of outsiders, whose success is based as much on sex appeal, looks, and connections as on ability or lineage, the Hollywood celebrity society is a peculiarly atomized elite. Whereas New York's literary-publishing-drama circles are notoriously inbred and intermingled, the Los Angeles entertainment elite generally lacks social cohesion. This is a common complaint among Easterners and European artists who have come to settle in Los Angeles over the past half century. The singer and composer Bob Dylan, for instance, recalls his earlier life in New York's musical community as a time of friendship and warmth, in contrast with the fragmentation and coldness of California's individualistic society. "It's too hard for people to relate to people out here," Dylan explained. "There's too much between them, too much space. They'll never be pushed together unless they want to come together—and if they don't have any reason to, they won't."

Treated as gods, living in splendor yet at the same time alone and insecure, the members of Hollywood's elite have distanced themselves from religious tradition, ethnic ties, and ethical considerations. In an oddly democratic manner, the ascension of the Hollywood celebrity culture has led to a cultural "breaking out." In the world of glitter and megabucks, all races and creeds are equally superfluous. Rona Barrett, once a pudgy Jewish girl from Queens named Rona Burstein, and now the glamorous "journalist" queen of Hollywood, dislikes the very idea of cultural distinctions. "Right now we're being inundated by minority groups who are pressuring the film industry to be more sensitive," the million-dollar "reporter" complains. "The issue is how long we are going to continue to perpetuate stereotypes that only divide America into cultural and ethnic factions. . . ."

The entertainment business also has had a sort of "bandit" mentality. In recent years business conduct has followed novel ethical principles. In their search for ever more profits, studio executives and producers have been accused repeatedly of "siphoning off" thousands of dollars supposedly due to their creative artists. The victims have reportedly included Sean Connery, Michael Caine, Judy Garland, and Cliff Robertson.

But perhaps no greater example of the casual morality of the "new" Hollywood has come to light than the case involving David Begelman, the former head of Columbia Studios. In May 1978, Begelman, one of the great powers in the movie industry, pleaded no contest to charges of grand theft stemming from the forgery of $40,000 in studio checks that were supposed to go to several actors. Begelman explained his thefts as "highly neurotic acts," unconnected to business. The court gave him a $5,000 fine and three years' probation in exchange for a promise to make a film about the dangers of "angel dust." Here was a man, a brilliant executive, earning over $300,000 a year, whose wife had just written a book about lavish living entitled *New York on $500 a Day,* who found it necesary to "borrow" from his own people. But in the amoral atmosphere of Hollywood, Begelman's actions were hardly criticized;

he was dismissed as Columbia's president, but still pulled a fat paycheck as an independent producer under contract with Columbia. Within two years of his grand theft conviction he was back on top, this time as head of another giant studio, MGM pictures. Discussing the Begelman affair with a reporter, Herbert Allen, chairman of the board of Columbia, commented: "Look, we trade every day out there with hustlers, deal makers, shysters and con-men.... That's the way businesses get started. That's the way this country was built."

In the electronic age, the ethical standards, social mores, and political beliefs of the stars and executives also influence the American culture as never before. As the social critic Ben Stein points out:

> ... what is on television comes almost exclusively from Los Angeles. This city has become the brain, the nerve center, of the electronic animal that rules civilized man. More than that, when the electronic god sends out its pictures and its guidance, they are pictures of L.A. and the L.A. commandments of life.
>
> All prime time, the heart of the beast, is made in L.A. If there is a cop, he is an L.A. cop. If there is a divorced mother, she is an L.A. mother, even if she is supposed to be in Indianapolis. If there is an Archie Bunker he might have a Queens accent, but he is speaking words written in Hollywood by two writers who live in Pacific Palisades and Malibu....
>
> The attitudes of L.A. are not only the dominant attitudes of prime time. They are the only attitudes. L.A. is the original in the Xerox machine.

THE GOSPEL ACCORDING TO J.R.

On the night the network promised to reveal the answer to "Who Shot J.R.?" more Americans watched "Dallas" than voted for the two main candidates in the presidential election of 1980. Through their televisions, Americans seemed to be escaping from the moral perplexities of the post-New Deal era and taking refuge in a world of fantasy where the needle of morality's compass swings aimlessly. Given the mass popularity and adulation accorded such entertainment, there seems little short of a mass switching off of the tube that can prevent the Hollywood values represented by J. R. Ewing, the Gucci cowboy, from becoming the mores of our society. It is also worth pausing to consider to what degree the equally avid television audiences in England and other countries might perceive "Dallas" as the reflection of the "real" America.

The free enterprise society of California has produced many wonders—engineering feats, a revolution in agriculture, unsurpassed computer technology, as well as some of the world's finest entertainment. But within that same entrepreneurial society often lies the heart of the bandit, the con-man, the swindler and thief, constantly in search of new "marks" who will naively swallow a line. Those who find J. R. fascinating, and his example worth emulating, might also adopt the values of his creators: an elite without a past, without conscience, without, in the end, a sense of the social contract that glues a civilized society together. In their stead, the fantasy packagers of Hollywood offer only the inverted golden rule of J. R. Ewing—"Do unto others before they can do unto you." Although California has provided the breeding ground and laboratory for these amoral values, the technology now available endows the state's dream merchants with the means to project their message to every corner of the globe. Indeed, these Hollywood "entertainments," as the critic and media expert Richard Hoggart has warned, could well end up poisoning not only the airwaves but all of society for the generations to come. Speaking of television over twenty years ago, Hoggart noted:

> They [mass entertainments] are full of corrupt brightness, of improper appeals and moral evasions. . . . They tend towards a view of the world in which progress is conceived as a seeking of material possessions, equality as moral leveling and freedom as the ground for endless irresponsible pleasure. These productions belong to a vicarious, spectator's world; they offer nothing which can really grip the brain or the heart. . . . They have intolerable pretensions; and pander to the wish to have things both ways, to do as we want and accept no consequences. A handful of such productions reaches daily the great majority of the population; their effect is both widespread and uniform.

VI.
California's Middle Class: The Free Enterprise Society

Elliot Sopkin is forty-five years old, single, and lives in a condominium in Sunnyvale, California—the heart of the state's Silicon Valley electronics complex. Director of communications for Advanced Micro Devices, he spends his leisure time, he says, "chasing broads and raising tropical fish." He commutes a little over a half hour each day to his job, in his $16,000 limited edition Volvo 262C sportscar. The son of a symphony orchestra conductor, Sopkin felt that he needed a little music to break the drudgery of the daily commute. After marveling over the sophisticated car stereo system an engineer friend had put into his automobile, Sopkin decided a cheap Panasonic tape deck just wouldn't do. He bought a German-made Blaupunkt AM-FM radio, a Becker model 355 cassette tape deck, a 100-watt Posgate amplifier, and four home stereo speakers adapted for use in a car. The whole system was custom-tailored to match the acoustics of his Volvo sportscar. The price tag was $1,100. Since installing his system, Sopkin's secretary has followed his lead and spent $500 for a stereo unit for her Volkswagen Rabbit. As Sopkin explains it: "I guess it's just bullshit snobbery. I'm sure we're not more avid fans of Tchaikovsky out here. It has something to do with just spending money. . . . The way I look at it, I can buy myself anything I can afford. We're just fast livers out here in California."

Sopkin is one of millions of high-income, middle-class Californians who comprise the nation's premier market for every manner of material fad and fantasy. Consumer goods that caught on first or faster in the West include water beds and hot tubs, stereo and quadrophonic equipment, cartridge tape recorders and microwave ovens, saunas and swimming pools, condominiums and mobile homes. California and Hawaii account for a quarter of all the swimming pools that exist in the entire country; people in California and the West own 31 percent more tape recorders and 25 percent more cassette recorders than those elsewhere in the nation. The number of Westerners paying $500 or more for a television set is 11 percent greater than the national average, and the Western states had 87 percent more planes per capita than the rest of the country.

When, in 1970, John J. Henderson & Associates examined the markets for new products in cities all over the country, they found that of the eight areas they ranked as "experimental," three were in California, and three others were in neighboring Western states. After several visits to California, Michael Davie, associate editor of *The Observer* (London), wrote in 1972:

> The acquisitive urge is the only characteristic that most Californians have in common. Even the hippies who most fiercely reject "materialist values" sometimes turn out to have powerful, if camouflaged, materialist drives. Californian salesmen, I found, even refer to the "hippie market." "If the Volkswagen is the hippie's car," said a Ford man in San Franciso, "then we must get a slice of the hippie market."

This same urge to acquire the "latest thing" extends into the realms of spirituality, religion, and new "consciousness" movements. California has been the home base for Erhard Seminar Trainings, the People's Temple, the Krishnamurti Foundation, Synanon, the Worldwide Church of God, and the Church of Scientology. Today it is estimated that from 25 to 40 percent of all alternative lifestyle groups in the country are located in California. One study found that California is the base for over 42 percent of the country's "spiritual growth centers." The *Yankelovich Monitor,* a publication that is standard reading for advertising agencies, found that the Western portion of the United States adjusts to and incorporates social trends faster than anywhere else in the nation, and nourishes far more of these "leading edge" trends than states to the east. "I strongly believe that if I wanted to make a million dollars in California," asserted Los Angeles attorney Paul Morantz, who has been an outspoken critic of the state's proliferation of cult groups, "I'd put up a sign and say, 'I have it, come and get it.' "

AMAZING GRACE

California's love affair with spiritual and material consumption has alternately enraptured, puzzled, amused, annoyed, and horrified observers from the East. To some, it is a mark of things to come, a fascinating peek into the nation's future. To others, it is a grim vision of the depravity and decadence that threaten to destabilize society, and requires that a section of the country should be isolated, like a rare, dangerous disease. As the Chicago *Sun-Times* columnist Mike Royko expressed it in 1979:

> . . . We could build a high fence around California and post psychiatrists at the border gates. Nobody would be permitted to leave it without passing a sanity test.
> . . . Whatever the reason, for years California's major export to the rest of the country has not been its fruits and vegetables; it has been craziness. It comes in many forms—bad TV shows, bad architecture, junk foods, auto worship and creepy life-styles that have ranged from the doped-up flower children to the souped-up motorcycle gangs, the Manson family to the Jones cult, the Symbionese Liberation Army to the Synanon brain shrinkers. You name it: If it babbles and its eyeballs are glazed, it probably comes from California. . . .
> Fencing the whole place in is something to consider. We could still have trade relations with them. They could sell us wine, and we could sell them straitjackets.

Many theories have been tentatively advanced to explain the state's fascination with the bizarre and the novel. Some have pointed to the migratory nature of the people in California—barely a third of the state's residents were born there. Many of its leaders, meanwhile, try to blame California's excesses on its status as the western edge of the national frontier, a place that attracts the rootless and alienated masses seeking one last go of it. "It's an end-of-the-line phenomenon," says Lester O'Shea, chairman of San Francisco's Republican County Central Committee, "and those that don't go off the Golden Gate Bridge stay here."

But in its search for values, California's middle class has not looked toward the fringe elements but to the top—to the entrepreneurial elite that has long dominated the state. Unlike the Eastern mandarins, with their aristocratic bloodlines and manners, a large number of California's rich are products of the great postwar boom. Few families, even the Chandlers, can boast of estates more than one century old. In California, and throughout the West, stories of successes abound concerning those who came to the state with a pocketful of pennies and, through guile or just plain luck, parlayed their meager assets into fortunes.

Perhaps in no other society has wealth seemed so attainable to so many. Since the 1940s, California has boasted far more new business starts per year than other states in the country. Rather than settle for mediocrity or rise up against the wealthy class, California's middle class

has instead struggled mightily to share the entrepreneur's dream. Some
do it by starting businesses, others by investing in gold or real estate or
growing marijuana; but the desire to join the wealthy class remains the
underlying motivation. Entrepreneur Jim Pinto, brought up in the caste
system of India and educated in class-conscious England, believes that
the universality of the entrepreneurial spirit dominates the behavior of
California's middle classes. Pinto observes:

> In England if you see someone driving a Rolls Royce, you say,
> "Some day I'm gonna tear him down to riding a Saab." Out here,
> you see someone in a Cadillac, you want to drive one yourself.
> ... The key thing on the West Coast is we have less polarization
> between most people and the businessman. When you lock someone
> in a room, the first thing [is] to get out. Then it's natural for [some-
> one] to say, "I'm gonna get you, sucker."
> ... If you talk about the East Coast, its roots are in Europe's class
> system. In the Western states you have the pioneers.... Here they
> are more agreeable toward the new kid, the fresh idea. They are not
> as interested in who you are and what you are.... Here you get the
> impression that capitalism is the game anyone can play.

From the day the first impoverished prospector sifted through the dirt
in his pan and found gold, playing the capitalist game has captivated
the imagination of California's middle class. The state has long had
what could be called a "free enterprise society," in which the quest for
wealth overcomes the traditional values of family, church, and neighborhood that prevailed in Europe and the East. In the "free enterprise
society," not surprisingly, the values that are most emulated by the
masses are those of the entrepreneurial elite, the esteemed winners of
the game.

THE BEST REVENGE

The high standard of living, made possible by the success of the
state's economy, has further diminished the perceived distance betwₑₑₙ
the middle and upper classes. Even modest affluence allows many
middle-class Californians to mimic on a small scale the extravagant
habits of the Hollywood and corporate jet-setters.

Although frequently characterized as a product of the state's demographic peculiarities, California's middle-class willingness to experiment flows largely from the state's transformation into a post-industrial
society. Rather than being a reflection of sociological mutation, the tu-
multuous condition of the state's middle class is more likely an augury
of the life awaiting all of American society. As the sociologist Ted K.

Bradshaw pointed out after an extensive study of the state's middle-class lifestyles:

> More of the characteristics of advanced industrialization may be found in California than anywhere else in the world. In addition, California is well-known for having some of the most dramatic changes in lifestyle patterns. Thus, in many ways it may be useful to think of California as a prototypical "advanced industrialized society," having grown rapidly during the last one hundred years, taking advantage of the world's newest, most sophisticated technologies. Even more than New York, California is an urban technological state, leading the world in electronics, aerospace, and entertainment. . . . Advanced industrialism is also found elsewhere . . . but nowhere is it as pervasive as in California.

Three of the key characteristics of "advanced industrial societies" are a high level of personal income; a concentration of employment in the "service" sector rather than heavy industry; and a generally high level of education. The healthy nature of the state's economy has produced a markedly higher standard of living in California and the West. In 1979, the per capita personal income in California was $9,913, over $1,200 more than the national average. Even more significant was the difference in median family income, a result of the increasing trend in which several members of a household in California hold down jobs. In 1980, family income in California was estimated to average $24,050, 14.5 percent higher, or over $3,000 more, than the national average. By 1985 it is estimated that that advantage will increase to 15.6 percent, with the average California family having $5,000 more in annual income than those elsewhere in the country. Per capita assets in California and other Western states, meanwhile, are $700 above the national average, a 39 percent difference.

The most dramatic examples of middle-class prosperity in the state are in California's booming electronics and aerospace sectors. In the Silicon Valley, an engineer with less than three years of college and only one or two years of experience draws an average salary of $22,000 a year. A computer programmer with four years in the field brings in $30,000 annually on the average. Even those with only a modicum of skills can quickly find a well-paying job in the electronics industry, where companies are starved for employees and "headhunting" firms are routinely employed to steal promising executives from other concerns. Matt Sarner of Search Specialists, Inc., in Cupertino, California, comments: "An industry friend of mine says that his firm has a standard technician's test. The applicants are told to spell 'technician,' and they get two mistakes."

The state's middle class is also unique in its sheer size. The state's economic base is concentrated in "service industries," such as finance, real estate, insurance, and trade. Since 1910, over half the state's employment has been in the service sector, while the rest of the nation did not reach that proportion until nearly thirty years later. Today, more than 75 percent of the employed population is in the service sector. While nationally 26.2 percent of all wage earnings came from manufacturing employment, in 1978 the percentage for California was only 21.3 percent.

California's entrepreneurial elite has rarely needed to recruit the services of the state's middle class for working in the fields and factories. While the literature of the industrial revolutions in Europe and the East abounds in tales of middle-class people brought low and forced to work in the mills or fields, in California there has usually been a large pool of immigrant laborers to do society's dirty work. These new migrants accounted for nearly 60 percent of the state's population growth between 1939 and 1979. Whenever the supply of "native" Anglo-Americans ran out, the California entrepreneurs could tap the virtually inexhaustible labor pools of Asia and Mexico to fill their needs. These migrants and racial minorities fueled the state's economic expansion, providing further opportunities for the middle class's relentless search to fulfill its vision of the entrepreneurial dream.

Rather than being relegated to employment in heavy industrial enterprises like steel or autos, California's middle class has been able to concentrate itself in service and professional occupations, where a more pleasant job environment and less rigid hierarchies allow for the maintenance of at least some entrepreneurial fantasies. Even in the state's manufacturing industries (such as high technology), California's middle classes labor in an ambiance much more akin to research laboratories than to the heavy manufacturing plants of the Northeast and Midwest. In the electronics hothouse of the Silicon Valley, for instance, plant sites often resemble college campuses, in stark contrast to the typical depressed factory town atmosphere of Detroit or Cleveland. Jac Fits-Ens, senior industrial relations director for Four Phase Systems, a Cupertino computer company, said after moving from San Francisco to the Silicon Valley, "The valley companies have a completely different atmosphere. Down here, it's flexible, entrepreneurial, informal, and definitely more challenging. You can talk to anybody in the company, anywhere, about anything. There's no question of going through a lot of channels. It's a family of peers, at least intellectually speaking, and your idea deserves to be heard."

THE SILICON CHIP SHALL MAKE YE FREE

Largely because of the skills needed by a high technology- and service-based economy, California has produced a middle-level work force that is significantly more educated than its counterparts in other regions of the country. An estimated one in four Californians over the age of twenty is enrolled in some form of continuing educational program, and over half the state's adult population has been enrolled at one time in a community college course.

While liberals have traditionally associated high levels of education with humanistic enlightenment, in California the middle class's educational achievements long have been weighted heavily in favor of technical and scientific skills. In 1977, the state boasted well over 36,000 engineers, by far the nation's largest number. In addition, the University of California as well as the state's private schools, anchored by CalTech and Stanford, have traditionally emphasized such economically practical skills as engineering, earth sciences, and computer science. Like the entrepreneurial elite above them, many in California's educated class approach the world from the viewpoint of the technician, with few of the cultural refinements traditionally associated with advanced learning. As one foreign-born engineer turned entrepreneur has observed: "There are many greatly skilled engineers in California. They know their fields very well but often little else. It's all business or money or sex or sports. Other things are not so easy to talk about. They are very bright, and very limited, a lot of them."

The middle classes, in effect, have absorbed the values of the business elite. California's advanced industrial economy, with its many spectacular success stories, helps preserve the capitalist mythology of the nineteenth century, in which entrepreneurial success was considered worthy only of respect and emulation, not attack and class hatred. The California dream is not to tear down the class system but rather to stake out one's own fortune and enter the ranks of the corporate elite. Randy Knapp, the forty-three-year-old founder of Wespercorp, a computer components manufacturer, comments:

We should have a privileged class in this country. I want to have everyone have a chance to get into the privileged class, to live in the house on the hill. But we only have so many hills and many more people. The approach in recent years has been to build more hills, so everybody can live on the hill. But you can't have that—if everybody lived on the hill it would have no value. You have to have an elite—it's an ego thing only, I know, but that's what it's all about.

The fantastic material drive of the members of California middle classes stems in large part from their desire to get as far as they can up Randy Knapp's "hill." Elliot Sopkin's boss at Advanced Micro Devices, Jerry Sanders, worked during high school delivering milk and digging ditches, and founded his company in the dining room of his home. Today Sanders, who is younger than Sopkin, is a millionaire, earns $300,000 a year, and owns a Rolls Royce Corniche, a Ferrari, and three Mercedes. He commutes between his Bel-Air mansion in Los Angeles and his twenty-room home near work in Atherton, 40 miles to the north. Sanders also retains a beach house in Malibu and a condominium at Aspen, Colorado. Far from feeling guilty about his many possessions, Sanders revels in them with an unabashed, youthful enthusiasm. "It's a hype that money isn't everything," Sanders asserts bluntly. "It may not be everything, but it sure beats whatever is second best."

WINNERS AND LOSERS

In a state where success stories abound, where today's mule skinner can be tomorrow's millionaire, people have tended to be more willing to take risks, depart from comfortable traditions and familiar settings in order to find their material nirvana. This gambling instinct has its earliest roots in the Gold Rush and the intrepid "Forty-niners," who almost overnight transformed an uncharted wilderness into the ultimate American land of opportunity. Thousands flocked to the gold-rich Mother Lode seeking their fortune. James H. Carson captured the "gold fever" that spread like a plague through the state's populace 130 years ago:

> I looked on for a moment; a frenzy seized my soul ... piles of gold rose up before me at every step; castles of marble, dazzling the eye with their rich appliances; thousands of slaves bowing to my beck and call; myriads of fair virgins contending with each other for my love—were among the fancies of my fevered imagination. The Rothschilds, Girards, and Astors appeared to me but poor people; in short, I had a very violent attack of the gold fever.

Even those left behind in San Francisco were consumed by the belief that they too could share in the fortunes being mined from the Sierra foothills. It was a boundless faith in the possibility of success that cut across all walks of life, as rags-to-riches stories swept through the town. Virtually everyone was in some way playing the gold or silver market and buying stocks in obscure companies in the hope that they might strike it rich. The historian Oscar Lewis captures the spirit of San Francisco during the decades following the first gold and silver finds:

Whatever his station, each citizen of the town was sure of its future, and of his own. The result was a mass restlessness, an urge to be up and doing.... It was, in short, a gambler's atmosphere.... The Comstock Lode was discovered in '59. Fifteen years later, speculation in Nevada mining stocks had become San Francisco's major industry. The spirits of the entire city rose and fell in unison with the daily quotations on the board at the Mining Exchange. Rich prizes had been won in the Comstock lottery and were still being won. Not only had it converted a score of saloon-keepers, pick-and-shovel miners, shoestring brokers and bankers into millionaires; it had elevated thousands of others to affluence. Fortune had smiled impartially on judges and hack-drivers and servant girls, on housewives and prostitutes, ministers and ex-jailbirds.... Few citizens did not personally know someone—no smarter than himself—who had turned a profitable deal in Comstock stocks; fewer still resisted the temptation to get some of the easy money for himself. The result was San Francisco's gambling fever of the '70s, a malady so widespread and acute as to impress every stranger who came to town.

The "gambling fever" that consumed San Francisco in the 1870s was soon repeated in somewhat different form in Southern California. There the target of middle-class expectations was even more basic than precious metals: land. The fortunes made by land barons, including Los Angeles *Times* editor Harrison Gray Otis, infected the population every bit as severely as the gold fever to the north was ravaging San Francisco. Literally thousands of Angelenos scraped together whatever they could to invest in the volatile real estate market. Louis Adamic describes the real estate hysteria that swept through the city in the 1920s:

... trailing after the big boys is a mob of lesser fellows ... thousands of minor realtors, boomers, promoters, contractors, agents, salesmen, bunko-men, office holders, lawyers, and preachers—all driven by the same motives of wealth, power, and personal glory.... They exploit the "come-ons" and one another, envy the big boys, their wives gather in women's clubs, listen to swamis and yogis and English lecturers, join "love cults" and Coue clubs in Hollywood and Pasadena, and their children jazz and drink and rush around in roadsters.

The all-consuming, often desperate drive to hit it big and catapult into the ranks of the state's elite is today a powerful imperative for the middle class. It can be found in the rural towns of Nevada City and Grass Valley, nestled in the Sierra foothills atop some of the richest gold veins that were mined over a century ago. There skyrocketing prices of precious metals have spawned a whole new generation of "Forty-niners" dredging streambeds and staking out old abandoned claims in search of their fortunes. The new gold rush has attracted everyone from savvy investors and small-time prospectors from urban areas to more local back-to-nature types who fled the cities years ago, but have now been caught up in the mad rush to make the big strike. John Vodonick, an attorney in nearby Reading who specializes in mining investments, has helped put together nearly twenty gold-mining ventures by would-be entrepreneurs. He comments:

> There's been a tremendous rekindling of interest in gold here. There is a desire for gold that transcends even the economic value it has. It's rampant in these hill counties, everybody is staking gold claims and a lot of old gold properties are being reactivated. The mining operations I'm affiliated with will be producing 2,000 ounces [of gold] a year within three years. . . . There are just a lot of people who by nature are gamblers. . . . It's a very emotionally charged activity.

Back in the Bay Area, meanwhile, the gambling fever is concentrated in the burgeoning electronics and high technology business, where hundreds of small-time entrepreneurs have set up shop trying to cash in on the region's booming economy. Some industrial parks in the area actually rent out a garage with two or three adjoining offices for the newcomers, following the lead of many of the area's corporate leaders who themselves started out in similarly humble surroundings. *Fortune* magazine has noted:

> The success ratio for company founders is so high that Santa Clara County can be said to mass-produce millionaires. There are at least a hundred, many in their early thirties. . . .
> People working for tiny enterprises . . . come to feel that they can do a segment of the work better than the company that employs them. And the hope of getting rich as scientific entrepreneurs provides a powerful goal, as do the striking examples of success all around them. So friends and associates form teams to strike out on their own.

But the world capital of overnight success stories lies to the south, in the fast-track atmosphere of Hollywood. There thousands move about anxiously, scouting the "in" bars, going to the right parties, dining out at the fashionable establishments, all looking to make a connection that will lead to overnight success.

It is often those who have failed fully to realize their entrepreneurial dreams who have the strongest drive to accumulate possessions. And nowhere is this drive for material satisfaction more evident than in the ultimate status symbol of the Western culture—the automobile. California leads the nation by far in the number of cars, with over 67 percent more vehicles than second-place New York. In addition, California and its Western neighbors completely dominate the market for the ultra-expensive foreign cars, with over 32 percent of all the Rolls Royces sold in America, over 30 percent of Mercedes Benz sales, over 41 percent of all Porsches, nearly 39 percent of Alfa Romeos, and close to 60 percent of Ferraris. "If you haven't quite made it to the top yet," explained one Silicon Valley executive, "you dream of buying a condo in the Sierra, retiring at thirty-five, and turning in your Porsche for a Ferrari."

But the Californian's quest for status does not stop with merely purchasing an expensive piece of foreign machinery. Frequently other "accessories," sometimes costing thousands of dollars, must be added to give the vehicle the proper image. Tom Collins, the man who sold Elliot Sopkin his car stereo system, built up his Auto Sound Works firm by advertising two sound systems priced at $1,299 and $2,199 each in local papers. In the first six months his store was open, Collins sold fifty of the cheaper systems and thirty more of the higher-priced model. In order to appeal to the status-seeking potential buyer, Collins has one of the systems installed in his own Porsche 911S sportscar. He explains:

I dress in blue jeans, Levi shirts, and Adidas tennis shoes to create a relaxed atmosphere. I bring [the customer] out to my Porsche and turn on my system. Once he hears it, he has got to buy that system to keep up with me. There's a lot of ego in this business.

A guy goes out and buys a new Porsche, he's kind of living a second childhood. The audio sound system is part of that car's image. And when he [buys] it, his buddies see it, and they want one.

It's ego, I'm appealing to their ego.

TOYS FOR GROWNUPS

In recent years the materialist drive of California's middle class has been channeled increasingly into the purchase of the electronic gimmickry on which many of the state's entrepreneurs have made their fortunes. Tom Collins helps sell his "auto sound systems"—he bristles at the crude phrase "car stereos"—with the aid of a $22,000 supersophisticated Sound Shuttle Mobile Audio Simulator. The unit consists of a soundproof enclosure with a couple of bucket seats and dozens of tape decks, radios, amplifiers, and speakers, all of which are hooked into a central computer system. The potential buyer can recline on a seat while Collins programs in one of thousands of combinations of stereo components until the listener finds the sound that's right for him.

When Shuttles were first marketed in the late 1970s, half of those sold were purchased by car stereo distributors in California.

The passion for high-priced electronic "toys" has made California the nation's premier market for home video games, and home computer sets. While Easterners are getting used to the necessary role of computers in modern-day business, Californians are on the way to turning them into regular home fixtures. In the Silicon Valley, for instance, numerous "home computer clubs" have popped up, including one called "Homebrew," organized back in 1975.

These computer clubs aid their members in setting up their own computer systems, as well as offering them an opportunity to exchange information on how to program their sets. "It's a bit like heroin," explains one club member; "a packaged program lasts about a year, and if you don't know how to do your own software, you're lost. Learning how to program is like learning how to drive a car—it's essential."

Also increasingly prolific are home word-processing machines, which some would-be California authors are installing before their first word ever appears in print. Liz Hyland, for example, who lives in San Francisco with her husband (a real estate broker) and is working on a fantasy trilogy, purchased a $20,000 home word-processing system. "It's only a matter of time before a lot of writers will use these things," she says. ". . . This is unusual because I'm not a published writer yet, but we consider writing like any new business, and you just try to get the best equipment."

The love affair of the California middle class with technology can extend beyond the grave. There are already two firms in California— the Institute for Cryobiological Extension (ICE) in Los Angeles, and Trans Time, Inc., in Northern California—that are freezing people shortly after death in the hope that advances in medicine and genetic engineering some day will allow them to be brought back to life. Trans Time currently has four whole bodies, two heads, and a brain in deep freeze at its storage facility in Emeryville, California, a run-down industrial town on San Francisco Bay. Trans Time's head of biological research, Paul Seagall, a physiologist, age thirty-eight, says: "The hope is that some day research will come up with a technique that will allow us to bring these people back. . . . If you have someone frozen now, cells of the brain are damaged. You have to replace the memory cells or transfer the memory in a frozen brain to a computer and then put the computer data back into a clone brain." In a similarly futuristic vein, two young entrepreneurs from Sunnyvale, California, have applied for a patent on a solar-powered talking tombstone that contains a recorded message from the departed.

THE ATOMIZED AMERICANS

In their zeal to succeed and acquire space-age status symbols, California's middle class has turned away from the "outworn" values which, in the past, provided meaning and context for individuals beyond the Darwinian struggle to succeed. Before the onslaught of "open" marriages and the prevalent, alluring, singles' lifestyles, the family structure often crumbles, dissolving into disillusionment and divorce. Home life itself loses meaning as people purchase houses, condominiums, or planned unit developments as "investments"; they are ready to move on to another, similar unit with a change in the real estate market or employment. Local political engagement has been rendered pointless by media slugfests between Hollywood-concocted image-candidates. Only the occasional chance to vote against a government assault on individual wealth or willfulness evokes any real enthusiasm. The same middle class that voted so heavily for Proposition Thirteen in June 1978, several months later turned down by a similarly huge margin an attempt by right-wing moralists to impose restrictions on homosexual teachers in the state's public schools.

In California's "free enterprise society" individuals are monads, disconnected units pursuing their own peculiar pleasures. It is not unlike the "mass society" concept popularized in the 1950s in such books as David Riesman's *The Lonely Crowd.* But the difference, to paraphrase Heidegger, is that in California the "dreadful" already has happened.

Nowhere is this clearer than in the dissolution of the family in California. The state's divorce rate is 20 percent above the national average, and over 44 percent of the state's once-married people were previously divorced. California has 10 percent fewer husband-and-wife households on the average than the rest of the country. One recent study found a "sharp" recent increase in the number of people who were simply living alone.

But perhaps the most damage to traditional family life has been done by the state's much-touted "sexual revolution." By virtually every measure available, California's middle class indulges in sexual pursuits with a Bacchanalian frenzy unmatched anywhere in the country. California, with one of the most liberal abortion laws in the nation, has a rate of legal abortions among women aged fifteen to forty-four that is 57 percent higher than the national average. One study found that one in nine girls in California between the ages of fifteen and nineteen became pregnant in 1977.

More remarkable than the mere numbers, however, is the brazenness with which California's middle class has celebrated its "liberation" from traditional moral values. In 1980 a male strip show opened in the "bedroom" suburban community of Fremont near San Francisco Bay, and was soon drawing five hundred women a night. In Southern California, a "clothing optional" condominium is being established by a property management company called LIBRE—Living in the Buff Residential Enterprises. The state corrections department, meanwhile, instituted a program to provide female sex hormones and bras to its transsexual inmates at a psychiatric prison. In 1978, in Livermore, the police chief was arrested for paying money out of the police informants fund to a young juvenile in exchange for sexual favors performed at his office in police headquarters. The chief was convicted of the crimes, put on probation and now is running a yogurt shop in the area. "He was a very progressive police chief," remarked one local. "We didn't know how progressive."

In its sexual exhibitionism, the state's middle class is again following the lead of California's corporate movers and shakers. The "jiggle" and "tits and ass" shows that Hollywood's TV moguls have made so popular set the standards for the state's sexual activities, while the much-publicized exploits of the jet-setting entrepreneurs make the explicit sexuality of Hollywood seem less an aberration than a call to arms. Chase Revel, age forty-three and founder nine years ago of International Entrepreneurs Association, a Los Angeles–based organization that provides business advice to people starting their own businesses observes:

> This is a free spirit area—it's pretty weird but it's weird in a strange and practical way. This town was built by a bunch of people who came here in search of a new idea, a new business. They didn't come here to become someone else's bureaucrat, they came here to catch the brass ring.
>
> Here people want to own their own piece of the action. Like me, they want the right to do whatever they want. Look, man, I have two chicks living with me for instance. I always have pussy. They keep house for me. If I tried to do that and still be a successful businessman in Chicago, I'd be thrown out of town. Here I'm perfectly acceptable. People are not afraid to be mavericks.

With the demise of the family in California, there also has come the steady destruction of the traditional neighborhood environment. In 1976, over 55 percent of all Americans reported they had spent their entire life in one state. In California, the figure was only 33 percent. From 1975 to 1977, nearly 35 percent of the people in California and the West changed their residence at least once, while the national figure was 26 percent, and in the Northeast only 19 percent. The desire to remain mobile is so ingrained in the cultural life of the state that when a satire appeared in a local magazine some years ago about a fictitious family that spent its entire life living in a mobile home constantly driving around the Los Angeles freeway system, the author was deluged with requests from other writers seeking interviews with the family members. A fellow journalist even chastised him for sloppy reporting—not taking the time to track down the real families that spent their lives on the freeways.

Such extreme mobility militates against the formation of the sort of strong familial, neighborhood, and community ties that have characterized the society back east. Interaction among neighbors tends to be infrequent and rather forced, with Eastern-style block parties replaced by the single's apartment-complex pool and sex parties. This alienation of the individual from a meaningful social environment exists not only in the heart of the state's cities but in the suburbs and small towns as well. As one sociological study of a semi-rural California town bleakly reported: "in spite of the consensus or the desire to maintain, protect or even extend the notion of community, the idea is greeted by public apathy. Public response to neighborhood planning, community elections, and similar activities has been minimal except for a few big issues."

POLITICS WITHOUT A PUBLIC

With the breakdown of the smaller units of society—the family, the neighborhood, the community—there has been a concomitant decline in the public and political life of California, a trend that reached its logical conclusion in the anti-government outburst of Proposition Thirteen. When ties to one's family, neighbors, or immediate surroundings have been severed, the government is seen as an alien presence that only interferes in the pursuit of personal pleasures.

Although the level of alienation has reached its highest in recent years, California has never possessed a strong tradition of political involvement. A society dominated by "outsiders" and business-oriented entrepreneurs, party affiliations have remained weak in most of the state. In fact, for generations political scientists have marveled at the Californian's propensity to split his ballot between the two parties on Election Day. Rather than being a Democratic or Republican state, California has promoted "non-partisanship," a tradition dating back to the upper-middle-class "progressive movement" at the turn of the century. While much attention has been focused on the "democratic" reforms ushered in by the Progressives—notably regulation of once dominant monopolies like the Southern Pacific Railroad, the referendum, the initiative and recall procedures—the movement also contained a strong anti-populist, anti-political strain. Progressivism was wedded closely to the scientism and pro-corporate ideology of the state's entrepreneurial classes, whose major goal was the rationalization of state government according to business principles.

The Progressives were concerned not only about the corrupting power of the Southern Pacific but also over the growing political organization among the state's white ethnic and working-class voters. The Progressives saw traditional politics as something dirty, and, by installing a government meritocracy and banning partisan elections on the local level, succeeded in breaking down the political "machine" structure then existing in many communities in the state. Under the Progressives, power flowed out of the ethnic neighborhoods and into the hands of the government technicians, men whose commitment would be to a "mass society" rather than to any particular unit or community within it. As the historian Spencer C. Olin, Jr., described the Progressive administration of Governor Hiram Johnson:

> The Johnson administration's devotion to efficiency and economy in government reached its apogee in John Francis Neylan's Board of Control. . . . As Neylan stated in a summary report to Governor Johnson, the major work of the Board of Control "was to systematize the business of the State of California in such a way that after a reasonable time it could challenge comparison of the State's system with the system in vogue in those great corporations that are models of modern commercial enterprise."

In Berkeley, for example, the city's reform-minded mayor proclaimed in 1909: "The administrative affairs of a city are a business matter, rarely a political issue. The object, therefore, [is] to provide a method which [will] result in the election of businessmen, not politicians, to office." The sentiment that the business spirit should govern the conduct of political affairs cut across all political lines. Two years after the Berkeley mayor's statement, the socialist J. Stitt Wilson sounded a strikingly similar theme when he won election as mayor of Berkeley: "I declare now that partisan politics shall not enter into the administration of the affairs of this city." He added later, "We propose nothing radical or impossible. It is a plain business proposition."

Within a few years, Wilson would abandon socialism altogether, and announce that he had become a born-again Christian.

The nonpolitical politics spawned in the Progressive reform era had a lasting impact on the California electorate. Voter apathy and ignorance became widespread. A 1948 study of voters in San Francisco revealed that 79 percent did not know the names of the candidates for the state legislature in the districts where they lived and 67 percent likewise were ignorant of the names of their congressional candidates. Traditionally, California had a higher proportion than other states of voters who "declined to state" their party preference when registering to vote. The political scientist Harold Gosnell observed in the 1940s: "Voters in California changed their party allegiances from election to election in accordance with changing issues and personalities, rather than adhered to any party symbol."

By the late 1950s, California political life was well on the way toward its ultimate transformation into little more than an extravagant media show. With image replacing content and issues in campaigns, voter turnout continued to decline from nearly 66 percent in 1960 to only 51 percent in 1976, a more precipitous drop than that experienced in the rest of the country.

Even when the voters bothered to come to the polls, they tended in California to vote in a way that repudiated politics and government itself. Well before the anti-bureaucratic rhetoric swept the country in the late 1970s, California's alienated, self-obsessed middle class was turning toward a form of "anti-politics." California voters have made it clear that to them public service has no honorable place in the "free enterprise society." This growing hostility toward public life has taken its toll on what was once a proud civil service. As Nancy Bohaty, a staff member of the California state personnel board, puts it: "There was once a sense of *esprit de corps,* a sense of mission. There were a lot of experts in state service, it was an honor to be in state service. Now you have to explain yourself to neighbors, with chagrin, that you work for the state. To the public and the Governor [Brown], state service is one step above being on welfare."

Paralleling the demise of family, community, and political life is the strong rejection in California of traditional religious organizations. The uprooted, mobile, and disconnected middle-class masses feel little attraction for the rich symbolism and traditions of established churches. When an effort was made recently to gather the nearly 500,000 signatures necessary to place a measure on the state ballot banning blasphemy against established church doctrines, its supporters could only find 4,000 people willing to sign the proposition. As Episcopal Bishop James A. Pike of San Francisco once explained:

There is less basic religious affiliation [in San Francisco]. There is a fresh new feeling that there are worlds to conquer, but the church was back there, and the need for it is felt less after the move to the West. San Francisco is the image of the last chance—the last place out—and it is a hub of anxieties and restlessness. It has the lowest degree of religious affiliation: 28 percent as against 32 percent in Seattle and 67 percent on the national average. With this low affiliation, it is not a coincidence that San Francisco is at the top of almost anything you name that shows unsolved personal anxiety.

Like the media politicians, the state's religious leaders have found themselves compelled increasingly to resort to showmanship and gimmicks in order to reel the fast-moving middle classes into their congregations. Southern California started "drive-in services" that do not require the parishioner to leave his car. A Los Angeles rabbi, Barry Levinger, goes to discos, singles' parties, and dances, looking for potential congregants for his "Synagogue for Singles." Levinger, or the "disco rabbi," as he is commonly called, is also involved in a commercial dating service and has openly embraced the singles lifestyle despite over two millennia of Jewish tradition to the contrary. In a further break with long-established practice, Levinger eschews establishing a home base for his congregation, instead renting halls around the city with money raised by his devoted, although highly transient, flock. "What's to support?" Levinger explains. "I don't need a lot of money for buildings, that's why I have a floating synagogue."

THE CONSEQUENCES OF FAILURE

In any society, failure is traumatic for the individual. But more traditional, hierarchical communities at least offer the solace of family, friends, and religion; for the Californian in the self-oriented "free enterprise society," there is often little place to turn for comfort or support. The result, in many cases, is a pervasive social anomie, as the middle-class individual finds himself or herself alone, seemingly about to catch the "brass ring," only to find it just out of reach.

For those caught without the traditional support systems, the failure to achieve the cherished status as a successful entrepreneur can be debilitating and its effect severe. Looking for panaceas, a way out from despair, the California middle class has distinguished itself by fleeing en masse to scores of half-baked self-improvement schemes, to bizarre religious cults, utopian organizations, and spiritualists, all serving to salve the severely bruised egos of those unable to claw their way to the top. Some join est, chant mantras, and meditate; others spend their weekends at mystical retreats and their weeknights reading what the latest human potential tract has to offer. In the extreme they withdraw from the world entirely, surrendering their barren souls to any one of a hundred cults only too eager to add one more lost sheep to their flocks.

Dr. Ronald Enroth, a sociologist at Santa Barbara's Westmont College and an expert on the development of California cults, points out:

> Our society is predisposed to this because of the marked decline of traditional religious values. . . . There's something of an authoritarian vacuum in this culture. We seem to need stern authoritarian figures to tell us how to talk, how to act, how to smile—whether it be Reverend Jim Jones, Reverend Moon, or Werner Erhard.
>   . . . Our culture here is obsessed with self-improvement and that makes self-help groups like est have more power. . . . There's a whole shift of consciousness. This preoccupation with the self is causing a retreat into these groups—people go into these groups for deeply personal reasons. People don't want to save the world, they'd rather save their own souls. It's all part of this self-centered spirit.

As long as California has been the nation's golden land of opportunity, it has been the breeding ground for scores of curious, sometimes frightening, religious orders, spiritual movements, and utopian communities. One survey found that from 1850 to 1950, California was the birthplace of seventeen different utopian colonies, while no other state in the nation could boast more than three. During the same period the state has spawned at least fifty new religious cults or sects, according to Dr. L. J. West, director of the UCLA Neuropsychiatric Institute.

The cult movement dates back to 1841 (or further), when a Scotsman named William Money came to Los Angeles and founded the "Reformed New Testament Church of the Faith of Jesus Christ." Known variously as Professor Money, Doctor Money, Reverend Money, Deacon Money, and Bishop Money, he offered his followers a hodgepodge of beliefs that author Curt Gentry described as "a blend of Catholic ritual, Protestant prohibitions, Greek philosophy, herbology, astrology, and utopian economics." He possessed no medical degree, but nonetheless promptly set up shop as a doctor, caring primarily for the area's large Mexican native population. He claimed to have treated over 5,000 patients, of which only 4 had died, he boasted.

While Money's religion paralleled the beliefs and practices of many of the state's latter-day cults, he was a pioneer in the field, predating by decades the bulk of his myriad successors. California's golden age of cults and crackpot movements began at the turn of the century, with the great influx of migrants who started settling on the western shore. In 1900, an expatriate of New England named Katherine Tingley started the Point Loma Theosophical Community near San Diego, part of a religious movement that soon claimed a following of 100,000 throughout the country. The "Purple Mother," as she came to be known, presided over a 500-acre retreat that included a Greek theater and Raja Yoga College. Based roughly on Theosophist principles first advanced in ancient Greece, Tingley's movement preached a blend of Buddhist and Brahman principles. In what was later to become a familiar pattern, the thrice-married Mrs. Tingley asked those blessed by her teachings to make a large "love offering" in the form of cash.

In Tingley's wake came a virtual caravan of salvation merchants. In 1911 still another Theosophist, Albert Powell Warrington, arrived in Los Angeles and founded the Krotona cult on a 15-acre site that later became the heart of the Hollywood film-making community. Krotona also boasted a Greek theater as well as an occult temple and a vegetarian cafeteria. One of the disciples of the group later established a school of "stereometry," which professed to unravel nature's secrets through a three-dimensional geometric alphabet.

In 1918 a young woman moved to San Diego and then to Los Angeles, and quickly established herself as the most successful religious leader of that era in Southern California. Aimee Semple McPherson, with her "Four Square Gospel" of fundamentalist religious beliefs, built up an immense following that by 1929 numbered well over 40,000 in the Los Angeles area alone. When she arrived in the city, McPherson had $100 in her pocket, but within three years she had collected more than $1 million in donations from her devotees and owned property worth $250,000. In May of 1926, McPherson mysteriously disappeared (it was later revealed that she had a secret rendezvous with a radio operator from the Temple), and the faithful mourned over what they believed was her drowning in the Pacific Ocean. When she suddenly reappeared days later, McPherson was paraded through downtown Los Angeles while 100,000 people looked on, then the largest turnout for any public figure in the city's history.

The cult movement also spread to the north, most noticeably with the establishment of Father William Riker's "Holy City" in the Santa Cruz Mountains in 1918. Earlier, Riker had started up the Church of the Perfect Christian Divine Way in San Francisco, but decided to relocate in Santa Cruz after his San Francisco operation was served with a grand jury indictment for larceny and embezzlement. Holy City, dubbed a "love cult" by its founder, sported fifty peepshow booths as part of its attractions, and was soon collecting $100,000 a year from those making the pilgrimage to the site. Some of the money later went to purchase six Cadillacs for Father Riker's personal use.

If California's early cults shared one thing in common, it was the strong determination of the founders to make a little money along the road to spiritual salvation. While other enterprising businessmen around them were staking out fortunes in land, rail transportation, farming, and oil, these religious entrepreneurs were likewise making a killing in the spiritual marketplace. "God winks his eye at any act we do," explained the enterprising Father Riker, "if we take him in on the deal."

But if greed motivated the cult-makers, so too did it spur those who followed them. Many middle-class cultists saw these groups not so much as the path to spiritual enlightenment but as formulas by which they could learn the way to share in California's rich bounty. "When they dream of Utopia, it is not of a well-planned, perfectly governed garden city, but of a perfect scheme or get-rich-quick system," Carey McWilliams said of the Southern Californians of that era. "Their archangel is not Sir Thomas More or Patrick Geddes, but the promoter who promises to deliver, the salesman with enticing phrases, the business magician."

The zenith of California's cult movement came in the 1930s, following a 66 percent jump in the state's population over the previous ten years. Drawn by California's reputation as the economic promised land, the immigrants soon found their expectations cruelly dashed by the grim realities of the Great Depression. Disappointed and desperate, they turned in droves to the new millennia being promoted by local spiritual leaders. Bruce Bliven describes the Los Angeles of the 1930s:

> Here is the world's prize collection of cranks, semi-cranks, placid creatures whose bovine expression shows that each of them is studying, without much hope of success, to be a high-grade moron, angry or ecstatic exponents of food fads, sunbathing, ancient Greek costumes, diaphragm breathing and the imminent second coming of Christ.

Many of the cults and spiritual movements of the period were little more than retakes on the earlier shows put on by Tingley, McPherson, and others. Astrologers, mystics, and fake psychic healers proliferated, drawing heavily on the insecure members of the Hollywood film community for their customers and converts. "Los Angeles leads the world in the advancement and practice of all the healing sciences," commented the journalist Morrow Mayo, "except perhaps medicine and surgery."

The cults of the 1930s also exhibited a growing tendency to draw on amateurish, half-baked scientific theories to attract their followers. In a state where the corporate leaders had for decades tapped the latest technology to tame the California wilderness, bring water to the arid wastes of Southern California, and usher in the age of radio, the fascination among the middle class with science was widespread.

WIRED FOR SAINTHOOD

In 1934 Guy W. Ballard, a transplant to Los Angeles from Chicago, published a paper entitled "Unveiled Mysteries," which became the doctrine for the "Mighty I Am" cult. Ballard claimed he had been visited by a saintly vision that presented him with a cupful of "pure electronic essence" and a wafer of "concentrated energy." Ballard offered to share the secret of the energy, which would bring untold riches to the takers. Soon the "love gifts" (i.e., cash) were pouring in. These offerings and other profits from the cult soon totaled $3 million, and the takers numbered 350,000 all over the country. Ballard later refined his theory, drawing on the pulp magazine science fiction craze, and claiming that the cult's saintly benefactor possessed an "atomic accelerator" to aid in the dispensation of truth.

Even more bizarre was the founding of Mankind United in 1934 by Arthur L. Bell in Los Angeles. Bell claimed that the world was dominated by a clique of "hidden rulers," but that salvation was at hand in the form of a superhuman race from outer space who had made contact with some lucky earthlings in 1875. The aliens had advanced brains inside their metallic heads and offered their assistance in overthrowing the dreaded hidden rulers. Bell himself claimed he had been outfitted with a ray machine that could knock the eyeballs out of enemies of the cult at great distances. He also promised those who joined the group that in exchange for surrendering their possessions, they each would receive a new $25,000 home equipped with air conditioning, radios, television, and movies, as well as an "automatic vocal-type correspondence machine." By 1939, 75,000 people had joined the cult, and Bell had distributed 220,000 copies of a book laying out the group's tenets. Interestingly, the group's membership was drawn primarily from longtime residents of California, one study found, rather than from recent immigrants to the state.

Southern California's reputation as the center for novel and messianic notions attracted even respected literary figures and intellectuals to sample the region's spiritual wares. D. H. Lawrence, Christopher Isherwood, Gerald Heard, and Aldous Huxley were among those who made the pilgrimage to lotus land in the 1930s and 1940s. The latter three became involved with the Swami Prabahavananda, a Hindu monk who in 1943 set up a monastery in California. Gerald Heard established his own monastery at Laguna in the 1940s. Isherwood came out with a translation of the *Bhagavad Gita,* and Huxley became a prolific writer about spiritualism.

But it was in 1961 that Huxley made perhaps the greatest contribution to the spiritualism thriving on the west coast. With his encouragement, two men, Michael Murphy and Richard Price, set up a residential community in the Santa Cruz Mountains to continue the quest for higher consciousness. The Esalen Institute would spawn a whole new generation of soothsayers and truthseekers, giving birth to much of what ultimately became known as the "human potential movement."

Esalen used a mélange of "rap sessions," "encounter groups," and seminars in spirituality and humanist psychology to help residents in their search for life's meaning. The group rapidly attracted writers from all over the country seeking to understand this mysterious exploration of the human psyche. Numerous prominent intellectuals, psychologists, and theologians came to Esalen, including the psychologists Norman O. Brown, Carl Rogers, R. D. Laing, and Rollo May; the Nobel Prize-winning chemist Linus Pauling, who later went on a one-man campaign promoting the virtues of Vitamin C; the theologian Paul Tillich; the futurist Herman Kahn; the behavioral psychologist B. F. Skinner; Zen Buddhism promoter Alan Watts; the poet Allen Ginsberg; and Carlos Castenada, whose *Teachings of Don Juan* would become a veritable bible of the spiritually minded drug-takers in the early 1970s. Others associated with Esalen in its early days were the humanistic psychologist Abraham Maslow, the educator George Leonard, and even the semanticist and later U.S. Senator S. I. Hayakawa.

The psychical exploration of the self promoted by Esalen caught on with the younger generations in California during the turbulent 1960s. Books like Laing's *Politics of Experience* and Alan Watts's *Psychotherapy East and West* became as popular among students of the New Left as Marx or Engels. The alliance between the human potential movement and the radical politics of the era, however, was always an uneasy one. The human potential groupies were sometimes violently anti-political, eschewing public activism for mystical retreats and inward psychological journeys.

This self-centered orientation flourished in the alienated, narcissistic decade of the 1970s. As the radical left found its adherents dwindling, the human potential movement won unprecedented acceptance among the members of the state's middle class. Popularizers of the psychological and spiritual concepts born in the ferment of the 1960s offered the middle class masses a hodgepodge of self-awareness truisms, interspersed with advice for achieving personal and professional goals. In the long-established California spiritual tradition, books like Thomas Harris's *I'm OK—You're OK* and George Bach's *The Intimate Enemy* promoted easy methods by which those unable to prove themselves in the "free enterprise society" could break out of their cycle of frustration and despair. By the beginning of the 1980s the human potential movement, whatever the goals of its founders, had degenerated into little more than a series of rationales for unabashed narcissism and selfishness. As the sociologist Edwin Schur comments:

> Especially in these popularizations, we see that the current interest in awareness strongly reflects our culture's long-standing emphasis on individualism and self-help ... the current tracts play down the conventional work ethic and competition for monetary success. Instead they emphasize what might be called psychological success. ... Even in the more theoretical works on the new awareness, a ... casual optimism prevails—tied to the notion that we must all accept "responsibility for ourselves."
>
> Along with the stress on continuously exploring one's feelings, this represents a clear invitation to self-absorption. The latent political implication seems equally apparent: complacency for those who have succeeded; resignation or self-blame for those who have not. ...
>
> While the movement provides middle-class consumers with an attractive new product, attention is diverted from the more serious social problems that plague our society. ...
>
> By inviting us to become preoccupied with our "selves" and our sensations, it is diluting our already-weak feelings of social responsibility.

As far back as 1965, one study found, spiritual groups in California accounted for a quarter of all such spiritual and cultural growth organizations in the country. Mark Satin, in his *New Age Politics,* published in 1978, reported that fully a third of all spiritual, political and other "alternative" groups were concentrated in California. One estimate put the number of Californians who have seriously participated in human potential type organizations at 1 million, with another 2 to 3 million having been marginally involved. The total represents up to 20 percent of the entire population of the state.

Among the most widespread of these middle-class–oriented human potential groups is Erhard's Seminar Trainings (est), founded in San Francisco in 1971 by Werner Erhard, a former salesman turned peddler of spiritual awareness. A mixture of self-help techniques, quasi-Eastern philosophy, and bastardized psychology, est has trained more than 150,000 persons, half of them Californians. In the San Francisco area alone, est claims to have trained one out of every nine middle-aged college graduates compared to one in thirty-three nationwide.

Like many of the California cult leaders, Erhard came to California with an undistinguished if somewhat checkered past. Born in Philadelphia as Jack Rosenberg, Erhard married his high school sweetheart and had four children, before running away with another woman. Although his official est biography describes him as having a "successful career in business management and executive development," Erhard was primarily a salesman, hustling used cars and even selling books door to door. Changing his name to avoid being located by his abandoned family, Erhard gravitated to San Francisco, where he landed a job as director of the child development materials division of *Parents* magazine for three Western states. While in San Francisco, he began sampling the city's vast supermarket of self-help and human potential groups, attending seminars at Esalen, as well as dabbling in Scientology and Mind Dynamics.

But Werner Erhard was not born to be a follower. When driving one day on a San Francisco freeway, he made the discovery that would provide this natural salesman with the ultimate product line. Somewhat grandly, the former Jack Rosenberg recalled:

> What happened had no form. It was timeless, unbounded, ineffable, beyond language. . . . Part of it was the realization that I knew nothing.
> . . . In the next instant—after I realized that I knew nothing—I realized that I knew everything. . . . It was so stupidly, blindingly simple that I could not believe it.
> I saw that there were no hidden meanings, that everything was just the way that it is, and that I was already all right.

Erhard decided not to keep his "blindingly simple" revelation to himself, but instead offered to share it with others—for a price. September 1971 saw his first est lecture at the Jack Tar Hotel in San Francisco. The training Erhard offered was something new, a sixty-hour affair lasting over two successive weekends at a cost of $350 (1978 prices). Attendees are instructed that they will not be allowed to relieve themselves during the course of the first morning's session. Smoking, drugs, and alcohol are strictly banned. Meanwhile they are subjected to a steady barrage of insults and provocations. They are told they are "turkeys," "tubes," and "machines," each insult aimed at breaking down defenses. Once properly subdued, the mass, usually numbering around 250 persons, is then imbued with Erhard's version of the truth: that political involvement, social responsibility, history, all are "bullshit"—obstacles in the way of personal fulfillment. If there is a perfect ideology for California's "free enterprise society," it is est.

Although most cults provide their adherents with excuses for self-absorption, few promote egoism and situational ethics with the zeal of est. "Est is concerned with transformation, not change," explains Erhard. "Est is not about content. Est is about altering the context in which one views and experiences everything in life. . . . Being enlightened is knowing that at any moment in your life, under any circumstances, you possess the ability to transform the quality of your life—to get off it. . . ." The self-obsessed, free enterprise approach to life advocated by Erhard has won est a respectability unmatched by any of California's new consciousness groups. On his advisory board sits Ted Connolly, a prominent Bay Area businessman and president of the Port of Oakland; Dr. George Brecher, chairman of the Department of Laboratory Medicine at the University of California School of Medicine in San Francisco; the actress Valerie Harper; and the singer John Denver.

Along with its growing respectability, est has also accumulated a vast amount of money. The organization's complicated financial set-up, which includes several offshore and overseas companies and a foundation in Switzerland, makes it virtually impossible to ascertain the total value of est's assets. But one investigation found that $6 million in revenues passed through the organization in a single six-month period in 1976.

Erhard's latest promotional scheme has been the Hunger Project, a nationwide effort to "end world hunger" in twenty years, by simply "making it an idea whose time has come." One outgrowth of the project was a $300,000 "Los Angeles World Hunger Event" held in May 1980. To raise funds for the effort to "inform, educate and enlighten powerful individuals to the realities of hunger and starvation in the world," a sumptuous dinner party was thrown at a Westwood penthouse. It included chocolate mousse cake, a kiwi tart pie, a rum and walnut cheese wheel, half a Boulogne gâteau of cheese, and bottles of wine and Perrier. Among those attending were the TV writer-producer Charlotte Brown; Gerald Isenberg, a producer and director of TV movies; the comedian Bill Dana; and the divorce attorney Marvin Mitchelson. "This is not about making people feel guilty," said public relations consultant Kip Morrison in response to a reporter's question about the quantity of food on display at a world hunger dinner. "That's not where we're at. Eating is a celebration of life."

HEAVEN FOR PROFIT—AND BEYOND

The financial success of self-help organizations like est is common to most of the contemporary cults and quasi-spiritual organizations that dot California's kinky cultural landscape. The Unification Church, for example, which each year draws a high proportion of its new recruits from California, has branched out into ownership of an auto repair service, a coffeeshop and delicatessen, and a carpet-cleaning company that has landed contracts with federal government agencies. Its young minions are strongly encouraged to round up as many bucks as they can for "Father"—the Reverend Sun Myung Moon. A Unification Church training manual explains to its devotees: "Do you like to make green bills happy? ... So many green bills are crying.... They are all destined to go to Father. This is our responsibility. Eventually unless everything goes through Father it can't be happy."

Even more brazen in its monetary urge was the Church of Hakeem, founded in the 1970s in Oakland by the Reverend Hakeem Abdul Rasheed. Members of the congregation were asked to donate $500 each to the church, in exchange for a promised 400 percent return on their investment that Hakeem said would be an "increase of God." Rapidly the church grew to 5,000 members, attending regular meetings where they would chant "richer faster, richer faster." Hakeem, meanwhile, purchased a 100-foot yacht and a Rolls Royce, and moved around Oakland decked out in a full-length mink fur coat and diamond rings in search of new converts. "The goal of this church is to make ten thousand millionaires," he said. He also planned to produce a nutrient-packed "prayer food" he claimed would energize the body in seven seconds, "solve the world hunger problem," and help alleviate baldness. "... I will not sell it, I will give it away," Hakeem said. "I will give it away in exchange for donations." Hakeem's plan never was brought to fruition, however, after his 1979 indictment on fraud charges. Authorities said the church was a classic "pyramid" scheme and Hakeem had taken church members and investors for a cool $20 million.

A famous movement in California reflects the state's love affair with high technology and futurist visions. Science fiction writer L. Ron Hubbard founded the Church of Scientology in 1954, based on the psychological "science" of "Dianetics." From its base on Hollywood Boulevard in Los Angeles, the group has expanded rapidly, and an estimated 2.5 million Americans have tried Scientology's self-improvement techniques.

In one of the most eerie moments in the history of California's cults, twenty-six people in 1975 sold their possessions, abandoned their families, and left Los Angeles with "The Two," Herff Applewhite and Bonnie Trusdale. "Bo and Peep" as they are also known, claimed to have made contact with extra-terrestrial beings, and were leading their following into "the next evolutionary kingdom." An estimated 1,000 people now belong to the group, organized into small clusters of people who travel mysteriously all over the country.

More down to earth is the Unarius organization in El Cajon, which has converted 67 acres of desert scrubland into a landing site for spaceships the group says will soon arrive from thirty-two separate planets. Eighty-one-year-old Ruth Norman, a retired realtor, started the group after she says she was contacted by extra-terrestrial beings back in 1953. Norman claims there are 50 dedicated members of the group, and numerous other backers to whom she regularly sends 1 of the 33 books she has produced on the expected space visitation: "We almost had to work underground for a long time. But now there's a great expansion of awareness. We're no longer just a little cult, we're really on the way—and that wonderful *Star Wars* really opened up the way. That 'force be with you' is preconditioning for the landing."

Members of the cult believe that the visitors from space are warm-hearted spacemen who want to help their less developed friends on earth. They are not clear on when the landing will actually occur, but in the interim, Unarians say, they have found peace of mind. "It filled in the enigmas of my own personal search for truth and identity," explained Vaughn Spaegel, a sixty-year-old one-time insurance salesman. "I could finally see beyond earth, beyond myself. I could see further out than ever before—I could see almost to an infinite degree."

Cults like Unarius seem quaint, and to some perhaps ludicrous, but generally harmless at first glance. But too often their escapism from society has led to extreme isolation. Cut off from the rest of the culture, directed ever more inwardly, some cults have fallen prey to paranoid delusions, viewing the "outside" world as a hostile enemy trying to undo their creation. When threatened with exposure or defections from within, they sometimes erupt in an orgy of violence.

The most tragic example of that phenomenon came in November 1978, when the Reverend Jim Jones led over nine hundred members of his People's Temple cult in a macabre act of mass suicide-murder. The People's Temple had moved to the Guyana jungles only a year before in the vain hope of establishing a utopian agricultural community there. But a visit by Congressman Leo Ryan and a fact-finding delegation triggered fears in Jones and his followers that there would be defections from the Temple, ushering in the demise of the cult itself. On November 18, 1978, Temple gunmen killed Ryan and three other members of his party. Hours later, Jones led the congregation in the mass suicide-murder ritual. Dr. J. Thomas Ungerleider of the UCLA Neuropsychiatric Institute observes: "This wouldn't have happened if they hadn't been so isolated. With no feedback from the outside world you can do incredible things with peer pressure. Paranoia becomes a useful tool. It's a binding force. With it, you'll engage in peer-pressure activities even more."

Today, three years after the Guyana massacre, there are indications that the People's Temple may not have been the last cult to turn toward violence. Two members of the Synanon cult were convicted in 1980 for planting a rattlesnake in the mailbox of attorney Paul Morantz, considered an enemy of the organization. The Unification Church, meanwhile, has been carrying out "suicide drills" among its members, in preparation for kidnappings by deprogrammers paid by parents to forcibly wean their children from the cult. A police raid on a farm in Northern California owned by the Hare Krishna sect uncovered a cache of automatic weapons and a grenade launcher. Krishna officials have claimed the weapons were purchased for use in self-defense, and asserted that several Krishna members arrested for illegal possession of weapons were disciples "fallen from grace."

ROUGH JUSTICE

This grim tradition stretches back to the California Gold Rush days, when vigilantism and mob violence were the order of the day. In January 1849, for example, two men were whipped and three others hanged by a mob for their involvement in robberies in Placerville. Around the same time in San Francisco the "Hounds" were organized by local citizenry, a vigilante group committed to hounding foreigners out of California. In July 1849, they attacked a tent city in San Francisco called Little Chile, murdering a mother and assaulting her daughter.

Two years later the Committee of Vigilance was formed in San Francisco, and quickly performed its first act of "justice"—the hanging of a local petty thief. In all that year, the Committee hanged four people, whipped one other, and sentenced twenty-eight more to deportation. Not to be outdone, the city of Los Angeles soon joined in the orgy of violence, when in 1851 the mayor and city council created a vigilance committee by formal decree. Three men, one of them later found to be innocent, were promptly hanged for the murder of a major in the California militia.

More often than not, the mob violence of white Californians has been directed at those lower down the economic ladder—the state's Indian, Mexican, and Chinese populations. On October 24, 1871, for example, 1,000 white locals invaded the Chinatown section of Los Angeles and lynched 19 Orientals.

Those in the white middle class who find that the California dream somehow has evaded their grasp can be left feeling failure, despondency, and betrayal. Nathanael West, writing in the 1930s, described the seething caldron of discontent among the newly arrived immigrants in Los Angeles:

Once there, they discover that sunshine isn't enough. They get tired of oranges, even of avocado pears and passion fruit. Nothing happens. They don't know what to do with their time. They haven't the mental equipment for leisure, the money nor the physical equipment for pleasure. Did they slave so long just to go to an occasional Iowa picnic? What else is there? They watch the waves come in at Venice. There wasn't any ocean where most of them came from, but after you've seen one wave, you've seen them all. The same is true of the airplanes at Glendale. If only a plane would crash once in a while so they could watch the passengers being consumed in a "holocaust of flame," as the newspapers put it. But the planes never crash.

Their boredom became more and more terrible. They realize that they've been tricked and burn with resentment. Every day of their lives they read the newspapers and went to the movies. Both fed them on lynchings, murder, sex crimes, explosions, wrecks, love nests, fires, miracles, revolutions, wars. This daily diet made sophisticates of them. The sun is a joke. Oranges can't titillate their jaded palates. Nothing can ever be violent enough to make taut their slack minds and bodies. They have been cheated and betrayed. They have slaved and saved for nothing.

VII.
Outsiders
to the Dream

For generations Mexicans have migrated north to work in the fields around Wasco, a dusty town set in the middle of California's fertile San Joaquin Valley. Laying down the irrigation pipes, pruning the fruit trees, driving tractors under the valley's brutal sun, they have helped turn a natural wasteland into one of the richest gardens in America. In the process they have enriched some of the state's most powerful agricultural interests.

Yet for all their work, these Mexicans—including those who settled in the new land and raised families—have shared little in the affluence of California's free enterprise society. Outsiders to the materialist dream, they have lived largely on the fringes of the dominant Anglo society, returning from their daily tasks to Wasco's barrio with its ramshackle cottages, stray dogs, and hostile police. Although they make up almost half of the town's 8,900 population, Wasco's Mexican Americans have been largely a voiceless people, little better off than the illegal migrants who pour into the hidden tent cities and fleabag motels outside town every spring.

By the late 1970s, however, there was something stirring among the long-quiescent Hispanic population in Wasco. Inspired by the examples of such leaders as farmworker union president Cesar Chavez, and prodded by Chicano militants from Los Angeles, 150 miles to the south, a handful of these local Chicanos made their first serious bid for political power. In 1977 two Mexican Americans tried to run for the traditionally all-white city council, only to be ruled off the ballot on technicalities. "It's blatant discrimination against us," charged an angry Marshall Rangel-Equilera, one of the abortive candidates and a local school custodian. "They try to stop us with their little rules. The Anglos know we're becoming the majority in the Southwest. They're afraid of the sleeping giant that might be waking up."

Yet four years later, Rangel-Equilera's "giant" still sleeps, in Wasco and throughout California. In 1979, two years after the initial electoral campaign, a Chicano candidate won a place on the Wasco municipal election ballot, only to lose badly in the election when the dispirited and apathetic barrio residents failed to come to the polls in significant numbers. As the 1980s began, things in Wasco still seemed as they had always been, with no Mexicans on the council and their community weak, disorganized, and in conflict with the local police. Frustration with the seemingly unmovable system expressed itself in occasional outbursts of rage, like that on July 1980 when three hundred "bottle wielding" Chicano men battled a contingent of heavily reinforced local police during the annual Fiesta of San Juan. The local police chief declared "war" on any future disturbances; some Chicanos saw it as just one more example of police "repression" against their downtrodden community. One of the few remaining activists, Mary Pollares, charged:

> We don't have any Hispanics in anything, the school boards, nothing. We have no power still. It's so hard to get people involved. If you try to do something, you get in trouble. My husband Rudy tried to run for office, get involved with the community, so the police broke his arm and put him in jail. I tell you, they were out to get him. . . . I work at the bank and at 4 o'clock every day all you have is Mexicans, in from the oil fields and the farms. All the work is done by us, but we've got nothing . . . everything belongs to the whites. They have all the power.

Pollares's frustrations with the status of Mexicans in California society are shared by many activists within the state's over 4.2 million-member Mexican-American community. Although linked by race to the Spaniards who founded the state, these Chicanos find themselves excluded from the sources of power and wealth in modern California. By far the largest minority group, with over one fifth of the total legal resident population, Chicanos hold only 6 out of 120 seats in the state legislature and have managed to elect only 1 congressman out of 43 sent to Washington from California. On the local level the lack of representation is perhaps even more marked. In Los Angeles, where over one third of the city population is Mexican-American, *no* Chicano has been elected to the city council or county board of supervisors for several decades.

Excluded from political power, the Chicanos of California and the swelling population of Mexican illegal aliens have largely been relegated to the bottom rungs of the California economy. Unlike the state's middle class and entrepreneurial elite, these outsiders have benefited little from the great high technology boom of the 1970s. Nationally, between 1959 and 1975, for instance, the mean earnings of Mexican Americans increased the least of any major ethnic group, including blacks, Puerto Ricans, and even Native Americans. The increasing demand for engineers, managers, and scientists among the state's fastest-growing industries, such as computers and aerospace, does little for a population whose level of education and job skills has long been low. Forty-two percent of all Chicanos fail to graduate from high school, according to one recent estimate. Nearly a quarter of all Mexican Americans have less than five years of schooling, compared to only 3.6 percent of the general population. In addition, although Chicanos constitute a fifth of all California high school students, they made up only 2 percent of the 1979 undergraduate class at the University of California at Berkeley. "It is not correct to say that just because things are better for the majority they are equally better for the minority population," asserts Vilma Martinez, head of the Mexican-American Legal Defense and Education Fund. " . . . The opportunities are increasingly in high technology fields, while 76.2 of all Hispanics employed in California are blue-collar workers."

MAÑANA NEVER COMES

Unqualified for positions in the burgeoning high-tech field, California's large Hispanic work force nevertheless has played a major role in the building of California's economic ascendancy. Although they earn on the average less than two thirds of the income achieved by the Anglos, California's Chicanos have largely avoided relegation to the sort of defeatist "welfare culture" that has afflicted black and Puerto Rican communities in the old Eastern industrial heartland. Hispanics in California, whether as citizens or illegal aliens, have provided the state's entrepreneurial elite with a large, cheap labor force without which many key sectors of the state's economy could not function efficiently.

Nowhere is the predominance of Hispanic labor greater than in California's largest industry, agribusiness. Ever since the 1940s, Mexican Americans and Mexican nationals, first as documented *braceros* and later as illegal aliens, have provided the bulk of the labor needed in the great fields of the state. Today, the bulk of the state's agricultural work force is comprised of either native or illegal Mexicans. Although the pay is often low—there are as many as 1 million rural poor in California—these Hispanics are considered essential by most growers for the industrialized form of agriculture perfected in the state. One labor contractor for a prominent central California grower commented: "For us there is no choice. . . . It's hard [work] and you have to be tough and those Mexicans will do it. These are good people, call them illegals or anything you want, but when you work with them you realize they're hard workers. We simply couldn't do without them."

In recent decades, however, the demand for farm laborers has diminished because of increased mechanization, leading many Mexican Americans, whether with or without the requisite working papers, to look for work in the big cities along California's industrialized coast. Already some 80 percent of the nation's Mexican-American citizens are urban dwellers, and an estimated 2.5 million Hispanics live in the Los Angeles area alone. In the large cities, these Hispanics find ample opportunity to work at the bottom levels of a fast-growing economy—as busboys, day laborers, domestics, and, increasingly, factory workers. A major part of this large, low-paid, and virtually unorganized work force is made up of illegal aliens, some 40 percent of whom are now employed in industrial enterprises, according to Immigration and Naturalization Service estimates.

Although working conditions are frequently poor and the pay low, these factory jobs attract thousands of Hispanics each year, some of whom brave immigration police and ride the rails from San Diego to get to the great industrial center of Los Angeles. Much of the reason for this vast influx lies in the poverty and desperation in the villages of Mexico, where the unemployment rate is 50 percent and wages frequently microscopic by American standards. Arturo Vallejo, an illegal alien aged thirty-four from Guanajuto, Mexico, came to Los Angeles in 1977 and went to work at a shoe factory on the city's heavily Hispanic East Side. Vallejo says:

> We don't come here to get anything from the government here. We all come because our government doesn't take care of anything. We had to come for opportunity, the chance to make a living for our families.
> The political situation and the economy back home is worse. The people without jobs are growing. People have nothing and come here to live better.

The prime beneficiaries of this desperate migration from the villages of Mexico are the entrepreneurs in such large cities as Los Angeles. Predominately Hispanic, heavily illegal workers provide the muscle for a myriad of California industries, ranging from restaurants and construction to plastics and garment manufacturing. For example, an estimated 90 percent of the Los Angeles garment industry work force of 125,000 is made up of illegal aliens, mostly from Mexico and Central America. These generally unorganized workers (no more than one in five belongs to a union) have been one of the main reasons behind the growth of the Los Angeles garment industry, which in the 1970s grew at a rate more than 50 percent higher than that of its longtime competitors in heavily unionized New York. "With the proximity of the Mexican labor pool, it's much easier to get the good workers in L.A.," explains one manufacturer, Mike Hopkins, founder of the Whiz Kids jeans factory in the city's downtown garment district. "The unions back east—they put you out of business. If unions came in here and took my people, I'd move everything to Mexico and become a Mexican corporation."

While the garment manufacturers have flourished, many workers in Los Angeles's garment district labor in conditions that more resemble New York's nineteenth-century Lower East Side sweatshops than the sterile, high-tech atmosphere of many California factories. In 1980, for instance, the U.S. Labor Department charged that sixty-four garment manufacturers in Los Angeles had violated labor laws by underpaying their predominately illegal work force. Donald Elisburg, Assistant Secretary of Labor for Employment Standards, said at the time:

> Because they are here illegally, workers are afraid of their employers and often do not know their rights, so they are more easily exploited.
> Exploitation through long hours of work under inhumane conditions at substandard wages is often no better today than what we had in garment industry sweatshops of 60 or 70 years ago.

Despite these and other revelations, few in California believe that this flow of illegal manpower will soon come to a halt. The demands of California's businesses for cheap labor, coupled with the grinding poverty and pervasive unemployment in lands south of the border, will ensure a continually expanding cheap Hispanic work force in the foreseeable future, unless there is a drastic tightening of immigration and border controls, most observers believe.

Anglo concern in some quarters about this mass "invasion" of Hispanics, has prompted political leaders such as Senator S. I. Hayakawa and Los Angeles Supervisor Pete Schabarum to call for tough new measures restricting the influx from the border region. With trepidation, men like Schabarum look toward the end of the decade when the poor Hispanic population could constitute an absolute majority in Los Angeles county. "In my opinion this probably is the most severe social problem pending. You're going to have periods of downturn in employment and the citizens will start raising hell on this," Schabarum, a leading conservative, claims. ". . . If the population balance gets skewed, we'll lose our [social] balance."

Despite such warnings, there appears to be little support among Los Angeles business leaders for slowing down the growth of this cheap yet hardworking Hispanic population. Many top business leaders believe that the illegals have become a vital part of the area's economy. Conrad Jamison, vice-president and chief economist for Los Angeles's Security Pacific National Bank, comments: "These people come to the United States, work real hard. They produce a lot and make for some of the richest little towns in Mexico. Our migrants are very economically motivated. They come for jobs. . . . There's no doubt they are helping out industry. If the illegals were rounded up, a lot of this town would grind to a halt."

THE FIRST CALIFORNIANS

A large, reliable pool of cheap labor has long been one of the essential ingredients in the development of the California economy. From the time of the first Spanish settlements in the late eighteenth century, the conquistadores and Catholic missionaries quickly worked to enslave the local Indian population for conversion to Christianity and work on mission farms. Blessed by a mild climate and the rich natural environment of the coastal region, California had one of North America's largest Indian populations, numbering at least 130,000 persons before the arrival of the Spaniards. Through subsistence farming, hunting, and gathering, these Indians, according to most accounts, built thriving, albeit primitive, tribal societies.

These aboriginal communities, however, did not fit comfortably into the pattern of development envisioned by the European intruders. Missionaries spoke grandly of saving the souls of Indians as they encouraged as many as possible to work on their expanding farms. Although they taught the Indians many useful farming methods and crafts, the monks all too often regarded the native Californians as children, capable only of working under the direction of more enlightened souls. Friar Geronimo Boscana, a Franciscan missionary attached to the San Juan Capistrano Mission on the Southern California coast, wrote:

The Indians of California may be compared to a species of monkey, for naught do they express interest, except in imitating the actions of others, and particularly in copying the ways of the "razon" or white men, whom they respect as being much superior to themselves; but in so doing, they are careful to select vice in preference to virtue. This is

the result, undoubtedly, of their corrupt, and natural disposition. . . .
[The Indian's] eyes are never uplifted, but like those of the swine, are
cast to the earth. Truth is not in him, unless to the injury of another,
and he is exceedingly false.

Conditions generally worsened for the Indians after Mexico won its
independence from Spain in 1821 and took control of the remote California possessions. Under Mexican rule the power of the missionaries
declined sharply, leading in 1834 to the secularization of the twenty-one
California missions. Without the paternalistic protection of the padres,
the Indians were forced either to escape into the wilderness or to go to
work for the private holders of sprawling ranchos, most of them established through old Spanish land grants. Throughout the period of Mexican rule in the 1830s and 1840s a small community of Mexicans, numbering no more than 7,000, established its domination of the slowly
shrinking Indian population. On the backs of the Indian's cheap labor,
the "Californios," as the Spanish Mexicans called themselves, developed a semi-feudal society based on large-scale ranching.

Freed from the demands of hard work by their passive and numerous
peons, the elite society of early California enjoyed an easy, leisure-
oriented life, dominated by lavish partying and elegant horsemanship.
Although only an estimated one hundred of these Californios were lit-
erate, observers noted that even the lowliest descendant of Mexicans
carried with him an air of aristocratic bearing and ease. But in many
ways the Californios' dependence on cheap Indian labor paved the way
for the destruction of this society. Unwilling to found new businesses or
adapt to changing trade patterns, the Californios, by the early 1840s,
found themselves increasingly dependent on Anglo merchants and
businessmen who brought them necessities and luxuries from the
workshops of New England. One American visitor to the California coast during the twilight of the Mexican era, Richard Henry Dana,
observed:

> The Californians are an idle, thriftless people and can make nothing
> for themselves. The country abounds in grapes, yet they buy bad
> wine made in Boston and brought round by us, at an immense price
> and retail it among themselves. . . . Their hides, too, which they value
> at two dollars in money, they give for something which costs sev-
> enty-five cents in Boston; and buy shoes (as like as not, made of their
> own hides, which have been carried twice around Cape Horn) at
> three to four dollars. . . .

The landmark events of the late 1840s—notably the American triumph over Mexican forces in the 1846–48 war and the discovery of gold
in California—shattered forever the balance of this pastoral society.

After putting up a spirited resistance, the Mexican forces in Los Angeles surrendered to American commander John C. Fremont in January 1847. In all only an estimated thirty top Mexican families, mostly in Southern California, managed to retain their power and wealth through the transition to American rule. Accepted into the upper echelons of the emerging Anglo society, some of the "dons" eventually ran for and won high office in the new State of California, including Don Romualdo Pacheco, who sat in the State Senate and eventually became lieutenant governor. Others, notably the landowning Sepulveda, Pico, and Castro clans, managed to hold onto their vast holdings long enough to play important roles in the early economic development of the American state. (The families' names survive today as the names of major streets and districts throughout California.)

But for the great majority of the Mexicans in California the American occupation proved a total disaster. A proud people, they watched in horror as thousands of fortune-seekers overran traditional grazing lands in a mad scramble for gold. Many others were swindled out of their holdings by unscrupulous Anglo businessmen such as Henry Miller. In the Sierra foothills Mexicans who attempted to mine for gold found themselves outnumbered, outbullied, and virtually thrown out of the gold fields by newly arriving Anglo-Americans. By 1850, the Mexicans were already a minority group within their own land, reviled by the more numerous newcomers who often considered them little more than "half-civilized black men." In the opinion of many of the new rulers, the Mexicans were simply incapable of playing a significant role in the development of the state. As the writer T. J. Farnham had expressed it:

> ... the Spanish population of the Californias [is] ... in every poor way a poor apology of European extraction; as a general thing, incapable of reading or writing, and knowing nothing of science or literature, nothing of government but its brute force, nothing of virtue but the sanction of the church, nothing of religion but ceremonies of the national ritual. Destitute of industry themselves.... In a word, the Californians are an imbecile, pusillanimous race of men and unfit to control the destinies of that beautiful country.

Pressured economically, driven from the gold fields, humiliated by crude pioneers and polished racists like Farnham, some Californios in the 1850s began to fight back against the Americans. Although outnumbered more than ten to one by the swelling population of fortune-hunting Anglos, these rebellious Mexicans concentrated their efforts in Southern California, where the majority of them lived. Much of the resistance took the form of desperado bands, made up both of political malcontents and of common criminals, which preyed upon American merchants, ranchers, and government officials. Desperadoes like Juan Flores, Joaquin Murieta, and Tiburcio Vasquez became folk heroes to generations of Mexican Californians. Most of these *bandidos* were hunted down and killed by vigilante Anglo bands. Shortly before his hanging in 1875, Vasquez explained what led him to his life of crime:

> My career grew out of the circumstances by which I was surrounded. As I grew to manhood I was in the habit of attending balls and parties given by the native Californians, into which the Americans, then beginning to become numerous, would force themselves and shove the native born men aside, monopolizing the dance and the women. This was about 1852. A spirit of hatred and revenge took possession of me. I had numerous fights in defense of my countrymen. The officers were continually in pursuit of me. I believed we were unjustly and wrongfully deprived of the social rights that belonged to us.

THE NEW ORDER

Even before the authorities hung the defiant Vasquez from the gallows, his people were a beaten, conquered race. Once the proud rulers of California, the Mexicans found themselves increasingly replacing the Indians they had subjugated at the bottom levels of society. The hapless Indians, after surviving the oppressions of the Spaniards and Mexicans, were almost completely wiped out by the impact of the American invasion. In the fifty-four years between the outbreak of the Mexican War and 1900, the California Indian population plummeted from about 100,000 to less than 16,000. Over 60 percent of the deaths in the Indian community were caused by disease, often brought by the Anglos; the balance of the fatalities came largely from malnutrition and starvation, brought about by the Anglo's annexation of traditional Indian lands.

By the 1860s the Mexicans, like the Indians before them, were rapidly becoming a landless people. Outmaneuvered, cheated of their ranches and farms, many Mexicans were reduced to taking work as menial laborers, bearing the water, washing the clothes, tending the fields of the dominant Anglo population. In the long established Mexican community of Santa Barbara, for example, between 1860 and 1870 the percentage of Hispanics with their own farms and ranches dropped from 24 to 6 percent. While Southern California boomed, the Chicano community suffered enormous economic setbacks; by 1880, between one half and three quarters of the total Hispanic work force in some large Southern California towns was unemployed. Not surprisingly, the Mexican population of the state began to stagnate, and by 1900 made up less than

5 percent of the total population of Los Angeles, which little over a half century before had been the capital of Mexican California. The vestiges of Spanish influence disappeared in town after town; brick replaced adobe, New England churches the old Catholic chapels, city parks the old plazas. Some observers wondered if the Mexican himself was not soon to follow the Indian on the path to virtual extinction as a people. One such observer, J. P. Widney, wrote in 1886:

> Death and Emigration are removing them from the land . . . they no longer have unnumbered horses to ride and vast herds of sheep, from which one for a meal would never be missed. Their broad acres now, with few exceptions, belong to the acquisitive American . . . grinding poverty has bred recklessness and moroseness. Simple healthful amusements have in many instances given way to midnight carousels; long continued dissipation and want are huddling them together in the most unwholesome localities in the towns.

Changing economic and political conditions at the turn of the century saved the California Hispano from historical oblivion. Rapid economic growth in the early twentieth-century California required the importation of large numbers of low-paid, menial laborers. In addition, the poverty during the declining days of the Díaz regime in Mexico, followed by the cataclysms after the 1910 Mexican Revolution, led thousands of desperate Mexican nationals to seek refuge in California. Between 1900 and 1910, the number of Mexican-born residents of California jumped 400 percent; in the years between the outbreak of the 1910 revolution and 1919, over 173,000 Mexicans immigrated into the United States.

These new Mexican immigrants revitalized California's declining Hispano population. They harbored few of the old resentments felt by the embittered Californios, and gravitated immediately to the menial jobs then in plentiful supply. Mexicans provided much of the muscle for the expanding California agribusiness, railroad, and manufacturing industries. By one estimate, Mexicans constituted between 25 and 66 percent of the work force in many of the state's industries in the 1910s and 1920s. World War I exacerbated the shortage of cheap labor, and the federal government soon started waiving virtually all controls in order to bring in the requisite numbers of Hispanic workers.

By the 1930s, the Mexican population of Los Angeles was estimated to be as high as 190,000, one seventh of the total citizenry of the burgeoning city. As the Depression set in, however, these Mexicans, so useful in times of economic prosperity, became targets of racial hatred and persecution. The small farmer blamed the Mexican for aiding the large, irrigated corporate farms, which were driving him out of business. On the other hand, growers and other employers of Mexicans tried to fight off moves limiting their immigration. "The Mexicans are wonderful people," commented one Imperial Valley resident at the time. "They are docile; I just love them. I was paying Pancho and his whole family 60 cents a day before the war [1918]. There were just no hours; he worked from sun to sun."

BACKFIRE

By the early 1930s the pressure to evict Mexican laborers had intensified, leading to mass deportations. In one year that decade, the Los Angeles *Times* reported, as many as 75,000 Mexicans were repatriated from California. Within ten years, between 1930 and 1940, the Mexican-born population of the United States had declined 41 percent. Many were shocked and outraged at the cruelty of the mass expulsion. The Mexicans of Los Angeles wrote many *corridos,* or folk ballads, lambasting their treatment by the Americans. As the *corrido* "El Deportada" put it:

> The blonds are very bad fellows,
> The blonds are very bad fellows,
> They take advantage,
> And to all the Mexicans,
> And to all the Mexicans,
> They treat us without pity.
>
> Today they bring a great disturbance
> And not without consideration
> Women, children and old people
> Women, children and old people
> They take us to the border,
> They eject us from this country.
>
> Good bye, dear countrymen,
> Good bye, dear countrymen,
> They are going to deport us.
> But we are not bandits,
> But we are not bandits,
> We came to toil.

But even as their *compadres* were being herded onto boxcars for the trip to the border, a new awareness was growing among the remaining Mexican-American population in the barrios of Los Angeles and other major southwestern cities. By 1940 a new, mostly American-born generation had come to maturity. Unlike their generally immigrant parents, these Chicanos refused to accept roles at the bottom of society. At the heart of this new self-assertiveness was the *pachuco,* usually in his late teens or early twenties, who donned the outlandish "zoot suit" or "drape shape" to express his own individuality. Neither Mexican nor assimilated American, the *pachuco* represented a new defiant breed of Chicano, with a swagger not seen in the barrio since the days of the bandit Vasquez.

The *pachuco* was also, in many ways, a product of the emerging "free enterprise society" that had rejected his people. His rebellion did not flow from Marxist or ultra-nationalist politics; *pachuquismo* expressed the uprooted Mexican's search for identity. Like the middle-class cultists of the period, the *pachucos* adopted the bizarre to deal with the confusion caused by living in California's society. The Mexican poet Octavio Paz, who studied the *pachucos* of Los Angeles, observed:

> They are instinctive rebels, and North American racism has vented its wrath on them more than once. But the *pachucos* do not attempt to vindicate their [sic] race or the nationality of their forebears. Their attitude reveals an obstinate, almost fanatical will-to-be, but this will affirms nothing specific except their determination . . . not to be like those around them. The *pachuco* does not want to become a Mexican again; at the same time he does not want to blend into the life of North America. His whole being is sheer negative impulse, a tangle of contradictions, an enigma. Even his very name is enigmatic; *pachuco,* a word of uncertain derivation, saying nothing and saying everything.

The *pachuco* came on the scene at a time of increasing paranoia and nativism among the dominant Anglo population of California. The outbreak of World War II had seen the mass internment of the Japanese Americans in concentration camps. In addition, wartime conscription and speeded-up industrialization, particularly on the west coast, created a massive labor shortage in the state. The anti-immigrant policies of the 1930s were cast aside, and in 1942, the federal government, in conjunction with the Mexican government, set up the *"bracero"* program that led to the importation of over 220,000 Mexican laborers into the country between 1942 and 1947. In their xenophobic state of mind, California's Anglos began to regard the suddenly increasing numbers of Hispanics—and particularly the highly visible, aggressive *pachucos*—as a dangerous threat to "the American way of life."

Hysteria over Mexicans and *pachucos* reached a climax when in August 1942, the body of José Diaz was found in an area called "The Sleepy Lagoon" section of Los Angeles's predominantly Hispanic East

Side. Twenty-three young Chicanos were indicted for the murder and placed on trial. All were later acquitted, but the highly publicized court proceedings deepened the division between the city's Mexican and Anglo communities. Typical of the racist sentiments then sweeping the Anglo community was a 1942 report issued by the Los Angeles County Sheriff's Office:

> The Caucasian, especially the Anglo-Saxon, when engaged in fighting, particularly among youths, resort to fisticuffs and may at times kick each other, which is considered unsportive; but this Mexican element considers all that to be a sign of weakness, and all he knows and feels is a desire to use a knife or some lethal weapon. In other words, his desire is to kill, or at least let blood. . . . When there is added to this inborn characteristic that has come down through the ages, the use of liquor, then we certainly have crimes of violence.

In early June 1943, the anti-*pachuco* feelings whipped up by police, politicians, and the press, exploded into full-scale rioting. A mob of 3,000, made up largely of off-duty Anglo servicemen, roamed the streets of downtown Los Angeles, assaulting the "zoot-suiters" under the watchful, tolerant eyes of the police. Although the Anglos initiated the attacks in most cases, all forty-four persons arrested were Mexicans. Few outside the Chicano community protested this revival of middle-class Anglo-Californian vigilantism. "Most of the citizens of the city," reported the suburban *Eagle Rock Advertiser*, "have been delighted with what has been going on."

The Sleepy Lagoon Case and the outrages of the "zoot-suit riots" of 1943, galvanized the long-suffering Mexican-American community. A Sleepy Lagoon Legal Defense Fund, supported by community residents and chaired by an Anglo journalist, Carey McWilliams, financed and appealed the original murder convictions of twelve of the *pachucos* and in October 1944 won their release, one of the landmark Mexican-American political victories in modern times.

As Mexican-American servicemen returned home from the war, they brought with them a new sense of pride and patriotism. Some engaged in trying to build new political and labor organizations, to create a respectable, mainstream alternative to the "anarchic" *pachuco*. One of the most successful of these new groups was the Los Angeles–based Community Service Organization (CSO), founded in 1947. Organized by middle-class Chicanos, the CSO was part of a "conscious attempt at further 'Americanization,' " and in 1949 helped elect Edward Roybal to the Los Angeles City Council, the first Hispano to sit on that body since 1881.

While organizations like CSO were trying to bring political unity to the barrios of California, others attempted to achieve a modicum of economic power. Starting in the 1920s and 1930s, labor organizers tried, usually unsuccessfully, to unionize Hispanic factory and farm laborers. Strikes were often brutally repressed, as during a 1934 lettuce strike in which local police routed 1,500 strikers with tear gas. To undercut the increasingly restless Chicano workers, California agribusiness interest had turned to the *bracero* program, which brought in an estimated 445,-000 workers to the country from Mexico by 1956. At the same time illegals continued to flock into the state and the Southwest; when their services were considered superfluous, massive crackdowns were ordered, as in 1953 and 1954, when nearly 2 million Mexicans were deported back to their homeland.

In 1962, an Arizona-born Chicano named Cesar Chavez quit his job as an organizer for the CSO and began a new farm union, the National Farm Workers Association. His union grew, aided by the end of the *bracero* program in 1964. Chavez organized all races, including Filipinos, Anglos, and Chinese farm laborers; but the vast majority of his members, like most of the workers in the fields, were Mexican illegals or Chicanos. In 1965 Chavez led his workers, reconstituted as the AFL-CIO–affiliated United Farm Workers (UFW), out of the grape fields of the San Joaquin Valley. Committed to nonviolence and an ideology of nonrevolutionary Catholic social welfarism, the UFW attracted wide national support from the liberal community when it initiated an international "grape boycott" to force the growers into signing with the union. Although four fifths of all Chicanos lived in the cities, the UFW's rhetoric spoke to the long-slumbering aspirations for full equality on the part of California's Hispanos. In May 1969 the strikers, who were based in Delano, declared:

> We have been farm workers for hundreds of years and boycotters for two. We did not choose the grape boycott but we *had* chosen to leave our peonage, poverty and despair behind.
> . . . Grapes must remain an unenjoyed luxury for all as long as the barest human needs and basic human rights are still luxuries for farm workers. The grapes grow sweet and heavy on the vines, but we will have to wait while we reach out first for our freedom. The time is ripe for our liberation.

Chavez won strong support from top Democratic leaders such as Senator Robert F. Kennedy, and from Governor Jerry Brown, who in 1975 successfully oversaw the passage of legislation proving free union access and supervised elections in the fields of California. In 1977 the UFW and its chief union rival, the Teamsters, signed a jurisdictional agreement, ending a bitter conflict and assuring the peaceful growth of the UFW. Yet even with the new legislation, the UFW, by the end of the 1970s, had managed to recruit no more than 30,000 members, less than 10 percent of the estimated total number of workers in California's agricultural industry. Chavez himself has admitted these numbers are still far too small for the UFW to consolidate its power, although the union leader pledges to carry on his struggle for as long as necessary. "We will continue whether it takes one year or twenty," Chavez has vowed. "We will never give up. We do not underestimate our adversaries because they are rich and powerful and they own land. But we know we will win in the end; we learned many years ago that the rich may have money, but the poor have time."

TREMORS ON THE FAULT LINE

By the late 1960s, however, such patient attitudes were increasingly rare among the expanding Hispanic populations of California's inner city barrios. There tensions between Chicanos, particularly the youth, and the police had been building since the days of the *pachuco*. In some barrios, as many as one in five Chicano families were directly affected by these confrontations with the law; 40 percent of the Los Angeles County Jail population was comprised of Mexican Americans. To many Chicanos, these statistics reflected an inbred anti-Mexican racism within the criminal justice establishment. More and more, they considered the police as an occupying army whose presence in their community—four times as numerous as in Anglo areas—was not justified by a crime rate not much higher than that of the dominant population.

Hispanic anger was further fanned by periodic displays of insensitivity, if not blatant racism, on the part of leaders of the Anglo-dominated criminal justice system. In the 1960s, for instance, Los Angeles Police Chief William Parker reportedly remarked that some Hispanics "are not far removed from the wild tribes of Mexico." Even more outrageous were the remarks in 1969 of Santa Clara County Juvenile Court Judge Gerald S. Chargin as he prepared to sentence a seventeen-year-old Mexican-American boy charged with incest:

Mexican people, after 13 years of age, think it is perfectly all right to go out and act like an animal. We ought to send you out of the country—send you back to Mexico. . . . You ought to commit suicide. That's what I think of people of this kind. You are lower than animals and haven't a right to live in organized society—just miserable, lousy, rotten people. Maybe Hitler was right. The animals in our society probably ought to be destroyed because they have no right to live among human beings.

Even before the blacks rioted in Watts, established Mexican leaders were fearful that these Anglo attitudes would someday lead to a full-scale racial confrontation between the authorities and the frustrated, powerless Chicano community. "In East Los Angeles," observed one local barrio newspaper in April 1964, "it has been rather noticeable lately that police officers have taken it upon themselves to search individuals without first obtaining a search warrant. Citizens of East Los Angeles are being pushed to the point of rebellion. . . ."

As hostility toward the Anglo police grew, new, more militant forces emerged in the barrio. Some took the form of street gangs, whose members, called *cholos,* resembled the *pachucos* of the 1940s in their brazen affirmation of an unconventional lifestyle. Others, such as the Brown Berets, founded in Los Angeles in 1967, took a more radical line, placing themselves as a quasi-defense force against the LAPD and the county sheriffs. The Brown Berets' ten-point program epitomized the attitudes of aggressive Chicano youths who claimed they were willing to battle the police on the streets, if need be. They pledged:

> To keep a watchful eye on all federal, state, city and private agencies which deal with the Mexican-American, especially the law enforcement agencies. . . .
>
> To protect, guarantee and secure the rights of the Mexican-American by all means necessary. How far we must go in order to protect these rights is dependent upon those in power. If those Anglos in power are willing to do this in a peaceful and orderly process, then we will be only too happy to accept this way. Otherwise, we will be forced to other alternatives.

On January 1, 1970, the "other alternatives" spoken of by the Berets and other militant Chicanos began to make themselves felt on the streets of the barrio. A crowd of 100 New Year's Day celebrants smashed some forty-two storefront windows and looted several shops, primarily those owned by Anglos from outside the community. But by far the most ominous incident took place eight months later, on August 29, 1970, when a coalition of Mexican-American groups called a National Chicano Moratorium March. Organized by Rosalio Munoz, a former UCLA student body president, an estimated 15,000 to 20,000 persons joined the demonstration, protesting the U.S. involvement in Southeast Asia. An attempt by police to disperse the marchers resulted in the largest expression of Hispanic rage since the American conquest. More than one hundred persons were injured and three—including one sheriff's deputy—were shot. One Chicano, Los Angeles *Times* reporter Ruben Salazar, died when he was struck by a tear-gas missile fired into a café by a sheriff's deputy. Some observers charged that the police purposely abused the demonstrators, hunting them through the streets of the barrio. One wounded demonstration leader, Raymond Hernandez, later stated: "It had just gotten dark and we were moving the crowd back, pushing them back. All of a sudden to my right side I heard four shots. I turned around and saw deputies aiming their rifles straight ahead . . . down in my direction. I said 'Don't shoot! Don't shoot!' But they fired again and I got hit. They were firing like a firing squad."

Despite the emotions stirred up by the 1970 East Los Angeles riots, little was done to rectify the conditions of poverty and suspicion of authority that led to its outbreak. As the nation moved into the conservative, self-oriented seventies, the problems of the barrios and ghettos receded in the minds of the ruling Anglo elite. After the brief flurry of activism in the late 1960s, the old traditions of political apathy reasserted themselves in the Chicano community. A study of one northern California county, for example, found Mexican-American registration and voting participation rates were 15 to 20 percent below the community average. Precious little progress had been made by Chicanos in attaining a strong voice in either state or local government. Looking back at the legacy of the 1970 riots, one prominent Chicano leader, Richard Martinez, commented bitterly: "I sometimes feel that out of the ashes just came more ashes."

TOWARDS AZTLAN

Still politically weak and economically depressed, Chicano leaders in the 1980s are counting on the force of their numbers to reverse their people's over-130-year sentence at the bottom rung of California society. High inflation, malnutrition, pervasive unemployment, and underemployment in Mexico, coupled with a rapidly expanding California economy, led to a new torrent of mostly illegal immigration. Along the border near San Diego, which accounts for as much as one quarter of all illegal alien apprehension in the nation, arrests of undocumented persons jumped from 62,000 in 1971 to 339,000 in 1979, an increase of more than 400 percent. At the same time the Hispanic citizen population—including children born to illegal aliens in California—continued to expand drastically. California's predominantly Mexican population of Spanish-surnamed residents grew much faster than the Hispanics in other major centers, like Texas and New York, during the 1970s, growing by over 91 percent compared to a national increase of 61 percent.

Perhaps even more significantly for the future, much of this swelling population is young. Today, nearly half of the students entering the Los Angeles school system are Hispanic, and by the mid-1980s, according to one UCLA study, Latinos will account for 30 percent of all the state's high school seniors. In 1984, Hispanics will surpass Anglos as the largest ethnic component in Los Angeles County, which has nearly one third of the state's total population; and by 1992, these Latinos will make an absolute majority of county residents, according to projections made by Security Pacific Bank. By the opening of the twenty-first century, some demographers predict, Hispanics, combined with increasing Asian and black populations, could make California the nation's first majority "Third World" state.

To some Chicanos, the prospect of a Hispanic-dominated "Third World" majority in California presents a major opportunity to redress many of the festering scars from their long history of subordination. A few radical activists even advocate a Quebec-style separatist movement, particularly in heavily Hispanic Southern California, which could seize power in the region from the United States. Rudulfo Acuna, a professor of Chicano studies at Cal State University at Northridge and leading Mexican-American intellectual, warns:

> ... if there are not dramatic changes in this society (then) ... the real talk of secessionism is going to come when you have shrinking resources and rising expectations. ... The economy is worse, there is less of a future for poor people. The structure alienates people and forces them out, pushes them into a situation where they have no alternatives. I say, if you're the majority, why not rule?

Nationalists like Acuna are still a small, if vocal minority among Mexican Americans in California, but many Chicanos share his dream of gaining political and even economic dominance in the state over the coming decades. Already a new, aggressive generation of middle-class Chicanos has begun to gain at least a modicum of power in the state. Groups like the church-sponsored United Neighborhoods Organization have given the Hispanic community a lobbying presence at Los Angeles City Hall not seen for generations. Significant numbers of Hispanics have also strived to enter the entrepreneurial class. Although most of their businesses remain small—almost 40 percent of businesses in Hispanic East Los Angeles grossed under $50,000 in 1976—there is potential economic and political clout in the growth of such groups as the Los Angeles–based Latin-American Businessmen's Association, whose membership jumped from 5 in 1972 to over 100 by 1980. "The opportunity is still in Los Angeles," claims Julio Rivera, a native of the East Los

Angeles barrio and now a successful businessman. "There are those who say because they are from the barrio they have to be failures. But I'm not a failure, I'm a business guy. I know what it's like to be Hispanic and not be allowed to grow—but that's changed now. They can't pull that shit now."

The emergence of this Hispanic middle class, coupled with the rapidly expanding Chicano population in general, has led some top Anglo politicians actively to court the Mexican-American community in ways virtually inconceivable just a decade ago. Most notable has been Governor Jerry Brown, who has openly told Chicanos that the 1980s is the time for them to take their "turn in the sun." Governor Brown has appointed thirty Mexican-American state judges, ten times the number appointed by Reagan, while placing an additional two hundred Hispanics onto various state boards and commissions. Although Chicanos still account for only 2 percent of all state judges and 10 percent of the membership on boards and commissions, some community leaders see in Brown's active courting the emergence of Mexican-American political power within the system. "When the numbers are high enough, it'll just change things. . . . We are finally going to have some leaders," said one Chicano official. "By setting an example of what people can aspire to—that changes people's heads about themselves."

The attorney's optimism is not shared, however, by many other Chicanos, particularly among the youth now growing up in California's barrios. To them, the appointment of a handful of middle-class Mexican Americans to state offices hardly compensates for deteriorating schools, increasing conflicts with police, Proposition Thirteen–inspired cutbacks in social programs, and a youth unemployment rate that reached 40 percent in East Los Angeles in 1980. Like the *pachucos* before them, these young people have adopted their own distinctive dress code—usually khaki pants, Pendleton shirts, and tattoos—and form tight-knit neighborhood gangs.

By 1980, barrio youth gangs had grown to a degree never before seen in California's Hispanic community. Mexican-American youths constituted the vast majority of an estimated 300 such gangs in Los Angeles alone, with an estimated membership of over 30,000. Frustrated, angry, faced with population pressures caused by high birth rates and illegal immigration, each group has become increasingly violent as it fights to protect its neighborhood "turf" from rival groups. In 1980, the number of gang-related deaths in Los Angeles was twice that of three years earlier. In 1979 there were 279 such deaths with Chicanos accounting for an estimated four fifths of the fatalities.

While this bloodshed has largely involved internecine battles between Chicano youths, the *cholos* generally share an extreme antagonism toward the police and other symbols of Anglo authority. In some neighborhoods a permanent state of siege already exists between police and local kids who consider the lawman as a foreign occupation force in their communities. Some *cholos* believe that armed conflict with the police, far greater than what occurred in the 1970 riots, may be inevitable given the worsening conditions in the barrio areas. As one *cholo* in the poverty-stricken Big Hazard section of East Los Angeles put it:

> Here you have no rights. There is no constitution. Down here the only law is the police law . . . [but] when we get tired, we get tired. We'll get rid of them someday. We'll shoot the cops to get them off our backs. We have an advantage over the cops. They don't know the area. We can shoot them and escape. . . .
> Someday this is going to be our world, our country, our streets, with our laws.

The rise of a Chicano and a "Third World" majority in California represents perhaps the greatest threat to the power of the state's entrepreneurial elite. Some middle-class Chicano leaders believe that eventually the Anglo elite must be convinced to voluntarily relinquish much of its political and economic hegemony to the Hispanics or face the possibility of street insurrection in the barrio areas. "They've been putting us down since, hell, 1848," explains attorney Miguel Garcia, leader of Californios for Fair Representation, a statewide coalition of Hispanic groups. "We have to have power and we will. You can only keep a people down so long. Look at South Africa. All we are trying to do now is accomplish the inevitable, hopefully in a peaceful way."

The rising level of barrio violence, along with warnings by leaders like Garcia, and the stark statistical evidence of massive demographic shifts in the state has led some corporate executives to begin taking seriously the challenge posed by California's Chicanos. Unless some political or economic accommodation can be reached soon, assert forward-thinking executives like Pacific Lighting president Joseph Rensch, California's business community may confront a rising tide of racial and class conflict, threatening the very structure of the state's society. Lunching at the exclusive Los Angeles Club in a high rise overlooking the city, Rensch admitted: "It's our biggest problem. We don't have too many years to go. It's a time bomb all around us. I watch the deterioration of this city, the crowding. The [Chicano] leaders come up to me just like that [and say], 'We're going to take our land back.' I think we are seeing such a sudden surge. How fast can our system absorb them? As things get worse, the standard of living drops, it can do nothing but explode."

THE BLACK ENIGMA

More than a decade and a half after California's racial "time bomb" exploded in the Watts section of Los Angeles, the burnt-out stores and rubble-strewn lots remain, testaments to the worst outbreak of civil disorder in recent California history. As they did in the time before the riots, which resulted in thirty-four deaths, scores of unemployed black men congregate in front of the liquor stores along Broadway, depressed, desperate, permanent "outsiders" to the California dream.

The figures used to measure the misery in Watts and other black communities in California show that, if anything conditions have worsened since the 1965 insurrection. Unemployment, according to 1980 estimates by the Los Angeles Urban League, stood at twice the level experienced in 1965—including up to one fourth of all adults and over 50 percent of youths within the ghetto. Other major social problems including crime, conflicts with law enforcement, drugs, have also generally worsened since the mid-1960s.

Perhaps most frustrating of all, this widespread economic and social deterioration has taken place despite impressive political gains achieved by California's 1.8 million blacks in recent years. Although less than 10 percent of the state's population, blacks have amassed a political clout to an extent that the far more numerous Chicano community is only beginning to envision for itself. Since the early 1970s, blacks have won control of such important statewide posts as lieutenant governor and Assembly speaker, as well as taking the mayor's office in major cities including Los Angeles, Oakland, and Berkeley. The apparent inability of these black politicians to improve conditions for the masses of California blacks points to the increasing irrelevancy and futility of politics to effect change in the state's "free enterprise society," particularly since the passage of Proposition Thirteen. Looking out over a bombed-out shopping district, Los Angeles NAACP president Paul Hudson remarked bitterly in 1980:

That clothing store next door burned down fifteen years ago and now look at it. It's a parking lot—and most of them [the other stores] are just vacant. Along Broadway, all over the place there's vacant lots. Nothing's changed in fifteen years, so why should people's feelings?

All the representation [at City Hall] doesn't mean increased opportunities for the districts they represent. Nothing's been done for us . . . we got nothing. The bottom line is this city has thrown up its hands—we can't do anything. South Central Los Angeles isn't being rebuilt.

The relative impotence of California's black politicians in effecting major improvements for their community stems largely from their community's status as only the state's second-largest minority, and their relegation to an increasingly peripheral role in the state economy. Unable to muster sufficient political or economic muscle from their constituents, California's skilled black politicians have gained power, for the most part, through alliances with the dominant sectors of the state's "free enterprise society," notably the leaders of the various local business communities. When San Francisco Assemblyman Willie Brown, for instance, became California's first black Assembly speaker in 1981, his victory was viewed more as a result of Brown's own personal savvy than an indication of statewide black political strength. Indeed, Brown's elevation to speaker was made possible only by an open alliance with Republican forces gathered around GOP Assembly leader Carol Hallett.

A similarly realpolitik marriage has developed in Los Angeles between Mayor Tom Bradley and the city's powerful business interests. Elected in 1973 by a coalition of blacks, liberals, labor, Jews, and moderate businessmen turned off by the theatrics of flashy, longtime Mayor Sam Yorty, former Police Lieutenant Bradley over the ensuing years has turned increasingly for support to the city's conservative business establishment. By 1981, when he won reelection by a landslide victory to a third term, Bradley was the unfailing darling of such top corporate leaders as the Los Angeles *Times* publisher Otis Chandler, (whose paper has endorsed virtually every Bradley move), Carter Hawley Hale's president Phil Hawley, and Pacific Lighting's Joe Rensch. While maintaining the conservative budget posture preferred by these corporate power brokers, Bradley has also served as chief cheerleader for such business-backed projects as the downtown "people-mover," the Wilshire Boulevard subway, the 1984 Los Angeles Olympics, and the Japanese-backed Little Tokyo Redevelopment Project. Under Bradley's administration, summed up Donald Hanauer, executive vice-president of the Los Angeles Chamber of Commerce, "business was made a managing partner in running the city."

While some black community leaders, such as the NAACP's Paul Hudson, have accused Bradley of abandoning the ghetto in favor of the boardroom interests, the mayor's top aides explain the corporate alliance as a logical response to the political and economic realities of Los Angeles. With less than 15 percent of the city's population, and little of its economic power, top Bradley aide Bill Elkins believes blacks can only improve their position with the support of the dominant white community, particularly the business elite. "If you look at [Bradley's] roots, you cannot escape the conclusion he is committed to improving the life of poor people," maintains Elkins. "[Bradley] also happens to be mayor of Los Angeles—that includes rich, poor, black, brown, yellow, and white. And you have to go with the people who have the capability to do things—the bankers, the business community."

Much the same sense of realpolitik is dominant 400 miles to the north, in Oakland, where blacks constitute nearly half the city's population and elected their first black mayor, Lionel Wilson, in 1977. Although not nearly as dependent as Bradley on white political support, Wilson soon realized that without the backing of the city's corporate leaders, his office would be able to do little but preside over the deterioration of the majority non-white city. Following the Bradley pattern, Wilson, shortly after taking office, took on an aggressive, pro-development, pro-business stance very similar to that of his Republican predecessor, John Reading. To a large extent, Wilson's election had more to do with his previous reputation as a moderate local judge than with the color of his skin. "I don't think racial or political affiliation is too important," observes Robert Shetterly, a key Wilson adviser and president of the powerful Oakland-based Clorox Corporation. ". . . I'm a registered Republican. However, that difference doesn't get in our way at all in my opinion."

Although a great source of pride, the remarkable emergence of California's black politicians could well prove economically disastrous for the community in the coming decade. Strong affirmative action programs and black influence within the government bureaucracy have led thousands of blacks, including professionals, toward careers in public service. In Los Angeles, for instance, blacks in 1980 accounted for more than 22 percent of city employees—significantly more than their percentage of the population. However, blacks in Los Angeles had gained far less in the private business world where both Asians and Hispanics had established ownership over more enterprises, with considerably higher total gross receipts, according to a 1977 federal study. Similarly in the San Francisco–Oakland area, black businesses generated less than half the gross receipts enjoyed by the less numerous Asian Americans. Given the strongly anti-government employment politics of post–Proposition Thirteen California, the concentration of blacks in the public sector could further exacerbate their already grim economic situation. "It's a big mistake for us to go after government jobs," believes Paul Hudson. "When you talk about the balanced budget and Proposition Thirteen, you're talking about cutting back the main employer of blacks. I just don't think the 1980s will be a good era for blacks. Bradley will probably be our last black mayor. . . . We may never see it as good again."

SEARCHING FOR THE GOLDEN STATE

Blacks have long lacked a secure position within California's society. While Mexicans of African descent were among the hardy band of settlers founding Los Angeles in 1781, few blacks emigrated to the state during the ensuing century. Black migration was actively discouraged in the initial period of American rule in California. Although it was admitted to the federal union in 1850 as a "free state," stiff discriminatory legislation, including a strict fugitive slave act and a ban against blacks testifying at judicial proceedings, was passed by early California legislatures. ". . . When Negroes are free, they are the freest of human beings; they are free from morals, free in all vices of a brutish and depraved race," one delegate to the state's constitutional convention of 1849 declared, reflecting the widespread anti-black sentiment of the state's new Anglo masters. "They are a most troublesome and unprofitable population."

Although there were only an estimated 2,500 blacks in California at the time, this racist attitude dominated state politics during and even after the Civil War. Pro-Confederate elements dominated in the southern part of the state, and California's discriminatory statutes concerning black rights to testify were not repealed until 1863, and in 1869 the state refused to ratify the Fifteenth Amendment to the U.S. Constitution guaranteeing blacks the right to vote.

It was not until the 1880s and the arrival of the railroad in Los Angeles that blacks began migrating to California in substantial numbers. With the establishment of a "Pullman Car" colony, the black population of Los Angeles County grew from 188 in 1880 to over 30,000 in 1930. Discriminatory housing covenants and other restrictions faced the city's growing black population; but, on the whole, blacks found conditions in Los Angeles generally more favorable than those existing in other contemporary American cities. Part of the reason, according to one study of early ethnic migration, was that the far more numerous Mexican and Japanese populations "drew off much of the racial hostility which might have been concentrated on the Negroes."

As early as the 1920s, a modest number of California blacks began making inroads into the middle class. Several small fortunes were made in real estate, hog farming, and scrap iron. Still restricted to the predominantly black section of Watts in south-central Los Angeles, some of these blacks began to aspire to a greater role in California society. Among the most articulate of the new, aspiring blacks was Ralph

Bunche, who graduated from UCLA in 1927 and later went on to become a leading American diplomat as well as winner of the Nobel Peace Prize. To illustrate the growing independence of blacks in California during the 1920s, Bunche told the story of the poor Texas black,

> who had been in a virtual state of slavery to his Southern white "boss." But by dint of careful saving he was able to take a short trip to Los Angeles and partake of the freedom and grandeur of the Southland, and more particularly, the pure liberty-inspiring atmosphere of our own Central Avenue.
>
> Needless to state, the Texas colored man returned home truant and rebellious. He didn't try to regain his old job—oh no. But his Southern master finally came to him and said: "Sam, you'd better come on back on the job. We've just killed a new batch of hogs and I've got some mighty fine hog jowls for you."
>
> But Sam just shook his kinky head wisely and, with a superior air, told the white man, "Uh, uh boss. You ain't talkin' to me, no suh. I've been to Los Angeles and I don't want yo' old hog-jowls, cuz I'm eatin' high on up on de hog now!"

The lure of California became irresistible to hundreds of thousands of blacks when the outbreak of World War II created a sudden need for their labor. A massive migration began from the poor black rural communities, particularly in Louisiana and Texas, to the booming war industry centers of Los Angeles, Oakland, San Francisco, and Richmond. Nearly a quarter million blacks migrated to California during the war, and even more followed as the state economy continued to expand in the ensuing decades. Between 1950 and 1965, California attracted more new black residents than any state in the union, with the state's percentage of blacks increasing from 1.8 percent in 1940 to over 5.6 percent in 1960.

Backed by their rapidly increasing numbers, blacks began to achieve a degree of political power in California. In 1959 the state legislature, reacting to black and liberal pressure, passed the "Unruh" Civil Rights Act, and four years later it enacted the Rumford Act, both designed to ban racial discrimination in the state. The Rumford Act was named after black Berkeley Assemblyman Byron Rumford, who was among the most prominent of a rising generation of black politicians, including Congressman Augustus Hawkins and Los Angeles City Councilman Tom Bradley.

But behind this facade of political progress, conditions were worsening within the fast-growing black ghettos in California. Nowhere was the deterioration more marked than in Los Angeles County, where the black population increased eightfold between 1940 and 1965, and accounted for over 600,000 residents. Unlike the earlier migrants of the 1930s and 1940s, many of these new black citizens found few employment opportunities in an increasingly high technology and aerospace-oriented economy. By the mid-1960s, unemployment in the heart of the Watts ghetto reached 34 percent, while one in five residents was on welfare. Many blacks who had trekked to the promised land of California found themselves increasingly segregated into overcrowded neighborhoods, their children forced to attend substandard, virtually all-black schools. "One can live, eat, shop, work, play and die in a completely Negro community," observed John Buggs, executive director of the Los Angeles County Commission of Human Relations, in 1963. "The social isolation ... is more complete than it ever was for the Negro rural resident in the South."

COMING HOME TO ROOST

Exacerbating tensions within the ghetto was an increasing fear of black encroachment by the dominant white majority. In 1964, for instance, California voters passed an initiative repealing the Rumford Act by a margin of more than two to one. A growing conflict also developed between the virtually all-white police force patrolling the ghetto—only 4 percent of the force was black—and the local populace. Charges of police harassment of blacks became commonplace; civil rights leaders and Los Angeles Police Chief William Parker engaged in a continuous war of words. On the warm summer night of August 11, 1965, that war became something much more. A white California Highway Patrolman pulled over two black youths driving in their mother's ten-year-old Buick. One of them resisted arrest and both were struck with batons by police. A crowd gathered, rumors of police "brutality" spread through the ghetto, and soon the most destructive race riot in recent American history broke out.

For several days there was a virtual insurrection in Watts. Thirty-four persons were killed, all but three of whom were black, and over two hundred buildings were completely gutted, with another four hundred severely damaged. Almost 3,000 blacks—whom Chief Parker accused of acting "like monkeys in a zoo"—were arrested. Yet though the blacks were routed, some of those who participated in the riots remember the events with a sort of nostalgia, like soldiers recalling a just war. Shay Drummond, then an eighteen-year-old Watts resident, said: "They came right down my street. It was like a new beginning. Blacks started saying they wanted their rights. You can't make us keep eating all this bad food. It was exciting—it was frightening. It was like the Fourth of July all week. I mean, you had a lot to fear but what else could they take from us? What did we have to lose? We woke up some of the upper-middle-class whites."

As Drummond suggests, white Californians were indeed awakened, although their initial reaction was to run to the gun stores, which experienced a 250 percent increase in business with the outbreak of the riot. Later, a blue-ribbon state commission, headed by Los Angeles banker John McCone, recommended a massive program of job creation by private industry to supply employment for the estimated 35,000 jobless adults in the immediate riot areas. The McCone Commission also called for "revolutionary" changes in attitudes between the races, and gratuitously suggested that blacks should "shoulder a full share of the responsibility for their own well-being."

Although little ultimately came out of the job-creating proposals of the McCone Commission, an increasing number of California blacks did begin assuming "full . . . responsibility" for their collective destiny. To the dismay of many whites, however, this new assertive attitude spawned not "Negro" Puritans but a new generation of black militant groups in California. But by far the most important of these was the Black Panther Party, which was founded at Oakland in 1966 by Huey Newton, the son of a Baptist minister.

Under Newton's charismatic leadership, the Panthers grew into a powerful force on the streets of Oakland, the most heavily black of all California's major cities. The party's "ten point program" called for a socialist-oriented change in the economic system and advocated the armed self-defense of black communities. Panther groups, including branches in Los Angeles, set up schools, defense units, and propaganda teams, designed both to aid urban black communities and to prepare for a possible revolutionary struggle in California and across the nation. "It is a fact that we will change the society," Newton proclaimed confidently. " . . . It will be up to the oppressors if this is going to be a peaceful change."

In May 1967, Newton shocked the state's white majority by leading a group of gun-toting, black-bereted militants to Sacramento as part of a lobbying effort against a gun control bill pending before the state legislature. While Newton's theatrical display actually hastened the bill's passage, the media impact was enormous, establishing the Panthers as a nationally recognized force in black politics. Three months later, Newton was arrested after a gun battle with Oakland police in which he was shot and one officer was killed. Charged with murder, Newton was ultimately found guilty of voluntary manslaughter in 1968 and sent to jail.

While Newton languished in prison, the Panthers—under the effective leadership of Bobby Seale, Eldridge Cleaver, and David Hilliard—expanded their following, establishing over thirty chapters in other cities, including Chicago and New York. Patronized by white liberals and radicals, the Panthers displayed a quintessentially Californian ability to manipulate the media. After his release from prison in 1970, Newton joined other Panther leaders in a series of alliances with prominent California politicians, including Berkeley Congressman Ronald Dellums and even Governor Brown, Jr. Top Panthers officials, such as Bobby Seale and Elaine Brown, publicly identified themselves with the Democratic Party, and in the 1970s launched impressive, albeit unsuccessful, campaigns for local office in Oakland.

Yet even as the Panthers were working to become accepted players in California politics, numerous reports of internal dissension, beatings, and underworld activities began to undermine this well-crafted new image. In 1974, Newton himself again was arrested and charged with the murder of an Oakland prostitute. Although he eventually was acquitted of the charge, the bad publicity resulting from the case and other incidents tarnished the party and particularly its leader. By the late 1970s, the Black Panther Party had all but disintegrated. Its demise was aided by an FBI campaign to destroy the party, but it was primarily a victim, according to some, of the same sort of inbred paranoia and megalomania that afflicted such groups as Jim Jones's People's Temple. Virtually every major party leader either broke with Newton or was unceremoniously dumped from the organization. Surveying the wreckage, one former Panther ally, Alameda County (Oakland) Supervisor John George, sadly commented in 1978: "I hear a very loud, a very eerie silence."

PERMANENT OUTSIDERS

The fading of such visible militant groups as the Black Panthers belies the increasing frustration and anger within California's black ghettos. Despite the well-publicized successes of prominent moderate black politicians, hostility toward the majority white population and establishment institutions has intensified among the state's minorities in recent years, according to a 1981 state-sponsored research project. The state report summarized:

> Frustration and helplessness lie on the surface of California's minority communities. Beneath the surface there lies growing anger.
> ... The good life, the capacity to buy a comfortable home in a good neighborhood, a new car and most of what people desire, is presented daily by all aspects of the media.

Most minority Californians, however, understand this everpresent definition of the good life as lying beyond their reach, frustrating, even taunting them.

Only too often this mounting frustration within the state's minority communities finds its expression in crime and violence. California's murder rate jumped 60 percent during the 1970s, a rate of increase almost twice that experienced in the Northeast. Much of this upsurge of violence was concentrated among California's blacks. Between 1973 and 1979, for instance, the rate of incarceration per capita among black Californians shot up 10 percent while dropping over 35 percent among the state's majority white population. In addition, police in such cities as Los Angeles and Oakland have noted an increasing tendency among assailants to commit violence outside their traditional neighborhoods and social circles. In Oakland, where nearly 90 percent of all murder suspects are black, murders by people apparently unacquainted with their victims accounted for some 48 percent of all homicides in 1976, compared to only 29 percent in New York. By 1980, killings by "strangers" had jumped to 63 percent of the total in Oakland.

Although blacks themselves remain by far the primary targets of these violent acts, a series of well-publicized killings in Los Angeles of whites by black youths during the last months of 1980 greatly intensified Anglo fears concerning restive ghetto residents. Within a matter of weeks, for instance, one black youth allegedly robbed and then murdered without provocation Sarai Ribicoff, a twenty-three-year-old newspaper reporter and niece of a former U.S. senator from Connecticut, and a group of three other young blacks, robbing a local Bob's Big Boy Restaurant, are said to have herded its employees and customers into a meat locker and began shooting them "execution style," police said, resulting in three deaths and the wounding of six other people.

Much of this rapid increase in crime can be traced to the widening gap between the state's prosperous white majority and the poverty-stricken ghetto residents. This imbalance has been exacerbated by the nature of California's high technology–based economic expansions during the 1970s, which benefited white-collar employees far more than manual laborers and government workers, the two occupation areas with high concentrations of blacks. In south-central Los Angeles, for instance, where more than 80 percent of the city's over 500,000 black people reside, only 39 percent of the male work force in 1977 was employed in white-collar positions, compared to a citywide average of over 52 percent. Meanwhile, the number of black undergraduates attending the University of California at Berkeley, located near the large black communities of Berkeley and Oakland, actually dropped over 20 percent between 1975 and 1979. Blacks constituted barely 3 percent of the total student body, and 2 percent of the engineering department. Largely lacking the educational skills needed by expanding high technology and communication industries, predominantly black areas like south-central Los Angeles enjoyed a rate of increase in median family income that was only one third that achieved by the city as a whole between 1970 and 1977. The total number of unemployed people in the area, meanwhile, increased at a 17 percent higher clip. By the end of a decade marked by a tremendous surge in economic growth throughout Southern California, objective economic conditions in the ghetto had actually declined to the point where over 32 percent of all south-central Los Angeles residents were living below poverty level, and 28 percent of the families were on public assistance. Commenting on these growing disparities, one frightened Los Angeles banker observed:

> This city is a boomtown compared to everywhere else, but you know the aerospace and electronics people are the ones who are booming and that just doesn't touch Watts.
>
> No, we don't have riots any more. We have a revolution going on instead, it's called crime. We just don't want to face it. Just spend a few minutes with those folks and you realize there's some real social dislocation going on.
>
> When I was a kid you saw the rich people in their houses on the hill, but today here these people have to watch these Rolls Royces every day.
>
> It must drive them crazy.

Further exacerbating the problems in California's black ghettos, some community leaders claim, has been the massive influx of Hispanic illegal aliens, rural Chicanos, and Asian immigrants into the state's major cities. These new arrivals are widely accused of successfully competing for many of the jobs once held by blacks—factory workers, construction laborers, and domestics—as well as slowly displacing blacks from their traditional inner city neighborhoods. Between 1970 and 1977, for instance, the Hispanic population in south-central Los Angeles jumped 28 percent. "The landlords are willing to accommodate in relocating blacks in favor of Hispanics," charges Linda Ferguson, a black legal aid attorney in the south-central area, who claims Hispanics are largely responsible for a doubling of the number of eviction cases in her office in 1980. "Black people are aware of this. It's easier to get mad at Mr. Gomez who took your apartment and your job at the service station than it is to blame the folks at the other end of town."

Unless much-needed development dollars are also brought into the ghetto from "the folks on the other end of town," some observers fear the state's black poor could end up as the nucleus of a permanent California "underclass"—a residue population with no place in the future of the free enterprise society. While individual blacks may continue to make great strides in politics and some professions, it is doubtful whether their successes will provide ample compensation for those left behind in the steamy slums of Oakland and Los Angeles. In the final analysis, observes longtime Los Angeles community leader Mary Henry, the presence of a Tom Bradley at City Hall is not what has prevented Watts from exploding once again. "Anything can happen," Henry predicted on a hot summer's day in 1980. "They cannot sit up there [at City Hall] and say there'll be no trouble." The only reason rioting hasn't already occurred, Henry said, is "self-preservation. It's not damned pride, it's just fear. Everyone knows in LA that if they start, they'll lose. . . . There's the mood to start another riot but we ain't got anything left to burn down."

"THE YELLOW PERIL"

Perhaps even more than the Mexicans and blacks, California's Asians have faced a long, bitter struggle to gain a foothold in the "free enterprise society." For most of the state's history, Asians have been the object of the Anglo-Californian's most deep-seated fears and prejudices. The result has been a shameful history of restrictions and persecutions, which terminated only recently. Yet today, California's Asians—who constitute over one third of all Asians in the nation—have emerged as the state's most economically successful growing ethnic minority, a testament to their skillful adaptation to the needs of California's economy and ruling elite.

Unlike the native Indians and Mexicans, who rightly considered California their home, or the blacks, who came to seek the freedom of a promised land, Asians at first crossed the seas to California with the intention of eventually returning to their native lands. The first wave of Asian immigrants came almost exclusively from the southeast coast of China during the middle of the nineteenth century. They left reluctantly and only after the chaos following the Taiping Rebellion had convulsed their poverty-stricken and still semi-feudal homeland. What the Chinese shared with other immigrants to the state at the time, however, was a strong desire to mine the gold that had been discovered in the streams flowing down from the Sierra Nevadas.

In 1850, there were only 1,000 Chinese in California; two years later, there were as many as 25,000, or one tenth of the state's total non-Indian population. Most came as virtual slaves who had sold their labor through subcontractors to large Chinese mining interests. With their creditor-employer network and numerous community associations, the Chinese retained a strong sense of separate identity. In densely populated neighborhoods or rural settlements, they continued to live according to their own customs which the white majority often viewed with derision. Hutchings's *Illustrated California Magazine* complained in 1857:

> Now permit us to introduce to your acquaintance celestial John and his lady, types and shadows of the empire of China—a large majority of whom are doubtless from the lower orders or coolies; exhibiting a cringing, abject sense of servility, to that degree that it appears a fixed character in all but a few of the more intelligent and wealthy . . . the Chinese have sent hither swarms of their females, a large part of whom are a depraved class; and though with complexions in some instances approaching to fair, their whole physiognomy but a slight removal from the African race.

Accused of being clannish, peculiar, and too willing to work at any wages under any conditions, the Chinese soon became an object of racial hatred to the American pioneers. As early as 1854 the Chinese were barred from giving testimony against whites, in order, as one court put it, "to throw around the citizen a protection for life and property, which could only be secured by removing him above the corrupting influence of the degraded classes." As the Chinese began arriving en masse at the gold fields, other restrictive legislation was enacted to discourage their working in the mines. In 1852 a foreign miners' license tax, originally $3.00 and later $4.00 a month, was levied, designed to stop the Chinese miners. To the chagrin of the Anglo majority, the Chinese readily paid this burdensome tax, which became a major prop for the state's finances, providing up to one fourth of all tax revenues in California until it was thrown out by a court in 1870. In 1858, the California legislature passed a law banning the immigration of Chinese and other Asiatics into California, but it too was later deemed unconstitutional by the courts.

Where state action had failed, local initiative often succeeded in driving the Chinese from the gold fields. As early as 1848, miners in Mariposa County had banned Asiatics from working the gold-rich streams of their district. In numerous gold-mining communities Chinese settlers were harassed, beaten, and robbed. Chinese miners found they could not trust any Anglo institution, even the Post Office, to refrain from stealing what they had earned through hard labor. Chinese miners and merchants set up their own "Chinese mail service" in order to secure the transshipment of their gold, goods, and even their bones, consigned to final resting places in China. David Cheng, an aged Chinese merchant in San Francisco, later remembered how his father carefully carried important parcels between the various Chinese settlements along the west coast. "My father was very cautious," Cheng recalled, "and never wore good clothing, or let on in any way that he was carrying thousands of dollars concealed among his rags."

Regulations and persecution gradually forced the Chinese from the gold fields. But they soon found employers who were more than willing to exploit their low-priced labor: the railroads. One of the first men to suggest using masses of "coolie" laborers to build private economic empires was Leland Stanford, one of the partners in the Central Pacific Railroad (later the Southern Pacific). Although in his 1862 inaugural address as governor Stanford had vehemently denounced Asian immigration, the critical shortage of the requisite cheap, reliable laborers to build the Southern Pacific's transcontinental rail link soon changed his mind. In 1865, Stanford and his desperate colleagues began an experiment using a crew of fifty "coolie" laborers on the rail line. It proved so successful that, at the height of Central Pacific's construction in the 1860s, over 10,000 Chinese, most of them freshly imported from China, were working at pitifully low wages for the railroad. The move to Chinese workers infuriated the emerging labor unions in San Francisco, but the "Octopus" kept their $30-a-month, largely docile Chinese employees on the job until the completion of the transcontinental link in 1869, when the railroad unceremoniously discharged virtually all of them.

Driven from the mines and railyards, the desperate Chinese, most too impoverished to return home, turned to agriculture. By 1884, Chinese laborers accounted for nearly one half of all farm workers in California, according to some estimates. As they had played an essential role in building the railroads, so too the Chinese made possible the transformation of California agriculture from a wheat-based economy to one centered on fruits and vegetables. "The availability of cheap Chinese labor gave the fruit growers hope," a rural California paper observed in 1893. "They extended their operations and the Chinese proved equal to all that had been expected of them. They became especially clever in the packing of fruit; in fact, the Chinese have become the only considerable body of people who understand how to pack fruit for eastern shipment."

While top businessmen were often impressed by the Chinese diligence and thrift, many Anglo-Americans, particularly those in the working and middle classes, considered the Chinese a major economic threat because they depressed wage rates and provided stiff competition for Anglo small businessmen. By 1870, nearly 50,000 Chinese resided in California; some prospered in such businesses as fishing and farming.

Chinese fishing villages, scattered from San Diego to Monterey, were exporting $1 million worth of abalone and millions more in dried shrimp annually by the end of the 1870s. Other Chinese became successful fruit and vegetable farmers, particularly in Southern California, and a handful succeeded through such illicit enterprises as opium dealing, prostitution, and their most common "vice," gambling.

Conflict between the competing "tongs" that controlled illegal activities in Los Angeles's growing Chinatown section set the stage for one of the worst outbreaks of anti-Oriental violence in California history. In October 1871, a Los Angeles policeman attempted to get in between two sets of "tong" street fighters armed with Colt .45s and Smith & Wesson six-shooters. When the unfortunate officer was shot as he pursued one of the Chinese, the long-simmering antipathy toward the Asians among the city's anglo majority exploded. A mob of 1,000, brandishing weapons, rushed to the city's Chinatown section. The San Francisco *Bulletin* later reported:

> Trembling, moaning, wounded Chinese were hauled from their hiding places; ropes quickly encircled their necks; they were dragged to the nearest improvised gallows. A large wagon close by had four victims hanging from its sides . . . three others dangled from an awning . . . five more were taken to the gateway and lynched. . . . Looting every nook, corner, chest, trunk, and drawer in Chinatown, the mob even robbed the victims it executed. . . .

In the end the mob murdered nineteen Chinese and stole some $40,000 in cash from their community. Although the outbreak was ultimately blamed on lower-class elements (150 men were indicted but only 6 served brief jail terms), there is still widespread suspicion that the city's police actually helped lead the riot.

By the 1870s, anti-Chinese sentiment in California had reached a fever pitch. Under the leadership of Denis Kearney, an Irish immigrant and former seaman, the newly formed Workingmen's Party (or "Sand-Lotters") became a major force in California politics. Formed in San Francisco in 1877, the party was built around two Kearney slogans: "a little judicious hanging" (for the rich gentlemen of Nob Hill) and "The Chinese must go!" Although they failed to capture a majority either of the state legislature or at the 1878 state constitutional convention, the vehemently anti-Chinese and politically radical faction exercised strong influence on both bodies.

Prodded by Kearney and other anti-Chinese forces, a statewide ballot was taken on the question of Chinese immigration in 1879; only 900 voted in favor of continuing the Chinese migration to California, while over 150,000 cast their votes against it. The Chinese, deprived of voting as well as other rights, were silent spectators as the legislature and convention, emboldened by "the people's voice," passed more discriminatory legislation. Laws were enacted to ban Chinese from fishing, owning businesses, or finding employment in the state's corporations. Even California's business leaders who had benefited immensely from the use of Chinese labor, became convinced that there should be a ban on Chinese immigration. "Indispensable as the Chinese are," one grower's report admitted, "they must go, as gradually as possible."

Under intense pressure from California, Congress in 1882 passed an act excluding Chinese from emigrating into the United States for 10 years. Although their battle had already been won, California Anglos continued to pass more discriminatory laws against the Chinese, including an 1891 measure designed to force the expulsion of Chinese already settled within the state, a law declared unconstitutional three years later. But the federal constitution was not powerful enough to prevent the virtual imprisonment of California's Chinese in small, overcrowded ghettos and segregated schools, the latter an indignity that was removed for blacks in 1890 but not for Chinese and other Asians until 1929. Not surprisingly, the number of Chinese in California began to decline sharply as the century ended, and then remained fairly low throughout the great growth years of California. Like the Mexicans before them, the Chinese became a small, insulated, powerless community in a state they had done so much to build.

NECESSARY ALIENS

The decline of the Chinese created major problems for California's agricultural enterprises. The loss of these hardworking and skilled laborers caused as many as a half million acres to go out of production in the last decades of the nineteenth century. Attempts to make up for the Chinese with existing Mexican and Anglo labor proved insufficient, so once again the agribusinessmen turned to the poverty-stricken peasants of Asia. In 1907, farm workers from India began to appear in the fields of California, the first wave of a "tide of turbans" that would see the employment of over 10,000 Indian farm laborers in the state before World War I. Bringing skills from their native land, these Indians helped establish California as a major cotton- and rice-producing area—two crops that would later become key components within the state's export-oriented agricultural economy.

Like the Chinese, however, the Indians aggravated American farm laborers by virtue of their hard work and their willingness to live under primitive conditions. In addition, the Indians also had a strong tendency toward entrepreneurship, and by 1918 owned or leased over

45,000 acres of California rice land. Despite their gains, the Indians fell victim to the Immigration Act of 1917, and further Indian entry into the United States was banned by Congress. Since most of the Indians in California were male, the immigration ban forced many of them to return home in search of wives. By the 1930s the Indian farm laborers, called "rag heads" by the Anglo Californians, had all but disappeared.

Even more tragic was the case of the Filipinos who started pouring into the fields of Central California in 1923. They appealed to the growers because as "American nationals"—their country had been annexed by the United States in 1899—they were not subject to immigration curbs. The Flipinos also made excellent workers and, at first, seemed satisfied with wages as low as 20¢ an hour. But as an agricultural depression began in the Midwest during the mid-1920s, the Filipinos soon found themselves competing with uprooted, equally desperate Anglo-Americans. As early as 1927, then California Senator Hiram Johnson was working to ban Filipinos from entering the country—a move that failed largely because their nation was still an American colony.

The problems of the Filipino laborers mounted in the troubled 1930s. Transient whites began violently forcing Filipinos out of the berry fields. Exacerbating their problems was the fact that out of 35,000 Filipinos in California during the early 1930s, it was estimated that only one in fourteen was female. Banned by anti-miscegenation laws from intermarriage, the Filipinos were often the targets of Anglo violence sparked by Filipino interaction with white women. Even worse, in the opinion of many growers, was the growing labor organization among the Filipino workers, designed to improve their wages and working conditions. In August 1934, some 3,000 Filipino laborers staged a strike in the lettuce fields of Salinas, only to be routed by an army of special deputies. The intrepid Filipinos were driven out of the area and their settlement burned down. No longer welcomed, they had become, in the words of one angry grower spokesman, "more disturbing and more dangerous than any other Asiatic group that has ever been brought into this state."

The passage by Congress of the Philippine Islands Independence Act in 1934 provided the pretext for the exclusion of Filipino laborers. The following year Congress even authorized funds for the free, one-way transportation of Filipinos living in the United States back to their native islands. Although some returned home, many Filipino laborers remained in California, a largely poor, isolated, and lonely community made up almost entirely of men. True to their reputation, many of these veteran Filipino farm workers, known in their community as *manongs,* continued to fight for better conditions in the fields and ultimately played an important, early role in the formation of Cesar Chavez's

United Farm Workers organization. Today several thousand *manongs* remain in California, still poor but deeply revered by a new, fast-growing community of Filipino Americans.

OPENING THE DOOR

It was the Japanese who constituted the largest, and ultimately most feared, replacements for the Chinese. Like the other new Asian immigrants, the Japanese had been invited into the state by the business interests, most particularly the agribusiness interests. The wave of Japanese emigration began in 1888 with the arrival of sixty Japanese laborers in the fruit orchards of Vacaville, outside the state capital of Sacramento. Soon other growers recognized that here was an ideal substitute for their lost Chinese workers. "The Japanese," a state document reported, "were regarded as very valuable immigrants and efforts were made to entice them to come."

By 1910 there were some 72,000 Japanese in the state, 30,000 of them working in the fields. Many arrived, like the Indian Hindus and Filipinos, without families, which was considered a great advantage by their hard-driving taskmasters. "The Japs and Chinks," said J. L. Nagle of the California Fruit Growers Exchange, "just drift—we don't have to look out for them. White laborers with families, if we could get them, would be liabilities."

This assessment of the Japanese quickly faded once the newcomers began to show some individual initiative and enterprise. Like the Filipinos, the Japanese began demanding better working conditions and higher wages. Even worse, in Anglo eyes, the Japanese proved themselves to be excellent entrepreneurs. Starting in 1901, they established a strong fishing community around Los Angeles's San Pedro Harbor, which grew into a village that included 500 fishermen, 150 merchants, and 450 dependents by 1940. Japanese farmers also became the dominant truck farmers of Southern California, by 1940 farming over 26,000 acres and controlling 90 percent of Los Angeles County's truck farming. Farther to the north, hardy Japanese entrepreneurs reclaimed thousands of acres of Sacramento delta "wasteland." Already in 1918 they had over 25,000 acres of rice in the state, mostly in the delta area. Others became major potato growers—such as "Potato King" George Shima—as well as important berry farmers. Although their remarkable success was mostly a simple product of hard work and thrift, many Anglos regarded the Japanese farmers with unconcealed loathing. As the Sacramento Valley's *Winter Express* complained in 1908:

The Florin district of Sacramento County affords one of the most convincing examples of the bad effects of the Japanese invasion.

Formerly it was inhabited wholly by white men and their families, who built up a large strawberry industry and planted numerous small vineyards.... But gradually the Japanese crept in, first as laborers then as renters, until nearly all the white growers of berries either rented to Asiatics or sold out entirely, in either case usually leaving the district. The result has been a great change for the worse. The Japanese have dominated the berry industry, having acquired and planted nearly all the acreage devoted to berries.

Their wretched, unsightly shacks are blots on the face of the country where there should be flower decked homes of American families. And so hundreds of alien unmarried Asiatics, caring nothing for the land or its future, have robbed the district of what was once its enviable attractiveness.

As early as 1905, the California State Legislature overwhelmingly passed a measure urging the federal government to exclude *all* Asian immigrants from entering the country. In that year the Japanese and Korean Exclusion League was formed in San Francisco and quickly attracted a membership of 80,000. Anti-Japanese rhetoric was also popular with the city's dominant politicians, including the corrupt Union Labor Party Mayor Eugene E. Schmitz and political "boss" Abe Ruef. Indicted by a grand jury for extortion of local businesses, these politicians found anti-Japanese rhetoric a fine way of diverting public attention from their own venality. Measures were passed by the city's school board to segregate Asian students, sparking strong protests from the increasingly powerful Japanese government. San Francisco officials agreed to reduce their attacks on the Japanese only after President Theodore Roosevelt promised to strictly limit Japanese immigration.

But these restrictions could not stop the Japanese already in the state from expanding their already significant holdings. To combat this "menace," the Alien Land Act was passed in 1913 to bar the Japanese from owning property. The measure was only partially successful as, particularly in Southern California, methods were found by some Japanese to hold onto their generally small farms. But the Japanese were forced increasingly into the state's towns and cities, where they came into conflict with the white merchants, who found that these immigrants could be as effective in the marketplace as they were on the land. As the Asiatic Exclusion League reported in 1908:

Merchants [are] getting tired of Japanese: Men of standing in the community who employ Japanese and have no race prejudice apparently, and who are distinctly opposed to labor unions, largely on account of the opposition of the latter to Orientals, declare the Japanese dishonest and inferior in this regard to the Chinese. When the

Japanese arrived in the Pajaro Valley they were welcomed by merchants; today the merchants bitterly complain that the Japs have become their very close competitors.

Although Roosevelt's restrictions on immigration significantly slowed the growth of the state's Japanese community, the hotheaded racists dominating California political life demanded additional, even more extreme measures. As Japan grew more powerful and its imperial visions began to conflict with those of the United States, the anti-Oriental forces in California promoted the idea that the local resident "Sons of the Mikado" were nothing more than advance agents for the ultimate takeover of California by Japan. As A. E. Sbarboro, president of San Francisco's Italian American Bank, warned in 1908: "I do verily believe that if the Japanese should be permitted to come to this country in unlimited numbers, they would in a few years, by their thrift, enterprise and frugality of living, transform California into a Japanese colony."

REMEMBER PEARL HARBOR

These deep-seated suspicions remained imbedded in the Anglo-Californian consciousness even after Congress passed the 1924 Immigration Act, which in effect ended Japanese immigration into the country. When the Japanese bombed Pearl Harbor, Hawaii, on December 7, 1941, the fruits of six decades of racist propaganda were harvested with shameless gusto. Almost immediately after the outbreak of war, leading California politicians including "liberal" Governor Culbert Olson, Attorney General Earl Warren, and Los Angeles Mayor Fletcher Bowron demanded immediate action against the Japanese from a reluctant General John L. DeWitt, head of the U.S. Western Defense Command. DeWitt soon caved in under intense political pressure and reported to Washington that the Japanese should be considered an "enemy race." In March, 1942, Roosevelt ordered their internment, and the evacuation began of some 112,000 Japanese on the west coast, 93,000 of whom were Californians and a majority Nisei, or American-born U.S. citizens.

Although widely accused of pro-Japanese Empire sentiments, most Japanese Americans were shocked and angered over the attack on their adopted land. "Couldn't it be possible," speculated one middle-aged Los Angeles Japanese upon hearing the news, "that Germans might have, in some manner, got hold of Japanese planes and carried out the bombing?" Despite their avowed loyalty to the U.S. the Japanese internees soon began arriving at Manzanar, California, in the Owens Valley, and nine other "relocation" centers primarily in the western United States. Although most accepted their condition with stoicism, many Japanese Americans, then as well as now, considered mass deportation a gross betrayal. As one internee, S. J. Oki, reported:

> Objectively, and on the whole, life in a relocation center is not unbearable. There are dust-storms and mud. Housing is inadequate with families of six living in single rooms in many cases. Food is below the standard set for prisoners of war. In some of the camps hospitals are at times understaffed and supplies meager, as in many ordinary communities....
> What is not so bearable lies much deeper than the physical make-up of a center.... [The prisoner's] faces look bewildered as they stare at the barbed wire fences and sentry towers that surround the camp. Their eyes ask: Why? Why? What is all this?

Despite the indignities of the camps, Japanese Americans more than adequately proved their patriotism during the war. Thousands of Japanese recruited from the "relocation" camps volunteered for army service. One all-Nisei unit, the 442nd Regimental Combat Team, suffered heavy losses in the 1943 invasion of Italy and emerged from the war as the most decorated regiment in the history of the U.S. Army.

Even the official history, *The United States Army in World War II*, admits there was "little support" for the supposed "military necessity" of the mass evacuation of Japanese on the west coast. After all, Japanese in Hawaii were largely left alone during the war because they provided the necessary labor and skills for the war effort as well as contributing men to the Hawaiian National Guard units defending the islands. Perhaps the real reason for the brutal treatment of the Japanese in California lies in the long history of conflict, often economic, between that community and the Anglo majority. Indeed, the wartime relocation forced many Japanese to sell their hard-earned homes, farms, and businesses at greatly reduced prices to willing Anglo buyers. After the war, the Japanese prisoners filed $400 million in claims concerning those losses and some 44,000 received a total of $38 million in settlements from the federal government. But, for the most part, the war all but wiped out Japanese-owned business in California, long the goal of many Anglos. "We're charged with wanting to get rid of the Japs for selfish reasons," a spokesman for Salinas Valley growers once admitted to a reporter. "We might as well be honest. We do. It's a question of whether the white man lives on the Pacific Coast or the brown man."

THE RISE OF THE EAST

Despite some Anglos' hopes to the contrary, World War II failed to stop the progress of the Japanese and other Asians on the west coast. Most

Japanese returned to their communities and started, like their racial brethren across the Pacific, a spectacularly successful process of rebuilding. By 1970, Japanese Americans averaged over 12.5 years of education (higher than the average among Anglos). By the 1970s, Japanese and Japanese-Americans accounted for some 4 percent of all undergraduates at the University of California at Berkeley, a rate three times greater than their percentage of the state's population. Accommodating themselves to the commercial and scientific needs of a high technology economy in states like California, the Japanese-American population achieved a median family income 30 percent above the national average, according to the 1970 census. In addition, for the first time, Japanese-American politicians began to achieve high office in the state. By 1980, California's Japanese-Americans could boast of having a U.S. senator, two U.S. congressmen, and two members of the State Assembly, as well as scores of local officeholders and government officials.

The remarkable success of the more than 260,000 Japanese people in California represents but one part of the growing Asian influence in the state over the last four decades. In 1943, Congress repealed the 1882 Chinese Exclusion Act in order to placate the nation's wartime ally and, in the words of President Roosevelt, "correct a historic mistake and silence the distorted Japanese propaganda." Under new regulations a small number of Chinese, perhaps as many as 10,000, were able to enter the country over the next two decades. In 1952 another piece of discriminatory legislation, California's thirty-nine-year-old Alien Land Act, was declared unconstitutional, while in the same year Congress passed a measure removing race as a reason for denying citizenship to naturalized aliens. But even these developments were overshadowed by the historic 1965 Congressional Act barring the national origins quota system that had sharply limited Asian immigration in the past.

While relatively few Japanese chose to emigrate, perhaps due to the memory of the relocation camps and to the prosperous condition of their own country, hundreds of thousands of Asians from less wealthy countries flooded into California during the 1970s. Drawing from the Pacific Rim lands of the Philippines, Hong Kong, Korea, Vietnam, and Thailand, California's Asian population between 1970 and 1980 soared 140 percent, to over 1.2 million, increasing to 5.3 percent of the state's total population. Attracted by the presence of other Asians and the state's fast-growing economy, this expanding community has only just begun to make its influence felt.

Within California's established Asian communities, however, the impact of this massive immigration has already been profound. The loosening of immigration restrictions after 1965, for instance, has brought about a rapid expansion of the state's Chinese population, which had been decreasing as a percentage of the state's population since the 1880s. Between 1970 and 1980, according to census data, California's Chinese population rose 90 percent, to over 320,000. Like their predecessors, these new immigrants have tended to crowd into the state's teeming Chinatowns, many of them working at menial jobs in restaurants and sweatshops.

THE BEHAVIORAL SINK

While many second-generation Chinese have managed to leave the Chinatowns and move into such middle-class enclaves as Berkeley, San Francisco's Richmond District, and suburban Monterey Park in Southern California, grinding poverty continues to afflict the old-time residents and the thousands of new immigrants who are left behind in the crumbling downtown neighborhoods. In San Francisco's Chinatown, where 40,000 residents are packed into an eighteen block-core area, nearly 40 percent of the people are estimated to be living in poverty. Seventy percent of Chinatown's housing is substandard, 82 percent of all families live in three or fewer rooms, the tuberculosis rate is the nation's highest, the suicide rate three times the national average.

Under such conditions, it is not surprising that over the last fifteen years San Francisco's Chinatown has been afflicted by a dramatic upsurge in crime. At the center of these problems have been the children of those non-English-speaking immigrants who work long hours in "bundle shops" and restaurants in Chinatown's many alleyways. These youngsters have formed tough new gangs, such as the "Joe Boys," which have engaged in bitter conflict with each other and with the long-established Chinatown tongs. The "Joe Boys" leader, Joe Fong, came to San Francisco from the slums of Macao in 1963 and began his criminal career at age eleven. During the late 1960s and early 1970s, Fong became the charismatic leader for hundreds of Chinese-born youths faced with a largely hostile local establishment. "The ABCs [American-born Chinese] called us FOBs—Fresh off the Boat—or China Bugs," Fong later recalled. "Even the American-born Chinese referred to us as 'Chinese'—as though they were not."

On Labor Day in September 1977 the growing, extremely complex internecine conflicts within Chinatown exploded into the "Golden Dragon Massacre" in which a gangland-style assassination squad ended up killing five innocent people and wounding eleven at a Chinatown restaurant. A dozen members of the "Joe Fong Gang" were ultimately convicted for crimes related to the incident, which attracted nationwide publicity. Since the Golden Dragon murders the Chinese youth gangs have avoided such brazen violence, while continuing to work with adult criminal organizations on more profitable activities like extortion, drug smuggling, and gambling. Some have joined up with sophisticated Chinese-led Pacific Rim international organized crime groups while also branching out to other parts of the U.S. The Wa Ching, for example, boasts over one hundred members in Los Angeles's Chinatown alone and has other branches in San Francisco, Seattle, and New York, according to Sergeant Shiro Tomita, an Asian crime expert for the Los Angeles Police Department. Tomita believes that the root of the growing Chinese gang problem lies in the difficulty of integrating so large an influx of new immigrants, many entering the state illegally and without marketable job skills, into Chinese-American society and the California economy:

> We get these youngsters from Hong Kong coming in illegally. They can't get a job, so all they know is how to extort from their own. They are attracted into worldwide organizations [like Wa Ching]. . . .
> They recruit these kids very young, right off the boat. They need to be accepted by somebody. They leave Hong Kong to get out of poverty and go to an Anglo high school where the other kids call them "Chink." It's degrading. They don't join just to commit crimes but because no one else will associate with them. It gives them a turf to defend.

A similar pattern of poverty, gang formation, and organized crime infiltration has also plagued California's large Filipino community. During the 1970s, tens of thousands of Filipinos fled the stagnant economy and repressive political climate of their native islands and more than doubled the state's Filipino population from 138,000 in 1970 to as many as 350,000 ten years later. A great many of these new immigrants were professionals—notably doctors, nurses, accountants, and businessmen—who, like the *manongs* before them, have shown strong organizational skills and achieved considerable political clout, particularly with the administration of Governor Jerry Brown.

But for thousands of other Filipinos, including farm workers and illegal aliens, California has yet to prove itself a promised land. Of all major Asian groups, Filipinos, according to 1970 census figures, were the only ones with a median income below the national average. Like their young Chinese counterparts, some Filipino youths in the rundown sections of San Francisco and Los Angeles have formed tough street gangs, including the Santanas and Temple Street Gangs of Los Angeles and the Exotics, Kearny Boys, the FM (Filipino Mafia) Boys, and Frisco Boys in the San Francisco area. These organizations, which may have a few dozen members or as many as three hundred, engage in activities ranging from street warfare to petty larceny, car theft, muggings, and occasional murders, according to local police, federal immigration, and drug enforcement authorities.

In addition, adult organized crime groups from the Philippines have established themselves inside the state's Asian community. One group was discovered to have operated a multi-million-dollar illegal car-export ring out of San Francisco. By the late 1970s, over fifty Filipinos were convicted for their part in the scam and other related crimes. A young associate of "The Syndicate," another Filipino organized crime group, claimed that his and other Pacific Rim–based organizations were manufacturing false passports and sending scores of thieves into several major Western cities. Over a beer, this mild-mannered father of five explained: "Let's put it this way. If you have a big house there's more for me to steal than if there's a small house. The U.S. is a much bigger house than the Philippines. It's just easier for us here. You protect everyone, the innocent, the guilty, the same. Our people laugh at it."

Also troubling to law enforcement officials in California, however, has been the rise of Thailand-based drug-smuggling rings in California. Although the Thais number only around 25,000 to 30,000 statewide, most of them concentrated in the faded stucco neighborhoods of Hollywood, members of this community are widely accused by law enforcement of being the source of much of the state's heroin supply. A small number of Thai merchants in the state—so federal officials claim—have strong ties to opium-producing regions of Southeast Asia's "Golden Triangle," which has emerged as one of the West's largest sources of heroin since the mid-1970s. "The Thai community here is our biggest problem," maintains Jerry Jenson, western regional director for the federal Drug Enforcement Administration. "They are trying to get together with American organized crime. If they do, it would be the biggest thing since the French Connection."

While admitting great "shame" over the arrests of several leading Thais in the West on drug-smuggling charges, Charman Malisunam, director of the Los Angeles–based Thai trade center, insists that "the majority of our people hate this kind of thing." Other Asian community leaders point out that gang membership and organized crime activity has long been part of the process of assimilation for many ethnic groups—including Irish, Jews, Greeks, Yugoslavs, and Italians—in many big Eastern cities. Today, in the era of large-scale Pacific Rim migration, a similar pattern is being carried out in the urban centers along the west coast.

One Asian group currently undergoing this process is the Korean community, whose population has mushroomed over 550 percent in California since 1970 to an estimated 103,000 people. Many Koreans, often lacking adequate English-language skills, have clustered since the early 1970s in the "Koreatown" section of Los Angeles, an area long inhabited by Hispanics and blacks. In the schools, Korean youngsters have followed the age-old American pattern of forming gangs to protect their "turf" from their racial rivals. Pointing to the formation of such new groups as the "A-Bs" and the "Korean Killers," Jane Kim, director of the Korean Youth Center in Los Angeles, observed:

> Our kids have had to organize to defend themselves from the blacks and Mexicans. They have to show the other groups they are *macho*.... The Korean community tends to be pretty silent about this. Asians have this sterotype that we are quiet, that there is no problem. But look inside and you will see a lot of trouble. The kids are taking drugs and selling them. This is happening more than ever before.

These and other problems among Asian youth, many community leaders believe, are the result of thousands of Asian families undergoing severe social dislocation, economic hardship, and culture shock as American influences severely challenge their traditional values. Most Asians, according to Dr. Mai Van Tran, a leading Los Angeles Vietnamese Catholic scholar and community leader, retain strongly Confucian beliefs concerning the primacy of the family and the community, with a special reverence for the role of the educated "mandarin" in society. These ideals, long embedded in the cultures of such countries as Korea, Thailand, and Vietnam, come under severe strain when confronted by the materialist and often philistine "free enterprise society" of California. Caught between two value systems, Asian children sometimes rebel against their parents. "They [the parents] don't want their children Americanized because they want to hold onto traditional values," Dr. Tran maintains. "But in school the kids learn American ways of acting that are very casual. The parents don't understand—they think the kids have picked up bad manners. And the kids think their parents are primitive, and that's when you have juvenile delinquency."

Exacerbating the generational conflicts within California's 165,000-strong Southeast Asian refugee population (three times larger than in any other state), is the presence of large numbers of single, male ex-servicemen from the defeated anti-Communist armies in Indochina. In both Los Angeles and Orange County, these ex-soldiers have formed gangs with such martial-sounding names as "The Pink Knights" and "The Frogmen." While these groups have been accused by law enforcement officials of extorting money from Vietnamese-owned businesses, they have become non-traditional role models to a small minority of Vietnamese youth. "Most of the refugee kids, they get really hurt because the American parents tell their kids to stay away from them, like they might catch diseases," explained Hieu Nguyen, a former Vietnamese Marine Corps lieutenant who is now working as a computer programmer in Southern California. "They feel hurt and some go to gangs. . . . It's terrible for us, but it's something we in the Vietnamese community have to solve."

CONFUCIUS IN SILICON VALLEY

Although the traditional Confucian ideals held by many Asian newcomers have led to deep generational and cultural rifts within their communities, many of these same beliefs are also helping Asians succeed within California's free enterprise society. Nowhere is this more important than in their emphasis on training and education, which reflects a continuing respect for "mandarin" ideals of the past. Adjusting to the needs of California's high technology economy, many Asians have concentrated their efforts on learning electronics and other science-related skills. By 1979, over 1,500 Indochinese refugees had been trained for and secured skilled and semi-skilled positions in the firms in Silicon Valley. They made up 60 percent of the enrollees at two large state-sponsored electronics training programs. "I don't want to see my people get into welfare," explained Phi Thai, a twenty-six-year-old volunteer electronics instructor and an engineer at Sunnyvale's Advanced Microdevices. "The only way I know how to help them is to teach them."

Although somewhat less than 50,000 of California's Indochinese refugees still required some income assistance by 1980, their children and those of other Asian newcomers have made remarkable strides within the state's educational system. Some 39 percent of all graduating Asian high school seniors in 1978 were academically qualified for places within the nine-campus University of California system, more than twice the rate for Anglos and over seven times that of other minority groups. Asians by 1979 accounted for over 18 percent of all undergraduates at the Berkeley campus, well over three times their percentage of the population. While the number of Chinese American undergraduates at Berkeley increased 12 percent between 1975 and 1979, the most radical growth occurred among Filipino students, whose number expanded over 50 percent, and Koreans, whose representation jumped over three times during the four-year period. "I think most Asians who have come here come for their children, so they can get an education and make it—over ninety percent of them," one Korean immigrant businessman observed. "Our kids work so hard, they become weak. Maybe we get carried away with this."

Asians, who of late have found more acceptance and less discrimination from the Anglo establishment than other minorities, have also spawned a growing population of entrepreneurs. Like the Japanese-American and early Chinese merchants before them, many newly arriving Asians have been able to start new businesses, often small shops and trading companies catering to fellow immigrants, including Mexican illegal aliens. In fact, Asian families owned or managed nearly one fifth of all businesses in the predominantly Hispanic East Los Angeles area, according to a 1976 study by the nonprofit East Los Angeles Community Union. "They take over mom-and-pop stores in areas where the former owners gave up," K. W. Lee, editor of the *Koreatown* newspaper in Los Angeles, says. "They provide private money orders for illegals to send home without any trace. They give better service than the previous owners. And Korean mom-and-pop stores who give service are never robbed. The Koreans give service, and the Latinos need service. It's a symbiotic relationship."

By 1977, Asians had established themselves as the largest minority business community in California. Despite their smaller numbers, Asians in the San Francisco-Oakland area in 1977 owned nearly two times as many businesses as blacks, with total receipts almost three times higher. In the Los Angeles area, where their numbers are dwarfed by far larger, long-established black and Chicano communities, Asians still possessed more enterprises than either group, with gross receipts 138 percent above those of Hispanic-owned business and more than twice the receipts of black entrepreneurs. With their increasing movement into the small business class, Asians have naturally experienced a marked improvement in their economic status. By 1977 the median family income of Los Angeles's Asian community had risen to $15,250, over 50 percent above that of other minorities and only $2,500 below that of the Anglo majority.

In the familiar California pattern, many of these small-scale Asian capitalists have been moving toward entry into the state's entrepreneurial elite. One enterprising Chinese-Cambodian refugee, Ngoy Bun Tek, started out as a manager trainee at a Huntington Beach, Orange County, donut shop in 1975; four years later, through hard work and perseverance, he had become a medium-scale entrepreneur with some eight donut outlets. At the same time California's Asians, particularly those with access to Hong Kong and other Pacific Rim capital sources, are becoming major landowners and developers. By 1980, for instance, Korean capitalists had purchased over two hundred parcels worth some $20 million in the Koreatown section of Los Angeles, many of them already developed as offices and shops. Similarly, Chinese have bought an estimated one third of the land and as much as 15 percent of all businesses in Monterey Park, a fast-growing and, increasingly, Asian-dominated Los Angeles suburb.

The rise of California's Asian entrepreneurs represents a unique development in the state's history—the first time that racial outsiders are being allowed to successfully integrate into the framework of the free enterprise society. Already, according to Korean-born entrepreneur Paul Kim, many Asian entrepreneurs look toward California as their ultimate land of opportunity, a place where the newly emergent industrial societies of the Pacific Rim and modern American capitalism can be fused. A Korean War refugee from Pyongyang, North Korea, Kim migrated to the United States in 1960 in order to study electromagnetics at the University of California at Santa Barbara. After working for several large American firms outside the state, Kim returned to California and in 1975 started U.S. Magnetics with several Korean-American investors. By 1980, his firm had grown from $100,000 annual sales and ten employees to over $3 million and over one hundred workers, almost all of them Korean immigrants.

Although he feels he could have done well on his own in another part of the country, only in California, Kim explained, could he remain part of a Korean community and still fully achieve his entrepreneurial dreams. Sitting over a traditional Korean lunch near his plant in Gardena, a heavily Asian industrial suburb near the port of Los Angeles, Kim explained:

> Here the communication for me is just much better. I can get Korean workers here. They work hard and are very accurate. Here we have our success and our way of doing things. The technology I know can only be used in the United States and we have the best computer people in California. But it's more than that. California is much easier, better for the emigrant. People in Oklahoma, I can't understand. People in California are used to the outsider. California is different from the rest of America. To me, it's like another country.

VIII.
The Pacific Rim

Eight decades ago, the port of Los Angeles was little more than a handful of wooden piers stuck precariously into the mudflats of San Pedro Harbor. With world economic and political power centered in the mature democracies of western Europe, it was New York that reigned virtually unchallenged as the bustling center of America's trade activities. Only Chicago, transfer point for the nation's agricultural production in the Middle West, could fancy itself as a serious competitor to legendary Gotham.

But the port of Los Angeles, long scoffed at as a poor cousin among the great natural harbors of the continent, today is one of the nation's fastest-growing centers of international trade. Relentlessly dredged over the years, the port is a gateway to the booming trade lanes and expanding economies of the Far East. Los Angeles, along with the adjacent port of Long Beach, could surpass New York as the nation's leading harbor by the beginning of the twenty-first century, according to the Army Corps of Engineers. As the Japanese and Taiwanese tankers and freighters steam into the clogged, smoggy harbor, Robert Kleist, director of planning for the port, senses the beginning of a new era, when national and international commerce is dominated by Los Angeles and California, Japan and the emergent powers of the Pacific:

We know damn well New York's declining as a shipping center and in every other way. We know we are becoming the greatest local market. It is quite realistic that we will be the largest city, the largest port. We can work on it quietly, building so we can handle it.

We're going to go about our business and not listen to those big mouths back east. They're frightened of us. They've had it their way for one hundred and fifty years and now it's changing. We're taking over as the major center. We're not tinseltown any more. We are the key place, located on the center of the coming world economy, which is on the Pacific Rim. We're entering, we're in, the era of the Pacific Rim.

Kleist's brash assertions reflect the growing confidence of California's business leaders that they will hold the pivotal position within the fast-changing international marketplace. Between 1970 and 1977, California's foreign trade expanded 600 percent, and by 1980 accounted for 15 percent of its gross state product and 1 million jobs—10 percent of total state employment. Perhaps even more impressive, the state's entrepreneurs, in the face of a persistent national trade deficit, have been able to boost exports far faster than imports. In 1980, for instance, exports from Los Angeles, now the nation's third-largest commercial port, rose 42 percent over the previous year, almost twice the rate of import growth. Similar economic successes were registered in the San Francisco Bay Area 400 miles to the north, where the nation's eighth-largest customs district enjoyed a remarkable $918 million trade surplus in the first half of 1980. Overall, California in 1980 was able to reduce its trade deficit by over 30 percent, placing the state's accounts close to balance.

THE CRUCIAL FACTOR

The drastic difference between the Golden State and the rest of the nation in the international trading market stems largely from California's unique role within the interconnected economic system of the Pacific Rim, the theater for two thirds of all California's overseas business. While the once mighty steel and auto industries back east have fallen prey to relentless Japanese, as well as other Asian competitors, California's entrepreneurs have concentrated their efforts on those key sectors—electronics, aerospace, and agriculture—where American industry retains an unmistakable superiority. Despite attempts by Asian and European firms to compete with them, California's aerospace industries, for instance, doubled their exports of nonmilitary aerospace products in one year to over $1.5 billion in the first half of 1980, accounting for a full quarter of the nation's civilian aerospace shipments. Similarly, California's farming entrepreneurs, with only 3 percent of the nation's acreage, captured 12 percent of all U.S. farm exports in 1979—with some 75 percent of their overseas shipments destined for the nations of the Pacific Rim.

Like Los Angeles's feisty Robert Kleist, many top state business leaders attribute California's overall strong trade position to its fortuitous geographic location and its increasingly symbiotic relationship with the world's ascendant economic powers. C. J. Medbury, chairman of the board of the Bank of America, observed in 1979:

> ... the state serves as a vital trade link between two of the world's fastest growing regions—Asia and the western United States. Its economy is aided by strong population growth, as many new immigrants (including those from Southeast Asia and Mexico) come here. It also stands adjacent to the soon-to-be-oil-rich Mexican economy. Meanwhile, demand for the state's important agricultural, electronic and aerospace products appears resistant to recessionary pressures.

Essential to the growth of California's economy and international trade has been the parallel development on the other side of the Pacific of the industrial economies of Japan and other Asian nations. While the East's traditional European trading partners staggered in the 1970s under the impact of flagging productivity, domestic political strife, inflation, and OPEC oil price increases, the economies of the nations bordering the Pacific experienced a period of unprecedented prosperity and, following the conclusion of the Vietnam War, relative political stability.

At the center of this new Pacific order stands Japan, today the world's third-largest industrial power. With a work force and industrial plant considered by many the most productive in the world, Japan by 1980 led the world in the production of consumer electronics, photographic equipment, merchant ships, and automobiles. From 1965 to 1975, Japan's share of world exports of photographic and sound equipment increased from 20 to 31 percent; in iron and steel, the Japanese share of world exports jumped from 17 to 26 percent; Japan's slice of the growing office machine and computer market rose from just 2 percent to nearly nine percent of exports; and, perhaps most dramatically, Japanese manufacturers during this period tripled their share of the international car and other vehicle trade, from 5 to over 15 percent. Since 1975, Japan's share of the U.S. automobile market alone jumped from 800,000 vehicles to over 1.9 million, leading to loud cries of protest from the U.S. auto industry, which was saddled with 200,000 unemployed workers and $7 billion in losses during 1980. Throughout the 1970s, despite a 99 percent dependence on foreign oil, Japan regularly turned in annual balance of payment surpluses that often topped $10 billion.

During the past ten years Japan and the emerging industrial complex of the Asian Pacific Rim—including Korea, Taiwan, and Hong Kong—vastly outperformed not only the aging economic machine of the Eastern United States but the economies of virtually every major country within the once dominant European/Atlantic community.

From 1970 to 1977, Japan's GNP grew at a real annual rate of 3.6 percent, Taiwan's at 5.5 percent, Hong Kong's at 5.8 percent, and South Korea's at 7.6 percent—compared to 3.1 percent in France, 2.2 percent in West Germany, 2.0 percent in Italy, and only 1.6 percent for Great Britain during the same period. In 1978, according to estimates by the Bank of America, the combined gross national products of Asian nations increased at nearly twice the rate experienced in western Europe. At the decade's end, the economy of the Pacific Rim countries had soared to $1.3 trillion, a staggering fourfold increase in only ten years.

The dramatic progress in these Asian industrial countries as well as the Western United States also helped spur increased growth among less developed, more resource-oriented economies in the Pacific Rim area. Indonesia, for instance, the only Asian member of OPEC, enjoyed a 5.7 percent annual GNP growth during the 1970–77 period, largely the result of the shipment of raw materials to Japan, other Asian industrial countries, and the Western United States. Indonesia, by 1977 the world's twelfth-largest oil producer, has already secured its position as California's principal source of imported oil and, though a controversial Brown administration–backed plan for a liquefied natural gas contract, is expected to supply up to one fifth of the state's gas requirements in the near future. Indonesia also possesses vast deposits of such key resources as tin, bauxite, copper, and nickel, as well as large supplies of timber and rubber. Its neighbor to the north, Malaysia, leads the world in tin and natural rubber production, and experienced an average annual growth rate of nearly 5 percent a year in the 1970s. Another key beneficiary of Pacific Rim industrial expansion has been Australia, a leading agricultural exporter which is also the world's top producer of alumina and possesses sizable reserves of such key minerals as coal and uranium. Sparked partly by growing demands from its Pacific Rim neighbors, Australia's economy was expected to grow 2.5 percent in 1980.

While many of the Pacific Rim economies already provide large markets for California's high technology and agricultural products, perhaps the most promising long-term customer, China, has barely been tapped. Although total U.S. trade with China in 1979 amounted to only $2.3 billion, businessmen, particularly on the west coast, are looking toward the world's most populous nation as a potential raw material supplier and consumer market on a grand scale. Already the Los Angeles–based Union Oil Company has agreed to sell major oil-refining process technology to the Chinese Communists and, along with three other companies, is negotiating to share in the development of Chinese petroleum reserves—estimated at some 20 billion barrels. Equally important to California will be the sale of food and fiber to the world's most populous country, yet another huge potential market for the state's agribusinessmen.

LOOKING SOUTH

Across the Pacific, on California's southern border, lies the only country that could rival the People's Republic as a future trading partner and source of raw materials: Mexico. Mexican oil reserves, by the most conservative estimates, are 20 billion barrels, placing the country within the top five potential petroleum-producing nations. (Other analyses claim Mexico may possess up to 200 billion barrels, making it the rival of Saudi Arabia as the world's most oil-rich country.) By 1980, Mexican oil exports topped 1 million barrels a day (approximately half of it to the U.S.), and U.S. intelligence estimates project that exports may increase to over 5 million barrels daily by the end of the 1980s. Although still decidedly an impoverished country by American standards, Mexico already ranks as the sixteenth-largest economy in the world, with an annual growth rate of 9 percent in 1979. Rich in uranium, iron, and copper, Mexico in recent years has been a focus of attention for California's business leaders, who are anxious to develop the nation's natural resources and tap its burgeoning, poorly utilized labor force.

Some California business leaders, such as Security Pacific National Bank Chairman Richard J. Flamson III, believe that resource-rich nations like Mexico will play an increasingly important role in the developing Pacific Rim economy. In a speech delivered to the American Chamber of Commerce at Mexico City in March 1981, Flamson declared:

> In the coming decade, external energy and resource dependency will be vital to the outlook for the industrial and other economies of the [Pacific] Rim. . . . This situation is bound to bring increased prosperity to such countries as Indonesia, Malaysia, Australia, China and, of course, Mexico. Rather than being just resource exporters as they would have been in the past, these countries will become economic powers in their own right. . . . In my mind Mexico is becoming an important new Rim force as we move into the 1980s.

Convinced that world trade is already "centered" on the Pacific Rim, Flamson, like other California business and political leaders, sees the state's economic future inextricably linked to the fate of Japan, China, Mexico, and other "Rim" nations. The California banker even accepts the notion that this growing Pacific economic region should have its prime "financial focal point" in Tokyo, along with the "development of international banking facilities" in such other key Rim cities as San Francisco, Los Angeles, and, perhaps, Mexico City. This Pacific-fixated view of the future was recently validated by the "Interfuture" report issued in 1979 by the Organization for Economic Cooperation and Development, which predicted the demise of America's position as the world's number one economic superpower by the end of this century in favor of a new Pacific Rim alignment dominated by Japan. B. K. Mac-Laury, president of the Brookings Institution based in Washington, D.C., comments:

> ... most observers expect Japan, in particular, to continue to outperform Europe and North America in productivity and growth rates of output. Indeed, in its high growth scenario, the OECD projects that Japanese output could grow half again as fast (7.6 percent) as the German rate (4.9 percent) between 1975 and 1990, and more than double the U.S. rate (3.6 percent). Even if the advantage for Japan were considerably less than these projections imply, it seems reasonable to assume a continuing shift in relative economic power toward Japan, and toward the Pacific Basin more generally.

Implicit in such projections is the anticipated gradual decline of many of the world's traditional economic centers—from London and Paris to New York and Boston. If they accept the projections, Americans have good reason to worry about this developing Pacific Rim ascendancy, with its bleak prospects for the residents of the Atlantic community—closed factories, forgotten cities, and the social turbulence that accompanies economic decline. But in California, due to its unique historical, cultural, and economic links to Asia, this future is frequently seen as the best of all possible brave new worlds. As Richard King, director of the California Office of International Trade, puts it:

> That's our market. We sit on the Pacific Rim. ... It's our feeling we can do better if we learn to get through the Japanese distribution system for our products. There's a hell of a lot of potential for more sales of our products in Japan.
> The Pacific Basin wants California agriculture. They love our oranges and our vegetables. We feel we can deal with them, state to nation. We're the third largest nation on the Pacific Rim, so let's start acting like a nation. We have more to offer them. They should consider us a separate national market. We don't want to rely on the Eastern establishment, they're more Europe-oriented. We have to fight our own economic battles.
> Our future is with the Pacific Basin. Sixty percent of humanity lives there, over forty percent of all world trade. We're right in the middle of it. If the Basin prospers, we prosper.

OIL FOR THE LAMPS OF CHINA

Even before California became an American possession, advocates of the nation's "manifest destiny" linked their calls for westward expansion to the eventual emergence of Asia and the Pacific Basin. The search for a western route to China and India, after all, had motivated Christopher Columbus's earliest journeys, and several expeditions were commissioned in the late seventeenth century by Virginia Governor William Berkeley "to find out the East India sea." Following the establishment of the United States as an independent nation, it was Thomas Jefferson who most passionately desired information about the Pacific. While he was with the U.S. embassy in France from 1784 to 1789, Jefferson studied everything he could get his hands on concerning America's western frontier.

Elected to the presidency in 1800, Jefferson quickly sought to establish an American presence along the Pacific. He commissioned Meriwether Lewis and William Clark on the famous journey that led them to the shores of the Pacific in 1805. Although himself a devoted believer in an essentially pastoral destiny for the new nation, Jefferson was not blind to the commercial opportunities that Pacific trade presented for American exports. "The object of your mission," Jefferson instructed Lewis, "is to explore the Missouri river, & such principal stream of it as, by its course & communication with the waters of the Pacific Ocean, may offer the most direct & practicable communication across this continent, for the purposes of commerce."

As so frequently happened in the history of American Western expansion, Lewis and Clark found others already claiming the rich, undeveloped lands along the Pacific. Indians and English traders were firmly established in the Northwestern frontier, while in California the Spaniards, with their system of mission settlements, held sway. It took another generation—and deeper penetration of the great hinterland west of the Appalachians—to start developing a more aggressive imperial vision of the American role in the Pacific. The bitter war with England between 1812 and 1815 heightened American nationalism. To men like Thomas Hart Benton of Missouri, a disciple of both presidents Jefferson and Jackson, the move toward the Pacific represented a form of national liberation, loosening the nation's ties to what Benton scathingly called "the English seaboard." With the assumption of the West and the Pacific region, Benton predicted in the early 1800s, the nation would no longer be "servile copyists and imitators" of Europe but a new people, free to shape a unique destiny.

The pressure for expansion to the Pacific grew in the early 1840s as

Anglo-American settlers began pouring into the rich, disputed territories of the Northwest and into Mexican-held California. Men like John C. Fremont, relentless explorer and son-in-law of Benton, and William Gilpin, a former soldier and newspaper editor, traveled to Oregon in 1843 and helped set up a rump American government in the still British-claimed Northwest. Gilpin's travels convinced him that the nation's ultimate future lay not in the East and the Atlantic, but in the West and the Pacific. In 1846, Gilpin fulminated:

> The untransacted destiny of the American people is to subdue the continent—to rush over this vast field to the Pacific Ocean—to animate the many hundred millions of its people, and to cheer them upward ... —to regenerate superannuated nations— ... to stir up the sleep of a hundred centuries—to teach old nations a new civilization—to confirm the destiny of the human race—to carry the career of mankind to its culminating point—to cause a stagnant people to be reborn—to perfect science—to emblazon history with the conquest of peace—to shed a new and resplendent glory upon mankind—to unite the world in one social family—to dissolve the spell of tyranny and exalt charity—to absolve the curse that weighs down humanity, and to shed blessings around the world!

America's ability to "shed blessings around the world" increased exponentially with the conquest of California and the solidification of American claims over the Northwest in the late 1840s. With the possession of the developing ports of the Puget Sound, Portland, and, most importantly, San Francisco, American merchants suddenly had a direct access to the fabled marketplaces of Asia. Now the most persuasive proponents of expansion of the nation's trade into the Pacific were not dreamers like Benton and Gilpin but hardheaded merchants like New York's Asa Whitney. Driven out of business by the Panic of 1837, Whitney had traveled to China and made a fortune as a mercantile agent there. Aware of the vast commercial potential of the Asian countries, Whitney as early as 1845 proposed the building of a railroad from the Great Lakes to the Pacific.

A practical businessman, Whitney did not wait for his dream to become reality before formulating an immediate strategy for taking advantage of Asian trade. The gunpowder was barely dry in Mexico and California before Whitney was calling for an all-out American trade offensive in the Pacific, built around the principle later known as the "Open Door." Speaking before the Pennsylvania Legislature in 1848, Whitney declared: "Here we stand forever, we reach out one hand to all Asia and the other to all Europe, willing for all to enjoy the great blessings we possess, claiming free intercourse and exchange of commodities with all, seeking not to subjugate any, but all ... tributary, and at our will subject to us."

This mercantile approach to Asia, at first, openly disavowed imperialist designs on any of the countries across the Pacific. But if Americans felt superior to the more colonialist Europeans, they soon showed themselves capable of resorting to intimidation in order to enforce what would become known as the "Open Door." American merchant ships and whalers had long complained of their treatment by the Japanese who had a strictly enforced policy of isolation from western "barbarians." By the 1850s, with California and the West under firm American control, this situation was deemed intolerable. Early in that decade, Acting Secretary of State C. M. Conrad ordered Commodore Matthew Perry to force open the reluctant Japanese market to American penetration. In his directions to Perry, Conrad noted:

Recent events—the navigation of the ocean by steam, the acquisition and rapid settlement by this country of a vast territory on the Pacific, the discovery of gold in that region, the rapid communication established across the isthmus which separates the two oceans—have practically brought the countries of the east in closer proximity to our own; although the consequences of these events have scarcely begun to be felt, the intercourse between them has greatly increased, and no limits can be assigned to its future extension.

Persuaded by the presence of Perry's warships in the waters outside Tokyo (then Edo), the Japanese government reluctantly signed the Treaty of Kanagawa in March 1854, guaranteeing the "perfect, permanent and universal peace" between the two nations. Four years later, diplomat Townsend Harris negotiated a full commercial treaty with Japan, establishing direct trade links and the exchange of ambassadors. By these actions the U.S. government secured for its new Pacific possessions a market that today is the west coast's primary overseas trading partner.

MANIFEST DESTINY DELAYED

Despite the grand hopes of men like C. M. Conrad, America's Pacific Rim trade developed slowly in the nineteenth century. As late as the 1890s, the bulk of California's rich grain crop was being shipped back east and to Liverpool, rather than to China as had long been expected. Although Chinese and Japanese Americans carried on a successful trade in such goods as abalone shells and dried shrimp to their native lands, few Anglo merchants successfully found large customers in the fabled Far East. In fact, by the late 1890s China and Japan had established an almost two-to-one trade advantage with the United States, while Pacific states, with 10 percent of the nation's wealth, controlled under 6 percent of America's overseas trade. Instead of becoming the highway to Asia, California in the 1890s, according to University of California President Benjamin Ide Wheeler, "stood at the end of a *cul de sac,* a fine decorative end of the continent—but the road went no further."

The American failure to exploit its Pacific opportunities was blamed on many causes, notably the lack of a sufficiently large merchant marine and the spheres of influence being carved out in China by the European powers and Japan. In stark contrast to the predictions of manifest destiny, some Americans began to feel their horizons closing in on them as others moved to slice up the rich trade of the Far East. "We have no longer a virgin continent to develop," declared Hubert Bancroft, an ultra-nationalist historian, in the closing years of the nineteenth century. "Pioneer work in the United States is done, and now we must take the plunge into the sea."

The nation's "plunge into the sea" began modestly when in 1867 Secretary of State William Seward successfully negotiated the purchase of Alaska from Russia. A New York Republican, Seward was an early believer in the need for an imperial American push beyond the shores of California, insisting that the Pacific Ocean and its Basin would ultimately emerge as "the chief theatre of events in the world's great hereafter." Few of Seward's immediate successors were quite so convinced, however, and American policy, under alternating Republican and Democratic administrations in the 1880s, remained basically moralistic and inward-looking. In fact, when American business interests in the islands organized a successful *coup d'état* in Hawaii in 1893, the Democratic Cleveland administration denied their pleas for immediate annexation.

It took the growing crisis over Spain's handling of nationalist rebels in Cuba—a crisis in part provoked by such imperially minded Californians as the newspaper tycoon William Randolph Hearst—to provide the pretext for a full venting of the pent-up ambitions of the American, and particularly the Western, business community. The blowing up of the American battleship *Maine* under mysterious circumstances at Havana Harbor in February 1898 ushered in a brief, successful conflict with the hapless Spanish. Theodore Roosevelt, Assistant Secretary of the Navy and a fervent believer in America's "manifest destiny," had, on his own, moved to put the U.S. Navy in a position to strike the Spanish fleet in Manila Bay *before* war was actually declared.

By the end of the year American soldiers had seized control of the former Spanish colony of the Philippines and, for good measure, Congress had authorized the annexation of Hawaii. Despite the spirited opposition of some Eastern senators, the Congress refused to grant or even promise independence to the Philippines, although this was a blatant repudiation of the oft-repeated American precepts about democracy and self-determination. America's takeover of the Philippines and Hawaii, however, was widely applauded throughout the West, where the leaders saw in the developing American Pacific Empire the realization of the earlier dreams of Benton, Gilpin, Conrad, and other promulgators of manifest destiny. Shortly after the American taking of the Philippines, the governor of Oregon brazenly declared the West's need for a new imperial American presence in the Pacific:

> All commercial nations are now fighting for trade and in their race of cupidity and inordinate ambition China is threatened with partition. We need the business of these islands. Exchange of products, natural and artificial, would be mutually beneficial to them and to us. We must find an outlet for the surplus product of our fields and forests, our factories and workshops; we must share on equal terms with all other nations the opportunity for trade in the Orient, which our possession of the Philippine islands affords us.

The strong American presence in the Pacific, born out of the Spanish-American War, sparked the long-awaited expansion of west coast trade with Asia. Under the leadership of President Theodore Roosevelt, the United States strengthened its naval presence in the Pacific and solidified the country's complete domination over the restive Filipinos. Feeling at last on an equal footing with their European and Japanese competitors, west coast businessmen intensified their efforts to penetrate the Asian market. Between 1913 and 1929, U.S. Pacific trade increased 375 percent, almost three times the jump in business on the Atlantic Coast. The victory over Spain had, at last, brought the promise of the Pacific Rim to California, whose foodstuffs, cotton, and oil now found captive markets across the ocean. The Spanish-American War had ushered in a new era. "As nearly as anything else," observed the Los Angeles writer Harry Carr, "this . . . period was punctuated by the Spanish-American War. When it began we were still a hick town. When it ended, we began to grow into a city."

EAST MEETS WEST

From its vantage point across the Pacific, Japan watched the development of American power with keen interest. American pressure had forced the country to open its ports, but it was the Japanese determination to modernize following the 1868 Meiji Restoration that brought the two countries into ever-increasing contact. By the 1890s, the United States was firmly established as Japan's leading customer. Raw silks, cocoons, and tea helped pay for purchases of cotton, machinery, and iron for the rapidly industrializing Japan of the late nineteenth century. American expertise and equipment also helped in the construction of Japan's basic railroad system. For America's business establishment, Japan proved to be a far more lucrative market than immense but chaotic China.

Although the Japanese themselves had engaged in an imperialist war against Korea and China in 1894–95, they were disturbed when the United States embarked on a similar course in 1898. A formal protest was lodged against the American annexation of Hawaii, for example, on which some 25,000 Japanese had settled. Some advocates of American expansion into the Pacific had indeed favored the takeover in Hawaii and the Philippines as a bulwark against Japan's (and Russia's) designs on China. Domestically there was also the growth of anti-Asian racist hysteria against "the yellow peril." These racist fears were further exacerbated in certain circles, particularly on the west coast, when Japan soundly defeated the Russian forces in the 1904–05 Russo-Japanese War. "Drunk with victory and fired by uncontrollable ambitions, these one million Japanese Napoleons will turn their eyes around for new territory to conquer," warned the San Francisco magazine *Organized Labor*, shortly after the decisive Japanese triumph at Mukden in 1905. "California in particular is an inviting field. . . ."

These hysterically anti-Japanese views were not widely shared by top officials in Washington or even by many of California's leaders. President Roosevelt, although wary about Japan's long-term Pacific designs, feared Russian imperial ambitions even more. Following the successful surprise attack on the Russian fleet at Port Arthur in 1904, Roosevelt revealed his true sympathies by exclaiming in delight: "Japan is playing our game." In 1905, Roosevelt helped assure Japanese compliance with his policies by acting as mediator in the peace talks between the beaten Russians and the triumphant representatives of the Emperor. Later, after gaining Japanese agreement to respect Washington's cherished "Open Door" policy toward the weak, disunited China, Roosevelt secretly agreed to recognize Japan's "sovereignty" over Korea.

Despite the fulminations of anti-Japanese propagandists like Hearst and many labor leaders, some Californians looked forward to a period of strong Pacific Rim growth and cooperation built upon a U.S.-Japan alliance. Reflecting these optimistic views, University of California President Wheeler told Japanese students at the Berkeley campus in June 1909:

The Japanese and the people of the Pacific coast must needs be good friends. They are to pursue the chief purposes of their being in the Pacific Ocean together. Their destinies bring them together. They must trade together, and one must supply what the other lacks. They must know each other and commune frankly with each other.

... We Americans, and expressly we Californians, admire very greatly the ready adaptability of the Japanese man to new conditions and strange tasks. ... We admire beyond all measure his devotion to his country and his Empire and his willingness to make personal sacrifice for the greater cause.

Similar sentiments were shared across the ocean in Tokyo, where a significant faction of the Japanese establishment worked to promote friendly commercial and political relations with the other rising power on the Pacific Rim. Key to the strong pro-American forces in Japan was the huge Mitsui Trading Company, one of the leading *zaibatsu,* Japan's business and financial oligarchy, which exercised almost feudal power, and was heavily involved in inter-oceanic trade with America's west coast. Their primary interest revolved around the raw silk trade with the United States, which accounted for one third of all Japanese exports into the early 1930s. Through the Seiyukai, or "conservative," Party in the Japanese Diet, the Mitsui interests worked for a policy of entente with the United States, based on increasing trade and political cooperation.

Somewhat less pro-American was the "liberal" Minseito Party, which was backed by the Mitsubishi *zaibatsu.* Concentrated in such heavy industries as steel, shipbuilding, and, eventually, airplanes, Mitsubishi-led economic interests tended to come more into conflict with American corporations over markets in China and Southeast Asia. Yet even the Mitsubishi interests in the highly controlled, concentrated political economy of Japan generally favored peace and good relations with the United States. Under both Minseito and Seiyukai leadership, Japan's government well into the late 1920s worked to preserve vital economic links to America. In fact, this approach reached its apogee under the tutelage of Baron Kijuro Shidehara, foreign minister of Japan through most of the 1920s, and a relation by marriage to the Iwasaki family, which founded Mitsubishi. In his analysis of *zaibatsu* influence of Japanese foreign policy, the historian Kazuo Kawai has observed:

Its keynote of "live and let live, prosper and let prosper" was based on the premise that Japan had to trade in order to live, that trade could flourish only if it was mutually profitable to both parties, that customers' good will had to be cultivated through conciliation, cooperation and friendship. The *zaibatsu* were thus strongly opposed to military adventurism, for as businessmen they believed that not only would taxes for armaments eat up the profits they were most interested in, but military activities would destroy profitable trade by antagonizing foreign customers and by arousing resistance in areas that could furnish raw materials to Japan. Acting on the sound business maxim that "the customer is always right," *zaibatsu* executives roamed the world exuding cosmopolitan good fellowship in the best Chamber of Commerce–Rotary Club manner.

This pragmatic, businessman's approach reaped huge economic benefits for Japan and its prime Pacific Basin trading partners in the first third of the twentieth century. Between 1897 and 1916, Japan's economy expanded at the rate of 7 percent per annum, from 1917 to 1936; following Japan's initial lunge into industrialization, growth rates continued to average nearly 6 percent annually. Following the logic of the *zaibatsu* politicians, much of this progress was linked to a strong increase in Japan's overseas trade, which soared over 188 percent between 1913 and 1929, more than three times the rate of increase experienced by Great Britain and almost twice the jump enjoyed by the still prospering Atlantic ports of the United States. Significantly, of all the world's leading trade areas only the American west coast ports enjoyed greater growth in this era than the Japanese. Although still secondary to the dominant Atlantic trading routes, the burgeoning trade between Asia and the west coast of North America helped boost the Pacific's share of total world trade from under 12 percent in 1900 to over 18 percent in 1933. After studying these trends, the British historian Gregory Bienstock predicted in 1937: "The history of mankind is now entering the Pacific era: that is to say, it is within the Pacific region that the great historical events of the next hundred years will take place."

But for the Pacific Rim economies to flourish, businessmen on both sides of the Pacific realized, there had to be a free flow of goods and resources across their common ocean. Nowhere was this more essential (particularly to the Japanese) than in the acquisition of oil, the all-important ingredient for industrialization in the twentieth century. Virtually without petroleum of its own, Japan very early in its industrial development turned to America, and most particularly the rich oil fields of California, for this vital resource. As early as 1874, oil man Demetrius G. Scofield, who would later become first president of the independent Standard Oil Company of California, had traveled to Japan to investigate the possible market for kerosene there. It was one of the earliest efforts at opening up what would become perhaps the key economic link between the United States and Japan in the period before World War II.

GROWING TOO FAST FOR COMFORT

As California moved toward becoming the nation's top oil producer, Japan's dependence on American sources grew, ranging from 50 to 60 percent of all its petroleum imports in the 1930s. Standard Oil of California was able to fulfill the early dream of Scofield by exporting oil across the Pacific at the turn of the century. By 1919 SoCal, as it is often called, controlled some 26 percent of all American production, more than any United States oil company. In 1936 SoCal teamed up with Texaco to form the CalTex marketing combine which would later become a major force in Japanese and other international petroleum trade.

These profitable two-way trade relations were interrupted, however, by the rising tension between the Japanese government and the United States. Japan, which joined the Allied side in World War I, had emerged from the conflict virtually unscathed while its chief European rivals—Germany, France, England, and, most importantly, revolution-convulsed Russia—were devastated. Seizing upon this weakness, Japanese military and commercial interests pressed their advantage in China, gaining increasing influence and economic possessions. Japanese armies, initially with Allied support, even invaded Siberia in the spring of 1918. They withdrew reluctantly in 1922, under intense pressure from the United States, which had grown concerned over Japanese imperial designs.

The Japanese withdrawal from Siberia reflected the essential pragmatism of the dominant *zaibatsu* forces in Tokyo. Anxious to placate the increasingly suspicious Americans, their largest and most important trading partners, the Japanese in 1922 agreed to limit their naval forces to a 5 to 3 ratio in favor of the United States. This agreement, the result of a nine-country naval conference in Washington, and other concessions to American policy considerations infuriated the growing number of right-wing extremists in Japan.

The far right was still raging about "Japan's defeat in a bloodless naval battle" when Congress passed the 1924 Immigration Act with its strict prohibitions against Japanese immigrants. The blatantly racist anti-Japanese provisions, pushed largely by California and other Western politicians, deeply offended even the moderate *zaibatsu*-oriented officials. In a note to U.S. Secretary of State Charles Evans Hughes, Ambassador Masanao Hanihara warned of the "grave consequences which the enactment of the measure retaining that particular provision [excluding Japanese] would inevitably bring upon the otherwise happy and mutually advantageous relations between the two countries."

The onset of a worldwide economic depression in 1929 further weakened the position of Japan's moderate business-oriented politicians and their hopes for the peaceful development of the Pacific Basin. As a trading nation with little in the way of natural resources, Japan was particularly vulnerable to the ravages of the Depression era. More and more Japanese, particularly inside the military, turned their backs on the apparently ineffective modern capitalist policies of the *zaibatsu* and started advocating the return to *Kodo* or "the Imperial Way" of ancient times. By 1931 advocates of this approach, which was in reality more fascist than samurai, launched the invasion of Manchuria without the approval of the duly constituted government. High-ranking offices, top government officials did nothing. "The units have already moved, so what can be done?" Premier Wakatsuki Reijiro asked pathetically.

From the Manchurian invasion on, the *zaibatsu* and their sponsored politicians proved increasingly unable, and ultimately unwilling, to halt Japan's slide toward total militarism. Although they continued to win elections and control key cabinet positions until the outbreak of war with the United States, the politicians and businessmen allowed themselves to be bullied, time and again, by militant officers who sought to replace the Pacific Rim with a Japanese-dominated "Greater East Asia Co-Prosperity Sphere." When the United States made clear its complete opposition to the Manchurian invasion in 1931, the pattern for growing U.S.-Japanese conflict was set.

As Japan expanded its war against China in the 1930s and the military forces grew in power within Japan, the fears of "the yellow peril" escalated once again in the United States. Rather than seeing Japan as a strong partner in the peaceful development of their shared Pacific Basin, American business interests began to view Japan as a competitor seeking to dominate all Asian markets to the exclusion of others. In 1937, *Fortune* magazine complained:

> The Japanese were no longer merely dressing up like a great power and talking like a great power—they were actually doing what the great powers had long reserved the special and peculiar right to do. They were appropriating pieces of Asia. And that wasn't all. Indeed it wasn't the half. Trade statistics began to come in. The Japanese, not content with pricking the diplomatic pride of the powers, were picking their purses as well. And not only picking their purses but picking them at a time of world depression when world markets were shrinking overnight.

From the British possessions of Malaya, India, and Kenya to the American-dominated markets of Argentina and Ecuador, *Fortune* reported, the Japanese were aggressively underselling and undercutting the once proud Western powers. Not surprisingly, these increased economic gains—at least in part traceable to Japan's de facto acquisition of such resource-rich territories as Manchuria (renamed the puppet state of Manchukuo)—softened the opposition to militarism on the part of some *zaibatsu*.

Some businessmen on the other side of the Pacific could well appreciate the dilemma faced by their Japanese counterparts. Companies like Standard Oil of California and CalTex provided much of the oil needed by Japan's growing war machine. Executives were divided between their traditional preference for "Open Door" exploitation of the markets of China and their business with European allies on the one hand, and their profitable sales to Japanese customers on the other. In his study *The Brotherhood of Oil*, Robert Engler points out the conflicts plaguing California's big oil exporters: "At the outset of World War II the President of Cal-Tex stressed the need to appear pro-British and anti-Japanese because of Cal-Tex's Chinese and British business, while the parent California company Standard of California 'must take as strong a pro-Japanese position as possible' to maintain its Japanese trade."

During the first years following the outbreak of war in Europe, the U.S. government proceeded slowly in trying to curb Japanese expansion. Strong protests were lodged against deepening Japanese intrusions into China, but no definitive move was made to cut off the vital flow of oil. But with the Japanese occupation of southern Indochina in July 1941, the Americans and the other European powers froze Japanese assets. On August 1, President Roosevelt ordered Standard of California and other oil exporters to embargo their shipments to Japan, moves that finally, according to one Japanese scholar, Saburo Ienega, "had thrown an economic noose around Tokyo's ambitions."

Even before the imposition of this "noose," Japanese militarists in control of the government were planning a possible invasion of the South Pacific area and war with the United States. Moderates still within the government tried to start negotiations for peace, but these forces lost their influence after Prime Minister Fumimaro Konoye, an aristocrat and relative moderate, resigned on October 16, 1941. He was succeeded by Tojo Hideki, the full-tilt militarist who would order the fateful attack on Pearl Harbor in December 1941 and lead his nation into the most devastating defeat in its long history.

Less than three years after the resignation of Konoye, the essentially pro-American advocates of the peaceful development of the Pacific Rim were again in ascendance in Japan. The militarist faction had lost the support of many *zaibatsu*-related politicians once it became painfully clear that Japan was suffering a terrible defeat at the hands of the Americans. On July 18, 1944, Konoye and other *jushin,* the statesmen of the old prewar order, gathered to begin plotting strategy for the war-ravaged country. That summer they managed to arrange the downfall of premier Tojo and his replacement by the more moderate Kuniaki Koiso. Operating carefully out of fear of assassination by diehard rightists in the military, the *jushin* sought a peace that would, in Ko-noye's words, "preserve the national policy."

THE FRUITS OF DEFEAT

When the Japanese government finally accepted the Allied unconditional surrender terms on August 15, 1945, there wasn't much else of Japan left to save. Two important commercial centers, Hiroshima and Nagasaki, had been devastated in the weeks before by atomic bombs; Tokyo and most other major cities had been leveled by repeated bombing attacks. Over 500,000 square miles of territory were suddenly stripped to an empire now reduced to four home islands. Hundreds of thousands of Japanese remained stranded in hostile lands overseas, taunted, even murdered by vengeful populations. On the home islands rations had dropped to 1,050 calories per person—about one half of the minimum for normal health—and people regularly dropped from malnutrition on the streets of Japan's ruined cities. Raw materials were virtually exhausted, while industrial production had dipped to one tenth of prewar levels. The old establishment feared the Emperor, and possibly capitalism itself, might not survive the ravages of the war.

Although the Americans quickly arrested such Japanese militarists as Tojo as "war criminals," the new occupiers had no intention of allowing Japan to alter its capitalist mold. American policy was to turn Japan into "a bulwark of democracy in the Far East," with an economy strong enough to prevent the development of a pro-Communist government. Even before the surrender of Japan, California entrepreneurs like Henry Kaiser were looking ahead to the rebuilding of the shattered Asian economies and the future preeminence of the Pacific Rim. In a speech before the San Francisco Chamber of Commerce in July 1945, Kaiser declared:

... We cannot prosper unless the nation prospers, and America cannot be an island of plenty in a world of despair.

I accept the judgment of the experts who proclaim that the Pacific Basin will be the theatre where civilization makes its next great advance. I am not impressed by those who say that the hundreds of millions in the Orient are doomed to a low standard of living because they have nothing with which to pay for the goods and services which would better their lot. From well-documented and carefully studied surveys, I am ready to accept the forecast that the Orient will be one of the best customers, even as we will be one of theirs.

The need to prop up California's traditional Asian trading partners also became a major priority at the state's leading financial institution, the Bank of America. Mario Giannini (son of A. P. Giannini) was appointed a member of the Committee for Financing Foreign Trade by President Truman in 1946, an elite twelve-member group set up to reinvigorate the private economies of nations threatened by possible Communist subversion. Reflecting the west coast's role as receptacle for over one third of all prewar trade with Asia, Giannini quickly expanded his bank's operations there and contributed to the reconstruction of the Pacific Rim economies. Between 1947 and 1951, the Bank of America set up eight branches in Asia—in contrast to one in equally war-ravaged Europe. All but one of these new additions succeeded; the one exception was the Shanghai branch, which was shut down less than three years after its founding in January 1949 due to the uncooperative attitude of China's new Communist rulers. But by far the most active field for new operations proved to be Japan, where four of the new branches were located. In 1947, the Bank of America played a pivotal role in securing a $60 million multi-institution loan designed to revitalize the Japanese textile industry. By 1952 the San Francisco–based bank, whose contribution of $10 million convinced the Wall Street bankers to go along with the industrial revitalization loan, could boast of assets in excess of $138 million in its Japanese operations.

Businessmen from both the United States and Japan also helped save the old *zaibatsu* concentrations that had been slated for extinction by the early occupation authority. From an original list of 1,200 corporations slated for dissolution, U.S. business pressure helped assure that only 9 ultimately suffered from the much-publicized "deconcentration" program. By the 1950s, most of the old *zaibatsu* had returned to dominate the Japanese economy; today the great houses of Mitsubishi and Mitsui stand at the center of the Pacific Rim multinational economy.

With the outbreak of the Korean War, Japanese industry received a tremendous shot in the arm. By providing the staging area and rear supply base for United Nations forces (overwhelmingly American), Japanese companies began to experience "gigantic" profits for the first time since Japan's defeat, according to one historian of the Occupation, Kazuo Kawai. From 1950 to 1962, Japan enjoyed a 14.4 percent annual growth rate, and by 1963 had regained the share of world exports it had achieved before the war. By the early 1960s, Japan began to grow at a faster rate even than that of West Germany, and its GNP jumped four-fold between 1961 and 1972.

As they had in Japan's earlier periods of growth, California-based corporations benefited tremendously from the success of their counterparts across the Pacific. Once again the most active partners of the Japanese proved to be the California-based oil companies; Standard of California, Union Oil, and Getty all became deeply involved in the profitable business of supplying postwar Japan's burgeoning oil requirements. Union Oil also worked in concert with the Japanese in developing the oil resources of Indonesia, a region of intense interest to businessmen on both sides of the Pacific Rim.

Today Japan, with the world's third-largest and by far most productive economy, presents a model for economic development most admired by countries throughout the world. Within the living memory of millions of Americans, Japan has grown from a shattered, poorly nourished land into a country which, in the minds of many, represents the future center of the world economic order. One Californian who has watched that remarkable transformation of roles is Jason Stewart, vice-president of Nippon Electric Company's new electron devices division in the Silicon Valley town of Santa Clara. A member of the U.S. Navy Occupation force in Japan between 1947 and 1952, Stewart believes the time has come for his fellow Californians to shed their old nationalist notions and join with Japan in building a new era of prosperity along the shores of the Pacific:

> We on the West Coast have long had these close connections with the rest of the Pacific Basin and now with the jet plane, the Pacific is no more a barrier than the Atlantic. There is a future for us in relations with Japan. Let's look at the way Japan is the richest nation on the Rim. That's how California's got to work. . . .
>
> Merchants have no nationality. Look at the globe from a satellite, you realize you have to see things on an internationalist basis. Look, Tokyo's robust—New York's going under. It's strange if you realize it, but for California, the orientation has to be to go with the winner and develop the Pacific trade.

ZEN FOREIGN POLICY

While Japan and its new "Co-Prosperity Sphere" emerged as the focus of world economic power in the 1970s, California's top political leaders moved quickly to adopt the "go with the winner" attitude advocated by Stewart. In contrast to the politicians of the industrial heartland, who often regarded Japanese success as something akin to an economic version of Pearl Harbor, the state's top elected officials virtually fell over each other in a rush to ally themselves with the new dominant force in the Pacific. Delegations from the port of Oakland, the cities of San Francisco and Los Angeles, as well as the state of California, traveled with increasing frequency to Tokyo, Osaka, Peking, Shanghai, Manila, and other key Asian economic centers. From these sojourns emerged numerous new trade links, cultural exchanges, and "sister city" agreements between California and Asian metropolises. Typical was the June 1979 trip to China by San Francisco Mayor Dianne Feinstein. From her ten-day tour resulted a "friendship city" relationship between San Francisco and Shanghai, and plans for a China tour by the San Francisco opera company, an educational exchange program, a Chinese promise to make San Francisco the first stop of a trade fair tour, and discussions of a joint San Francisco–China expedition up Mount Everest. "Our destiny in the future, as in the past, will be inexorably tied to China trade," Feinstein enthused upon her return. "Our port, our airport will be gateway ports for China. The friendships we made there will flourish and grow."

But no California politician more brazenly coveted the friendship of the Orient than did Governor Brown, Jr. A longtime devotee of Zen Buddhism and other Asian philosophies, Brown was peculiarly suited for the role of California's supreme ambassador to the economic mandarins of the Pacific. While on a trip to Japan in 1977, for instance, Brown expressed his admiration for Asian cultural values by making a visit to a Zen monastery outside Tokyo, a far cry from the Christian insularity of such American leaders as Jimmy Carter. Brown portrayed himself to his Japanese hosts as a kindred soul, with an appreciation for Asian approaches to trade, environmental, and foreign policy considerations that often seemed to contradict those advocated by the national government at Washington. So total was Brown's ideological commitment to a pro-Japanese Pacific Rim policy that his leading trade official, Dick King, spoke openly about the state's desire to sign up with other Pacific "nations" in a Japanese-led "Co-Prosperity Sphere." Another key Brown aide, energy adviser Wilson Clark, publicly announced his proposal to set up a "Pacific Rim Council," which would allow California the opportunity to formulate regional policy in concert with representatives of Japan, Australia, and other Rim nations. "We have an internationalist idea," explained Brown's legal adviser Anthony Kline. "I think nationalism is a reactionary force anyway."

Brown's affinity for Asia, however, was not motivated solely by his philosophical tendencies. Behind his administration's courtship of Asia, and particularly Japan, lay a firm grasp of California's economic self-interest. Fundamental to Brown's approach was the understanding that, in an era dominated by multinational corporations, the actual boundaries of individual nation-states had become largely irrelevant. California, Brown's advisers reasoned, stood to gain from the Japanese-led Pacific Rim economic rise, even though it came largely at the expense of the American industrial heartland. Andy Safir, director of the California Office of Economic Policy, explained in 1979 the Brown administration's economic perspective:

> There is a tendency now to look to imports for our industrial goods, that used to come from the East Coast. There is a growing interdependence, that while we used to look toward the East Coast, now we look to Japan. People are more sophisticated, they look to see if the American goods are better. The east will definitely have to compete for California with the Japanese. . . . There is, on the other hand, a convergence of interest between California and the West with Japan.
> . . . For us the Japanese are a close market. It's 5000 miles away so the transport costs are similar to going back East. Their products are geared to a consumer market. Japan has a big market here. . . . You have [in Japan] an economy that can respond to specialized demands of a place like California while you have no such ability in the East.

Most important of all, these essentially pro-Japanese, anti-Eastern sentiments are shared by many key entrepreneurs both in California and throughout the West, men who have long benefited enormously from Asian trade. For instance, many California agribusinessmen have built their fortunes through serving as Japan's leading supplier of fruits and second-largest source of cotton. California, Washington, and Oregon ranked first, second, and third as exporters of vegetables to the food-poor Japanese. Montana, Idaho, and Washington farmers all reaped the benefits of being among Japan's top suppliers of wheat, while Alaska has done a multi-million-dollar business in fish, oil, and timber with the rising dynamo of Asia. Similarly profitable trade relations with Japan and other Asian nations also grew during the 1970s in such key Western-oriented industries as aerospace and high technology electronics. Finally, California's location as the ultimate assembly point for imports from Asia helped produce over 1 million jobs in the state's expanding trade sector. In contradiction to the Eastern and Midwestern regions, the massive flow of Asian manufactures into the U.S. west coast "actually helped this area," observes Eric Thor, a vice-president and senior economist for the Bank of America. "We're really becoming a financial center of the Asian community."

Seeing Japan and other Asian nations as more of a potential market than a menace, California's entrepreneurs tend to oppose virtually all restrictions on "free trade." Still riding the crest of an economic expansion every bit as impressive as Japan's, these Western businessmen are convinced they can compete head-to-head with any foreign company. John McPherson, president of the Vector General Company, a leading computer graphic equipment manufacturer in suburban Los Angeles, bristles at the very thought that his company cannot take on the most innovative Japanese firms. "We are moving very aggressively into the Japanese market," he boasts, "I think we can compete with them because of our Western atmosphere of freedom, which makes people more innovative. We can out-create anybody."

THE RIGHT PLACE AT THE RIGHT TIME

Given the economic parameters and entrepreneurial attitudes common in California today, it is not surprising that the state's leaders have often clashed sharply with their Eastern peers on foreign trade matters. Proposed quotas and other trade restrictions on Asian imports, designed to save the sagging fortunes of the industrial heartland, have engendered stiff opposition throughout the West. Despite strong pressure from Eastern corporate lobbyists, even the ultra-nationalists around President Reagan have consistently refused to impose direct import quotas on the Japanese auto manufacturers, preferring instead the less drastic remedy of temporary, voluntary export reductions by the Japanese themselves. The staunchly conservative, pro-Reagan Los Angeles *Herald Examiner* has consistently criticized Eastern-inspired protectionist moves and even blasted a proposal in the California Legislature to promote the buying of American-made steel, pointing out that it would cost the state up to $154 million more to buy the higher-priced domestic product. Similarly, the Los Angeles *Times,* the great gray bastion of the California establishment, displayed uncharacterisic passion in a strong editorial attack on a 1981 congressional proposal to set limits on foreign car imports:

> Protectionism only invites retaliation, which would not serve the U.S. economy at all. Protectionism in this case would also deny Americans a freedom of choice that, as they have shown, they are keen to exercise. It would also have the unhappy side effect of retarding the encouraging decline in gasoline demand that has been occurring. Import quotas aren't the answer; competition is.
> The U.S. auto industry's blind and even arrogant refusal to recognize that fact has helped force more than 200,000 auto workers off the payroll. The industry's long indifference to fuel economy im-

provements, its too casual attitude toward production quality, its smug rationalizing year after year that it was giving the public what it wanted are very much at the heart of the current problems. . . .

This tendency to adopt what, in effect, is a pro-Japanese position on trade matters reflects the deep sense of admiration for and fraternity with Japanese business that has developed in California in recent years. Increasing numbers of California corporations, for instance, have begun to adopt Japanese-style management techniques, some quite consciously. This trend has been most marked among the high-tech firms of Northern California's Silicon Valley, where many companies have installed recreation facilities—tennis courts, swimming pools, running paths—of the sort commonly provided by Japanese corporations for their employees. At the new San Francisco high-rise headquarters of the Shaklee Corporation—a major maker of vitamins and office products—one floor has been reserved as a sports and recreation center, all encircled by an indoor jogging path. In a novel effort to make the work environment more pleasant and fraternal, Tandem Computers of Cupertino has even initiated the practice of sponsoring company "beer busts" every Friday afternoon for its employees.

On a more serious note, some top California firms have extended their adoption of Japanese management techniques far beyond the playground and have attempted to incorporate their methods into the very structure of corporate life. These companies have hired private consultants, such as Professor William Ouchi of the UCLA Graduate School of Management, in order to teach them the Japanese way of doing business. Ouchi, a Japanese American, has developed his own "Theory Z" management approach, which incorporates the Japanese "consensus" style with the traditional Western-style brand of individualistic entrepreneurism. In essence, Ouchi advocates that corporations make a greater effort to help their employees cope with the mounting problems of mobility, alienation, and the deterioration of home and community life—the basic negative side effects of the modern free enterprise society—by providing them with a Japanese-style corporate-created "community" at work. The author of a widely acclaimed book on "Z" management theory, Ouchi has written:

> In the Z organization, this wholism includes the employee and his or her family in an active manner. . . . That means that family members regularly interact with other organization members and their families and feel an identification with the organization. . . .
> If it is true that American society in general is moving toward a low affiliation state, if it is true that neither the church, the family, the neighborhood, the club, nor the childhood friendship is likely to

make a comeback, then it falls to the work organization to provide the glue which will hold this society together.

Several major California companies such as Hewlett-Packard, as well as some outside the state, have incorporated elements of Ouchi's thinking into their corporate planning. At Hewlett-Packard, a "Z"-style "corporate spirit" among employees is promoted by putting everybody—including the company founders David Packard and William Hewlett—on a first-name basis. Similarly, in an attempt to break down alienation and spur productivity, the company offers the same wide list of benefits, stock option plans, and profit-sharing arrangements to every employee from the highest-ranking executive to the assembly-line workers. Other entrepreneurs, such as Action Instruments' founder Jim Pinto, have adopted Japanese-style precepts completely on their own in order to raise employee productivity toward the high levels enjoyed in Japan. "The purpose of the future revolution in the West is to eliminate the difference between workers, managers, and the owners by making all the same," Pinto claims. "If you own a part of the place, you can do everything you can to increase efficiency and productivity. In many ways Action Instruments is very Japanese. We tend to be more team-oriented and focus on team success."

THE INSCRUTABLE WEST

California's flourishing romance with the nations of the Pacific Rim, however, is not a one-sided love affair. As the state's political and business leaders have sought closer relations with their Asian trading partners, the nations across the Pacific have also shown a growing attraction for California and the West. The American West—many foreign leaders seem to believe—is where the future of American society and economic life is being shaped. The United States International Communications Agency, which sets up tours for foreign officials visiting America, reported that the vast majority of these leaders chose California as the area in the country they most wanted to visit.

But perhaps it is the Japanese more than any other group who see California as the key to the future of the United States. Maseo Tsuyama, chairman of the board of the Japanese-owned California First Bank, speaks of the strong attraction the state holds for today's Asian business executive:

To a certain extent there's a historical tie here. Our people like California, feel comfortable here. . . . When Japanese people come to America, they think of California first. They like the climate, it's so near, it's just one flight. There are more Orientals in California and that makes it more comfortable. They are more tolerant of Orientals here. People would rather work here than in New York.

And another high-ranking Japanese banker echoed Tsuyama's assessment. "California is almost like home," the nattily dressed executive said, breaking into a broad smile. "Yes, California prefecture. . . . You still have some advantages in a few areas, airplanes, space, oh, and Disneyland. We're still far behind in the Disneyland kind of technology."

Indeed perhaps nothing reflects the Japanese zest for things Californian more clearly than their passion for Hollywood and its numerous confections. Today, under an agreement with Walt Disney Productions, the Mitsui Real Estate Development Company is constructing a $350 million Japanese version of Disneyland outside of Tokyo. Other Hollywood productions, especially police thrillers set in the modern West, have become perennial favorites with Japanese television audiences: "Starsky and Hutch," "Columbo," and "CHiPs" have soared into the top ten of Japan's Nielsen ratings. Hollywood's influence has become so pervasive across the Pacific that in 1979 three hundred commercials featuring Hollywood personalities were shot for commercials advertising products in the Japanese media. In Tokyo, you can watch Charles Bronson pitch after-shave, Peter Falk model men's wear, Faye Dunaway hawk her favorite soap, and Candice Bergen explain, to the Japanese, the virtues of their own Minolta cameras. Occasionally, minor wars even break out between rival Tokyo ad agencies, each competing against the other with their own Hollywood pitchman. In one instance, ad agencies representing various coffee firms all come out with media blitzes featuring such stars as Kirk Douglas, Peter Fonda, Paul Newman, Pat Boone, and Telly Savalas. "Western-inspired products are better sold by Westerners," Kanshi Tanabe, regional manager in Los Angeles for Dentsu, Japan's top ad agency, explains. "We need new images to sell new products and, in Japan, new means Western."

To many Japanese, however, the ultimate status symbol of the West is not a tough Hollywood star like Charles Bronson but the tall, blond, tanned California girl. One Japanese company recently shelled out some $50,000 just for the rights to use a tape of the movie The Misfits for a blue jeans ad. All they used, according to an agent involved in the deal, was a six-second shot of "Marilyn Monroe's Levi's-clad rear end" as she jumped onto a horse. Less morbid but equally absurd was a recent advertisement for "Cup O' Noodles" that showed a popular Japanese singer stepping out of a plane at Southern California's Palmdale Airport, almost drowning in a bevy of radiant California blonds. Another campaign, launched by Coca-Cola of Japan, featured Tracy

Peters, a seventeen-year-old blond high school student from Burbank. All the commercials using Peters were shot in the United States, Hawaii, or western Canada. She was often clad in a bikini. Peters spoke no Japanese, was unknown, and had never even visited the Land of the Rising Sun. "They told me they wanted the California look," she explained later, "blond hair, blue eyes, I guess." In one of the commercials, Peters stood holding a bottle of Coke, with a banner stretched across her thighs that read: "Come On In." Trying to explain this bizarre Japanese infatuation with Western pop culture, Jared Cook, a Hollywood producer who has worked in Japan, commented:

> The Japanese have a very narrow idea of beauty for Western women, and they are immensely attracted to the tall blond type. I remember a Playboy bunny contest in Tokyo where the judges were Japanese. The winner was the tallest and blondest girl, the runner-up was the next tallest and blondest, and so on. They had them all lined up according to size. I mean, what can you say, opposites attract.

A perhaps more reasoned expression of the Japanese bias can be seen in their conscious decision to concentrate a disproportionate amount of their U.S. business activities in California and other Western states. "The western part [of the U.S.] is growing faster than the rest, I think," explains Katzutoshi Satta, a high-level San Francisco-based executive with the powerful Mitsui Trading Company. "Our people are working harder here because that's where the opportunities are greatest. We have to go where the industries are growing." By 1980, 835 Japanese firms had picked California as the location for their U.S. headquarters, including 16 Japanese-owned banks, 2 of which, California First and Sumitomo Bank of California, rank among the state's 10 largest. Equally clear is intense Japanese interest in the resource-rich West, where their overseas investments are most concentrated; Japan is already the leading foreign investor in such states as Oregon, Idaho, and Washington.

But it is in Southern California, more than any other single place in the continental United States, that the Japanese have made their deepest economic penetration. Between 1970 and 1979, over 400 Japanese companies and 3,000 individuals invested in Los Angeles and Orange counties alone, according to Tadao Uchida, editor of *U.S.-Japan Business News*. Among the most important investments in southern California was Sony's sparkling $25 million television factory at Rancho Bernardo outside San Diego, which opened in 1972 and now employs 1,800 local workers. Another twenty-four Japanese companies have moved into the massive Irvine Industrial Park in Orange County, while new major Japanese-owned business facilities are currently under construction at Carlsbad, north of San Diego, and in Compton outside Los Angeles.

Japan's intense interest in Southern California is in part traceable to the presence of the region's large Japanese-American community. Although separated by a vast ocean and certain cultural differences, there remains a strong sense of commitment between the Japanese in both countries; Japanese Americans, in addition, play an important function in providing needed translators and other services for their cousins from overseas. Nothing better reflects this powerful interconnection than the Japanese-financed revitalization of the Little Tokyo section of Los Angeles. Long the hub of the city's Japanese-American community, the area near Los Angeles's downtown had decayed during the 1950s and 1960s as upwardly mobile Japanese Americans moved out into the city's sprawling suburbs. In the 1970s, however, Japanese overseas interests, joined by local Japanese Americans and the Los Angeles Community Development Agency, started a concerted effort to rebuild the historic quarter. By 1980 the once decrepit district was thriving once again, filled with throngs of shoppers from both sides of the Pacific. On the edge of one of Los Angeles's toughest barrios, Little Tokyo now boasts a brand-new skyline dominated by high rises emblazoned with the names of such Japanese corporate giants as Sumitomo and Mitsubishi, as well as the elegant new $30 million New Otani Hotel. Hayihiko Tokunaga, architect and manager for Los Angeles of the worldwide Kajima Construction Company, which has designed much of the new construction in the area, explains the massive Japanese commitment to the Los Angeles development:

> We are sort of obligated to develop the Little Tokyo area. The Consul General [of Japan] asked us to come up with a plan to help the Japanese Americans. It hasn't been done purely on a commercial basis, it's a community project. We want to renew the area.
>
> You know, the name is Little Tokyo but the real Tokyo is different, much more modern. This area was thirty, forty years behind modern Japan. A lot of people who come from Japan come here and are disappointed.
>
> Our objective in coming to Southern California is not to achieve radical growth but to make a solid base of supply and delivery for all over the United States. The American attitude is that they accept everything—they have a big capacity. California itself is a country.

The Japanese initiatives in Southern California constitute only one part of a growing tide of foreign capital now flooding into the booming economy of the Western states. In 1978, the U.S. Conference Board reported that California had surpassed New York, long the lodestone for international investment capital, as the top state in new foreign acquisitions and manufacturing facilities, "California," concluded one survey of the flow of international investment capital into the United States by *Saturday Review,* "is the hottest area of foreign investor activity."

Besides courting the Japanese, California trade officials and business executives have actively encouraged numerous investors from around the world to put their millions into the Golden State's economy. Reflecting this rampant internationalism, California's bankers, who have strongly resisted attempts by Eastern financial institutions to enter the state's lucrative market, have welcomed foreign banks. When added to the two large Japanese-owned banks, the California Canadian Bank and the British-controlled Lloyds Bank of California and Barclays Bank have placed foreigners in dominion over five of the fifteen largest banks in California. "I don't think we are anti-foreign bank by any stretch of the imagination," asserts Richard J. Borda, executive vice-president of Wells Fargo Bank. "If anything, we welcome the competition."

Part of the reason for this open arms approach to foreigners lies in the need for increased capital in order to fuel the continuing expansion plans of relentless entrepreneurs. With the national economy in a tailspin and interest rates skyrocketing, foreign investments have played an increasingly important role in providing capital for state agribusiness projects, electronics industry research and development schemes, and construction projects. In addition to the Japanese, major investments have come from Switzerland, Germany, France, Canada, England, Saudi Arabia, Hong Kong, and Thailand.

In contrast to other states, where strong legislation has been enacted to prevent or limit foreign ownership of farm land, California generally has welcomed millions in overseas investments into its highly mechanized, capital-intensive agricultural sector. Italian, French, German, and other foreign interests have invested very large sums in the rich farmlands of the San Joaquin Valley, and contributed to a dramatic inflation in local land prices. Baron Philippe de Rothschild has entered a joint venture with the Robert Mondavi winery to produce a Bourdeaux-style wine in the Napa Valley grape-growing area north of San Francisco. Swiss, French, German, Canadian, and Thai investors have also purchased wineries in the state.

Another lure for foreign capital has been the fast-growing electronics industry. The German firm of Rober Bosch jointly owns 20 percent of the American Microsystems Company in the Silicon Valley with another firm, while down the road at Sunnyvale the German electronics giant Siemens has taken control of 20 percent of Jerry Sanders's Advanced Micro Devices, as well as one fifth of another promising California high technology firm, Litronics. In addition, British-owned Lucas Industries owns 24 percent of fast-growing Siliconix Corporation, while the Canadians have weighed in with one third of yet another high-tech firm, Intersil.

But it has been in the real estate and development sector where the foreign impact has been most profound. One major worldwide power in banking and real estate—Adnan Khashoggi of Saudi Arabia—has chosen to make Los Altos, a posh San Jose suburb, the headquarters for his widespread $400 million Triad Corporation, while the potent real estate giant, Canadian-owned Daon Corporation, had purchased nearly 2,500 acres of California real estate and developed 18 apartment complexes by 1979. Another middle Eastern financier, Daryoush Mahboudi-Fardi, is currently developing a $20 million complex of boutiques and stores in Beverly Hills's swank shopping district. In the central Los Angeles area alone, according to real estate magnate John Cushman III, investors from Canada, Germany, Britain, France, Abu Dhabi, and Iran have all poured tens of millions of dollars over recent years into new construction projects and acquisitions.

A similar rush of foreign investment capital has invaded the San Francisco Bay Area. One major San Francisco real estate exchange reported that up to 40 percent of all its transactions in 1977 involved foreigners. But perhaps the most dramatic example of the increasingly important role of foreign capital in California took place in Oakland, across the bay from San Francisco. Unique among California's cities, Oakland with its antiquated heavy industrial base and huge poor black population has long resembled one of the deteriorating urban centers commonly found in the Eastern half of the country. Determined not to become a Pacific Rim version of Newark, Oakland in 1971 unveiled a massive $120 million City Center redevelopment project featuring three new high-rise office buildings, a 500-room hotel, and a regional shopping center. But just three years afterwards the project faced disaster as the national recession pushed the prime developer, Oakland-based Grubb and Ellis, into receivership. Only two of the office buildings had been completed and one of them was unable to attract sizable numbers of clients into what seemed to be a doomed city. Staring at the huge four-square-block hole left unoccupied by the project's demise, one desperate city official asked in 1974: "What are we going to do with those open pits? It will look like Berlin after the war."

But by 1981 the project, and Oakland, were back on track. Once again it was foreigners, hungry to buy a piece of the California dream, who put up the key development funds. In the late 1970s Canadian firms moved in, bought those two existing high rises, and are paying for the construction of the third. Nearby, three Hong Kong–based companies have plunked down $50 million for a new Trans Pacific Centre, which has led to a veritable rush of Pacific Basin investors into the central Oakland area. "They [foreign investors] are coming here with cash," exclaims D. Christopher Davis, executive director of the revived city's Convention and Visitors Bureau. "It's kind of scary the money they're throwing around. But downtown development—it would never have happened except for that. It would have never gotten off the ground if it weren't for foreign investment."

FOREIGN AID

The impact of massive foreign investment has served further to intensify the essentially internationalist Pacific Rim pespective shared by California's business and political leadership. Disdainful of traditional national and state boundaries, these Californians have worked assiduously to formulate a new order of interrelations beneficial to the state's economic system and entrepreneurial aspirations. This quest has led not only to the increasing marriage with Asia but towards formulating a closer relationship with the other two leading "nations" on the North American side of the Pacific Rim, Canada and Mexico. Perhaps the most conscious expression of this initiative by California has been the proposal by Governor Jerry Brown to form a "North American Common Market" with Ottawa and Mexico City. The plan, which has also won support from Ronald Reagan, calls for the movement of Alaskan natural gas to Canada in exchange for the shipment of gas from Canada's border regions into the energy-short Northern United States, with considerable savings and efficiency for both sides. More important to California, the North American Common Market would also provide both for the transfer of Mexican oil riches and cheap labor across the border to the American Southwest. "This would provide the United States with a large, low-cost labor force," explained Kenneth Hill, a director of Standard Oil of California and major advocate of the North American Common Market; " . . . But above all this would provide an outlet for the millions of unemployed, under-utilized Mexicans who cannot obtain jobs in Mexico."

The common market idea thus far has been largely ignored by Eastern leaders. But while neither Congress nor the Carter administration bought his idea, Brown characteristically continued to woo the leaders of both foreign countries, meeting twice over four years with both Premier Pierre Elliot Trudeau and President Jose Lopez Portillo. In addition, Brown has carried on his own negotiations with Alberta's Peter Lougheed, a fellow provincial ruler from a wealthy western region of

Canada. Lougheed and Brown are scheduled to continue their negotiations for increased gas shipments from Alberta to California.

Brown's courtship of Mexico has been even more exuberant. He has set up regular communication with several top Mexican officials and established ties with Roberto de la Madrid, governor of neighboring Baja California. In 1977, Brown aide Gray Davis proudly announced that California would receive up to 15 percent of Mexico's natural gas exports to the United States in the future, yet another example of the state's increasingly independent diplomatic efforts. And Brown's adviser Richard Silberman, himself a former business partner of the Bustamante Mexican oil family, has proclaimed his uniquely Californian approach to foreign policy:

> Indeed the future of the entire continent of North America is more dependent now on the economic, cultural and political relationships between Canada, Mexico and the United States than ever before. Again, California is ideally positioned to maximize the economic and trading potential presented by our common border with Mexico.
> By virtue of our historic and cultural bonds, we will be able to benefit from the development of Mexico, while at the same time influencing the economic growth of that country.
> ... The oil and gas reserves in Mexico believed to be as great, if not greater, than those of Saudi Arabia. It is not difficult to understand therefore that the long term development of Mexico is important to the United States and California. It has great potential, not only in terms of providing future sources of fuel, but expanded trade and domestic jobs.

CALIFORNIA'S COLONIAL POLICY

California's efforts to tap into the energy wealth of its foreign neighbors—Canada and Mexico—has been matched by moves to dominate its own resource-rich western hinterland. In 1976, almost 80 percent of all the crude oil reserves in the United States were in California, Alaska, Texas, and five other Western states. In November 1979, the United States was importing daily 1,503,000 barrels of oil, while the western District Five total was only 91,000 barrels. The Rocky Mountain states alone are estimated to have 50 percent of the nation's recoverable reserves of coal. Wyoming has eight times as much low sulfur coal as West Virginia and Kentucky combined, while Utah has sufficient coal reserves to supply the entire United States for the next thirty-eight years. Coal production in the West increased six times over its level of a decade ago. Wyoming, Montana, Colorado, New Mexico, and

Utah between them will be producing 316 million tons of coal a year by 1985, up from only 22 million tons annually in 1967, according to a recent Department of Energy estimate.

The West also stands as the nation's principal source of numerous other important minerals. An estimated 93 percent of the uranium in the country lies in the Western mountain states. The same area produces 70 per cent of the nation's gold and 50 percent of its silver. Arizona mines more than half of all the nation's copper each year, while one open pit mine in Utah has already produced more copper than any other single mine in the history of the world.

Even more impressive are the projections for future production of Western resources in the synthetic fuels area. The oil shale deposits in western Colorado, Utah, and Wyoming contain more energy potential than all the oil fields of the Middle East. Although it is estimated that only one third of that may be ultimately recoverable, such an amount alone is more than five times the current U.S. petroleum reserves. Already there are thirty-six separate projects in the synfuels area under way in the West. "The time has come for shale," Roger Loper, president of the shale oil subsidiary of Standard Oil of California, boasted in 1980. "It's going to be a whole new world in five years."

Much of the excitement in California's corporate boardrooms is focused upon a narrow, 40-mile-wide belt of land that runs for 2,300 miles from Mexico up to Alaska. The "Overthrust Belt," as it is called, contains up to 100 trillion cubic feet of natural gas, approximately half of all the proven reserves in the United States. This same long sliver of the continent also possesses some 10 to 15 billion barrels of oil—enough to supply all the petroleum needs of the nation for two years. While ignored for years because of the costs and risks involved in extracting the petroleum products from the ground, such technological advancements as the use of computers in analyzing exploration data have produced a modern-day land rush by energy firms trying to stake out claims in the belt.

California corporate enterprises have been at the forefront of the push to exploit the vast resource potential of the Western United States. Three engineering firms—Bechtel of San Francisco, and the Fluor Corporation and Parsons Company of Southern California—have been the most active engineering and construction concerns in the area. Thornton Bradshaw's ARCO has teamed up with another California concern to build a $1.2 billion oil shale plant in the Colorado Rockies that could be producing 45,000 barrels of synthetic crude oil a day by the mid-1980s. In September 1980, five firms, including subsidiaries of two California utilities, applied to the federal government for permission to build a 583-mile-long natural gas pipeline from the Rocky Mountains to California. The line would eventually deliver 800 million cubic feet of natural gas a day to the state, and will cost $515 million to construct. Other California firms heavily involved in developing shale oil and other synthetic fuels in the mountain states include Tosco Corporation, Union and Getty Oil companies, all Los Angeles–based. In addition, San Francisco's Chevron has spent $350 million since 1974 on oil exploration in the area, and now lays claim to one third of the total oil and gas reserves uncovered thus far. Chevron's parent firm, Standard Oil of California, also holds mineral leases on 176,000 acres of land in the belt in southwest Wyoming.

The current California initiatives to draw on the immense wealth of resources in neighboring Western states are the culmination of a decades-long exploitation of the area by California that at times has bordered on colonialism. As a financial and business behemoth, dwarfing the smaller local economies of its sparsely populated and underdeveloped western neighbors, California has often used its corporate and political muscle to squeeze out the resources it needs. As Carey McWilliams explained in 1949: "Essentially, California is to the West what New York, for many years, was to the industrial East: a great center of power with lines of influence radiating outward in all directions. But there is this important difference: California, within the West, has no rivals."

Traditionally, California has exercised its power over other Western states by drawing heavily on their water- and electrical-generating capabilities—two critical elements in the state's expanding agricultural and industrial sectors. The most spectacular example has been the state's involvement in harnessing the Colorado River, principally since the completion of the Hoover Dam in 1936. At the time, California could claim only a small, 4,000-square-mile stretch of land in the desert as the state's part of the Colorado River's watershed. Yet with only this tenuous claim on the river, California was able to negotiate a deal by which it would receive over one quarter of all the water diverted from the river for use by Western states.

In an area where, as one Utah planner once phrased it, water is "the testicles of the Universe," the state's greed has engendered no small amount of ill feeling among its Western neighbors. For instance, during California's great drought of 1948, when $100 million in crops and livestock production was lost, both Montana and Colorado balked at requests from California cattlemen for those states to open their ranges for grazing to thirsting herds shipped in from the Golden State. When the Pacific Gas and Electric Company in the 1940s tried to win approval for a pipeline nearly 1,000 miles long to draw natural gas from San Juan, Colorado, to San Francisco, the Colorado state government bitterly fought against the plan. Another plan in the late 1940s to tap the Columbia River in Oregon and divert it to California to meet the state's critical water needs drew sharp retorts from Oregon officials angry over California's appetite for gobbling up the resources of its Western neighbors. Oregon's Senator Guy Cordon sneered at the time: "If this fantastic project goes through, Oregon would like to have a corresponding conduit going north, pulling into it the income of California oil plus the income of Hollywood. If a few stars fall into the sluiceways, we'll gladly accept them."

Such concerns have not dampened the efforts of California corporate and political officials to draw on the resources of other Western states to meet their water and energy needs. Pacific Gas and Electric Company of San Francisco has purchased coal leases in central Utah that are expected to fulfill the needs of the firm's two planned coal-fired plants in California for their entire thirty-five-year lifespan. Three other utility companies, including Southern California Edison and San Diego Gas and Electric Company, share an interest in 30,000 acres of land in the rich Kaiparowits coal area of southern Utah. There are also plans to build 237 miles of new rail lines to help ship the coal to California. Overall it is estimated that 75 percent of the coal in the area will go to California, with most of the rest exported on to Japan. "Utah looks good to us," explained California Energy Commission head Richard Maullin. "[California] is planning to use coal in the 1980s, and it has to come from somewhere outside California."

Faced with strict air quality standards and an already severe air pollution problem, California utilities have also pushed hard for the construction of coal-fired plants in other states that they can tap for their electricity needs. Southern California Edison, for example, draws on the 2,085-megawatt Four Corners Power Station located in northwestern New Mexico. Another project proposed for Utah, the Intermountain Power Project, represents a $4 billion effort to build the largest coal-fired plant in the United States. The 3,000-megawatt generating facility would consume 10 million tons of coal a year and send up to 75 percent of its electric output to the Los Angeles Department of Water and Power and other California utilities. Yet another ambitious California scheme is the Allen-Warner Valley Energy System, which would include two generating plants in Utah and Nevada and a massive strip mine near Bryce, Utah. A joint venture by PG&E and Southern California Edison, the 2,500-megawatt project would send 90 percent of its power to California. The plant, supported by Utah, would consume 10 million tons of coal a year, transported in a slurry pipeline from an 8,300-acre strip mine. "Utah has coal, it has water, it's prudent to husband both those resources for the highest and best use," summed up

Lewis Winnard, chief engineer for the Los Angeles Department of Water and Power. "The water we have is best used to grow our vegetables, in [Utah] it's best to use water for power plants."

HOW DRY WE ARE

While development-minded state officials in Utah have supported the large-scale exploitation of their resources by California, there has been mounting opposition in other quarters to the schemes of the Golden State. Environmentalists have protested vehemently over what amounts to the export of air pollution from Los Angeles to the vast unspoiled stretches of the mountain states. Even more important have been the grumblings of agricultural interests, who are concerned that the projects will consume immense quantities of water and dry up their farmlands. The Intermountain Power Project, for example, will require 50,000 acre feet of water a year for cooling and other purposes, leading to the drying up of at least 15,000 acres of land currently under cultivation. Similarly, the Allen-Warner project will drain 9,700 acre feet of water a year from that area. Overall, the Western States' Water Council estimates that new energy projects in the eleven Western states—including nuclear plants, coal gasification facilities, electrical generators, slurry pipelines, and oil shale mining—will require an additional 2.3 million acre feet of water by 1990, enough to irrigate almost 1 million acres of cropland.

This trend could prove catastrophic for a region already thirsty for water. Arizona is faced with the grim prospect of losing an estimated third of its current 1.4 million acres of irrigated cropland in the future because of water shortage. In Texas, there is concern that 3.2 million acres of irrigated crop land may go out of production in twenty years.

The growing anxiety in Western states over the impact California's imperial designs will have on their energy and water resources, however, pales in comparison to the powerful Western-wide estrangement and revolt against the policymakers of the Eastern establishment. Leaders in states throughout the West have been angered by the heavy-handed tactics of Washington officials, who are accused of trying to exploit the mountain states to reduce the dependency on foreign imports of the resource-starved East. In the West, where the majority of the land is still owned by the federal government, there is pervasive fear that the East is simply oblivious to Western concerns over water and other issues. Western leaders were particularly rankled in 1977 when President Jimmy Carter temporarily suspended the development of numerous Western water projects in order to reevaluate their cost effectiveness. "They want to take our coal and take our water, and what do we have left?" complained Governor Thomas Judge of Montana. "A couple of national parks."

BLUE-EYED ARABS

Suspicion of the motives of the Eastern power brokers has sparked a widespread alienation in the West that is now threatening to erupt into outright rebellion. The hostility has reached the point where many Westerners are developing the same attitudes toward the industrial East that the OPEC oil producers have exhibited toward the industrialized nations as a whole. People in Montana have started to refer to themselves as "blue-eyed Arabs," for example, while bumper stickers reading: "Drive Faster, Freeze a Yankee" have proliferated in the Southwest. "There's a whole complex of resource issues, especially water, which sets the West apart," explained Colorado Senator Gary Hart. "They build on an anti-Eastern, anti-government feeling that was already there. I look upon the West as a kind of New South in which there is a basic alienation."

The distrust of easterners stems from a long history of neglect and exploitation of the mountain states by the nation's political and corporate leaders. Early in the nation's history, for example, many Easterners viewed the vast expanses of the territorial West not as the nation's manifest destiny, but rather as a desolate and largely worthless appendage to the more civilized Atlantic seaboard. In 1852, U.S. Secretary of State Daniel Webster from Massachusetts remarked: "What do we want with this worthless area, this region of savages and wild beasts, of shifting sands and whirlwinds of dust, of cactus and prairie dogs? To what use could we ever hope to put these great deserts and these endless mountain ranges?" Later, when Eastern interests became more aware of the potential of the "worthless area," they moved quickly to exploit its resources. Mining firms appeared overnight, stripped the land bare, and departed, leaving behind them hundreds of acres of scarred mountainside and prairies pockmarked with gaping holes. Eastern financiers and railroad owners also exploited their Western subjects, charging them exorbitant interest rates on loans and stiff shipping charges on their crops and livestock. "Billions of dollars came out of here, and none of the money remained," observed Governor Richard Lamm of Colorado. "Can you blame us for feeling like a colony?"

Today, that suspicion of Eastern designs explains numerous efforts by Westerners to take control of their own destiny. Whereas the Southern half of the country has historically been the hotbed for states' rights sentiments, it is now the West that is the most openly hostile toward the federal government and pushing hardest for cutbacks in Washington spending as well as self-determination for state governments. The most prominent expression of that feeling has come in the modern-day "Sagebrush Rebellion," a drive by the Western states to take control of the huge federal landholdings in the area. Alaska, for example, is 96 percent owned by the federal government, while 87 percent of Nevada, 66 percent of Utah, 63 percent of Idaho, 54 percent of Oregon, 47 percent of Wyoming, 42 percent of Arizona, and 45 percent of California are likewise set aside as federally supervised acreage.

Already the state of Nevada has passed legislation to appropriate the federal land, and similar moves have been considered in California and Alaska. Spearheading the movement is the League for the Advancement of States' Equal Rights (LASER), a coalition of ranchers and state and local government officials. Nevada Senator Paul Laxalt, who served as Ronald Reagan's 1980 campaign chief, has been one of the advocates of the effort. The President himself has gone on record in support of the Western revolt. "I happen to be one who cheers and supports the Sagebrush Rebellion," Reagan told a group of Utah Republicans in 1980. "Count me in as a Rebel."

While the Sagebrush Rebellion has in large part stemmed from disaffection over federal regulation of Western lands, it also reflects what has become virtually a secessionist movement in the West. Frustrated over bureaucratic restrictions imposed on them by the federal government, fearful of Eastern desires to plunder their natural resources, many leaders in the Pacific half of the country have begun to call for what amounts to a second civil war between the states. Kent Briggs, administrative assistant to Utah Governor Scott Matheson, expresses the resentment building in the West:

> It all parallels France after Charlemagne. The Balkanization out here is becoming a perfect parallel. . . .
> We see the Yankees putting restrictions on our development, to continue colonial shackles. My vision is we might need a new nation from the Mackenzie River to the Rio Grande, Alberta to the Mexican border, one Western nation, rich in resources, in control of these resources.

There are some severe contradictions behind such expressions of independence in the West. The region has for years been heavily dependent on federal outlays for water projects, and much of the industrial growth in the area has come from the electronics and defense industries heavily subsidized by Washington. Overall, the Rocky Mountain states have received $20.5 billion from the federal government in various subsidies, while contributing only $14.5 billion in revenues.

But the current fast-paced economic growth throughout the West has reinforced the smug sense that the region might be better off on its own. From 1970 to 1977, for example, the rate of population growth in eleven Western states was double that of the rest of the country, labor force expansion 55 percent greater, and the increase in personal income nearly 13 percent above the national average. In the California pattern, much of the economic expansion in the mountain states has taken place in the high technology area—the sector that holds the key to the nation's economic future. Hewlett-Packard has built a new plant in Boise, Idaho, employing 2,800 people; National Semiconductor has opened a new factory in Tucson, Arizona, along with IBM; Intel and Internetics are establishing new facilities in Salt Lake City. Texas Instruments, Honeywell, and TRW Corporation have all recently moved into Colorado Springs as well. Overall the Census Bureau has predicted that during the 1980s seven mountain states will rank among the nation's ten fastest-growing states. Ferris Taylor, Western regional manager for Data Resources, a leading Massachusetts-based economic forecasting firm, explained in 1979:

> Economic growth has to come for some tangible reason. It isn't regulated by the government, it's regulated by resources—labor, land, minerals. As you look at those, the West has them all. . . .
> We have the Alaskan oil here while places like New England have to get all the crude from overseas. They're much more vulnerable back there. We still have commodities to offer the world. . . .
> The mountains cut us off from the rest of the United States economy. We can instead be more receptive to what happens in the Asian community. The West is going to be the leader, the dynamic part of it. I don't see anything happening to the East that will change that in the 1980s.

The tide of Western power has not been lost on Eastern leaders. While the West may still be fearful of Eastern efforts to colonize its area, in the East there has been growing concern that the Atlantic seaboard may soon fall prey to the imperial designs of the Pacific states. Atlantic leaders point, for example, to the windfall that the Western states will be getting from oil deregulation in the form of increased state royalties as oil production rises. It is estimated that in the decade of the 1980s, $128 billion in new royalties will be generated, with fully 70 percent of that total ($92 billion) going to California, Texas, and Alaska. "What we're talking about is a massive shift in the competitive relationship between states," warns Tom Cochran of the Northeast-Midwest Institute, a congressional research firm, "[leading to] a small group of extremely wealthy, extremely powerful states—sort of a United American Emirates."

While Easterners grow increasingly apprehensive about the rising wealth of the mountain states and the West, California's leaders believe it will only serve to hasten their ascension as the new economic and political power center of the United States. Sandwiched between the resource-rich Rocky Mountain states and the rapidly developing nations of the Pacific Rim and the Far East, California's leaders are confident they are destined to become the key power brokers in the United States for decades to come. As Joseph Rensch of the Pacific Lighting Corporation observes:

> It's a bunch of pieces you put together. It's the Pacific Basin, the Overthrust [Belt], Canada and Mexico. It's all of these. We must remain close to all of them. . . .
> It's a massive flow. The myopia we have on the Potomac makes them slow to realize the changes. They don't see California and the West. They look across the Atlantic, it's right there, and the Pacific seems remote. . . . But we will go after it ourselves. I know the Orient. I grew up with a lot of Japanese kids out in Pasadena. We know the Mexicans, the Japanese. It's a good thing too. With the possible exception of West Germany, and they're having their problems, things are aging along the Atlantic. They are in trouble in England, Italy, France. . . . It's not wise at all to ignore where the future is, the Pacific.

IX.
Brave New World Visited

"Bring me men to match my mountains." This inscription, etched upon the facade of the State Capitol at Sacramento, stands as witness to the two great converging factors which do much to explain California's rise to economic, political, and cultural supremacy. Nature's generosity and a massive shift in global power relations have provided the context for success, but the determined effort of the California entrepreneurs has remained the catalytic agent. Collectively they form one of the most innovative and relentlessly ambitious groups of men ever to set upon the path of self-aggrandizement. From the days of land baron Henry Miller and press lord Harrison Gray Otis, conditions in California—the rapid rate of settlement, lack of inhibiting tradition and rigid social classes, an arid climate and imposing geography, the easy availability of cheap, exploitable Asian and Mexican labor—conspired to create a capitalism brasher than any previously seen in the East or in Europe. "California," Karl Marx noted in 1880, "is very important . . . because nowhere else has the upheaval most shamelessly caused by capitalist centralization taken place with such speed."

The impact of California's entrepreneurial synthesis, blending futurism with primitive capitalism, has extended far beyond the confines of the state's business elite. California's middle class "free enterprise society" has long reflected essentially entreprenurial values—from it's distinctive "do you own thing" morality to its passion for the consumption of the latest technological gadgetry. Similarly, the state's enormous communications and entertainment industry has amplified these same themes.

Not surprisingly, entrepreneurial perspectives have also dominated the politics of California. The state's leading political figures—Ronald

Reagan and Jerry Brown—have fought in their own way to promote the Western businessman's anti-New Deal, anti-bureaucratic ethos. While Reagan has more faithfully followed the ultraindividualism of the older generation of entrepreneurs, Brown has moved to embrace the more future-oriented, although no less hardhearted, ideology of the emerging corporate "new class." With the state's economy booming, particularly when contrasted with the declining East, California's political leaders seem determined to impose the state's formula for success—Proposition Thirteen-style tax cuts and increased reliance upon the economic wizardry of the entrepreneur—on the rest of the nation. "Our performance in California—at least it puts to task all the doom and gloom, the dire predictions that Proposition Thirteen would cause all this catastrophe," chortels University of Southern California economist Arthur Laffer, one of Reagan's top economic theorists. ". . . We're just doing very, very well. We could be virtually paradise . . . we should show [the rest of the country] how to do it. We should annex them."

Even as they seek the imperial mantle, California's business and political leaders must face some of the harsher realities resulting from their systematic denigration of the New Deal state in favor of the private sector. Moves such as cutting taxes and promoting technological innovation clearly benefit the entrepreneurial elite and, to a lesser extent, the state's middle class. But they leave little hope for the working poor and the welfare recipient most in need of government assistance. Cuts in government-sponsored jobs programs, coupled with technology-induced structural changes in the labor market, have sent youth unemployment rates spiraling upward to near 40 percent in some of the state's ghettos and barrios. Young blacks alone suffer from nearly five times the amount of unemployment experienced by the white population as a whole. Surrounded by a predominantly Anglo and prospering high-technology-based economy, youthful high school drop-outs and other unemployables have grown increasingly bitter and resentful toward the mainstream "winner" society.

Although this mounting minority anger could ultimately explode into widespread civil disorder or even insurrection, the most direct impact so far can be seen in the dramatic increase in crime throughout the prospering Western states. Between 1970 and 1979, for instance, the murder rate in California and the West jumped 60 percent, nearly twice the rate of increase experienced in the East. At the decade's end, California's murder rate was 9 percent higher than the rate in economically strapped New York, 21 percent above Illinois, 60 percent above unemployment-ridden Ohio, and nearly twice the rate of the nation's most urbanized state, New Jersey. In addition, booming Los Angeles County has been plagued in recent years with one of the worst outbreaks of youth gang violence, predominantly Mexican-American, in the nation's history, resulting in 351 gang-related slayings in 1980 alone. Cruz Valdez, a thirty-two-year-old *veterano* gang leader from East Los Angeles, explained:

> Those [Anglo] folks have no idea what's happening on the streets. If you want to stop kids from killing, you've got to deal with unemployment. Now you have a lot of kids coming up who don't care about anything but having a bad reputation. Gangs is all they know and they want to get into the fun. They go crazy and kill someone to make a name for themselves real quick. I guess it's their way of making it, part of the attitude that's all over the country. It's this competitive thing. Everybody's getting down and dirty.

Although their economic prospects are considerably brighter, California's middle class has also shown an increasing tendency to get "down and dirty." Threatened by the destabilizing tendencies of the state's "free enterprise society," California's middle class appears headed towards greater alienation and anomie. For some, refuge has been found in such relatively harmless activities as physical culturalism and quaint spiritualism, or through involvement in the state's plethora of cults and "self-help" groups. At the same time, however, the growing anger of the poor, often expressed through criminal violence, has engendered more dangerous, violent expressions of middle class fear. Between 1975 and 1980 Los Angeles experienced a 60 percent jump in gun ownership. Similarly, a 1980 poll found that 37 percent of all California families possessed at least one firearm, a total of over 3 million households.

In recent years some of these gun-toting Californians have started turning their weapon against those they consider a threat to their homes and communities. The Posse Comitatus, a vigilante organization founded in 1968, had an estimated 10,000 members nationwide by the late 1970s, the majority of them in California. These right-wing zealots have long been prominent in antitax movements and have pledged to use their guns to protect "tax resisters" from federal agents. They have also taken on minority groups, notably Cesar Chavez's United Farm Workers, in defense of what they consider "property rights." Posse leaders once even sought to establish their own middle class bastion in thinly populated Alpine County in the California Sierra. "Once we get our people up there, then we'll elect our own sheriff, and our own county council," explained one Los Angeles posse leader in 1976, while he proudly wore the posse symbol, the hangman's noose, on his lapel.

"We can get what we want then—mortars, machine guns, anything."

Far more often, however, California's disturbed middle class rebels tend to freelance when it comes to expressing their violent rage. The 1969 Manson gang murder spree, the 1978 assassination of San Francisco Mayor George Moscone and Supervisor Harvey Milk by Supervisor (and ex-policeman) Dan White, the Hillside strangler murders and the 1980 shotgun slaying of Playboy Playmate of the Year Dorothy Statten all reflect the same deeply disturbed pattern of aberrant middle class behavior. San Francisco Psychologist Gayle Bates has observed:

> A lot of people come here to find new possibilities that didn't exist back home. All these people come here looking for something. Out of these are a certain group on the margin, people for whom the lack of structure and limits here creates enormous anxieties. There's nothing here to keep this craziness under control.

While California's rapid rate of change threatens to further rend its social fabric, the tremendous demands placed upon the state's natural endowment by the entrepreneurial elite have, in turn, created equally severe strains on the land, energy, air, and water resources of California. The very engineering marvels which have underlain the state's tremendous growth have produced some critical ecological problems. Largely through the efforts of engineers and entrepreneurs, cities like Los Angeles have been transformed within a half century from natural paradises into overcongested, polluted exemplars of man's destructive capabilities. Shocked by the devastation of Los Angeles and other regions across the state, Californians have given birth to much of today's environmental movement—both the Sierra Club and the Friends of the Earth trace their origins to the Golden State. Due largely to the presence of this home-grown environmentalist sentiment, California has imposed some of the nation's strictest controls on air pollution and nuclear power plant construction, and virtually has banned the building of new fossil fuel energy plants near its polluted urban areas. While many of California's entrepreneurs appreciate the necessity of such controls, other interested parties, notably labor unions and the construction/development industries, complain these safeguards could pose a major threat to the future of the California economy. By the 1990s, predicts the California Council for Environmental and Economic Balance, a leading labor-industry group, up to $4.7 billion in earnings and over 300,000 jobs could be lost annually due to these environmental restrictions. They also foresee widespread power "brownouts" developing over the next twenty years as a result of the recent slow-downs in power plant construction.

Looming water shortages, however, represent by far the greatest direct threat to the state's continued economic prosperity. By the mid-1980s Arizona is expected to begin tapping into California's current supply of water from the Colorado River, cutting the Golden State's share by 50 percent. A shortfall of as many as 500,000 acre-feet could develop by the late 1980s, forcing a frantic scramble for scarce water supplies among the state's farming, industrial and municipal interests. Although the state's largest industry, the most likely loser in this struggle would be agribusiness, which consumes up to 85 percent of all the state's precious water. Combined with growing salinity problems in the state's underground water supplies, state-mandated water conservation policies could end up taking as many as 600,000 acres out of production in the San Joaquin Valley alone within the next decade. If controls are not imposed, however, some experts fear a repeat of the great December, 1977, Arvin "windblow" which covered thousands of acres with dry topsoil in the southern San Joaquin Valley. "We have the landscape but we simply don't have the water," warns Huey Johnson, California Resource Agency secretary under Governor Edmund G. Brown, Jr. "We have to stop growing. Sure we can do it in a wet year but in another dry period, the winds are going to come along and blow all the topsoil from Colorado to Wyoming. It happened to us in 1977 and it's happening now. The classic symptoms are repeating themselves."

Environmentally-oriented Californians like Johnson might worry about the state becoming a late-twentieth-century "dust bowl" but powerful entrepreneurial interests, likely to possess far more power over the long run, cling to their long-held faith that new, massive engineering achievements can meet the needs of the state's fast-growing economy. Responding in part to these interests, the Brown administration has backed away from applying its "era of limits" philosophy to several large projects, and supported the massive plan for a Liquified Natural Gas facility on the pristine central California coast and the $5 billion Peripheral Canal, a plan to divert one million acre-feet of water from northern California to the arid, more densely populated south. An even more ambitious plan has been proposed by the Pasadena-based Parsons Engineering Company, calling for the transfer of some 36 trillion gallons of water from the continent's water-rich northern tier—Alaska, British Columbia and the Yukon Territory—down to seven Canadian provinces, thirty-three American states and three states of the Mexican Republic. The $80 billion project would include a 500-mile-long reservoir in the Rocky Mountains and theoretically could satiate the West's thirst through the next century.

Another, particularly poignant, illustration of the strain put upon California's resources by the state's fast-paced economic growth has been the spiraling inflation in the price of its real estate. Between 1975 and 1980 the median price of a home in California more than doubled with San Francisco and Los Angeles boasting the highest housing prices of any major urban areas in 1977. These high costs have already posed severe difficulties for California firms seeking to attract new employees to the state. With the price of the average house in the state nearly $100,000, housing promises to remain one of the great challenges to California's future development.

Despite the severity of the problems facing California, they pale in comparison with the afflictions besetting the declining centers of the East. Inflated land prices, massive immigration, strains on water and power resources, even social dislocation are all symptomatic of an ascendant society, seeking ways to cope with its rapid progress. For the Eastern half of the nation the situation is reversed; a region in the process of decay, the East finds itself in a struggle just to stay solvent, to keep its creaking machinery operable in the unpromising future.

A half century ago the East was the nation's dominant region, with per capita incomes in Northeastern states ranging as high as 60 percent above the national average. Today the average citizen of the Northeast has a "real" income slightly below the national average. In recent years major Eastern cities such as New York, Chicago, Cleveland, Baltimore, and St. Louis have all experienced population declines while urban centers in the West—notably San Diego, San Jose, Phoenix, Dallas, Denver—have enjoyed remarkable population and economic growth. While real estate prices in cities like Los Angeles exploded exponentially during the 1970s, property values in Chicago, once one of the world's most dynamic economic centers, increased a mere 3 percent, while demands for government service soared. Similar problems afflict virtually every major Northern and Eastern metropolis, forcing severe cuts in such essential city services as mass transit, police, and education.

These trends are expected to continue well into the 1980s. Manufacturing employment growth in the West, according to the projections made by Chase Econometrics, will increase at an annual rate more than three times that predicted for the Northeast and Midwest. Similarly, personal income growth in the Northeast and Midwest, according to Chase, will be 20 percent lower than in the West. Not surprisingly, as many as 3.3 more million people are considered likely to desert the old industrial heartland for more prosperous regions by the end of the current decade.

While many of these problems can be traced to exterior factors, much of the blame for the East's accelerated decline can be traced to the weaknesses of that region's own business community. Comfortable in their own heavily guarded islands of affluence, these business leaders have found themselves surrounded by increasing misery, in cities largely deserted by the middle class fleeing to the suburbs or to the promised lands of the West. In some cities, such as Chicago, as many as one-third of all residents now receive some sort of federal aid. Apparently unable to curtail this debilitating reliance on government by speeding up economic growth, the enlightened, liberally minded Eastern elite—such as the Fords and Rockefellers—have instead turned to the noblesse oblige of welfarism, public works, and the token hiring of minority group professionals. Meanwhile, they themselves have appeared increasingly out of touch and effete, indulging their cultivated tastes for fine wines and intellectual diversions while the urban society around them has slowly collapsed. In some ways, in fact, the elite of the East and Midwest has come increasingly to resemble the doomed French aristocracy before the 1789 Revolution, a class that became, in the words of historian Alexis de Tocqueville, "... through its indifference, its selfishness and its vices, incapable and unworthy of governing the country."

Starting in the 1960s, the Eastern business establishment began to seemingly lose faith both in itself and the capitalist system. Embracing the welfarist solutions first of the New Frontier and later the Great Society, the Eastern leaders tended to downgrade the role of the entrepreneur in the creation of new wealth. With more promising investment opportunities overseas and in the West, they failed to capture the capital needed to modernize the aging Eastern economy. Between 1959 and 1980 the number of Fortune 500 companies based in New York State dropped from 150 to 98, while in the 1970s the New York–New Jersey region, the center of the nation's banking community, suffered from "net disinvestment," according to a 1979 report. Nor was big business the only victim of this capital flight from the East. During the 1970s Chicago suffered a net loss of some 18,000 small businesses, over 15 percent of the city's total, while Los Angeles and other Western centers were experiencing a renaissance of new entrepreneurial ventures. "There's a quantum difference in the character of today's businessmen and the old-timers who built Chicago," observed Northwestern University professor of industrial relations Frank Cassell. "Today's businessmen are highly mobile, going from company to company and job to job. They have no genuine roots. They live in the suburbs, not in the city. And they're professional managers who are committed to managing a firm, not building a city."

Facing a dismal future of diminished economic opportunities, swelling populations of the unemployed, and decaying physical plants, some Eastern leaders now believe that only a quasi-socialist program, based on massive federal aid, can save their beleaguered region. The chief spokesman for this point of view, New York financier Felix Rohatyn, openly advocates the redistribution of "surplus" Western wealth for the purposes of propping up the faltering Eastern economy. Unless quick remedial action is taken by Washington, Rohatyn argues:

> Existing trends are likely to exacerbate rather than attenuate this situation with the result that another decade like the last one will divide the country into "have" and "have not" regions with unpredictable but probably highly unpleasant consequences. As taxpayers leave older urban centers, the remaining tax base collapses inward, requiring higher taxes for a population that is unable to pay them and fewer services to people in increasing need of them. In these trends are the makings of social strife.

Although many Eastern and Midwestern leaders share Rohatyn's sense of impending doom, few possess his ardor for the sort of strong new initiatives that will be necessary to prop up the aging "have not" half of America. More typical of the "old" leadership were the members of the Presidential Commission for a National Agenda for the Eighties, headed by former Columbia University President William McGill, who concluded that the problems of the old industrial heartland were almost beyond solution. Opposed to remedial action to slow the exodus from the older regions, they could do no better than suggest allowing the current trends to continue, notwithstanding what they admitted to be the "traumatic consequences" for the Northeast and Midwest. Increasingly, it seems, the Eastern elite has taken as its motto the famous fatalistic statement of France's Louis XV: *"Apres moi, le deluge."* Among other Eastern leaders there is the sense that the eleventh hour has already arrived for their cities. "How much time do we have?" asked George Ranney, chairman of the Task Force on the Future of Illinois and vice-president of Inland Steel. "We have actually no time. We should have been thinking about these things five or ten years ago."

Against its dispirited competitors, California has been able to assert its growing hegemony virtually without firing a shot. Over the last few years there has been an increasing acceptance of the basic Western political and economic program—reduced government spending, deregulation, increased reliance on entrepreneurship and the tyranny of the market. When President Reagan pushed through his program of gutting a half century of progressive social and economic legislation, the old New Deal order in Congress was barely able to put up even a respectable fight.

Remarkably, many Eastern and Midwestern leaders have acquiesced to Reagan's programs despite clear evidence they will do irreparable damage to their own regions. While Reagan's budget cuts will hurt California's poor and working class population, the state—as the prime beneficiary of the administration's rapid military build-up program—will suffer an annual net loss of only one billion dollars in federal funds. Beleaguered New York State, on the other hand, is expected to absorb $5 billion federal funding loss due to the Reagan Administration's highly selective assault on government spending. "The Reagan budget will have its most substantial impacts on those states which are least able to cope with them," concludes Thomas J. Anton of Michigan's Institute for Social Research. "It is a program of focused inequity."

Once in place, such "focused inequity" is sure to further accelerate the widening gap between California and once dominant economic centers of the East. In 1980, for instance, large American firms suffered a profit decline of 2.7 percent while California's giants enjoyed a 13.5 jump. Even more impressively, in the face of growing structural unemployment in the East and Midwest, California in 1980 created 30 percent of all the nation's new jobs. Already many states are looking to California for their economic models, setting up their own "mini" Silicon Valleys in such places as Austin, Texas; Tucson, Arizona; Boulder, Colorado; and Chapel Hill, North Carolina, all in the hope of duplicating the Golden State's high-technology-oriented success story.

In a similar way, the nation is also likely to continue adopting more and more of its cultural patterns from California. Playing a key role in this process will be the expanding Hollywood mass communications industry, which expects tremendous growth in the incipient era of cable, video-cassettes, and video-discs. Shaping the beliefs and tastes of Americans regardless of their region, Hollywood-made confections will continue to usurp the traditional role of the family, the church and community with mounting effectiveness. Indeed, one recent poll by the Roper Organization found that more people presently derived more pleasure from their televisions than from their friends. Among people in rural communities television was identified as the single most pleasurable occurrence in their daily lives.

Even the California lifestyle, once widely seen as a bizarre aberration by most of the country, has begun to gain an increasingly firm hold on national patterns of behavior. In 1970 the Yankelovich Monitor discovered a 15-point differential between Western and national attitudes toward such things as naturalism, introspection, sexual permissiveness, and mysticism. Seven years later, the gap had shrunk to only three percentage points, with the nation moving ever closer to the attitudes shaped in California. People from all sections of the country—in their political attitudes, lifestyles, and tastes—are becoming slowly, but perceptibly, "Californians."

These recent trends demonstrate how dramatically things have changed since those days when a cool and confident Eastern elite could look at California as a fascinating, somewhat comical mutation, lying a continent away from the presumed center of civilization. Even the late Carey McWilliams, perhaps the most perceptive modern observer of California, still considered the state as something removed from the rest of the nation, a "Great Exception." Today, one might well wonder if New York City with its high-rise canyons and rotting subways, Cleveland with its soot-covered smoke stacks, or the small Midwestern towns still somehow untouched by the great homogenizing power of Hollywood, are now really the exceptions, particularly to young people brought up on television and imbued with the values of California's "free enterprise society." "The experimental phase in California is now over. The rest of the country has now adopted us," proclaims Hank Koehn, a native New Jerseyan and now chief of the futures research division at Los Angeles's Security Pacific National Bank. "They don't fully realize it back east but the fundamental change has already occurred. We are no longer the Great Exception. We are the norm."

Notes

Chapter I. THE CALIFORNIA ASCENDANCY

3. **Presidential Commission** The President's Commission for a National Agenda for the Eighties, A National Agenda for the Eighties (Washington: 1980), pp. 18, 67–70, 103–105, 167.

4. **unemployment rates** *Oakland Tribune,* "Jobs: Old dreams, new realities," June 28, 1981.

5. **largest firms** Standard & Poor's Corporation, Stock Market Encyclopedia (New York: 1979); *Los Angeles Times,* "The *Times* Roster of Top Financial Institutions," May 18, 1980.

5. **manufacturing employment** Security Pacific National Bank, "The Sixty Mile Circle: The Economy of the Greater Los Angeles Area," May, 1981.

5. **gross state product** California Office of Economic Policy, Planning and Research, "California Economic Forecast," November 1, 1979.

5. **per capita income** *San Francisco Examiner,* May 11, 1980.

5. **California's rank as a nation** Security Pacific National Bank, "Gross Regional Product of California and the Los Angeles Area Compared with Gross National Product in Leading Nations of the World," January 16, 1980.

5. **California's oil imports** Authors' interview with Jim Woods, executive vice president of the California Independent Producers Association.

5. **"The center for ..."** Interview with authors.

5. **Pacific nations' growth** *Information Please Almanac, Atlas & Yearbook: 1981,* Simon and Schuster (New York: 1980).

5. **foreign trade growth** State of California, "Economic Report of the Governor," 1978.

5. **export growth** United California bank, "Forecast 1981," September, 1980.

6. **"Out here there's a sense ..."** Interview with authors.

6. **"California has recaptured . . ."** Interview with authors.

7. **alternative energy** *San Francisco Examiner,* "Energy: California may have it made," April 18, 1978.

8. **overthrust belt** *Los Angeles Times,* "Overthrust: A Belt That Could Energize U.S.," March 30, 1980; *Wall Street Journal,* "In West, a Long Strip of Land Stirs Hopes Among Oil, Gas Men," August 27, 1979.

8. **Fluor synfuel plant** *Los Angeles Times,* "Fluor Expects 1st U.S. Synfuel Plant by 1985," March 12, 1980.

8. **oil reserves** U.S. Department of Commerce, Statistical Abstract of the United States, U.S. Government Printing Office (Washington, D.C.: 1979), p. 760.

8. **uranium and coal** *Washington Post,* "Old Frontier Sees Bright New Future," June 17, 1979.

8. **energy potential** *San Francisco Chronicle,* "Oil shale: How the west is lost?" November 18, 1979.

8. **"Over the next few decades ..."** Interview with authors.

8. **"colonial"** Interview with authors.

8. **Four Corners station** *Los Angeles Times,* "Cal Plants Ignite Pollution Protests," October 5, 1979.

8. **gas pipeline** *Los Angeles Times,* "Large Gas Pipeline to State Sought," September 9, 1980.

8. **"The history of this area ..."** Interview with authors.

9. **population growth** Security Pacific National Bank, "Estimated Population Increase in California," January 31, 1980.

9. **personal income growth** Security Pacific National Bank, "'Real' Disposable Income per Capita in California, 1929–1980," October 1, 1980.

9. **NASA and DOD contracts** United California Bank, "Forecast, 1981," op. cit.

9. **professional and technical employees growth** Kirkpatrick Sale, *Power Shift*, Random House (New York: 1975), pp. 31–32.

9. **"The fruits and nuts ..."** Interview with authors.

9. **aerospace growth** United California Bank, "Forecast, 1981," op. cit.

9. **backlogged orders** Wells Fargo Bank, "California Aerospace and Electronics: Another Strong Year Ahead?" October, 1979.

9. **Hughes growth** Information supplied by Hughes Aircraft.

10. **"I know it's weird ..."** Interview with authors.

10. **bank earnings growth** A. W. Clausen, president of BankAmerica Corporation, speech to the Los Angeles Society of Financial Analysts, September 18, 1979.

10. **corporate profits** *Los Angeles Times,* "Despite Softening Economy, Profits of Roster Firms Jump," May 18, 1980.

10. **unemployment rates** United California Bank, "Forecast, 1981," op. cit.

10. **wealthy people** *The World Almanac & Book of Facts 1980,* Newspaper Enterprise Association (New York: 1979), p. 93.

10. **highest-paid executives** *Los Angeles Herald Examiner,* "The results of last year's executive earnings derby," June 2, 1980.

10. **new business formations** United California Bank, "Recent Economic Trends and Indicators," August, 1980.

11. **business expectations** Prudential Insurance Company of America, "Western Business Forecast," 1980.

11. **economic growth** Bank of America, "Economic Outlook, 1981,

California Report," undated; Bank of America, "Economic Outlook, 1981, U.S. Report," undated.

11. **investment patterns** *Wall Street Journal,* "Energy to Foster Boom in West; Sun Belt Investment Will Slow," October 28, 1980.

11. **employment growth** Wells Fargo Bank, "California to 1990," March, 1978.

11. **gross state product** Center for Continuing Study of the California Economy, "California Growth in the 1980s," 1979.

11. **"The country's lagging ..."** Interview with authors.

11. **"We have been going"** Interview with authors.

12. **"God's great blueprint"** Cited in Stephen Longstreet, *All Star Cast: An Anecdotal History of Los Angeles,* Thomas Y. Crowell Co. (New York: 1977), p. xii.

12. **new jobs** Security Pacific National Bank, "The Sixty Mile Circle: The Economy of the Greater Los Angeles Area," op. cit.

12. **income growth** ibid.

12. **employment projections** Chase Econometrics, "Metro Area Forecasts," New York and Los Angeles, July 1980.

12. **"I don't think there's ..."** Interview with authors.

12. **apparel industry statistics** U.S. Department of Labor, "Employment and Earnings, States and Areas, 1939–78," undated. See same report for figures on publishing, entertainment, and financial employment.

13. **immigration** Security Pacific National Bank, "Monthly Summary of Business Conditions," March 31, 1980.

13. **Motion picture and television workers** Security Pacific National Bank, "Monthly Summary of Business Conditions: Southern California," July 31, 1979.

13. **recorded entertainment production** Federal Reserve Bank of San Francisco, "City of the Angels," August 29, 1980.

13. **"If you want ..."** Cited in *Forbes,* "Los Angeles: The New Look" (special

advertising supplement), January 8, 1979.

14. **book publishing** *Los Angeles Times,* "The West—New Chapter in Publishing," May 23, 1979.

14. **"In a certain sense ..."** Cited in *The New Yorker,* "The Blockbuster Complex—II," October 6, 1980.

14. **"Clearly there's an element..."** Interview with authors.

15. **"It is sad because ..."** Interview with authors.

Chapter II. THE ENTREPRENEURIAL SPIRIT

17. **"Look man, the entrepreneur..."** Interview with authors. See also, *San Francisco Examiner,* "Business' little giant sees gold," June 25, 1980.

17. **drop in aerospace employment** Wells Fargo Bank, "California to 1990,-" op. cit.

17. **population figures** Security Pacific National Bank, "Estimated Population Increase in California," op. cit.

18. **semiconductor growth** Semiconductor Industry Association, "1980-1981 Yearbook and Directory," 1981.

18. **manufacturing growth** Security Pacific National Bank, "California, Pacific Giant, A Statistical Profile," 1979.

18. **"And we're not going ..."** Interview with authors.

18. **fastest-growing firms** *Inc.* Magazine, "The Inc. 100," May, 1980.

18. **"Old-fashioned east coast ..."** Interview with authors. See also, *Investment Dealers' Digest,* "Exacting Technology, Aggressive Marketing Position Printronix For Strong Growth," March 11, 1980.

18. **high tech statistics** California Governor's Office, "Investment in Economic Strength," February, 1981; Bank of America, "Perspectives on the California Economy in the Eighties," undated.

19. **Worldwatch Institute** *San Francisco Examiner,* "A challenge for Silicon Valley firms," October 6, 1980.

19. **integrated circuits** California Governor's Office, "Investment in Economic Strength," op. cit.

19. **foreigners visiting plants** Authors' interview with Nancy Honig, Regional Director of the U.S. International Communications Agency in San Francisco.

19. **"There are guys ..."** Interview with authors.

20. **population increase** *California Yearbook: Bicentennial Edition,* California Almanac Company (La Verne: 1975), p. 292.

20. **Henry Miller** Edward F. Treadwell, *The Cattle King,* Western Tanager Press (Santa Cruz: 1981); Carey McWilliams, *Factories in the Fields,* Peregrine Publishers (Santa Barbara: 1971), pp. 29–39; Walton Bean, *California, An Interpretive History,* McGraw Hill Book Company (New York: 1968), pp. 225–226, 279; Warren A. Beck and David A. Williams, *California: A History of the Golden State,* Doubleday & Company (New York: 1972), p. 259.

20. **foodstuff production** Margaret S. Gordon, *Employment Expansion and Population Growth, The California Experience: 1900-1950* University of California Press (Berkeley: 1954), p. 100.

20. **Hugh Glenn** Bean, op. cit., pp. 225–226, 271–272; McWilliams, *Factories in the Fields,* op. cit., p. 51; Beck and Williams, op. cit., p. 259.

21. **William Chapman** McWilliams, *Factories in the Fields,* op. cit., p. 20; Bean, op. cit., p. 225.

21. **surveyors' land deals** McWilliams, *Factories in the Fields,* op. cit., p. 20.

21. **farm sizes** U.S. Bureau of the Census, 1870 Census, Vol. III, p. 340.

21. **500 men** McWilliams, *Factories in the Fields,* op. cit., p. 20.

21. **Southern Pacific early history** Bean, op. cit., pp. 209–218, 224; Beck and Williams, op. cit., pp. 324–325, 339; Carey McWilliams, *The Great Exception,* Peregrine Smith, Inc. (Santa Barbara: 1979), pp. 178–179; Oscar Lewis, *The Big Four,* Alfred A. Knopf (New York: 1946); Neill C. Wilson and Frank J. Taylor, *Southern Pacific,* McGraw-Hill Book Company (New York: 1952).

22. **"(this) symbol of power ..."**

Frank Norris, *The Octopus, a Story of California*, Bantam Books (New York: 1963), p. 33.

22. **"bring together the businessmen"** Cited in Bean, op. cit., p. 320.

22. **reform movement against the Southern Pacific** Bean, op. cit., pp. 320–325; McWilliams, *The Great Exception*, op. cit., pp. 180–181; Spencer C. Olin, Jr., *California's Prodigal Sons*, University of California Press (Berkeley: 1968), pp. 7–8.

22. **Luther Burbank** McWilliams, *Factories in the Fields*, op. cit., pp. 61–62; Rockwell D. Hunt, *California's Stately Hall of Fame*, College of the Pacific (Stockton: 1950), pp. 453–458.

22. **pioneering in new technology** McWilliams, *Factories in the Fields*, op. cit., pp. 55–56, 61; Bean, op. cit., pp. 272, 274; Beck and Williams, op. cit., pp. 279–280.

23. **Stockton gang plow** Bean, op. cit., p. 272.

23. **"The plows, thirty-five in number . . ."** Norris, op. cit., p. 84.

23. **wheat production** McWilliams, *Factories in the Fields*, op. cit., p. 50.

23. **oranges, lemons and wine** Bean, op. cit., pp. 273–274.

23. **leading agricultural counties** Carey McWilliams, *Southern California Country*, Duell, Sloan & Pearce (New York: 1946), p. 213; Information supplied by the California Department of Agriculture.

23. **agricultural research** *The Nation*, "Agribusiness On Campus," February 16, 1980; *Newsweek*, "Big Farming's Angry Harvest," March 3, 1980; *Los Angeles Times*, "U.S. Won't Aid Labor-Saving Research," February 1, 1980.

24. **farm ownership** *Sacramento Union*, "Who'll control our farmlands?" July 10, 1977.

24. **"farming has been replaced . . ."** McWilliams, *Factories in the Fields*, op. cit., pp. 6–7.

24. **California farm production** Security Pacific National Bank, "California's International Trade," November, 1980.

24. **Boswell company** *Los Angeles Times*, "Agricultural Giant Sows the Political Field," November 18, 1979.

25. **Jewish immigrants** Longstreet, op. cit., pp. 56–57; Neil Morgan, *Westward Tilt*, Random House (New York: 1963), p. 59.

25. **Joseph Chapman** Longstreet, op. cit., p. 20; Bean, op. cit., p. 80.

25. **"Over the years . . ."** Interview with authors.

26. **"Few Californians of today . . ."** Cited in Hunt, op. cit., p. 493.

26. **Harrison Gray Otis** Robert Gottlieb and Irene Wolt, *Thinking Big, The Story of the Los Angeles Times, Its Publishers and Their Influence on Southern California*, G. P. Putnam's Sons (New York: 1977), pp. 17–18; McWilliams, *Southern California Country*, op. cit., p. 274.

26. **"No city in the United States . . ."** Cited in Hunt, op. cit., p. 493.

27. **Los Angeles aqueduct** Gottlieb and Wolt, op. cit., pp. 127–143; Bean, op. cit., pp. 348–352; John D. Weaver, *El Pueblo Grande*, The Ward Ritchie Press (Los Angeles: 1973), pp. 43–46.

27. **William Mulholland** Weaver, op. cit., pp. 43–46. Bean. op. cit., pp. 350–352.

27. **"I would rather give birth . . ."** Cited in Remi Nadeau, *The Water Seekers*, Doubleday & Company (New York: 1950), pp. 15–17.

28. **"I am a foresighted man . . ."** Cited in McWilliams, *Southern California Country*, pp. 133–134.

28. **Henry Huntington** Bean, op. cit., pp. 281–282; Weaver, op. cit., p. 48.

28. **Los Angeles' population** McWilliams, *Southern California Country*, p. 14.

28. **food-processing employment** Bean, op. cit., p. 373; Gordon, op. cit., p. 28.

28. **oil boom** Western Oil and Gas Association, "Highlights of California's Petroleum History," undated; Bean, op. cit., pp. 368–374; McWilliams, *Southern California Country*, pp. 135–136; *Smithsonian* magazine, "In the Los Angeles oil boom, derricks sprouted like trees," October, 1980.

28. **Union Oil** Bean, op. cit., pp. 371–372; Western Oil and Gas Association, op. cit.

29. **"I observed the rapid growth . . ."**

John Paul Getty, *As I See It*, Prentice-Hall (Englewood Cliffs: 1976), p. 33.

29. **largest corporations** *Fortune*, "The 500 Largest Industrial Corporations," May 5, 1980.

29. **Getty Oil** Authors' interviews with Getty Oil officials; *Getty News*, "The story of two men and the companies they made," March, 1977.

29. **Western Geophysical** Authors' interview with Henry Salvatori.

29. **Atlantic Richfield** *Fortune*, "The Escalating War for Alaskan Oil," July, 1972.

29. **Armand Hammer** *Los Angeles Times*, "Hammer at 82 Sets Pace of Defiance," May 21, 1981; *San Francisco Examiner*, "Armand Hammer: Wheeler-dealer with Midas touch," March 26, 1978; *San Francisco Chronicle*, "$1 Billion Move to Tap Shale Oil," August 10, 1979; *Los Angeles Times*, "Hammer Pushes Hard for U.S. Oil Shale Project," March 21, 1977.

30. **"There are two and a half times . . ."** Cited in *California Business*, "Decision makers of California's eight key industries master-plan the '80s," January, 1980.

30. **"Somebody has to be first . . ."** cited in ibid.

30. **exports growth** Benjamin C. Wright, *The West, the Best, and California, the Best of the West*, A. Carlisle & Co. (San Francisco: 1913), p. 5.

30. **oil industry growth** Bean, op. cit., p. 373.

30. **Fluor Corporation** *Business Week*, "Fluor gambles on a flock of new orders," November 9, 1974; *Engineering News Record*, "Emphasis on sales makes Fluor the largest construction firm," July 15, 1976; *Los Angeles Herald Examiner*, "Theatrics aside, J. Robert Fluor has sound reasons for St. Joe Bid," April 3, 1981; *Fortune*, February 26, 1979.

31. **"The idea is . . ."** Cited in *Los Angeles Herald Examiner*, "Theatrics aside, J. Robert Fluor has sound reasons for St. Joe bid," op. cit.

31. **"Here is a hundred-dollar bill . . ."** Cited in *Los Angeles Herald Examiner*, "Theatrics aside, J. Robert

Fluor has sound reasons for St. Joe bid," op. cit.

31. **Bechtel** Robert L. Ingram, *A Builder and His Family*, private printing (San Francisco: 1961); *Fortune*, "Bechtel Thrives on Billion-Dollar Jobs," January, 1975; *San Francisco Examiner*, "The engineer who's planning an Arabian city," May 8, 1978; *Los Angeles Times*, "Southland Firms Work in Moscow," September 12, 1976; *Mother Jones*, "The Bechtel File," September, 1978; *San Francisco Examiner*, "Bechtel reports record profits but slumping sales," January 17, 1979; *San Francisco Examiner*, "Bechtel Earnings Continue to Rise," February 13, 1980; Bechtel Corporation, "Today's Bechtel," December, 1980.

32. **Kaiser** Kaiser Industries, "The Kaiser Story," 1968; Marquis James and Bessie R. James, *Biography of a Bank*, Harper & Brothers (New York: 1954), pp. 467–468.

32. **"Necessity is the great creator. . ."** Henry Kaiser, speech before the San Francisco Chamber of Commerce, July 19, 1945.

33. **"Word of the project . . ."** Kaiser Industries, "The Kaiser Story," op. cit.

33. **Hoover Dam** Bean, op. cit., pp. 397–398; Kaiser Industries, "The Kaiser Story," op. cit., pp. 16–20; Ingram, op. cit., pp. 31–37.

33. **early banks** Bean, op. cit., pp. 199–201; Security Pacific National Bank, "Security Pacific, The Story of a Bank," 1978; Wells Fargo & Company, "1972 Annual Report," 1972.

33. **Giannini and the Bank of America** *San Francisco News*, "The Story of the Bank of Italy and A. P. Giannini," 72 part series, March 6, 1928–May 28, 1928; *San Francisco Post-Enquirer*, "Giannini, Maker of Fortunes, Outlines Secret of Success," 14-part series, March 8, 1928–March 23, 1928; James and James, op. cit.; McWilliams, *The Great Exception*, op. cit., pp. 230–232; Neil Morgan, *The California Syndrome*, Ballantine Books (New York: 1971), pp. 256–258.

34. **largest banks and financial insti-**

tutions *Fortune*, "The Fortune Directory of the Largest Non-Industrial Companies," July 14, 1980.

34. **bank assets** U.S. Department of Commerce, *Statistical Abstract of the United States*, op. cit., pp. 528, 529.

34. **First Interstate Bancorp.** First Interstate Bank, "UCB Becomes First Interstate Bank of California," June 1, 1981.

34. **"West Coast banking ..."** Cited in *Wall Street Journal*, "A Jolted Wells Fargo Keeps Punching Away in California Slugfest," March 4, 1981.

34. **Home Savings and Loan** *Los Angeles Times*, "The Times Roster of Top Financial Institutions," May 17, 1981.

34. **"We have always been different ..."** Interview with authors.

35. **population figures** *California Yearbook*, op. cit., p. 294; McWilliams, *Southern California Country*, p. 14.

35. **immigrants** McWilliams, *Southern California Country*, pp. 14, 160–162.

35. **"Like a swarm of locusts ..."** Cited in ibid., p. 135.

35. **"a parasite ..."** Cited in Morgan, *The California Syndrome*, op. cit., p. 255.

35. **Count of Monte Cristo** McWilliams, *Southern California Country*, op. cit., p. 331; Robert Glass Cleland, *California in Our Time*, Alfred A. Knopf (New York: 1947), p. 267.

36. **early Hollywood** Leo Rosten, *Hollywood, the Movie Colony, the Movie Makers*, Harcourt, Brace and Company (New York: 1941), pp. 67, 177; *Penthouse*, "Los Angeles, A Celebration," September, 1979.

36. **"The demand was ahead ..."** Cited in John Caughey and LaRee Caughey, eds., *Los Angeles: Biography of a City*, University of California Press (Berkeley: 1976), p. 255.

36. **movie industry growth** McWilliams, *Southern California Country*, op. cit., pp. 332–333, 339, 341; Rosten, op. cit., pp. 378–379.

36. **entertainment industry** United California Bank, "Recent Economic Trends and Indicators: California," August, 1980.

37. **"The plastic asshole ..."** Cited in Longstreet, op. cit., p. xii.

37. **growth during the war** McWilliams, *Southern California Country*, op. cit., p. 371; Bean, op. cit., p. 426.

37. **Kaiser during the war** Bean, op. cit., pp. 426–427; Beck and Williams, op. cit., pp. 416–417; James and James, op. cit., pp. 466–468; Kaiser Industries, "The Kaiser Story," op. cit.

38. **"created the role ..."** Cited in *San Francisco Examiner*, "An era ends for a Kaiser," November 30, 1979.

38. **early aircraft pioneers** Cauthey and Cauthey, op. cit., pp. 374–378; Bean, op. cit., 428–430.

38. **aircraft production** McWilliams, *The Great Exception*, op. cit., p. 225.

38. **post-war growth** McWilliams, *The Great Exception*, op. cit., pp. 8, 9, 243; Security Pacific National Bank, "Estimated Population Increase in California," January 31, 1980; McWilliams, *Southern California Country*, op. cit., p. 372.

38. **postwar unemployment** Beck and Williams, op. cit., p. 435.

38. **"Peace threatens industrial dislocation ..."** Cited in Weaver, op. cit., p. 107.

39. **Howard Hughes** Donald L. Bartlett and James B. Steele, *Empire: The Life, Legend and Madness of Howard Hughes*, W. W. Norton & Company (New York: 1979), pp. 37–38, 65, 124, 53–54, 68–78; Hughes Aircraft Company, "Local Firm Made 'Electronics' Before Word Was Widely Known," May, 1980; Hughes Aircraft Company, "Hughes Aircraft Company, 1980," January, 1980; Authors' interview with Charles Thornton.

39. **"When Mr. Hughes ..."** Interview with authors.

40. **Litton Industries and Charles Thornton** Authors' interview with Charles Thornton; *The Executive*, "Litton Industries' Charles B. (Tex) Thornton," January, 1980; *Fortune*, "A Rejuvenated Litton Is Once Again off to the Races," October 8, 1979.

41. **top industrial firms** *Los Angeles Times*, "The Times Roster of California's 100 Top Industrials," May 17, 1981.

41. **Nobel laureates and scientists** Morgan, *Westward Tilt,* op. cit., pp. 6, 39; Federal Reserve Bank of San Francisco, op. cit.; Morgan, *The California Syndrome,* op. cit., p. 110; *Los Angeles Times,* "Californians Among 20 Awarded Medal of Science," January 15, 1980.

41. **college rankings** *The Chronicle of Higher Education,* "The Well-Known Universities Lead in Rating of Faculties' Reputation," January 15, 1979.

42. **"It is not the University . . ."** Cited in University of California Office of University Relations, "A Brief History of the University of California."

42. **early university history** ibid.

42. **Hearsts Bean,** op. cit., pp. 258, 458; University of California Office of University Relations, op. cit.

42. **university engineers** Berkeley Chamber of Commerce, "Berkeley, California," 1970; University of California Office of University Relations, op. cit.

42. **university funding and growth** ibid.

43. **"Science is the mother . . ."** Cited in ibid.

43. **Ernest Lawrence** ibid.; Morgan, *The California Syndrome,* op. cit., p. 112; Beck and Williams, op. cit., pp. 419–420; Berkeley Chamber of Commerce, op. cit.

43. **university master plan** University of California Office of University Relations, op. cit.; McWilliams, *The Great Exception,* op cit., pp. 265–266.

43. **"Universities have become . . ."** Clark Kerr, *The Uses of the University,* Harper & Row (New York: 1963), pp. 89–90.

44. **private donations** Stanford University News Service, press release, May 24, 1979; Authors' interviews with Stanford officials.

44. **genetic engineering** *Time,* "Shaping Life in the Lab," March 9, 1981; *San Francisco Examiner,* "Genentech stock: big money in designer genes," October 15, 1980; *Los Angeles Times,*

"DNA: 2 Obscure Firms See It as Key to Vast Profits," March 10, 1980.

44. **"Southern California faces . . ."** Cited in McWilliams, *The Great Exception,* op. cit., pp. 267–268.

44. **CalTech history** ibid., pp. 260–263; Morgan, *Westward Tilt,* op. cit., pp. 47–49; California Institute of Technology, "Facts about CalTech," June, 1977; Authors' interviews with CalTech officials.

45. **Stanford history** *Fortune,* "California's Great Breeding Ground for Industry," June, 1974; Stanford University News Service, press release (Terman biography), October 3, 1977; *San Francisco Chronicle,* "Why It's Happening on the Peninsula," September 22, 1980; Hewlett-Packard Company, "Hewlett-Packard, a brief sketch," June, 1980; Authors' interviews with Stanford officials.

46. **"There wasn't much here . . ."** Cited in *Fortune,* "California's Great Breeding Ground for Industry," op. cit.

46. **banking legislation** *Oakland Tribune,* "N.Y. bankers want California branches," November 20, 1979.

46. **"I wouldn't trade two blocks . . ."** cited in ibid.

47. **"We have a different . . ."** Interview with authors.

47. **employment growth** California Employment Development Department, "Job Growth in California, 1979."

48. **brain drain** Authors' interview with Tom Schroth, coordinator of engineering internship programs, the University of Michigan at Dearborn.

48. **decline of the Northeast** *Business Week,* "One Country, Five Separate Economies," June 1, 1981.

48. **"If we don't stem . . ."** Interview with authors.

49. **"What we have to do . . ."** *New York Review of Books,* "Reconstructing America," March 5, 1981.

49. **"We've had enough . . ."** Authors' interview with Fluor executive who wished to remain anonymous.

Chapter III. THE RISE OF REAGAN

51. **Salvatori and "the speech . . ."** Authors' interview with Salvatori. See also, Joseph Lewis, *What Makes Reagan Run*, McGraw-Hill (New York: 1968), pp. 1–12.

51. **"After that speech . . ."** Interview with authors.

52. **"Nothing's sacred . . ."** Interview with authors.

52. **Friends of Ronald Reagan** *San Francisco Chronicle*, "Christopher Backers Go for Reagan," August 20, 1966; *Los Angeles Times*, "McCone Named to Reagan's State Executive Committee," August 19, 1966; Kent Steffgen, *Here's the Rest of Him*, Forsight Books (Reno: 1968), pp. 96–97.

53. **"We raised a little money . . ."** Interview with authors.

53. **"We knew then . . ."** Interview with authors.

53. **Behavior Science Corp.** Bill Boyarski, *The Rise of Ronald Reagan*, Random House (New York: 1968), pp. 142–145.

53. **Lyn Nofziger** Authors' interview with Nofziger; Boyarski, op. cit., pp. 140–141.

53. **"No. Jimmy Stewart . . ."** Cited in Edmund G. Brown, *Reagan and Reality*, Praeger Publishers (New York: 1970), p. 41.

54. **Reverend McBirnie** Authors' interview with McBirnie; Lou Cannon, *Ronnie and Jessie: A Political Odyssey*, Doubleday & Company (Garden City: 1969), p. 77.

54. **Spencer-Roberts** Boyarski, op. cit., p. 137.

54. **"The most manageable candidate . . ."** Interview with authors.

54. **"Ronnie always played Ronnie . . ."** Interview with authors. See also, *Newsweek*, "Ronald Reagan Up Close," July 21, 1980.

55. **"It's a sense of mission . . ."** Interview with authors.

55. **"We had to convince them . . ."** Interview with authors.

55. **new Reagan supporters** *San Francisco Chronicle*, "Christopher Backers Go for Reagan," op. cit.; *Los Angeles Times*, "McCone named to Reagan's State Executive Committee," op. cit.; Steffgen, op. cit., p. 98.

56. **Reagan's gubernatorial victory** Cannon, op. cit., pp. 79–88; Boyarski, op. cit., pp. 151–155; Lewis, op. cit., pp. 123–155.

56. **early childhood** Authors' interviews with Neil Reagan; Ronald Reagan's daughter, Maureen Reagan; Reagan's boyhood friend, Edward O'Malley. See also Cannon, op. cit., pp. 3–6; Boyarski, op. cit., pp. 29–38; Lewis, op. cit., pp. 21–22; Ronald Reagan, *Where's the Rest of Me?* Best Books (New York: 1965), pp. 7–24.

56. **"one of those rare . . ."** Reagan, op. cit., p. 15.

56. **hard times in Dixon** Authors' interviews with Neil Reagan, Edward O'Malley, and Joseph Sharkey, the Reagan family's barber in Dixon; Reagan, op. cit., pp. 11, 12, 40; Cannon, op. cit., p. 6.

57. **"Ronnie hung out . . ."** Interview with authors.

57. **Eureka College** Reagan, op. cit., pp. 23–38; Cannon, op. cit., pp. 7–8; Boyarski, pp. 42–51; Lewis, pp. 23–25; Authors' interview with Neil Reagan.

57. **radio career** Reagan, op. cit., pp. 45–64.

57. **arrival in Hollywood** ibid., pp. 64–68.

57. **early film career** Reagan, op. cit., pp. 69–95; Cannon, op. cit., pp. 29–33.

58. **"Ronnie was always . . ."** Interview with authors.

58. **war years** Reagan, op. cit., pp. 97–112; Authors' interview with Al Levitt, who served with Reagan in the military.

58. **"I found him totally changed . . ."** Interview with authors.

59. **"near hopeless, hemophilic liberal . . ."** Reagan, op. cit., p. 126.

59. **"He was often at the Colonel's . . ."** Interview with authors.

59. **"It isn't that he's a bad guy . . ."** Interview with authors.

59. **Union strife in Hollywood** Au-

thors' interviews with Hollywood figures Karen Morley, Jack Wrather, Robert Dornan, Al Levitt, and Anne Revere. See also, Reagan, op. cit., pp. 115–181; David Caute, *The Great Fear*, Simon and Schuster (New York: 1978), pp. 487–520; Boyarski, op. cit., pp. 76–92.

60. **Nancy Reagan** Authors' interview with Mervyn LeRoy; Reagan, op. cit., pp. 208–215; Boyarski, pp. 96–97.

61. **"He woke up ..."** Interview with authors.

61. **"We're all business people ..."** Interview with authors.

62. **"I don't read much ..."** Interview with authors.

62. **"Let's face it ..."** Interview with authors.

62. **The Reagan crowd** Authors' interviews with Irene Dunne, Jack Wrather, Frank McCarthy, William Wilson, Armand Deutsch. See also *New York Times*, "Reagan's Inner Circle of Self-Made Men," May 31, 1980; Cannon, op. cit., p. 196; *Los Angeles Times*, "Wives of 'Kitchen Cabinet' Speak Out," November 14, 1980.

62. **money problems** Authors' interview with Reagan associate who wished to remain anonymous; Reagan, op. cit., p. 219; Boyarski, op. cit., p. 97.

62. **GE Theater** Reagan, op. cit., pp. 224–243; Boyarski, op. cit., pp. 99–102; Cannon, op. cit., p. 69; Lewis, op. cit., pp. 48–51.

63. **"We brought these women ..."** Interview with authors.

63. **inauguration** Boyarski, op. cit., p. 164; Cannon, op. cit., p. 130; Lewis, op. cit., p. 160.

63. **"We are going to squeeze ..."** Cited in Cannon, op. cit., p. 142.

63. **"Any major business ..."** Cited in Cannon, op. cit., p. 130.

64. **business supporters** Cannon, op. cit., pp. 137, 196; Lewis, op. cit., p. 176; Boyarski,, op. cit., pp. 160–162; *Rolling Stone*, "Reagan's Millions," August 26, 1976; *Los Angeles Times*, "Record Doesn't Always Support Reagan's Claims," April 12, 1980.

65. **"When you can stop ..."** Interview with authors.

65. **"Is going to have to be ..."** Cited in *San Francisco Chronicle*, "Reagan Says PT&T Needs Higher Rates," May 17, 1967.

65. **"No other Governor ..."** Interview with authors.

65. **PUC decisions** Authors' interviews with Bill Dunlop and other PUC staff members; information provided by William Bennett former PUC Commissioner; *Los Angeles Times*, "State Utilities Watchdog—A Pattern of Ineptness," December 22, 1974; California Joint Legislative Audit Committee, "Public Utilities Commission," September 12, 1973.

66. **William French Smith** Information drawn from various biographical sources and PUC files.

66. **campaign contributions** Campaign contribution records on file at the California state archives.

66. **"Reagan Undoubtedly got support ..."** Interview with authors.

66. **DART decision** Authors' interviews with PUC staff members; California Public Utilities Commission, "Application of DART Industries, ... Statement of Commission Staff," June 30, 1972.

66. **DART and Tuttle contributions** Campaign contribution records on file at the California state archives; Financial Disclosure Statement of Ronald Reagan, for period of April 1, 1974 to January 6, 1975, filed with the California Secretary of State's Office; *San Francisco Chronicle*, "How Much Reagan Is Worth," February 26, 1976.

67. **"The big utilities ..."** Interview with authors.

67. **Newport Bay land swap** California Joint Legislative Audit Committee, "State Lands Division: Review of Upper Newport Bay Proposed Land Exchange," August, 1972; authors' interviews with SLC staff members.

67. **Irvine's new city** University of California Board of Regents, "Minutes of Meetings," May 15, 1970, July 17, 1970, September 18, 1970, November 20, 1970; *Cry California* magazine, "Irvine: the case for a new kind of planning," Winter, 1970.

68. **Smith and the Irvine Co.**

Authors' interview with William French Smith; Campaign contribution records on file at the California state archives.

68. oil tax bill *Sacramento Bee*, October 24, 1970.

68. race horse bill *Los Angeles Times*, October 8, 1970.

68. motion picture taxes bill *Rolling Stone*, "Reagan's millions," op. cit.

68. Reagan's land deal *Rolling Stone*, "Reagan's Millions," op. cit.; *Sacramento Bee*, October 20, 1970; *New York Times*, "668-Acre Ranch on Coast Is a Key Holding for Ex-Governor, Reticent on Details," October 6, 1980; *Wall Street Journal*, "Film Company Paid the Candidate a Steep Price for Some Steep Land to Make Him a Millionaire," August 1, 1980; Cannon, op. cit., p. 195.

69. Governor's mansion *Sacramento Bee*, March 25, 1969; Cannon, op. cit., p. 139.

69. "They are the only people ..." Authors' interview with former Reagan staff member who wished to remain anonymous.

69. Reagan and the right Kent Steffgen, op. cit.; *Los Angeles Herald Examiner*, "He May Be a Lot More Liberal Than Conservatives Suspect," March 26, 1980; *Los Angeles Herald Examiner*, "Reagan downplaying right-wing links," July 30, 1980; *San Francisco Examiner*, "Far right looks aslant at Reagan's 'mixed' transition teams," November 16, 1980.

70. budget and taxes *Los Angeles Times*, "Record Doesn't Always Support Reagan's Claims," op. cit.; *Washington Post*, "The Leader He Was, the Leader He Wasn't," April 26, 1980; *San Francisco Chronicle*, "The Record, and Reagan's Claims," April 2, 1980.

70. "Ronnie believes in God ..." Interview with authors.

70. abortion bill Capitol Hill News Service, "Ronald Reagan," 1976.

71. fair housing Cannon, op. cit., p. 270; Steffgen, op. cit., pp. 30–38.

71. welfare *Los Angeles Times*, "Record Doesn't Always Support Reagan's Claims," op. cit.; *California Jour-nal*, "Is Reagan taking too much credit for 'slaying' the welfare monster?" December, 1974; *California Journal*, "Welfare Reform Revisited," December, 1972; California Joint Legislative Audit Committee, "California Work Experience Program (CWEP)," May, 1974; Authors' interviews with legislative staff members in Sacramento.

71. "He was trying ..." Interview with authors.

71. UROC United Republicans of California, "Be It Resolved . . . Subject: Oppose Candidacy of Reagan," May 4, 1975.

71. "I thought he was terrific ..." Interview with authors.

72. 1968 and 1976 campaigns Authors' interviews with Reagan campaign officials Lyn Nofziger, Henry Salvatori, William Wilson, Peter Hannaford, Jeff Bell. See also Lewis Chester, Godfrey Hodgson, and Bruce Page, *An American Melodrama, the Presidential Campaign of 1968*, Dell Publishing Company (New York: 1969); Jules Witcover, *Marathon, the Pursuit of the Presidency, 1972–1976*, The Viking Press (New York: 1977).

73. supply siders Interviews with Jeff Bell and Art Laffer; *Wall Street Journal*, "Supply-Side Economics and How It Grew from a Theory to a Presidential Program," February 18, 1981; *Business Week*, "A guide to understanding the supply-siders," December 22, 1980; *Los Angeles Times*, "Reagan's Economic Team," February 15, 1981; *San Francisco Chronicle*, " 'Supply-Side' Economics—What It Means," February 20, 1981.

73. "the Gordian knot ..." Ronald Reagan speech to the Executive Club of Chicago, September 26, 1975.

73. "Nixon is worried ..." Interview with authors.

73. Nixon and Reagan supporters Campaign contributions records filed with the California Secretary of State's Office; *New York Times*, September 21, 1952.

73. "Defeat changed him ..." Authors' interview with Reagan campaign staff member who wished to remain anonymous.

75. "Ronald Reagan represents..." Interview with authors.

76. **tax cut movement** *San Francisco Examiner,* "Jarvis revolt taxing other states as well," August 27, 1978; *San Francisco Examiner,* " 'Spirit of 13' survives in 12 states but fizzles in 4," November 8, 1978; "Prop. 13-itis win in Massachusetts," September 20, 1978.

76. **Jarvis impact on state's economy** California Department of Economic and Business Development, "The Impact of Proposition 13 on the California Business Climate," July 17, 1979; Larry J. Kimbell and David Shulman, "The Impact of Proposition 13 on Rates of Return for California Intensive Firms," presentation before the Financial Management Association Annual Meeting, October 11–13, 1979; California Council for Environmental and Economic Balance, "The Fiscal Impact of New Residential Development After Proposition 13," August, 1979.

76. **1980 campaign** Authors' interviews with Reagan campaign officials and supporters Jim Lake, Charles Black, Lyn Nofziger, Pat Hillings, Peter Hannaford, William Wilson, Casper Weinberger, Ted Cummings.

77. **"Since the death ..."** Interview with authors.

77. **"I know my friends ..."** Interview with authors.

78. **Reagan appointees** *San Francisco Chronicle,* "The President and His Cabinet," February 6, 1981; *The Washington Post,* January 11, 1981.

78. **"We don't buy that ..."** Interview with authors.

79. **"Out here we know ..."** Interview with authors.

Chapter IV. JERRY BROWN AND THE NEW CLASS

80. **Pat Brown** Robert Pack, *Jerry Brown, The Philosopher Prince,* Stein and Day (New York: 1978), pp. 2–5.

80. **California growth** Security Pacific National Bank, " 'Real' Disposable Income Per Capita in California, 1929–1980," October 1, 1980; Security Pacific National Bank, "Estimated Population Increase in California," January 31, 1980.

80. **"As the momentous shift ..."** Cited in Weaver, op. cit., p. 121.

80. **state budget growth** California Governor's Office, "Governor's Budget for 1981–82," January 10, 1981, p. A-12.

80. **Pat Brown's accomplishments** Bean, op. cit., pp. 482–483; Curt Gentry, *The Last Days of the Late, Great State of California,* Ballantine Books (New York: 1969), pp. 50–51.

81. **Freeways, education and water** Bean, op. cit., pp. 483–484; Gentry, op. cit., p. 50.

81. **"Jerry's attitudes developed ..."** Interview with authors.

82. **seminary life** Pack, op. cit., pp. 17–19.

82. **"Life was very simple ..."** Cited in *Playboy* Magazine, "Playboy interview: Jerry Brown," April, 1976.

82. **"There was a wasteland quality..."** Cited in *Playboy,* op. cit.

83. **Tuttle and Taylor** Pack, op. cit., p. 34.

84. **"Reagan. And Reagan does have..."** Cited in *The Village Voice,* "At Home with Jerry Brown: Loser Tells All," July 2, 1980.

84. **Los Angeles Community College** Pack, op. cit., pp. 37–38.

84. **"He was a loner then ..."** Cited in Pack, op. cit., p. 38.

84. **Secretary of State campaign** Pack, op. cit., pp. 41–43.

84. **gubernatorial campaign** J. D. Lorenz, *Jerry Brown: The Man on the White Horse,* Houghton Mifflin Company (Boston: 1978), pp. 2–6; Pack, op. cit., pp. 55–60.

85. **"Jerry Brown continues..."** Cited in Lorenz, op. cit., p. 5.

85. **campaign contributions** Campaign contribution records on file at the California state archives. On John Factor, see Ovid Demaris, *Captive City,* Lyle Stuart, Inc. (New York: 1969), pp. 122–124; Wallace Turner, *Gambler's Money,* Houghton Mifflin Company (Boston: 1965), p. 109; *Los Angeles Times–Washington Post* Wire Service,

"Jake the Barber Put Up 350G for HHH," January 4, 1969.

85. general election campaign Pack, op. cit., pp. 63–70.

86. "not too sure of ..." Cited in Pack, p. 64.

86. "Jerry Brown came to Sacramento ..." Interview with authors.

87. "I think that order ..." Interview with authors.

87. "The whole Jeffersonian ideal ..." Edmund G. Brown, Jr., Thoughts, City Lights Books (San Francisco: 1976), p. 44.

88. Governor's mansion and asceticism Pack, op. cit., pp. 94–95; Newsweek, "The Pop Politics of Jerry Brown," April 23, 1979.

88. University budget Authors' interview with Lawrence C. Hershman, director of the budget, University of California.

88. "The problem with the university ..." Interview with authors.

88. "cheap shots" Interview with authors.

88. employee growth rates California Governor's Office. "Governor's Budget for 1981–82," op. cit., p. A-12.

88. "If you ask the people ..." Interview with authors.

89. budget cuts San Francisco Chronicle, "Senators Call Brown 'Unrealistic' on Budget," January 3, 1979; Oakland Tribune, "Brown 'failed to support' mental health programs," October 5, 1978; Los Angeles Times, "Antipoverty Director Quits, Charges State Indifference," December 22, 1976; Los Angeles Times, "Brown Vetoes $300 Million in Budget, Mostly Pay Hikes," July 14, 1979; Los Angeles Herald Examiner, "Brown to Colleges: Trim the Fat," November 30, 1978.

89. "When Jerry Brown talks ..." Cited in Washington Post, "Crisis Grows in Calif. Mental Hospitals," April 16, 1979.

89. Homemaker Chore cuts California Joint Legislative Audit Committee, "A Management Review of the Homemaker-Chore Services Program," June 11, 1975; Authors' interviews with legislative and county staff members involved in the Homemaker Chore program.

89. "Brown's people ..." Interview with authors.

89. community centers Sacramento Bee, "Handicapped Group Calls Brown a Miser," January 28, 1976; Sacramento Bee, "Aid for the Retarded," editorial, March 21, 1976; G. Vern Beckett, President of the California Association for the Retarded, "Memorandum to Members of the Senate Finance Subcommittee," March 22, 1976.

90. "have to sacrifice something ..." Interview with authors.

90. state mental hospitals Washington Post, "Crisis Grows in Calif. Mental Hospitals," op. cit.; Los Angeles Times, "California's Shame: the Mental Hospitals," November 21, 1976; Los Angeles Times, "Charges May Be Filed in Deaths at Mental Hospital, Probers Say," October 12, 1976.

90. "Things went fairly well ..." Cited in Washington Post, "Crisis Grows in Calif. Mental Hospitals," op. cit.

90. social program cuts Los Angeles Times, "The Legislature Has a Cruel Gift for the State's Poor," December 28, 1980; Los Angeles Times, "Brown Goes to Court on Medi-Cal Limit," January 9, 1979; California Workers' Compensation Reporter, "Special Report: Proposed Budget Cuts Increase Pressure on WCAB," March 1979; Wall Street Journal, "Jerry Brown, Bullet-Biter," January 29, 1981.

90. Chicano appointments Pacific News Service, "Jerry Brown's 'Hispanic Strategy' Stirs White Backlash," February 20, 1978.

91. "He is a master ..." Authors' interview with state legislator who wished to remain anonymous.

91. Dow Chemical San Francisco Chronicle, "Dow's President Raps Brown," January 28, 1978.

91. nuclear power stance San Francisco Chronicle, "Brown Attacks N-Power, Defends Energy Policy," October 2, 1978.

91. "He would come into ..." Interview with authors.

92. "I came off the streets ..." Interview with authors.

93. "I doubt there's a person ..." Interview with authors.

93. Richard Silberman Interview with authors; *San Diego Union*, "Executive on Go Unable to Stop," July 11, 1976; *San Diego Union*, "Silberman: Asset or Liability to Brown?" March 30, 1979; *San Diego Union*, "Silberman's Influence Widespread," March 30, 1979; *San Diego Union*, "Banking Remains the Vital Thread Marking Several Silberman Careers," March 31, 1979; *San Francisco Chronicle*, "Selling Government Like Hamburgers," September 15, 1978.

93. kitchen cabinet Authors' interviews with Brown aides Mickey Kantor, Tom Quinn, Jodie Krajieski, Don Gevirtz.

94. "There will be an increasing role ..." Interview with authors.

94. high tech proposals *Business Week*, "California's own reindustrialization program," January 26, 1981; *Oakland Tribune*, "Brown's staff pushes industrial plan," February 4, 1981.

94. "This nation did not become ..." *Washington Post*, "Edmund G. Brown, Jr.: Reagan Is Wrong," March 1, 1981.

95. "No one is going ..." Cited in *Los Angeles Herald Examiner*, "Chairman Manatt's quotation: 'The New Deal is far too old,'" March 1, 1981.

95. "Until the last couple of years ..." Interview with authors.

95. pro-business efforts *San Francisco Chronicle*, "State Inventory Tax Is Finally Repealed," April 21, 1978; *Wall Street Journal*, "California Gov. Brown Shifts Position, Begins to Woo New Business," July 12, 1977; *San Francisco Chronicle*, "Brown Signs Bill to Ease Paper 'Flood,'" September 12, 1979; *San Francisco Examiner*, "Brown softens his insistence on 160-acre farm limit," November 9, 1977; *San Francisco Chronicle*, "Brown Vetoes Bill on Real Estate Broker Standards," July 31, 1979; *New York Law Journal*, "New California Law Forecasts Access Growth," October 11, 1979.

96. Robert Anderson *Los Angeles Herald Examiner*, "Is Anderson of ARCO Pushing Brown to the Right?" January 24, 1979.

96. Brown and businessmen *San Francisco Chronicle*, "Brown Is Wooing the Farm Vote," August 31, 1978; *San Francisco Examiner*, "Brown in pursuit of big business," September 5, 1976; *San Francisco Examiner*, "Brown patching up his business image," December 16, 1976.

96. "Brown's just great ..." Interview with authors.

96. "He's gone to the corporations ..." Interview with former Brown aide who wished to remain anonymous.

96. promotion of high tech and space efforts *Sacramento Bee*, "Expanded Electronics Apprenticeships Asked," May 11, 1978; *San Francisco Chronicle*, "The Governor's New Programs," January 10, 1978; *San Francisco Chronicle*, "Brown's Space Quest," February 21, 1978; *Los Angeles Times*, February 19, 1978.

96. Japan trip *Sacramento Bee*, "Talking Business: Governor Wooing Japanese Auto Makers," April 10, 1977; *San Francisco Examiner*, "Brown's sales pitch to Fukuda," May 6, 1978.

97. foreign trade Security Pacific National Bank, "California's International Trade," October, 1979.

97. Office of International Trade *Oakland Tribune*, "Gains seen very quickly," May 21, 1978.

97. "We don't want to rely ..." Interview with authors.

97. trips to Mexico Pacific News Service, "Brown Forges Foreign Policy for California," December 9, 1977; *Los Angeles Herald Examiner*, "Brown-Portillo meeting in Mexico," July 28, 1979.

97. LNG proposal *Los Angeles Times*, "Brown Will Seek Speedy Approval of LNG Facility," February 11, 1977; *San Francisco Examiner*, "Impatience over picking LNG site," May 16, 1977; Authors' interviews with PUC and Coastal Commission staff members, and officials of Pacific Lighting Corporation; *Los Angeles Herald Examiner*, "New Look at Brown Holdings," April 18, 1979.

97. Bustamante family *New York Times*, "Gov. Brown Supporting Proj-

ects That Aid a Mexican Contributor," March 11, 1979; *Los Angeles Herald Examiner,* "Bustamante Ties to California Firms Probed," March 13, 1979.

98. **campaign contributions** California Fair Political Practices Commission, "Campaign Contribution and Spending Report, June 6, 1978. Primary Election," September 28, 1978; California Fair Political Practices Commission, "Campaign Contribution and Spending Report, November 7, 1978, General Election," May 15, 1979. See also, *San Francisco Examiner,* "When it comes to money, Gov. Brown is Mr. Practicality," August 3, 1979; *San Francisco Chronicle,* "$2 Million Raised for Brown," September 30, 1978.

98. **"Jerry Brown's attitude ..."** Interview with authors.

98. **outspends Republican** *Los Angeles Times,* "Brown Outspent Younger by More Than $1 Million to Win Re-election in 1978, " February 1, 1979.

98. **Proposition 13** Authors interviews with Howard Jarvis, staff members of the pro- and anti-Jarvis campaigns and officials at several county assessor's offices; Howard Jarvis, *I'm Mad as Hell,* Times Books (New York: 1979), see especially, pp. 8–10, 39–40; *San Francisco Chronicle,* "The Men Behind the Big Tax Revolt," February 2, 1978; *San Francisco Examiner,* "The man whose mission is tax reform," March 19, 1978; *San Francisco Chronicle,* "The Strategists in the War on Jarvis," March 23, 1978; *San Francisco Chronicle,* "A Prop. 13 Talk with Brown," July 26, 1978; *Oakland Tribune,* "Brown predicts '13' will sweep nation," September 21, 1978; *Los Angeles Times,* "Prop. 13: Change but Not Disaster," June 3, 1979.

99. **Brown and Younger** *San Francisco Chronicle,* "Brown Widens Lead in Poll," October 4, 1978.

100. **"We have our marching orders ..."** Cited in Jarvis, op. cit., p. 55.

100. **layoff estimates** Jarvis, op. cit., p. 167.

100. *Los Angeles Times* **poll** Cited in Jarvis, op. cit., p. 150.

100. **"better wake up ..."** Cited in

Los Angeles Times, "GOP Manager Stuart Spencer Praises Governor Brown's Political Skills," August 4, 1978.

101. **Reinhardt claim** *Los Angeles Times,* "Brown Cast Eye on White House Early," June 6, 1976.

101. **Brown enters race** ibid.; Pack, op. cit., p. 186.

101. **"We had no staff ..."** Interview with authors.

101. **campaign contributions** Campaign contribution records on file with the California Secretary of State's Office.

102. **1976 presidential campaign** Pack, op. cit., pp. 257–262; Orville Schell, *Brown,* Random House (New York: 1978), pp. 32–34; *New West* magazine, "Brown, Reagan and Self-Destruction," June 7, 1976.

102. **"We didn't lose ..."** Cited in Pack, op. cit., p. 262.

102. **"The media needs conflict ..."** Cited in Schell, op. cit., pp. 120–121.

102. **1980 campaign** Authors' interviews with Brown aides Tom Quinn, Mickey Kantor, Gray Davis, Don Gevirtz, Andy Safir; *Oakland Tribune,* "Just what does Gov. Moonbeam stand for, anyway?" August 5, 1979; *San Francisco Examiner,* "Most New York politicos yawn as 'Jerry-Who' flies into town," October 10, 1979; *San Francisco Chronicle,* "Brown Is Still Not Taken Seriously," October 16, 1979; *Los Angeles Herald Examiner,* "Is the nation ready for Jerry Brown, cosmic candidate?" November 12, 1979; *Los Angeles Herald Examiner,* "Uh, wow!—it's Gov. Mork of California!," November 30, 1979; *Los Angeles Times,* "Jerry Brown's Dream-Turned-Nightmare," March 28, 1980; *Los Angeles Times,* "Brown's New Campaign Team Criticized," March 23, 1980.

103. **"Jerry Brown is brilliant ..."** Interview with MCA official who wished to remain anonymous.

103. **financial supporters** Authors' interviews with Brown campaign aides Tom Quinn and Jodie Krajieski.

104. **"simply couldn't produce ..."** Interview with authors.

104. **"I didn't have a strong ..."** Cited in the *Village Voice*, "Loser Tells All," July 2, 1980.

104. **shift away from Hayden** Authors' interviews with Brown aides who wished to remain anonymous.

105. **"I think Brown is developing ..."** Interview with authors.

Chapter V. THE POLITICS OF CULTURE

106. **"There's a tremendous ..."** Interview with authors.

107. **ARCO and public TV** Atlantic Richfield Company, "Participation III, Atlantic Richfield and Society," October, 1980. *Los Angeles Times*, "Do-Goodism Is Fast Becoming Company Rule," April 22, 1979.

107. **"The United States ..."** Interview with authors.

107. **Movie, TV, and recording statistics** Federal Reserve Bank of San Francisco, "City of the Angels," op. cit.; Security Pacific National Bank, "Monthly Summary of Business Conditions, Southern California," op. cit.

108. **record sales** Figures supplied by the National Association of Recording Manufacturers.

108. **movie box office grosses** Figures supplied by the Motion Picture Association of America.

108. **TV viewing** Figures supplied by A. C. Nielsen and Company.

108. **"I'm going to talk in ..."** Cited in *Forbes*, "Video Fever," September 1, 1980.

108. **"We really are children ..."** Cited in *Los Angeles Times*, "Hollywood Whiz Kids, Over the Hill at 30?" March 8, 1981.

108. **Hollywood parents** *Ladies Home Journal*, September, 1979.

109. **time watching TV** *Los Angeles Herald Examiner*, "A Nation on Remote Control," January 11, 1981.

109. **"Children who have been taught ..."** Cited in Martin Mayer, *About Television*, Harper & Row (New York: 1972), p. 128.

109. **People magazine** *Los Angeles Herald Examiner*, "Up from the racks," March 15, 1981.

109. **advertising revenue** *Los Angeles Herald Examiner*, "A Nation on Remote Control," op. cit.

109. **political advertising** ibid.

109. **Hollywood and politics** *Variety*, "Showbiz & Politics Not Odd Fellows," November 9, 1978; *Los Angeles Herald Examiner*, "Celebrity Politics: The All-American Star Wars Version," December 27, 1979; *Los Angeles Herald Examiner*, "Political Star Wars," February 10, 1980; *New York Times*, "The Stars Come out to Raise Funds," April 16, 1978; *Newsweek*, "The Battle of the Bands," May 31, 1976; *San Francisco Examiner*, "Gov. Brown's flashy array of donors: That's show biz," May 7, 1978; *San Francisco Examiner*, "The candidates of the celebs," March 8, 1980.

110. **"Electronic communication ..."** Richard Sennett, *The Fall of Public Man*, Vintage Books (New York: 1978), p. 282.

110. **"The entertainment people ..."** Cited in *Esquire*, "California," February, 1978.

111. **beginnings of Hollywood** Caughey and Caughey, op. cit., pp. 254–258.

111. **"a safety valve ..."** Cited in Henry Nash Smith, *Virgin Land*, Harvard University Press (Cambridge: 1976), p. 254.

112. **"big, tough boy ..."** Cited in Jerzy Toeplitz, *Hollywood and After*, George Allen & Unwin, Ltd. (London: 1974), p. 138.

112. **early Hollywood** McWilliams, *Southern California Country*, op. cit., pp. 331–332.

112. **Birth of a Nation** Robert H. Stanley, *The Celluloid Empire*, Hastings House (New York: 1978), p. 22; McWilliams, *Southern California Country*, op. cit., p. 332.

112. **$20 million payroll** McWilliams, *Southern California Country*, op. cit., p. 333.

112. **Mary Pickford** Stanley, op. cit., pp. 24–25.

113. **Theda Bara** Stanley, op. cit., pp. 26–27.

113. **social acceptance** Leo C. Rosten, *The Movie Colony, The Movie Makers*, op. cit., pp. 165–166.

113. **production expenditures** Rosten, op. cit., p. 375.

113. **Chaplin salary** Stanley, op. cit., p. 31.

113. **financing Hollywood** Stanley, op. cit., pp. 33–34, 45, 47–48, 58.

113. **wealthy investors** Stanley, op. cit., pp. 66, 100–101.

114. **Howard Hughes** Bartlett and Steele, *Empire, The Life, Legend, and Madness of Howard Hughes*, op. cit., pp. 39–47; Stanley, op. cit., pp. 100–101.

114. **Joseph Kennedy** Rosten, op. cit., pp. 253–254.

114. **problems with Eastern control of filmmaking** ibid., pp. 251–255.

114. **"The men on the west coast ..."** Cited in Rosten, op. cit., p. 251.

114. **production costs** Rosten, op. cit., p. 375.

114. **"in the crisis of 1929 ..."** *Los Angeles Times*, "Hollywood, 1915: Reminiscence of a Simple Time," advertising supplement, August 31, 1980.

115. **Warner's, sound and growth** Stanley, op. cit., pp. 55–57.

115. **Warner's in the 1930s** Stanley, op. cit., pp. 59–62.

115. **"the movies (were) ..."** Cited in Rosten, op. cit., p. 367.

115. **size of the movie industry in the 1930s** Rosten, op. cit., pp. 3–4, 375.

115. **movie industry size and salaries** Rosten, op. cit., pp. 379–381.

115. **Mayer salary** ibid., p. 80.

115. **stars' salaries** ibid., p. 83.

115. **Shirley Temple** Stanley, op. cit., p. 83.

115. **life of luxury** McWilliams, op. cit., pp. 345–346.

116. **"Men have always ..."** Rosten, op. cit., pp. 12–13.

116. **divorces** Rosten, op. cit., p. 400.

117. **"It was Pollyanna time ..."** Interview with authors.

117. **Dorothy Parker** Cited in Rosten, op. cit., p. 133.

117. **Meriam-Sinclair campaign** Rosten, op. cit., pp. 134–139.

117. **Hollywood liberalism** ibid., p. 160.

118. **migratory workers** Rosten, op. cit., p. 154.

118. **"We are accused ..."** Cited in Rosten, op. cit., pp. 154–155.

118. **SAG formed** *Screen Actor* magazine, "SAG history: In the eye of the beholder," Summer, 1979.

118. **Hollywood Anti-Nazi League** Rosten, op. cit., pp. 140–143; David Caute, *The Great Fear*, op. cit., p. 487.

118. **Congressman Dies** Rosten, op. cit., pp. 144–153.

118. **Hollywood Communists** Caute, op. cit., p. 487.

118. **pro-Soviet films** ibid., pp. 490–491.

118. **"to help a desperate war effort"** Cited in Caute, op. cit., p. 491.

118. **anti-communism in Hollywood after the war** Caute, op. cit., pp. 488–500.

119. **Walt Disney** Caute, op. cit., p. 493.

119. **"tinged with Communistic ..."** Cited in Caute, op. cit., p. 492.

120. **"The Great Chief ..."** Cited in Caute, op. cit., p. 497.

120. **250 blacklisted** Caute, op. cit., p. 515.

120. **"these people were deserted ..."** Interview with authors.

120. **Salt of the Earth** Caute, op. cit., p. 514.

120. **Motion Picture Alliance** ibid., p. 502. Stanley, op. cit., p. 128.

121. **"It was boy meets girl ..."** Interview with authors.

121. **televisions** Mayer, op. cit., p. 21; Stanley, op. cit., p. 127.

121. **movie industry losses** Stanley, op. cit., pp. 126–128.

121. **"The 1950s saw ..."** Longstreet, op. cit., p. 241.

121. **Klaus Landsberg** *Los Angeles Times*, "L. A. Television: The Early

Days," advertising supplement, August 31, 1980; *Back Stage,* "Studios Shift to Television: Hollywood Tele-production, 1945–55," September 5, 1980; Authors' interview with Syd Cassyd of the Academy of Television Arts and Sciences.

122. **"Back then this was ..."** Interview with authors.

123. **Hollywood action dramas** Stanley, op. cit., pp. 168, 169, 173.

123. **migration to Hollywood** Toeplitz, op. cit., pp. 90–91.

123. **"When television came out here ..."** Authors' interview with local journalist who has covered Hollywood for many years and wished to remain anonymous.

123. **Disneyland** Christopher Finch, *The Art of Walt Disney,* Abrams (New York: 1976), pp. 145–152; Neil R. Peirce, *The Pacific States of America,* W. W. Norton & Company (New York: 1972), pp. 172–173; *New West,* "Disneyland Is Good for You," December 4, 1978.

124. **Knott's Berry Farm** *Los Angeles Times,* "Knott's: 60 Years of Family Fun," February 24, 1980.

124. **Stars for Barry** Stars for Barry (record), American United, 1964; Interview with Tony Hilder, producer of Stars for Barry.

124. **"I suppose a lot ..."** Stars for Barry, op. cit.

124. **"These relationships go back ..."** Interview with authors.

125. **Reagan inaugural** *Los Angeles Times,* "A Candlelight Evening of Inaugural Festivities," January 20, 1981; *Oakland Tribune,* "Reagan's Day," January 18, 1981.

126. **"The old Hollywood ..."** Interview with authors.

126. **decline of Hollywood in the 1960s** Toeplitz, op. cit., pp. 37, 39; Morgan, *Westward Tilt,* op. cit., p. 151.

126. **takeovers** Peirce, op. cit., p. 163.

126. **Gallup poll** Toeplitz, op. cit., pp. 100–101.

126. **Cleopatra** ibid., pp. 46–48.

127. **"at best a major ..."** cited in Toeplitz, op. cit., p. 48.

127. *The Green Berets* Toeplitz, op. cit., pp. 104–106.

127. **"There is no shortage"** Cited in Toeplitz, op. cit., p. 77.

127. **new directors, producers and films** Toeplitz, op. cit., pp. 94–98.

128. **"The old heroes ..."** Cited in Toeplitz, op. cit., p. 116.

128. **"You wish you could ..."** Interview with authors.

128. **"There is a new problem ..."** Interview with authors.

129. **record production** Authors' interview with John Sippel.

129. **Brown and music figures** *Los Angeles Herald Examiner,* "Political Star Wars," February 10, 1980; *Newsweek,* "Battle of the Bands," May 31, 1976; *Oakland Tribune,* "Gov. Brown, Ronstadt on way to Kenya," April 9, 1979; Authors' interviews with music industry figures Irv Azoff and Jeff Wald, and Brown campaign aides Gray Davis and Tom Quinn.

129. **"Brown's perfect for ..."** Authors' interview with television executive who wished to remain anonymous.

129. **"We need a leader ..."** Interview with authors.

130. **Mike Curb** *New West,* "Will the 'Sixth Osmond Brother' Be the Second Ronald Reagan?" March 27, 1978; *Los Angeles Times,* "Nofziger to Advise Curb on the Media," September 27, 1979; *San Francisco Chronicle,* "GOP's Toss-Up for Lieutenant Governor," May 9, 1978; Lawrence A. Armour, *The Young Millionaires,* Playboy Press (Chicago: 1973), pp. 123–138.

130. **"The activists within Hollywood ..."** Interview with authors.

130. **Curb on social issues** *Oakland Tribune,* "Uproar over GOP candidate's racy film ties," September 28, 1978; *San Francisco Examiner,* "GOP candidate Curb is opposed to Prop. 6," September 7, 1978.

130. **"In terms of pot ..."** Cited in Armour, op. cit., p. 136.

131. **fundraising for Curb** Authors' interviews with Republican party officials Arnie Steinberg and Jack Courtemanche.

131. "The day of the bosses ..." Interview with authors.

131. California cable firms New York Law Journal, "Cable TV Deregulation," October 11, 1979.

131. cable TV legislation Los Angeles Times, "New Cable Bill Widely Hailed," September 17, 1979; Cablevision magazine, "The Making of a Law," October 8, 1979; New York Times, "A New California Law to Deregulate Cable TV," September 29, 1979.

131. Oak Communications Los Angeles Herald Examiner, "Oak Communications looks to 'leapfrog' cable television," February 3, 1981.

131. "The cost of transportation ..." Cited in Los Angeles Herald Examiner, "Oak Communications looks to 'leapfrog' cable television," op. cit.

132. publishing and Hollywood Los Angeles Times, "The West—New Chapter in Publishing," May 23, 1979; Los Angeles Herald Examiner, "Bringing American Book Publishing to Its Knees," March 20, 1980; Los Angeles Times, "The L.A. connection: publishers find talent, entertainment tie-ins," December 10, 1978; Los Angeles Times, "Selling Books—TV Often Writes Story," October 17, 1979; The New Yorker, "The Blockbuster Complex," October 6, 1980; New Times, "Star Wars," February 6, 1978.

132. employment decline U.S. Department of Labor, "Employment and Earnings, States and Areas, 1939–78," op. cit.

132. "talk shows for the semi-literate" New Times, "Star Wars," op. cit.

132. power of stars over publications ibid.

133. "In some strange way" Cited in New Times, "Star Wars," op. cit.

133. "an I for an I" Cited in Rosten, op. cit., p. 45.

133. conspicuous consumption The Washington Post, "California, Christmas and the Stars" December 23, 1977.

133. "It's not really business ..." Cited in ibid.

134. "It's too hard ..." Interview with authors.

134. "Right now we're ..." Cited in Los Angeles Herald Examiner, "Rona Barrett: Can we take her seriously," February 22, 1981.

134. Hollywood ethics New York Times, "Critics of the Movie Business Find Pattern of Financial Irregularities," January 29, 1978; Oakland Tribune, "David Begelman's heritage: a generation of chaos," April 16, 1978; Los Angeles Herald Examiner, "New Hollywood's creative bookkeeping isn't a hit or miss proposition," January 22, 1981; New York Times Magazine, "Hollywood's Wall Street Connection," February 26, 1978.

134. Begelman affair New West, "The Incredible Past of David Begelman," February 13, 1978; New York Times Magazine, "Hollywood's Wall Street Connection," op. cit.; San Francisco Chronicle, "Movie Mogul Tells Why He Stole," July 23, 1979; San Francisco Chronicle, "Controversial President Fired at Columbia Pictures," July 21, 1978; San Francisco Chronicle, "MGM Hires Begelman as President," December 19, 1979.

135. "Look we trade ..." Cited in New York Times Magazine, "Hollywood's Wall Street Connection," op. cit.

135. "what is on television ..." Penthouse, "Los Angeles a Celebration," op. cit.

135. Dallas Los Angeles Herald Examiner, "The 'Dallas' Phenomenon," January 11, 1981.

136. the California corporate conscience See, for example, "Occidental accused in $600,000 payoffs," San Francisco Examiner, May 4, 1977; Morton Mintz and Jerry S. Cohen, America, Inc. Dell Publishing Company (New York: 1971), pp. 211–212; New York Times, "A Bribery Scandal—the Give and the Take," July 3, 1977; J. Anthony Lukas, Nightmare: The Underside of the Nixon Years, the Viking Press (New York: 1976); Arthur H. Samish and Bob Thomas, The Secret Boss of California, Crown Publishers (New York: 1971).

136. "They are full of" Cited in Martin Mayer, op. cit., p. 381.

Chapter VI. CALIFORNIA'S MIDDLE CLASS: THE FREE ENTERPRISE SOCIETY

137. **"I guess it's just ..."** Interview with authors.

137. **consumer goods** *Sunset* magazine, "Western Market Almanac," 1978.

138. **markets** ibid.

138. **"The acquisitive urge ..."** Michael Davie, *California, the Vanishing Dream*, Dodd, Mead & Company (New York: 1972), p. 22.

138. **spirituality and religion** *San Francisco Chronicle*, "Cults: America's Growth Industry," June 6, 1979; *San Francisco Chronicle*, "Those Burgeoning 20th Century Cults," June 7, 1979; *San Francisco Chronicle*, "Cults: Their Stunning Proliferation," June 8, 1979; Ted K. Bradshaw and Edward J. Blakely, *Policy Implications of California's Changing Life Styles*, Institute of Governmental Studies (Berkeley: 1978), p. 21; Ted K. Bradshaw, "Life Styles in the Advanced Industrial Society," paper presented before the American Sociological Association, August, 1978.

138. **Yankelovich Monitor** *Sunset* magazine, "Western Market Almanac," op. cit.

138. **"I strongly believe ..."** Interview with authors.

139. **"We could build ..."** *Los Angeles Times*, "Should America Fence Off California," April 23, 1979.

139. **mobility** U.S. Department of Commerce, Statistical Abstract of the United States, op. cit.

139. **"It's an end of the line ..."** Interview with authors.

139. **new business starts** Neil R. Pierce, *The Pacific States of America*, op. cit., pp. 161–162; United California Bank, "Recent Economic Trends and Indicators California," op. cit.

140. **"In England if you see ..."** Interview with authors.

141. **"More of the characteristics ..."** Bradshaw, "Life Styles in the Advanced Industrial Society," op. cit.

141. **income statistics** *San Francisco Examiner*, "Per capita income in '79: $8,706," May 11, 1980; United California Bank, "Recent Economic Trends and Indicators California," op. cit.

141. **assets** *Sunset* magazine, "Western Market Almanac," op. cit.

141. **high tech salaries** *San Francisco Chronicle*, "California Casual—Plus a Lot of Hard Work," September 23, 1979.

141. **"An industry friend"** Cited in *San Francisco Chronicle*, "The Headhunters of Silicon Valley," June 23, 1978.

142. **service sector** Bradshaw, "Life Styles in the Advanced Industrial Society," op. cit.; Wells Fargo Bank, "California to 1990," op. cit.

142. **wage earnings** California Governor's Office, "Economic Report of the Governor, 1980, Statistical Appendix," 1980.

142. **immigrants** Security Pacific National Bank, Estimated Population Increase in California," January 31, 1980.

142. **"The valley companies ..."** Cited in *San Francisco Chronicle*, "California Casual—Plus a Lot of Hard Work," op. cit.

143. **education** Bradshaw, "Life Styles in the Advanced Industrial Society," op. cit.

143. **engineers** U.S. Department of Commerce, Statistical Abstract of the United States, op. cit.

143. **"There are many ..."** Authors' interview with engineer who wished to remain anonymous.

143. **"We should have ..."** Interview with authors.

143. **Sanders' background** Authors' interview with Sanders; *San Francisco Chronicle*, "Instant Tycoons in Silicon Valley," September 24, 1980.

144. **"It's a hype ..."** Cited in *San Francisco Chronicle*, "Instant Tycoons in Silicon Valley," op. cit.

144. **"I looked on for a moment…"** Cited in Bean, op. cit., pp. 111–112.

144. **"Whatever his station …"** Oscar Lewis and Carroll D. Hall, *Bonanza Inn*, Ballantine Books (New York: 1971), pp. 4–5.

145. **"trailing after the big boys"** Cited in McWilliams, *Southern California Country*, op. cit., p. 160.

146. **"There's been a tremendous"** Interview with authors.

146. **"The success ratio"** *Fortune*, "California's Great Breeding Ground for Industry," op. cit.

146. **automobiles** *Sunset* magazine, "Western Market Almanac," op. cit.

147. **"if you haven't …"** Cited in *San Francisco Chronicle*, "California Casual—Plus a Lot of Hard Work," op. cit.

147. **"I dress in blue jeans …"** Interview with authors.

147. **Tom Collins** Authors' interview with Collins.

148. **home computers** *San Francisco Chronicle*, "The New Boom—Home Computers," September 24, 1980.

148. **"It's a bit like heroin …"** Cited in ibid.

148. **"It's only a matter of time…"** Cited in *San Francisco Chronicle*, "Writers Plugging into the New Technology," November 28, 1980.

148. **"The hope is …"** Cited in *San Francisco Chronicle*, "Berkeley Outfit Still Freezing People," May 4, 1979.

148. **tombstone** *Los Angeles Times*, "Entrepreneurs Who Help You Go in Style," March 13, 1981.

149. **Briggs' initiative** *San Francisco Examiner*, "Proposition 6," November 8, 1978.

149. **Social attitudes of Californians** See also *Oakland Tribune*, "California No. 1 in 1979 divorces, report says," June 9, 1981; *San Francisco Chronicle*, "The Singles Business," September 3, 1979; *Sunset* magazine, "Western Market Almanac," op. cit.

149. **divorces** U.S. Department of Commerce, Statistical Abstract of the United States, op. cit., Bradshaw and Blakely, op. cit., p. 11.

149. **sexuality** U.S. Department of Commerce, Statistical Abstract of the United States, op. cit.; *Oakland Tribune*, "Teen-age pregnancies high in California," July 29, 1978.

149. **open sexuality** *Oakland Tribune*, "Male strip show rocks Fremont," February 21, 1980; *San Bernardino Sun-Telegram*, "It's 'clothing optional' at S. B. apartment," December 3, 1977; Authors' interviews with officials of LIBRE; *San Francisco Chronicle*, "Ex-Cop Pleads No Contest in Sex Case," March 25, 1978; *San Francisco Chronicle*, "Ex-Police Chief Faces 3 Sex Charges," February 8, 1978.

150. **"He was a very …"** Authors' interview with Livermore resident who wished to remain anonymous.

150. **"This is a free spirit …"** Interview with authors.

150. **mobility** U.S. Department of Commerce, Statistical Abstract of the United States, op. cit., *Sunset* magazine, Western Market Almanac, op. cit.

151. **freeway living** Curt Gentry, *The Last Days of the Late, Great State of California*, Ballantine Books (New York: 1968), pp. 171–172.

151. **"in spite of …"** Bradshaw and Blakely, op. cit., p. 11.

151. **non-partisan tradition** McWilliams, *The Great Exception*, op. cit., pp. 192–198.

151. **progressives** George Mowry, *The California Progressives*, University of California Press (Berkeley: 1951).

152. **"The Johnson administration's"** Spencer C. Olin, Jr., *California's Prodigal Sons*, University of California Press (Berkeley: 1968), p. 173.

152. **"The administration's affairs …"** Beverly Hodghead, "The General Features of the Berkeley Charter," address delivered before the Convention of California Municipalities, September 21, 1909.

152. **"I declare now …"** Cited in *Berkeley Daily Gazette*, March 30, 1911.

152. **"We propose nothing …"** Cited in *Berkeley Daily Gazette*, March 31, 1911.

152. **Stitt Wilson** Information contained in Berkeley campaign files at the University of California at Berkeley's Bancroft Library.

152. **voter apathy and ignorance**

McWilliams, *The Great Exception,* op. cit., pp. 195–196.

153. **"Voters in California ..."** Cited in ibid., p. 196.

153. **voter turnout** U.S. Department of Commerce, Statistical Abstract of the United States, op. cit.; *New York Times,* "West Taking South's Place as Most Alienated Area," March 18, 1979.

153. **"There was once ..."** Interview with authors.

153. **blasphemy initiative** Information supplied by California Secretary of State's Office.

153. **"There is less basic ..."** Cited in Neil Morgan, *Westward Tilt,* op. cit., p. 162.

154. **disco rabbi** *Los Angeles Times,* " 'Disco Rabbi' Forms Singles Synagogue," March 14, 1980.

154. **"What's to support ..."** Cited in ibid.

155. **"Our society is predisposed"** Interview with authors.

155. **cults and utopian communities** Bradshaw and Blakely, op. cit., p. 25; *San Francisco Examiner,* "California's history of cults: from kooks to the violents," November 23, 1978.

155. **William Money** McWilliams, *Southern California Country,* op. cit., pp. 250–251; Gentry, op. cit., pp. 245–248.

155. **"a blend of Catholic ritual ..."** Gentry, op. cit., p. 245.

155. **Katherine Tingley** McWilliams, *Southern California Country,* op. cit., pp. 252–253; Beck and Williams, op. cit., p. 384; Andrew F. Rolle, *California, a History,* Thomas Y. Crowell Company (New York: 1963), p. 528.

156. **Krotona cult** McWilliams, *Southern California Country,* op. cit., pp. 254–255; Gentry, op. cit., p. 248.

156. **Aimee Semple McPherson** McWilliams, *Southern California Country,* op. cit., pp. 258–262; Bean, op. cit., pp. 411–412; Beck and Williams, op. cit., pp. 386–388; Caughey and Caughey, op. cit., pp. 280–282.

156. **William Riker** Robert V. Hine, *California's Utopian Colonies,* W. W. Norton & Company (New York: 1973), pp. 154–157; Gentry, op. cit., pp. 249, 256, 260.

157. **"God winks his eye ..."** Cited in Gentry, op. cit., p. 256.

157. **"when they dream ..."** McWilliams, *Southern California Country,* op. cit., p. 304.

157. **population increase** California Yearbook: Bicentennial Edition, op. cit., p. 294.

157. **"Here is the world's ..."** Cited in McWilliams, *Southern California Country,* op. cit., p. 250.

157. **Hollywood and the spiritualists and astrologers** Rosten, op. cit., pp. 225–228.

157. **"Los Angeles leads ..."** Cited in Beck and Williams, op. cit., p. 383.

158. **Mighty I am** McWilliams, *Southern California Country,* op. cit., pp. 262–265; Gentry, op. cit., p. 257.

158. **Mankind United** Beck and Williams, op. cit., pp. 384–385; McWilliams, *Southern California Country,* op. cit., pp. 265–266.

158. **literary figures and intellectuals** McWilliams, *Southern California Country,* op. cit., p. 271; Davie, op. cit., pp. 196–198.

159. **Esalen Institute** Marilyn Ferguson, *The Aquarian Conspiracy,* J. P. Tarcher, Inc. (Los Angeles: 1980), pp. 137–140; Davie, op. cit., pp. 173–180.

160. **"Especially in these ..."** Edwin Schur, *The Awareness Trap,* McGraw-Hill Book Company (New York: 1977), pp. 3–4.

160. **"While the movement ..."** ibid., p. 7.

160. **spiritual groups** Bradshaw, "Life Styles in the Advanced Industrial Society," op. cit.; Bradshaw and Blakeley, op. cit., pp. 21–24.

160. **Werner Erhard and est** Materials supplied by the est organization; Authors' interviews with est graduates; Bradshaw, "Life Styles in the Advanced Industrial Society," op. cit.; W. W. Bartley, *Werner Erhard,* Clarkson N. Potter, Inc. (New York: 1978); *Los Angeles Herald Examiner,* "Est seekers get the message," November 19, 1979; *New York* magazine, "Powers of Mind, Part II: The EST Experience," September 29, 1975; *The Village Voice,* "Erhard's Interior Design," March 5, 1979.

161. "What happened had no ..." Cited in Bartley, op. cit., pp. 166–167.

161. "est is not about ..." "What is est?" provided by the est organization.

162. est advisory board "The est Advisory Board," provided by the est organization.

162. est finances Mother Jones, "Let Them Eat EST," December, 1978.

162. hunger project Materials supplied by the Hunger Project organization; Mother Jones, "Let Them Eat EST," op. cit.

162. "inform, educate and enlighten ..." Cited in Los Angeles Times, "Food for Thought at a Hunger Party," March 13, 1980.

162. dinner party ibid.

162. "this is not about ..." Cited in ibid.

162. Unification Church Records on file at the Alameda County, California, courthouse; San Francisco Chronicle, "U.S. Hiring Moonies to Clean Its Carpets," March 7, 1980; Pacific News Service, "Holy mackerel: Moonies go fishing," January 4, 1979; Authors' interviews with former members of the Unification Church.

163. Church of Hakeem San Francisco Examiner, "Church charges illegal police search," January 3, 1979; Oakland Tribune, "Hakeem loses documents fight," January 16, 1979; Oakland Tribune, "Riding the red Rolls Royce: an interview with Rev. Hakeem," March 11, 1979; Oakland Tribune, "Hakeem's women talk about church leader," April 26, 1979; San Francisco Chronicle, "Church Founder Indicted for Fraud," May 30, 1979; San Francisco Chronicle, "Cults: America's Growth Industry?," op. cit.

163. "I will not sell it ..." Cited in Oakland Tribune, "Riding the red Rolls Royce: an interview with Rev. Hakeem," op. cit.

163. Scientology San Francisco Chronicle, "Those Burgeoning 20th-Century Cults"; Information supplied by the Church of Scientology organization.

163. The Two San Francisco Chronicle, "Cults: Their Stunning Proliferation," op. cit.; Authors' interview with a California psychologist who has studied the group, and who wished to remain anonymous.

163. Unarius Authors' interviews with Unarius officials and members; San Francisco Chronicle, "Waiting for the Space Fleet to Come In," March 11, 1979.

164. "We almost had ..." Interview with authors.

164. "It filled in the enigmas" Interview with authors.

164. People's Temple Authors' interviews with former Temple members and survivors of the Jonestown incident.

164. "This wouldn't have happened ..." Cited in Charles A. Krause, Guyana Massacre, Berkeley Publishing Corporation (New York: 1978), p. 115.

164. Synanon San Francisco Chronicle, "Big Synanon Gun Purchase Reported," January 26, 1978; San Francisco Chronicle, "Rattlesnake 'Ambush' of Synanon Foe," October 12, 1978; Oakland Tribune, "Synanon's founder held in murder try," December 3, 1978; Los Angeles Times, "Dederich Tape: 'Going to Crack Some Bones,'" December 9, 1978; New York Times, "A Changed Synanon the Subject of Inquiry," December 10, 1978; San Francisco Chronicle, "Court Transcript Lists Alleged Synanon Abuses," March 1, 1979; New Times, "Synanon's Tragic Journey," November 27, 1978.

165. Unification Church San Francisco Chronicle, "Moonie Drills for Suicide Are Reported," February 20, 1979; Authors' interviews with former members of the Unification Church.

165. Hare Krishna's Oakland Tribune, "Hare Krishna Sect Faces Growing Police Scrutiny," May 25, 1980; Berkeley Independent and Gazette, "Krishna Weapons Probe Widens," March 20, 1980; Authors' interviews with California state and local police officials and former members of the Hare Krishna organization.

165. vigilantism Bean, op. cit., 138–143; Stanton A. Coblentz, Villains and Vigilantes, A. S. Barnes & Company (New York: 1961); George R. Stewart, Committee of Vigilance, Ballantine Books (New York: 1971).

165. **Chinatown lynchings** McWilliams, *Southern California Country*, op. cit., p. 91.

165. "Once there, they discovered..."

Nathanael West, *Miss Lonelyhearts* and *The Day of the Locust*, New Directions Publishing Corporation (New York: 1962), pp. 177–178.

Chapter VII. OUTSIDERS TO THE DREAM

167. **Wasco** Authors' interviews with Miguel Garcia, chairman of Californios for Fair Representation, and Mary Pollares, Rudi Pollares, Margaret LaRue, and Marshall Rangel-Equillera, Chicano activists from Wasco.

167. "It's blatant discrimination..." Interview with authors.

168. **Wasco disturbance** The Wasco News, "300 riot in Barker Park; six arrested," July 2, 1980.

168. "We don't have any..." Interview with authors.

168. **Mexican population** Pacific News Service, "California Promises to Become Nation's First 'Third World' State, December 30, 1977.

168. **political power** Time, "It's Your Turn in the Sun," October 16, 1978.

169. **mean earnings** Joan W. Moore, "Minorities in the American Class System," undated (provided by Moore).

169. **schooling** Time, "It's Your Turn in the Sun," op. cit.; University of California at Berkeley Office of Student Affairs Research, "Fall 1979 Enrollment by Ethnicity and Five-Year Trends at Berkeley," November 27, 1979; San Francisco Examiner, "36% of State's Pupils Are Ethnic Minorities," October 19, 1978.

169. "It is not correct..." Interview with authors.

169. **earnings** Moore, "Minorities in the American Class System," op. cit.; Los Angeles Times, April 13, 1980.

169. **Chicanos and welfare** Los Angeles Times, "New Middle Class Emerging in City—Persevering Asians," April 13, 1980.

169. **farmworkers** Authors' interviews with officials of the United Farm Workers union, several growers, and Dean MacConnell, Chairman of the Department of Applied Behavioral Sciences at the University of California at Davis.

169. "For us there is no choice..." Authors' interview with contractor who wished to remain anonymous.

170. **city dwellers** Newsweek, "Chicanos on the Move," January 1, 1979; Los Angeles Times, "No Ethnic Majority," January 25, 1981.

170. **illegals in manufacturing** Authors' interview with Robert Seitz, Los Angeles area spokesman for the U.S. Immigration and Naturalization Service.

170. **Mexican unemployment** Time, "It's Your Turn in the Sun," op. cit.

170. "We don't come here..." Interview with authors.

170. **garment industry** Los Angeles Herald Examiner, "'I'm not Joan of Arc. I'm a garment manufacturer,'" January 21, 1981; Los Angeles Herald Examiner, "Undercover in the Garment Industry," January 16, 1981; Los Angeles Herald Examiner, "Who are the players? What are the problems?" January 28, 1981.

171. "With the proximity..." Interview with authors.

171. **wage allegations** San Francisco Chronicle, "Garment Workers Underpaid, a Probe of L.A. Firms Shows," June 26, 1980.

171. "Because they are here..." Cited in ibid.

171. "In my opinion..." Interview with authors.

172. "These people come..." Interview with authors.

172. **early mission work** McWilliams, Southern California Country, op. cit., pp. 24–37; Robert F. Heizer and Alan J. Almquist, The Other Californians, University of California Press (Berkeley: 1977), pp. 4–16.

172. "The Indians of California..." Cited in Heizer and Almquist, op. cit., p. 4.

173. the Californios Bean, op. cit., pp. 70–72; McWilliams, *Southern California Country*, op. cit., pp. 37–40.

173. "The Californians are ..." Cited in John Caughey and LaRee Caughey, *California Heritage*, Ward Ritchie Press (Los Angeles: 1962), p. 123.

173. Mexican-American War Bean, op. cit., pp. 101–104.

174. decline of the Mexicans Wayne Moquin and Charles Van Doren, *A Documentary History of the Mexican Americans*, Bantam (New York: 1972), pp. 309–315; Heizer and Almquist, op. cit., pp. 143–148.

174. "Half-civilized black men" Cited in Heizer and Almquist, op. cit., p. 141.

174. "the Spanish population ..." Cited in Heizer and Almquist, op. cit., p. 140.

175. bandidos Rodolfo Acuna, *Occupied America, the Chicano's Struggle Toward Liberation*, Canfield Press (San Francisco: 1972), pp. 110–117.

175. "My career grew ..." Cited in ibid., p. 115.

175. Indian deaths Bean, op. cit., pp. 169–170.

175. Economic decline Albert Camarillo, *Chicanos in a Changing Society*, Harvard University Press (Cambridge: 1979), pp. 128–129, 135.

175. population decline ibid., p. 200.

176. "Death and Emigration" Cited in McWilliams, *Southern California Country*, p. 65.

176. Mexican laborers Acuna, op. cit., pp. 127–128; Moquin and Van Doren, op. cit., p. 33.

176. population increases McWilliams, *Southern California Country*, op. cit., pp. 315–316; Acuna, op. cit., p. 132.

176. employment figures Camarillo, op. cit., p. 211.

176. population growth in LA ibid., p. 200.

176. depression era hostility Acuna, op. cit., p. 141.

177. "The Mexicans are wonderful ..." Cited in ibid., p. 142.

177. deportations Moquin and Van Doren, op. cit., p. 386; Armano Mo-rales, *Ando Sangrando, I Am Bleeding*, Perspectiva Publications, (La Puente: 1972), p. 15.

177. "The blonds are very bad ..." Cited in Morales, op. cit., p. 15.

178. pachucos Moquin and Van Doren, op. cit., pp. 409–415.

178. "They are instinctive rebels ..." Octavio Paz, *The Labyrinth of Solitude, Life and Thought in Mexico*, Grove Press (New York: 1961), p. 14.

178. bracero program Acuna, op. cit., pp. 168–169.

178. Sleepy Lagoon McWilliams, *Southern California Country*, op. cit., p. 319.

179. "The Caucasian, especially ..." Cited in Weaver, op. cit., p. 103.

179. zoot suit riots Weaver, op. cit., pp. 102–105; McWilliams, *Southern California Country*, op. cit., pp. 318–320.

179. "Most of the citizens ..." Cited in Weaver, op. cit., p. 105.

179. Defense Committee Weaver, op. cit., p. 104.

179. CSO Acuna, op. cit., pp. 208–210.

180. lettuce strike ibid., p. 163.

180. bracero program ibid., p. 172.

180. deportations Stan Steiner, *La Raza, the Mexican Americans*, Harper & Row (New York: 1970), p. 128.

180. UFW Acuna, op. cit., pp. 176–184.

180. "We have been ..." Moquin and Van Doren, op. cit., p. 473.

181. UFW growth "Biographical Sketch, Cesar Chavez," provided by the United Farm Workers; Authors' interviews with UFW officials.

181. "We will continue ..." "Biographical Sketch, Cesar Chavez," provided by the United Farm Workers.

181. crime statistics *Social Casework* magazine, "Institutional racism in mental health and criminal justice," July, 1978.

181. "are not far removed ..." Cited in Longstreet, op. cit., p. 267.

181. "Mexican people ..." Cited in Morales, op. cit., p. 43.

182. "In East Los Angeles ..." Cited in ibid. pp. 22–23.

182. **Brown Berets** Acuna, op. cit., pp. 231–233; Luis Valdez and Stan Steiner, *Aztlan, an Anthology of Mexican American Literature,* Vintage Books (New York: 1972), pp. 303–305.

182. **"To keep a watchful eye ..."** Valdez and Steiner, op. cit., p. 305.

182. **riots** Morales, op. cit., pp. 100–109; Weaver, op. cit., p. 129.

183. **"It had just gotten dark ..."** Cited in Morales, op. cit., pp. 108–109.

183. **voter apathy** Joint Committee for the Revision of the Elections Code, "Memorandum to Chairman Mervyn M. Dymally," August, 1972.

183. **"I sometimes feel ..."** Cited in Weaver, op. cit., p. 129.

183. **illegals** *Los Angeles Times,* March 25, 1980.

183. **population growth** *Los Angeles Times,* "Minorities gaining in California," March 27, 1981; *Los Angeles Times,* "L.A. Unified Schools Principally Latino," April 13, 1980; *Los Angeles Times,* "No Ethnic Majority," January 25, 1981; Pacific News Service, "California Promises to Become Nation's First 'Third World' State," op. cit.

184. **"if there are not ..."** Cited in *Los Angeles Herald Examiner,* May 29, 1980.

184. **United Neighborhoods** *Los Angeles Times,* "Latino Activists from UNO Turn Backs on Ballot Box," July 27, 1980.

184. **Chicano businesses** Authors' interview with Julio Rivera, former president of the Latin-American Businessmen's Association; *Los Angeles Times,* April 13, 1980.

184. **"The opportunity is still ..."** Interview with authors.

185. **"turn in the sun"** *Los Angeles Times,* April 13, 1980.

185. **political gains** Pacific News Service, "Jerry Brown's 'Hispanic Strategy' Stirs White Backlash," op. cit.

185. **"When the numbers ..."** Cited in ibid.

185. **youth unemployment** Authors' interview with Richard Zumiga, director of a job training program in Los Angeles.

185. **youth gangs** *Los Angeles Herald Examiner,* "Ex-gang members tell hearing what it was like," October 21, 1980; *Los Angeles Herald Examiner,* "Straight talk from the streetwise," March 8, 1981; "Justice and the Administration of Justice in the Chicano Community," paper delivered before the Third Annual Solidarity Conference of Hispanos Unidos, October 11, 1980.

186. **"Here you have no rights ..."** Authors' interview with a gang member who wished to remain anonymous.

186. **"They've been putting us down ..."** Interview with authors.

186. **"It's our biggest problem ..."** Interview with authors.

187. **black unemployment** Authors' interview with John Mack, director of the Los Angeles Urban League.

187. **black population** *Los Angeles Times,* "Minorities gaining in California," op. cit.

187. **"That clothing store ..."** Interview with authors.

188. **Willie Brown** *California Journal,* "The powder-keg speakership: How long can Brown hold it?" January, 1981.

188. **Tom Bradley** *New West,* "Inside Tom Bradley," January, 1981.

188. **"business was made ..."** Cited in ibid.

189. **"If you look ..."** Interview with authors.

189. **Lionel Wilson** Authors' interviews with Oakland political and community leaders; *Oakland Tribune* "Lionel Wilson's outer circle," February 28, 1978.

189. **"I don't think"** Cited in *Oakland Tribune,* "Lionel Wilson's outer circle," op. cit.

189. **blacks in government** Authors' interview with Julian Klugman, regional director for community relations resources of the U.S. Health, Education and Welfare office in Los Angeles.

189. **minority businesses** U.S. Department of Commerce, "1977 Survey of Minority-Owned Business Enterprises," December, 1980.

189. **"It's a big mistake ..."** Interview with authors.

190. **early discriminatory legislation** Bean, op. cit., pp. 165, 170; Heizer and Almquist, pp. 93–97, 104–119, 128.

190. **"When Negroes are free ..."** Cited in Heizer and Almquist, op. cit., p. 114.

190. **blacks in LA** McWilliams, *Southern California Country,* op. cit., pp. 324–325.

190. **"drew off much ..."** Cited in ibid., p. 325.

190. **black advancements** Weaver, op. cit., pp. 125–127; McWilliams, *Southern California Country,* op. cit., p. 325.

191. **"who had been in a ..."** Cited in Caughey and Caughey, op. cit., p. 284.

191. **WWII migration** Bean, op. cit., p. 513; McWilliams, *Southern California Country,* op. cit., p. 325; Caughey and Caughey, op. cit., p. 426.

191. **civil rights legislation** Bean, op. cit., p. 515.

191. **LA and Watts** *Washington Post,* "Coast Disturbance Called Battle of Have-Nots Against the Haves," August 16, 1965; Caughey and Caughey, op. cit., pp. 426–427.

192. **"one can live ..."** Cited in *Washington Post,* August 8, 1965.

192. **repeal of Rumford Act** Bean, op. cit., p. 515.

192. **police** Gentry, op. cit., pp. 204–217; *Washington Post,* "Los Angeles Riot Was Prophesied in Report to Officials Last Year," September 3, 1965.

192. **Watts riot** Gentry, op. cit., pp. 199–206, 212–228; Bean, op. cit., p. 517.

192. **"They came right down ..."** Interview with authors.

193. **guns** *Washington Post,* August 17, 1965.

193. **McCone Commission** *Washington Post,* December 13, 1965.

193. **Black Panthers** *New Times,* "The Party's Over," July 10, 1978; Davie, op. cit., pp. 128–131; Edward C. Hayes, *Power Structure and Urban Policy, Who Rules in Oakland?* McGraw-Hill Book Company (New York: 1972), p. 38.

193. **"It is a fact ..."** Cited in Davie, op. cit., p. 131.

193. **Huey Newton** *New Times,* "The Party's Over," op. cit.; Authors' interviews with former Black Panther Party members.

194. **Panther problems** *New Times,* "The Party's Over," op. cit.; *San Francisco Examiner,* "Newton mistrial: jury deadlocked from the start," March 25, 1979; *Berkeley Gazette,* "Black Panthers now in disarray," April 21, 1978.

194. **"I hear a very loud ..."** Cited in *Berkeley Gazette,* "Black Panthers now in disarray," op. cit.

194. **"Frustration and helplessness ..."** Cited in *Oakland Tribune,* "Panel finds minority anger is growing," March 12, 1981.

195. **violence and crime** United States Department of Justice, "Crime in the United States, 1979," September 24, 1980; Statistics supplied by the FBI in Washington, D.C.; *Oakland Tribune,* "Panel finds minority anger is growing," op. cit.; *Oakland Tribune,* "Murder: Epidemic of violence, Special Report," January 11, 1981; Authors' interviews with police officials in Oakland and New York. *Los Angeles Times,* "Rising Tide of Violence Shocks City," December 16, 1980.

195. **black employment** South-central Economic Research and Development Associates, report on six manpower planning areas of Los Angeles.

195. **black students** University of California at Berkeley, Office of Student Affairs Research, "Fall 1979 Enrollment by Ethnicity and Five year Trends at Berkeley," op. cit.; Statistics supplied by UC Berkeley.

196. **black economic performance** South-central Economic Research and Development Associates, op. cit.

196. **"This city is ..."** Authors' interview with banker who wished to remain anonymous.

196. **black problems with new immigrants** Authors' interviews with blacks in Los Angeles, including Paul Hudson, Mary Henry, Shay Drummond, Linda Ferguson, John Mack, and Charles Hammond.

196. **hispanic increase** South-central Economic Research and Development Associates, op. cit.

196. **"The landlords are willing ..."** Interview with authors.

197. "Anything can happen ..." Interview with authors.

197. early Chinese immigration Bean, op. cit., pp. 163–164.

197. numbers Bean, op. cit., p. 164; Heizer and Almquist, op. cit., p. 154.

198. "Now permit us to ..." Cited in Heizer and Almquist, op. cit., p. 166 ff.

198. "to throw around ..." Cited in ibid., p. 129.

198. discriminatory legislation Bean, op. cit., pp. 164–165; Heizer and Almquist, op. cit., p. 161.

198. attacks and thefts Beck and Williams, op. cit., p. 150; Westways, "Celestial Couriers," August, 1980.

199. "My father was very ..." Cited in Westways, "Celestial Couriers," op. cit.

199. working for the railroad Bean, op. cit., pp. 215–216; McWilliams, *Factories in the Fields,* op. cit., p. 70.

199. in the fields McWilliams, *Factories in the Fields,* op. cit., pp. 70–72; McWilliams, *The Great Exception,* op. cit., p. 152.

199. "The availability of ..." Cited in McWilliams, *Factories in the Fields,* op. cit., p. 73.

199. Chinese population McWilliams, *The Great Exception,* op. cit., p. 67.

199. Chinese fishing McWilliams, *Southern California Country,* op. cit., pp. 87–88.

199. Chinese farming ibid., pp. 81–90.

200. vice Longstreet, op. cit., pp. 75–76.

200. anti-Chinese riot Longstreet, op. cit., pp. 78–84; Weaver, op. cit., p. 32; McWilliams, *Southern California Country,* op. cit., pp. 91–92.

200. "Trembling, moaning, wounded ..." Cited in McWilliams, *Southern California Country,* op. cit., p. 91.

200. Workingmen's Party Bean, op. cit., pp. 237–239; McWilliams, *The Great Exception,* op. cit., pp. 172–176.

200. 1879 ballot Heizer and Almquist, op. cit., p. 166.

201. anti-Chinese laws Heizer and Almquist, op. cit., pp. 170–175.

201. "Indispensable as the ..." Cited in McWilliams, *Factories in the Fields,* op. cit., p. 77.

201. immigration exclusion Heizer and Almquist, op. cit., p. 158.

201. expulsion law Heizer and Almquist, op. cit., p. 175.

201. segregation laws ibid., pp. 175–176.

201. population ibid., p. 203.

201. labor shortage McWilliams, *Factories in the Fields,* op. cit., p. 105.

201. Indians McWilliams, *Factories in the Fields,* op. cit., pp. 116–119.

202. Filipinos McWilliams, *Factories in the Fields,* op. cit., pp. 130–133; *Harvard* magazine "The manongs of California," May, 1981.

202. "more disturbing and more dangerous ..." Cited in McWilliams, *Factories in the Fields,* op. cit., p. 387.

203. arrival of the Japanese McWilliams, *Factories in the Fields,* op. cit., pp. 105–106.

203. "The Japanese ..." Cited in ibid., p. 105.

203. "The Japs and Chinks ..." Cited in ibid., p. 107.

203. Japanese fishing McWilliams, *Southern California Country,* op. cit., pp. 321–322.

203. Japanese farming ibid., p. 321; McWilliams, *Factories in the Fields,* op. cit., pp. 109–115.

203. "The Florin district ..." Cited in Heizer and Almquist, op. cit., pp. 185–186.

204. Japanese in San Francisco ibid., pp. 181–183.

204. Alien Land Act Bean, op. cit., pp. 334–335; McWilliams, *Factories in the Fields,* op. cit., p. 116.

204. "Merchants (are) getting ..." Cited in Heizer and Almquist, op. cit., p. 190.

205. "I do verily believe ..." Cited in ibid., p. 392.

205. Japanese internment Bean, op. cit., pp. 430–436; Caughey and Caughey, op. cit., pp. 366–370.

205. "Couldn't it be ..." Cited in Weaver, op. cit., p. 94.

206. "Objectively and on the whole ..." Cited in Caughey and Caughey, op. cit., pp. 370–372.

206. Japanese during the war Bean, op. cit., pp. 434–436.

206. **"We're charged with ..."** Cited in Weaver, op. cit., p. 102.

207. **Japanese-American achievements** University of California at Berkeley, Office of Student Affairs Research, "Fall 1979 Enrollment By Ethnicity and Five-Year Trends at Berkeley," op. cit.; Urban Associates, Inc., "A Study of Selected Socio-economic Characteristics of Ethnic Minorities, Based on the 1970 Census," undated.

207. **political gains** San Francisco Chronicle, "The Political Clout of State's Minorities," August 7, 1978; Asian American Studies Center, "The National Asian American Roster," 1980.

207. **"correct a historic ..."** Cited in Bean, op. cit., p. 513.

207. **other laws** ibid., pp. 512–513.

207. **population increases** Oakland Tribune, "Minorities gaining in California," March 27, 1981; Los Angeles Times, "Filipinos California's Largest Asian Group," July 27, 1981.

207. **Chinese population** Los Angeles Times, "Filipinos California's Largest Asian Group," op. cit.; Authors' interview with Walter Hollman, chief of population research for the California State Department of Finance.

208. **Chinatown conditions** New Times, "The Golden Dragon Labor Day Massacre," October 28, 1977.

208. **Chinatown gangs** New Times, "The Golden Dragon Labor Day Massacre," op. cit.; Pacific News Service, "A Chinese Connection Behind San Francisco Gang Wars?" September 30, 1977; San Francisco Examiner, "Two faces of a Chinatown tong," October 23, 1977; Mother Jones, "Turning Reporters into Orphans," June, 1977.

208. **"The ABC's ..."** Cited in New Times, "The Golden Dragon Labor Day Massacre," op. cit.

208. **Golden Dragon massacre** New Times, "The Golden Dragon Labor Day Massacre," op. cit., Oakland Tribune, September 14, 1980.

208. **organized crime** Pacific News Service, "A Chinese Connection Behind San Francisco Gang Wars?" op. cit.; San Francisco Examiner, "Two faces of a Chinatown tong," op. cit.;

Authors' interviews with youth gang specialists at several police departments in California.

209. **"We get these youngsters ..."** Interview with authors.

209. **Filipino migration** Los Angeles Times, "Filipinos California's Largest Asian Group," op. cit.; Harvard magazine, "The manongs of California," op. cit.

209. **median income** Urban Associates, Inc., op. cit.

209. **Filipino gangs** Authors' interviews with youth gang specialists at several police departments in California.

210. **Filipino organized crime** San Francisco Examiner, "Vast illegal car ring between S.F., Philippines, uncovered," December 9, 1979; Authors' interviews with law enforcement officials investigating the Filipino groups.

210. **"Let's put it this ..."** Interview with authors.

210. **Thai population** Authors' interview with Charman Malisunam, director of the Thai trade center in Los Angeles.

210. **Thai drug smuggling** Authors' interviews with law enforcement officials in California investigating narcotics; Los Angeles Times, "Six Arrested in Seizure of $7 Million in Heroin," January 19, 1980; U.S. Drug Enforcement Administration, press release, June 3, 1976.

210. **"The Thai community ..."** Interview with authors.

210. **"the majority of ..."** Interview with authors.

210. **assimilation** Authors' interviews with several Asian community leaders in Los Angeles.

210. **Korean population** Los Angeles Times, "Filipinos California's Largest Asian Group," op. cit.

211. **Korean gangs** Authors' interviews with Korean community leaders and police officials.

211. **"Our kids have had ..."** Interview with authors.

211. **Asian cultural problems** Authors' interviews with several Asian community leaders; Tran Van Mai, "Cross-Cultural Understanding and Its

Implications in Counseling," undated; Los Angeles County Commission on Human Relations, "Expressions Shared by Vietnamese in America," July, 1975.

211. **"They don't want ..."** Interview with authors.

211. **Southeast Asian refugees** *Los Angeles Times*, "California No. 1 State for Refugees from Indochina," November 29, 1979; *Los Angeles Times*, "Filipinos California's Largest Asian Group," op. cit.

211. **Vietnamese gangs** *Los Angeles Herald Examiner*, " 'Curtain of silence,' shrouds victims of Vietnamese gang," February 2, 1981; Associated Press, "Extortion Rings Prey on Vietnamese Refugees," November 21, 1979; Authors' inverviews with gang experts in several police departments in California.

211. **"Most of the refugee kids ..."** Interview with authors.

212. **refugees in high tech** *San Francisco Chronicle*, "Jobs in Santa Clara County Attracting Refugees," August 18, 1979.

212. **"I don't want to ..."** Cited in *Los Angeles Times*, "Self-Help Is Refugees' Key to 'Dream,' " December 17, 1980.

212. **Asians and education** University of California Joint Planning Committee, "The University of California a

Multi-Campus System in the 1980s," September, 1979; University of California at Berkeley Office of Student Affairs Research, "Fall 1979 Enrollment by Ethnicity and Five-Year Trends at Berkeley," op. cit.

212. **"I think most Asians ..."** Authors' interview with Asian businessman who wished to remain anonymous.

213. **Asian businesses** *Los Angeles Times*, "New Middle Class Emerging in City—Persevering Asians," April 13, 1980.

213. **"They take over ..."** Cited in ibid.

213. **Asian businesses** "U.S. Department of Commerce," 1977 Survey of Minority-Owned Business Enterprises," op. cit.

213. **median family income** *Los Angeles Times*, "New Middle Class Emerging in City—Persevering Asians," op. cit.

213. **Ngoy Bun Tek** *Santa Ana Register*, "Refugee Success Formula: Work," November 29, 1979.

213. **land purchases** *Los Angeles Times*, "New Middle Class Emerging in City—Persevering Asians," op. cit.

214. **Paul Kim** Interview with authors.

214. **"Here the communication ..."** Interview with authors.

Chapter VIII. THE PACIFIC RIM

215. **corps of engineers** Authors' interview with Everett Chasen, spokesman for the Army Corps of Engineers.

215. **"We know damn well ..."** Interview with authors.

216. **trade statistics** *Los Angeles Times*, "State Seeks Hike in Trade-Related Jobs," May 22, 1978; *California Business*, "World Trade," May, 1980.

216. **trade increases** Security Pacific National Bank, "California's International Trade," November, 1980.

217. **"the state serves ..."** C. J. Medberry, remarks before the Los Angeles Society of Financial Analysts, September 18, 1979.

217. **Japan** *Time*, "How Japan Does It," March 30, 1981; *U.S. News and*

World Report, "Worry for World Business: How to Compete with Japan," September 26, 1977.

217. **Pacific Rim economies** *Information Please Almanac*, op. cit.; Bank of America, "Economic Outlook, 1980, Global Report," October, 1979; Financial World, "Paydirt along the Pacific Rim," April 1, 1981.

218. **Indonesia** *Information Please Almanac*, op. cit., p. 213; Security Pacific National Bank, "California's International Trade," op. cit.; Stanford Research Institute, "Business in Indonesia," 1974.

218. **Malaysia** *Information Please Almanac*, op. cit., p. 235.

218. **Australia** Security Pacific Na-

tional Bank, "California's International Trade," op. cit.; *Oakland Tribune*, "Aussies look to California cousin," December 13, 1979.

218. **China** *San Francisco Examiner*, "A slow road to U.S.-China trade," September 14, 1980; *San Francisco Chronicle*, "China Needs More of Everything," July 16, 1979; *San Francisco Chronicle*, "Union Oil Sells Refining Process to China," January 20, 1979; *San Francisco Examiner*, "Four U.S. oil firms seeking share of China's oil reserves," August 14, 1978.

219. **Mexico** Security Pacific National Bank, "The Sixty Mile Circle," op. cit.; Security Pacific National Bank, "California's International Trade," op. cit.; U.S. National Security Council, "Presidential Review Memorandum, Number 14," August 14, 1978; *Los Angeles Herald Examiner*, "Why Mexicans are reluctant to sell their oil to the U.S.," November 10, 1980; *Los Angeles Times*, " 'Miracle' boom: millions are left behind," July 15, 1979; A. Gary Shilling and Company, Inc., "Mexico: Its Miracle May be Postponed," February 1, 1980.

219. **"In the coming decade ..."** Richard J. Flamson, remarks before the American Chamber of Commerce of Mexico, March 24, 1981.

220. **Interfuture** *Los Angeles Herald Examiner*, "Led by Japan, East Asian nations predicted to become top powers," July 15, 1979.

220. **"Most observers expect ..."** B. K. MacLaury, "Banking Beyond the Five-Year Plan," remarks before the International Monetary Conference, June 3, 1980.

220. **"That's our market ..."** Interview with authors.

221. **"to find out the ..."** Cited in Henry Nash Smith, *Virgin Land*, op. cit.

221. **Jefferson** ibid., pp. 15–17, 20–21.

221. **"The object of your mission ..."** Cited in ibid., pp. 20–21.

221. **Thomas Hart Benton** ibid., pp. 22–26.

222. **"The untransacted destiny ..."** Cited in ibid., p. 37.

222. **Asa Whitney** ibid., pp. 30–34.

222. **"Here we stand ..."** Cited in ibid., p. 33.

223. **conflict with Japanese** Lawrence H. Battistini, *The United States and Asia*, Frederick A. Praeger (New York: 1955), pp. 18–21.

223. **"Recent events ..."** Cited in ibid., p. 20.

223. **"perfect, permanent ..."** Cited in ibid., p. 21.

223. **early Asian trade** Hubert Howe Bancroft, *The New Pacific*, The Bancroft Company (New York: 1912), pp. 7, 304, 314–315, 318; McWilliams, *Southern California Country*, op. cit., pp. 87–88.

224. **"stood at the end ..."** Cited in McWilliams, *Southern California Country*, op. cit., p. 134.

224. **failure to exploit** Bancroft, op. cit., pp. 302.

224. **"We have no longer ..."** Bancroft, op. cit., p. 13.

224. **William Seward** Battistini, op. cit., p. 26.

224. **"The chief theater ..."** Cited in The Pacific Basin Economic Council United States National Committee, "A New Pacific Era," undated.

224. **Hawaii** Battistini, op. cit., p. 27.

224. **Spanish American War** ibid., pp. 28–41.

225. **"All commercial nations ..."** Cited in Bancroft, op. cit., p. 301.

225. **expansion of trade** Gregory Bienstock, *The Struggle for the Pacific*, The MacMillan Company (New York: 1937), p. 21.

225. **"As nearly as ..."** Cited in McWilliams, *Southern California Country*, op. cit., p. 134.

226. **Japan-U.S. trade** Bancroft, op. cit., pp. 314–316.

226. **Hawaii protest** Bancroft, op. cit., pp. 384–385.

226. **"Drunk with victory ..."** Cited in Heizer and Almquist, op. cit., p. 179.

226. **"Japan is playing ..."** Cited in Battistini, op. cit., p. 64.

226. **Roosevelt** ibid, pp. 64–70.

227. **"The Japanese and ..."** Benjamin Ide Wheeler, *The Abundant Life*, University of California Press (Berkeley: 1926), p. 287.

227. **zaibatsu** Bienstock, op. cit., pp.

179–180; Kazuo Kawai, *Japan's American Interlude,* The University of Chicago Press (Chicago: 1974), pp. 153–156.

227. **"It's keynote of ..."** Kawai, op. cit., pp. 153–154.

228. **Japan's growth and trade** Bienstock, op. cit., p. 21; Japan Development Bank, "Facts and Figures on the Japanese Economy, 1964," July, 1964.

228. **"The history of mankind ..."** Bienstock, op. cit., p. 17.

228. **Demetrius Scofield** Gerald T. White, *Standard Oil Company of California, Formative Years in the Far West,* Appleton-Century-Crofts (New York: 1962), p. 41.

229. **Japanese oil imports** Bienstock, op. cit., p. 219.

229. **Standard Oil** White, op. cit., pp. 283–284; Anthony Sampson, *The Seven Sisters,* Viking Press (New York: 1975), p. 36.

229. **Japanese initiatives** Battistini, op. cit., pp. 92–95, 98–99.

229. **naval agreements** Battistini, op. cit., pp. 101–107; Frank Gibney, *Japan, the Fragile Super Power,* W. W. Norton & Company (New York: 1979), p. 57.

229. **"Japan's defeat in ..."** Cited in Gibney, op. cit., p. 57.

229. **"grave consequences ..."** Cited in Battistini, op. cit., p. 109.

230. **growth of the right wing** Kawai, op. cit., pp. 43–45.

230. **"The units have already..."** Cited in Saburo Ienaga, *The Pacific War,* Random House (New York: 1968), p. 62.

230. **Manchuria** Battistini, op. cit., pp. 131–132; Gibney, op. cit., pp. 57–60.

230. **"The Japanese were ..."** Cited in Gibney, op. cit., p. 59.

231. **softening opposition** Gibney, op. cit., p. 58.

231. **"At the outset ..."** Robert Engler, *The Brotherhood of Oil,* University of Chicago Press (Chicago: 1977), p. 135.

231. **American moves** Battistini, op. cit., pp. 131–139, 163–170; Ienaga, op. cit., pp. 131–132.

231. **"had thrown an ..."** Ienaga, op. cit., p. 132.

231. **going to war** Battistini, op. cit., pp. 165–167, 170–173.

232. **jushin and peace** Ienaga, op. cit., pp. 229–235; William Craig, *The Fall of Japan,* Dell Publishing Company (New York: 1968), pp. 24–25.

232. **postwar Japan** Kawai, op. cit., pp. 134–137; Ienaga, op. cit., pp. 233–235; Battistini, op. cit., p. 205.

232. **"a bulwark of democracy ..."** Cited in Ballistini, p. 215.

232. **"We cannot prosper ..."** Henry J. Kaiser, "remarks before the San Francisco Chamber of Commerce," July 19, 1945.

233. **Giannini and the Bank of America** James and James, op. cit., pp. 479–482.

233. **saving the zaibatsu** Kawai, op. cit., pp. 142–147.

233. **Korean War and prosperity** Gibney, op. cit., pp. 41, 178; Kawai, op. cit., p. 179.

233. **economic growth** Japan Development Bank, op. cit., pp. 3–4; Gibney, op. cit., p. 178.

234. **oil companies** John G. Roberts, *Mitsui, Three Centuries of Japanese Business,* Weatherhill (New York: 1973), p. 478; Union Oil Company, "The Sign of the 76," 1976; Getty, *As I See It,* op. cit., p. 266.

234. **"We on the west coast ..."** Interview with authors.

234. **SF-China** San Francisco Examiner, "The mayor's report on China," June 24, 1979; San Francisco Examiner, "S.F. to get first China trade fair," June 19, 1979.

235. **"Our destiny ..."** San Francisco Examiner, "The mayor's report on China," op. cit.

235. **Brown trip** Associated Press, November 16, 1977; Los Angeles Times, "Brown stays open to Japanese incentives," March 11, 1977; Schell, op. cit., pp. 188–206.

235. **"co-prosperity sphere ..."** Interview with authors.

235. **"Pacific Rim Council ..."** Interview with authors.

235. **"We have an internationalist ..."** Interview with authors.

236. **"There is a tendency now ..."** Interview with authors.

236. **Japan and the west** Japan External Trade Organization, "Japan & the West Coast, Trans-Pacific Neighbors," undated; Peirce, op. cit., pp. 270, 287, 292.

236. **"actually helped..."** Cited in Los Angeles Times, "Leaving out Oil Firms, Top California Companies Had Weak Profit Year," May 17, 1981.

237. **"We are moving ..."** Interview with authors.

237. **Los Angeles Herald** Los Angeles Herald, "Protectionism: Whom does it really protect?" editorial, February 22, 1981.

237. **"Protectionism only invites..."** Los Angeles Times, "Cars, not Quotas," editorial, March 10, 1980.

238. **Shaklee** Oakland Tribune, "Shaklee takes to the park," June 20, 1979.

238. **Tandem** Authors' interview with Patricia A. Becker, manager of public relations for Tandem Computers.

238. **Theory Z** William Ouchi, Theory Z (uncorrected proof), Addison-Wesley Publishing Company, (Reading: 1981); Los Angeles Times, "Theory Z: Hot New Plan to Revitalize Corporate America," April 12, 1981.

238. **"In the Z organization..."** Stanford Business School Alumni Bulletin, "Theory Z Organization: a Corporate Alternative to Village Life," Fall, 1977.

239. **Hewlett-Packard** Authors' interviews with Hewlett-Packard executives; Hewlett-Packard Corporation, "The HP Way," January, 1980.

239. **"The purpose of ..."** Interview with authors.

239. **foreign visitors** Authors' interview with Nancy Honig, Regional Director of the U.S. International Communications Agency in San Francisco.

239. **"To a certain extent ..."** Interview with authors.

240. **"California is almost ..."** Authors' interview with Japanese banking executive who wished to remain anonymous.

240. **Hollywood in Japan** Los Angeles Herald Examiner, "Japan's Superstar TV Blurbs," May 18, 1980.

240. **"Western-inspired products..."** Cited in ibid.

240. **"Marilyn Monroe's Levi's-clad ..."** Cited in ibid.

240. **Tracy Peters** ibid.; Los Angeles Times, "Coke of Japan Goes Californian," May 29, 1979.

240. **"They told me ..."** Cited in Los Angeles Times, "Coke of Japan Goes Californian," op. cit.

241. **"The Japanese have ..."** Cited in Los Angeles Herald Examiner, "Japan's Superstar TV Blurbs," op. cit.

241. **"The western part ..."** Interview with authors.

241. **Japanese investment** Los Angeles Times, "Leaving out Oil Firms, Top California Companies Had Weak Profit Year," op. cit.; Japan External Trade Organization, op. cit.; Los Angeles Herald Examiner, "Foreign banks invade state," July 15, 1979.

241. **Japan and southern California** Los Angeles Times, "Japanese Southern California Land Holdings Balloon," July 1, 1979; Time, "Consensus in San Diego," March 30, 1981.

242. **Little Tokyo** Los Angeles Times, " 'Not so Little' Tokyo to Gain Another Shopping-Restaurant Mall," November 9, 1980; Los Angeles Times, "Japanese Southern California Land Holdings Balloon," op. cit.

242. **"We are sort of ..."** Interview with authors.

242. **Conference Board** Authors' interview with James Green, executive director, International Business Programs, U.S. Conference Board.

243. **"California is the hottest ..."** Saturday Review, "Invasion of the Americana Heartland," October 15, 1977; See also Oakland Tribune, "Why foreign buyers flock to California," June 11, 1978.

243. **"I don't think ..."** Cited in Los Angeles Herald Examiner, "Foreign banks invade state," op. cit.

243. **agricultural investments** San Francisco Chronicle, "The California Land Owned by Foreigners," September 11, 1979; Fresno Bee, "Curbing Foreign Investment," May 6, 1978; Stockton Record, "Italians Buy Mandeville

Island," April 12, 1978; *Los Angeles Times*, "Foreigners Plowing Cash into Rich U.S. Farmland," February 1, 1978.

243. **wineries** *San Francisco Examiner*, "The foreign taste for state wineries," June 29, 1980; *California Business*, "Mondavi & Rothschild," July, 1980.

243. **high tech investments** *California* magazine, "A Piece of the Action," September, 1979.

244. **other investment** *Washington Post*, "The Arabs," September 18, 1975; *Wall Street Journal*, "Saudi Who Tried to Buy California Bank Returns to Controversy in Northrop Affair," June 9, 1975; *San Francisco Chronicle*, "A Small Score for Khashoggi," January 14, 1978; Daon Development Corporation, "Annual Report, 1979"; *San Francisco Chronicle*, "The Canadian Investment Invasion," June 14, 1979; *Oakland Tribune*, "Condo conversions put Daon in the spotlight," June 22, 1980; *Oakland Tribune*, "Why foreign buyers flock to California," op. cit.; Earl H. Fry, *Financial Invasion of the U.S.A.*, McGraw-Hill Book Company (New York: 1980), p. 113; Kenneth C. Crowe, *America for Sale*, Doubleday & Company (New York: 1978), pp. 60–61; *California* magazine "A Piece of the Action," op. cit.

244. **San Francisco area** *San Francisco Chronicle*, "For Sale," April 26, 1978.

244. **City Center** Authors' interviews with Oakland redevelopment officials and business executives.

244. **"What are we going ..."** Authors' interview with Oakland city official who wished to remain anonymous.

244. **foreign investment in Oakland** Material supplied by Oakland Convention and Visitor's Bureau; *Oakland Tribune*, "Oakland's Chinatown Development resumes," November 12, 1980.

245. **"They are coming ..."** Interview with authors.

245. **North American Common Market** Kenneth E. Hill. "North American Energy: a Proposal for a Common Market Between Canada, Mexico and the United States," January, 1979; *Oakland Tribune*, "Vision of North American Common Market," April 23, 1981; *San Diego Union*, "Brown's Aide Optimistic, Points to Job Increase," June 11, 1978; *Christian Science Monitor*, "Reagan '80 campaign goal: positive foreign-policy image," October 15, 1979.

245. **"This would provide ..."** Hill, op. cit.

245. **Jerry Brown efforts** Pacific News Service, "Brown Forges Foreign Policy for California," op. cit; *New York Times*, "Gov. Brown Supporting Projects That Aid a Mexican Contributor," op. cit.

246. **"Indeed the future ..."** *San Diego Union*, "Brown's Aide Optimistic, Points to Job Increase," op. cit.

246. **western resources** U.S. Department of Commerce, Statistical Abstract of the United States, op. cit.; *Time*, "Rocky Mountain High," December 15, 1980; Information supplied by the American Petroleum Institute; *Los Angeles Herald Examiner*, "Oil from 'them thar rocks' is closer to reality," February 24, 1980; *Los Angeles Times*, "Battle Expected on Utah Power Project," May 22, 1977; *Los Angeles Times*, "Synfuel—the West's New Range War," July 18, 1979; *Washington Post*, "States Demand a Share of Wealth," June 19, 1979.

247. **"The time has come ..."** Cited in *Los Angeles Times*, "Shale Oil: Peak Appears Near on Mountain of Hope," June 22, 1980.

247. **overthrust belt** *Los Angeles Times*, "Overthrust: a Belt That Could Energize U.S.," March 30, 1980; *Wall Street Journal*, "In West, a Long Strip of Land Stirs Hopes Among Oil, Gas Men," August 27, 1979; *Los Angeles Herald Examiner*, "Overthrust Belt: Great oil potential," February 18, 1980.

247. **California firms** *Los Angeles Times*, "Engineering Firms to Get a Big Piece of Synfuel Action," April 20, 1980; *Wall Street Journal*, "Firms Lobby for Funds for Their Pet Projects on Synthetic Fuels," February 25, 1980; *Los Angeles Times*, "Overthrust: a Belt That Could Energize U.S.," op. cit.; *Los Angeles Times*, "Large Gas Pipeline to State Sought," September 9, 1980.

248. "Essentially, California..." McWilliams, *The Great Exception*, op. cit., p. 344.

248. Colorado River McWilliams, *The Great Exception*, op. cit., pp. 293–316.

248. "testicles of the..." Authors' interview with Utah planner who wished to remain anonymous.

248. great drought McWilliams, *The Great Exception*, op. cit., pp. 273, 351.

248. pipeline ibid., p. 352.

249. "If this fantastic..." Cited in ibid., p. 348.

249. Kaiparowits *Los Angeles Times*, "Dispute Grows over Coal Mining in Utah," February 5, 1979.

249. "Utah looks good..." Cited in ibid.

249. Four Corners *Los Angeles Times*, "Coal Plants Ignite Pollution Protests," October 5, 1979.

249. Intermountain Power Project *San Gabriel Valley News*, "Electrical Plant Site Draws Suit Threats," December 6, 1977; *Los Angeles Times*, "Battle Expected on Utah Power Project," May 22, 1977; Authors' interviews with IPP and other utility company officials; *High Country News*, "Coal plant planners eye Southern Utah," May 6, 1977.

249. Allen-Warner *Los Angeles Times*, "Bryce Canyon: Choosing up Sides over Coal, Beauty," December 31, 1979; *Los Angeles Times*, "Conflicts on Utah Power Grow Heated," July 21, 1980; *San Francisco Examiner*, "California utilities in crucial battle to strip mine Western coal," June 29, 1980.

249. "Utah has coal..." Interview with authors.

250. water problems *Wall Street Journal*, "Colorado River, Vital to Southwest, Travels Ever-Rockier Course," February 12, 1979; *San Francisco Examiner*, "Booming Arizona: fountains now, shortages later," April 26, 1981; *Los Angeles Herald Examiner*, "Why California could run short of water in 1985," January 7, 1979; Authors' interviews with Los Angeles Department of Water and Power officials, residents of Utah; information supplied by Western States Water Council; Authors' interviews with federal officials, and Texas and Arizona governmental officials.

250. "They want to..." Cited in *Time*, "Rocky Mountain High," op. cit.

251. "blue-eyed Arabs..." Cited in *Washington Post*, "Old Frontier Sees Bright New Future," June 17, 1979.

251. "Drive Faster..." Cited in ibid.

251. "There's a whole..." Cited in ibid.

251. "What do we want..." Cited in *Time*, "Rocky Mountain High," op. cit.

251. "Billions of dollars..." Cited in ibid.

252. sagebrush rebellion *San Francisco Examiner*, "Sagebrush rebellion against Uncle Sam," April 19, 1979; *San Francisco Chronicle*, "Western Council Calls for Selloff of Federal Lands," September 27, 1979; *San Francisco Chronicle*, "A Discouraging Word for Land Rebels," September 6, 1979; *Oakland Tribune*, "California supports Sagebrush Rebellion," October 27, 1980; *Los Angeles Herald Examiner*, "And now, the West vs. the rest," April 21, 1979.

252. "I happen to be one..." Cited in *New West*, "Sagebrush," November 17, 1980.

252. "It all parallels..." Interview with authors.

252. federal outlays *Time*, "Rocky Mountain High," op. cit.

252. western growth Nevada National Bank, "Western Economic Overview, 1970–1977," undated.

253. high tech growth *Time*, "Rocky Mountain High," op. cit.

253. "Economic growth has..." Interview with authors.

253. oil royalties *Los Angeles Times*, "Eight States Strike It Rich on Oil Tax," January 6, 1980; *San Francisco Examiner*, "Decontrol boon for oil states," January 10, 1980; *San Francisco Examiner*, "Crude oil decontrol could mean billions to California," December 25, 1979.

253. "What we're talking..." Cited in *Los Angeles Times*, "Eight States Strike It Rich on Oil Tax," op. cit.

254. "It's a bunch of pieces..." Interview with authors.

Chapter IX. BRAVE NEW WORLD VISITED

255. **"California is very ..."** Cited in McWilliams, *Factories in the Fields*, op. cit., p. 56.

256. **"Our performance ..."** Interview with Katherine Macdonald, *Washington Post* correspondent, provided to authors.

256. **unemployment** *Oakland Tribune*, "Murder: epidemic of violence," January 11, 1981; *Oakland Tribune*, "Jobs: Old dreams, new realities," June 28, 1981.

256. **murder rates** Federal Bureau of Investigation, "Crime in the United States," op. cit.

257. **"These folks have no ..."** Interview with authors.

257. **guns** *Los Angeles Herald Examiner*, "Fighting crime with guns, dogs and gadgets," December 13, 1980.

257. **Posse Comitatus** Authors' interviews with Posse Comitatus members and numerous police officials in California; *San Francisco Examiner*, "The New Posses and Their War Against Lawmen," September 7, 1975.

257. **"Once we get our people ..."** Authors' interview with Posse Comitatus leader.

258. **"A lot of people ..."** Interview with authors.

258. **jobs loss** California Council for Environmental & Economic Balance, "California's Electric Power Future Revisited," July, 1979.

259. **water problems** *Los Angeles Herald Examiner*, "Why California could run short of water in 1985," op. cit.; *Oakland Tribune*, "Why L.A. thirsts for Peripheral Canal," May 18, 1980; Authors' interviews with California state government and federal water officials.

259. **"We have the landscape ..."** Interview with authors.

259. **Peripheral Canal** *San Francisco Chronicle*, "The War over the Peripheral Canal," June 26, 1980.

259. **Parsons proposal** *The Lethbridge Herald*, "Water," February 7, 1976; Ralph M. Parsons Company, "North American Water and Power Alliance, Project Description," undated.

260. **housing** Bank of America, "Perspectives on the California Economy in the Eighties," op. cit.; *San Francisco Chronicle*, "Homes Cost Most Here," June 5, 1980; *San Francisco Examiner*, "Why few executives want to move to California," February 20, 1980.

260. **relative real income** Ken Auletta, *The Streets Were Paved with Gold*, Random House (New York: 1979), p. 20.

260. **population declines** *New York Review of Books*, Reconstructing America," op. cit.

261. **Chicago** *Chicago Tribune*, "City's needs grow while tax sources dwindle," May 12, 1981.

261. **employment and income** *Business Week*, "America's Restructured Economy," June 1, 1981.

261. **population shift** ibid.

261. **federal aid** *Chicago Tribune*, "City's needs grow while tax sources dwindle," op. cit.

261. **"through its indifference ..."** Alexis de Tocqueville, *Recollections*, Meridian Books (New York: 1959), p. 13.

261. *Fortune* **companies** *Fortune*, "The 500 Largest Industrials," July, 1960; *Fortune*, "The 500 Largest Industrial Corporations," May 4, 1981.

261. **"net disinvestment"** The Port Authority of New York and New Jersey Committee on the Future, "Regional and Economic Development Strategies for the 1980s," May, 1979.

261. **small businesses** *Chicago Tribune*, "Parts of city have become economic wastelands," May 13, 1981.

261. **"There's a quantum ..."** Cited in *Chicago Tribune*, "Chicago: city on the brink," May 11, 1981.

262. **"Existing trends ..."** *New York Review of Books*, "Reconstructing America," op. cit.

262. **"traumatic consequences"** President's Commission for a National Agenda for the Eighties, op. cit.

262. **"How much time ..."** Cited in *Chicago Tribune*, " 'How much time do we have? ... no time,' " May 10, 1981.

262. **Reagan budget impact** *Oakland Tribune*, "Reagan is losing image of political Tom Sawyer," June 3, 1981.

263. **"The Reagan budget . . ."** Cited in ibid.

263. **profits** United California Bank, "California Fourth Quarter Profits and Sales, California Again Outperforms the Nation," May 15, 1981.

263. **jobs growth** Bank of America,

"Perspectives on the California Economy in the Eighties," op. cit.; Authors' interview with Bank of America and UCLA economists.

263. **television** United Press International, June 4, 1981.

263. **Yankelovich monitor** *Esquire*, "California vs. the U.S.," op. cit.

264. **"The experimental phase"** Interview with authors.

Index